The Veiled Discord

The Veiled Discord

Book One of The Visions of Lodas Series

Michael Prusnofsky

Printed in the United States of America

First Printing, 2020

Michael Prusnofsky Publishing

ISBN: 978-0-578-71184-3

Dedication

For my wonderful girlfriend, Sasha.

Acknowledgments

I want to start by thanking my girlfriend, Sasha, who was the first one to believe in me when I decided to pursue writing and storytelling. As someone who has rarely been comfortable with putting my words or work on public display, her sincere and consistent motivation and encouragement made me more confident in myself.

I would also like to thank my parents for allowing and encouraging me to pursue whatever interests I have been drawn to. From a business degree to writing a fantasy novel, I thank them for all of their support. The two of them are always there for me.

I also want to thank my brother, Joe, for always being on my side.

I would like to give the biggest acknowledgment to my father, Jeff, who took the lead on making edits to my novel. Without the several rounds of revisions he helped me with, there would not be *The Visions of Lodas*.

Lastly, I would like to thank my illustrator, Simona Molino, who created the book cover, the Map of Lodas, and the ten illustrations included in the book. Her artistry and expertise in creating fantasy characters continue to amaze me and help bring my story to life.

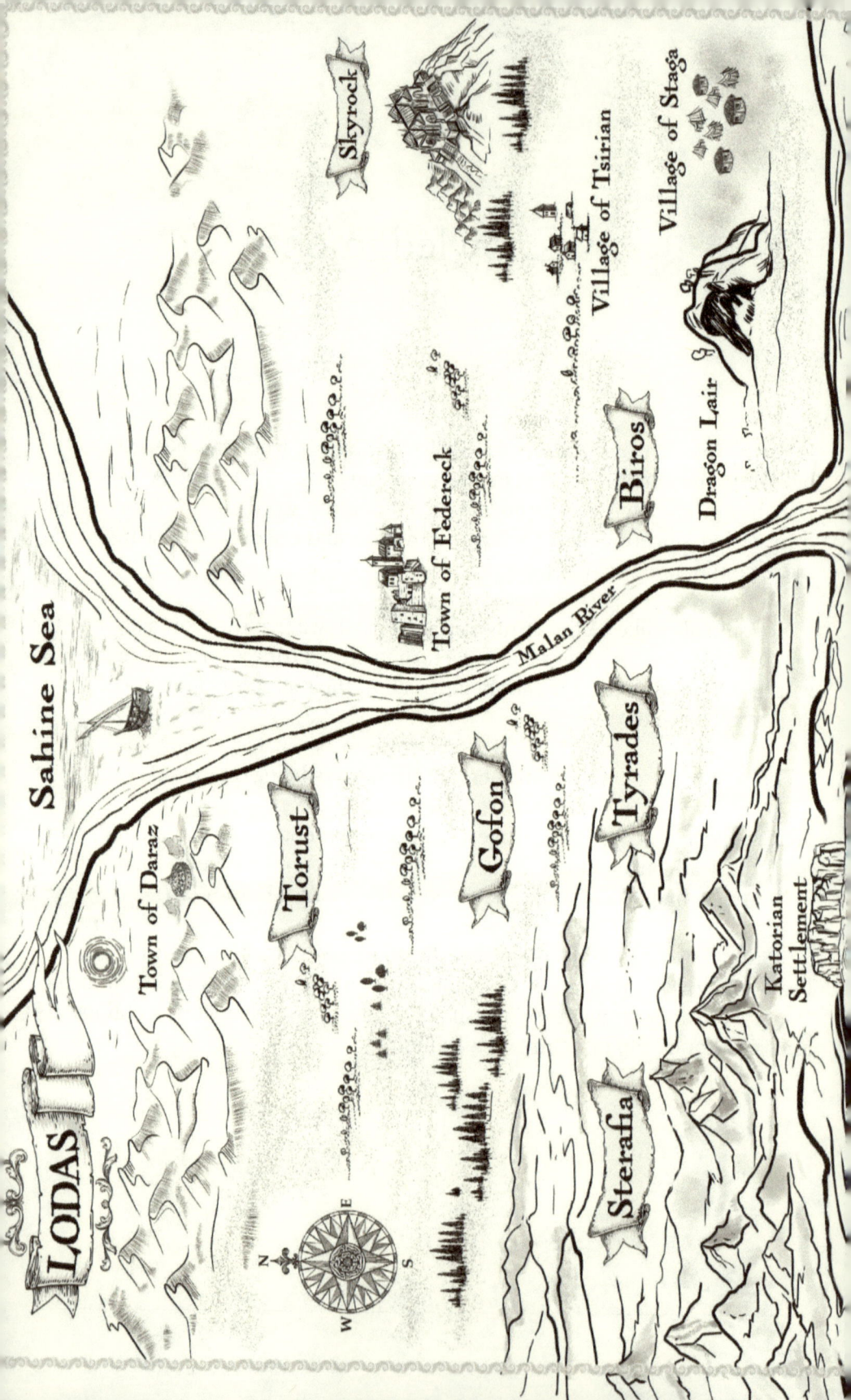

Table of Contents

Chapter One: The Bucket and the Fight

Roy Syssian, Tyrades – Roy Syssian sat in the armory mentally preparing himself for the duel that would define his life and the legacy of the Syssian bloodline. In a short time, he would be facing another finalist in the Grand Gladiator Arena of Tyrades. The Grand Gladiator Council hosts these tournaments once every three years to honor one notable person deserving to be a gladiator. Although many men dream of achieving this honor, only a select few have the skill and courage to participate in these tournaments.

Roy Syssian stood at six feet and a single inch, possessing light-skin with brown eyes and brown hair that puffed up in the front. He had an athletic body and was still young at the age of twenty-eight. He used his great strength and mobility to prevail against his opponents in combat. Despite being talented as a fighter and having attractive features, Roy was not married and had no children, but this did not matter to Roy at this time. His sole focus was to become an elite gladiator and wield the elite gladiator armor and weapon. Roy's father, Lucas Syssian, participated in the same tournament eighteen years earlier, but failed to become an elite gladiator. He lived to train Roy, and Roy shared his aspirations. Lucas always taught Roy to fight to make the world a better place. Roy understood the importance of this grand event, and the pride his success would bring his family back home in the city of Biros. 'The city will sing songs of my bravery and the Syssian legacy will bloom', Roy thought to himself. Roy's hope for the Syssian legacy was more than just about his family name and power. Roy intended to use that power and influence to make the world a better place.

Roy's moments of serenity quickly faded as he grew more apprehensive as the fight was about to happen. The opponent was a fighter named Peter Fardine, from the city of Torust. He had built up an impressive record of combat wins in Torust in the forty-two years of his age. This fight would be the most intense, difficult, and potentially deadly Roy would experience at this point in his life.

Roy tried to shake off his nerves as he put on his plate armor and readied his weapon, a long, slightly curved blade that was attached to a long handle. An arena coordinator entered Roy's room and asked, "We are about to begin the Grand Gladiator duel, are you almost done completing your preparations, Roy?" Roy took one last gulp of water from the bucket and placed it back on top of the bench where he sat and then responded, "Yes, the fight that will write the next chapter in my life, whether good or bad, I am ready to face it."

Roy stood up and looked down at the bucket, which was more than half full of water. The water was still swishing from side to side. His eyes peered at the water in the bucket as the coloring started to change. First the color started to redden, then the water turned goldish, then back to red. As Roy stood staring at the bucket the color of the water kept switching back and forth and became more and more distinct in smaller patches of water. The color shift was mesmerizing Roy as it sped up and then settled on each side. Finally, Roy got the message he was expecting and needed, the right side of the water went red, the left side went gold, right side red, left side gold.

Roy nodded at the arena coordinator and started walking through the tunnel leading to the arena. He could hear the excitement of the crowd as he got closer to the arena entrance. With each step the arena came more to life. As Roy entered the arena, he was overwhelmed by the excitement of the crowd, the screaming, cheering and blaring horns. As Roy stood in the sand of the arena, he looked around and observed thousands of citizens in the crowd who were now in a frenzy.

Despite the enormous boisterous crowd, Roy was now only focused on Peter who walked into the arena directly across from him. Peter Fardine stood at six feet and four inches, was bulkier than Roy and weighed close to forty pounds more. Peter possessed long brown, slightly curly hair that went down to his neck. As the two walked closer together Roy could see that Peter was equipped with a long, thick sword, which required two hands to hold it up, and plate armor. The two stopped about thirty feet apart and their attention was directed to the Grand Gladiator Council. The Grand Gladiator Council consisted of seven gladiators who had won the tournament in the past. They all wore their elite gladiator armor to honor the tournament.

James Farenter, the most recent gladiator, stood and shouted, "We have all fought in that arena and we are proud to see you here today trying to accomplish the extremely difficult task of becoming a gladiator. As always, we let combat decide the worthy. Please wield your weapons and prepare to battle." As James looked around the arena and crowd, he could not help but to admire this new perspective of the tournament. His eyes then focused back on the men below as he shouted, "Fight!"

Roy slowly walked closer to Peter taking each footstep with extreme care. Peter walked with long strides toward Roy until they were only a few feet apart. Peter, initiating the combat, swung his sword upward at Roy then swung left. Roy blocked both of Peter's attempts but was forced back a few steps. Roy gathered his footing and responded with a swing at Peter's left arm then left leg, but both attempts were stopped and the two were locked against each other.

The stalemate lasted a moment as Peter threw a shoulder thrust at Roy that sent him flying back and down to the ground. Roy was able to compose himself and quickly stand back up. The two came back at each other swinging, the blades loudly clanking as they met. Roy swung again with his lighter and quicker weapon and caught Peter in the back of the knee. "Rhaaaaa!", Peter yelled in pain as he retaliated with an intense elbow to Roy's jaw that sent Roy falling back to the ground. As Peter walked ahead with a limp, Roy grabbed his weapon and was able to block Peter's strong downward thrust of his sword. Roy then used the long handle of his weapon to hit Peter's weak knee and rolled his way back so that he could stand again.

The two now faced each other again, but this time with greater fury and intensity. Roy was bleeding from the lip and Peter's knee was injured. Peter swung a long thrust at Roy that was blocked, and Roy went for another counterattack that Peter defended with his blade. As Roy took a step back, his vision shifted to the colors of the water. He saw left side gold and right side red. Roy instantly shifted his body left as Peter's hard thrust was aimed at Roy's right side. As Roy evaded Peter's swing, Roy's blade came swinging from the left side and caught part of the armor protecting Peter's upper back, which bounced off and caught Peter in the back of the neck. Peter suddenly fell to his knees as his neck was bleeding from a large and possibly fatal gash. The crowd roared with spirited energy and shouted, "Gladiator! Gladiator! Gladiator!"

Peter's injury was so severe that he could not stand back up on his feet. Once Roy realized that Peter had been defeated, Roy swung his arms in the air with his weapon in his right hand. The feeling was euphoric and overwhelming, and Roy could not help but smile at his thrilling victory. Roy turned his head to view the audience and saw the entire Grand Gladiator Council standing and loudly clapping. After a few moments, a gate opened leading to the gladiator chamber of the arena and Roy started walking to enter. He took one last look back in awe to absorb the intensity of the crowd and could not help but feel a strong sense of pride. Peter's friends from

Torust rushed into the arena to try to help save his life. Although Roy wondered whether Peter would survive, that concern retreated to the back of his mind as he now entered the gladiator chamber from the long corridor.

The room was dark but lit with large torches on the wall and filled with relics of armor and weapons from past gladiators. On the wall Roy could see white with blue trim armor; lettering on a slab of wood below the armor indicated it belonged to the very first gladiator, Grand Gladiator Howard Flox. His sword and buckler with the white and blue trim were placed to the right of the armor. Roy moved to the next set of equipment on the wall to the right. Grand Gladiator Yerad Tarendarn used white and silver plate armor with a matching buckler and a one-handed mace.

James Farenter called out from a doorway upstairs leading to the arena viewing area, which was reserved for the gladiators, "Come Roy, we can look through the gladiator chamber later. The Grand Gladiator Council would like to congratulate and welcome you." James was a tan-skinned man with brown-blondish hair. He was six feet tall and slightly more muscular than Roy. James was in his early thirties. Like Roy, he had a scruff of facial hair covering his jaw. Roy, now looking at James, said, "This...this room is so astonishing; I never knew it existed and I have always had a strong interest in gladiator history." As Roy walked toward James, James said, "I was amazed my first time here too, crazy to think it was just three years ago." James and Roy walked through the room into the arena viewing area where all the gladiators were talking among themselves.

One of the men approached Roy and said, "Good day, sir, and congratulations on your very impressive victory. I am Grand Gladiator Lemit Osrone." As he handed Roy a silver and blue emblem he said, "Welcome to the Grand Gladiator Council, you are now officially one of us. When you wear this pin in most cities, you will be treated and accommodated respectfully."

Roy looked at the emblem pin and noticed the detail up close. It was a silver helmet with blue trimming just like the one he had seen on Grand Gladiator Howard Flox, the very first gladiator. Roy asked, "Are the colors of the gladiator emblem supposed to honor Grand Gladiator Howard Flox or is it just a coincidence?" Lemit, with a surprised reaction, said, "Impressive catch Roy, I knew from watching you fight you had a good eye. The way you evaded that sword thrust at the end was splendid, it really brought back memories from my younger days when I used to be sharper at dueling." Roy, now smiling, responded, "Thank you, Lemit. I like to think I have the proper training for many situations. However, I must say my jaw and mouth are a bit sore from the elbow Peter hit me with." Roy and Lemit both chuckled together making light of the situation after such an intense fight.

As Roy finished speaking with Lemit, he felt a tap on his right shoulder. Once Roy turned around another gladiator said, "My name is Daniel Rahlin. Very impressive performance today, sir. You are the first person to reach gladiator using your type of weapon, it was quite entertaining to see."

Roy noticed that Daniel was clearly the smallest of the gladiators. Roy responded, "Thank you, Daniel. When I was younger, I really enjoyed using swords and spears so when it came time to master one, I went with a weapon that combined the two." Daniel said, "Interesting, I excel in swords and daggers, if you ever want to practice, let me know, I would be happy to train with you. Also, as you know, all gladiators receive custom pieces of plate armor and a jaxion steel weapon of choice. We will have the blacksmith's assistant take your measurements shortly, but while we are waiting do you know what type of weapon you want to choose?"

Roy smiled as he lifted his weapon and said, "This, I used it to defeat all my opponents in these tournaments and Peter Fardine today. I have practiced with many weapons in my life, but I have mastered this blade like no other combatant in our history." Daniel responded, "Very well, give us a few weeks' time and we will have it ready for you. What coloring would you like your armor and weapon to be?" Roy, in an instant, said, "Gold and Red." Daniel nodded and said, "That should look really nice with that weapon, I am eager to see how it will turn out. As I mentioned, give us a few weeks and a letter will be sent to you requesting that you visit Tyrades for the ceremony."

James, in a loud and clear voice, announced, "Fellow gladiators, I have brought us some wine to celebrate and honor Roy's victory and becoming a gladiator. With him, our council grows to eight of the most elite fighters Lodas has ever witnessed. Roy has become the only living gladiator from Biros, let us toast to that." As all the gladiators picked up a chalice of red wine and lifted them in the air they bellowed together, "To Roy." James continued speaking and said, "To properly honor Roy, King Lance Hasting of Tyrades is hosting a royal banquet."

The group of gladiators walked nobly throughout Tyrades until they arrived at the entrance of King Hasting's chambers. James said, "Take out your pins so that these fine guards know who we are." Roy and the gladiators did as James instructed and proceeded past the guards.

Roy was amazed at the architecture of the king's buildings. In front of the chambers there were six columns made from marble with carvings in each of them. Roy was not certain what the mysterious designs were, but he figured he could ask later.

The gladiators entered the royal dinner hall of the chambers where many of Tyrades' royals and council members were starting to sit. King Hasting, Queen Nora, and the royal family all sat at long tables and on tall chairs in the front of the room while everyone else had seating at round tables with regular chairs. The royal family consisted of Lance and Nora's three children: Leora Hasting, who was in her early twenties, Sophie Hasting, who was a teenager, and Blake Hasting, who was ten. The gladiators found their places at the table closest to the king and his family and went to be seated. A few moments later the king stood and shouted, "We all feast tonight as a tradition of the great city of Tyrades. Tyrades is the only city that creates gladiators. Even though they come from many backgrounds and many places, they understand that Tyrades will always be here for them. Congratulations to our newest gladiator, Roy Syssian of Biros."

James Farenter leaned toward Roy and said, "He isn't lying, Tyrades has always treated gladiators like their own royal family. Some cities look down upon the art of combat, but here the kings have always embraced us, allowed us to fight to become gladiators, and fueled our legacies with power. I know it is easy for me to say all of this because I am from Tyrades, but my parents were not rich, they did not eat at fancy banquets like this. Once I became a gladiator, my life significantly changed thanks to the king. Now I am paid handsomely to train young students who want to learn how to fight so that one day they can end up like me. I just had my first born child two years ago and I can rest easy every night knowing that even if he doesn't want to become a gladiator, at least his future will be taken care of thanks to my efforts and the king providing the opportunity. Go speak with him, he will help you like he has helped us."

Roy nodded and stood up from his chair to greet the king. As Roy walked up to the royal table he bowed and said, "King, queen, royal family, thank you for the feast and for the opportunity to be what I have become today. I have been incredibly blessed with the gift of a fighter's skills and to live in a world where I can use those skills, like an artist or a musician, to stand out like a masterpiece. I do understand that this gladiator status will hopefully bring me power and influence. My intention is to make Biros, Tyrades, and all the lands a better place for all to live and I hope you can be a supporter of my mission."

The king and queen smiled as the king responded, "Very kind words you have spoken". As he faced his wife and saw her genuine smile he continued, "It seems my queen would agree with me. You have proven yourself a Grand

Gladiator and I have always supported the gladiators throughout my kingship. The power and influence you speak of can be used in numerous ways, you can ask your fellow gladiators, but I must say I am impressed with how you intend to build your legacy. My oldest daughter Leora here shares your interest in charity."

Roy turned his head and faced Leora who had been sitting to the left of the king. Leora had long blonde hair with some curls, she was five feet and six inches tall. She had dark blue eyes and was wearing a light-blue silk dress. Roy was astonished by Leora's beauty and he wondered if the king knew that he was not married.

Roy, finally finding the words, addressed Leora, "I am glad to hear this, perhaps I should also be asking for your assistance with my mission." Leora smiled and said, "I have been working to help those without food and jobs find work around the city. Compared to your goal it is a small task, but I would be interested in speaking with you about ideas that can, as you said, make the world a better place." Roy responded, "That would be very helpful, thank you, my lady."

Roy turned back to the king and said, "I am heading back to Biros tomorrow morning, but I will be back in Tyrades in a few weeks to receive my gladiator weapon and armor. I look forward to seeing you all again." Lance said, "Be sure to send my regards to the king, I haven't seen him in quite some time, but hopefully we can all gather together soon."

Roy headed back to his table and had another drink of wine with his fellow gladiators. Several courses and drinks were consumed before everyone left the banquet. As Roy and James were leaving the royal chambers, James said, "Roy, you are now one of the most elite fighters in Lodas. If you ever need our support, you should know that we gladiators have undying loyalty to each other. I look forward to seeing you again for the gladiator ceremony in a few weeks when you will receive your gear." Roy responded, "Thank you for your help today, James. You and the gladiators are good men; I look forward to working with you on the council."

Roy walked back to a building where he would spend the night and get some rest. As he got into bed, he felt jubilant about his day, 'Such an eventful one', he thought. 'The vision, whether Peter Fardine had survived, becoming a gladiator, meeting the king, queen and the royal family, could Leora be attracted to him as well, looking ahead to the gladiator ceremony.', All these events ran through Roy's mind, but what he focused on the most was his legacy and making it one step closer to where he wanted to be.

Chapter Two: The Threat to a Kingdom

Phillip Denvion, Gofon - King Phillip Denvion adored the outdoors and wine, making his vineyard a popular place on days when the weather was good. To Phillip, this meant almost every sunny day, of which there were many in his kingdom of Gofon. Phillip Denvion stood at six feet and zero inches, possessing light-skin with light brown eyes and black hair. He had a stocky frame and was fifty-two years of age. The king was serving in his seventeenth year as king after his older brother, Kendrin, died from an illness. When Phillip was growing up, he never expected nor really wanted to inherit the kingship, but he knew how important it was for his family's legacy and understood that he needed to accept the crown. When he was younger, he was interested in writing stories and scripts for plays to be performed in his city of Gofon. Those days were great and carefree he thought, and time went slower too. Now time was too precious as a king and Phillip loved any free time he could get.

Timothy Milton, the king's hand who also served Phillip's brother and father, walked into the vineyard and said, "My king, I have just heard new reports of an illness spreading in some of the towns between Torust and Gofon. A high amount of deaths has been reported as well." Phillip, now quite unsettled, said, "It's been close to two decades now since the last epidemic, and that was the one that took my brother's life. I had a feeling another was bound to occur. I have always had a soft spot in my heart for those who suffer from these scourges, especially after Kendrin's passing. Many of these farmers supply our cotton, wheat, and other necessities and it is our duty to help them in their time of need. Let us show our support and send aid parties to distribute blankets, food, medicinal herbs, or whatever these people need. Make sure these aid parties learn whatever they can about the sickness so that our potion makers can start working toward a cure. The gates of Gofon must be closed at once, no one leaves or enters without specific permission from myself or the Gofon council members."

At this time, Gofon was the largest kingdom in Lodas and had maintained the most powerful military for several centuries. Under Phillip's kingship, Gofon strategically prolonged and enhanced its military strength, built and maintained good relations with other kingdoms, and grew trade for Gofon by welcoming new foreign traders and goods. But, despite all of this, Phillip knew how dangerous a severe illness like this one, which was so close to home, could be on the enormous Gofon population. Moments like this put a tremendous strain on Phillip, but he took comfort in the fact that at least he was a king who empathized with his people.

Timothy nodded and responded, "Yes, my king. I believe that is a wise choice. The last illness outbreak was not a focus for your brother and unfortunately a tenth of the city's population was killed before potions master Jol Parantis found a cure. And even then, it took weeks to gather and produce enough to distribute to everyone. If I may suggest one piece of advice, my king." "Of course," replied Phillip. "I would recommend that you send Jol Parantis with one of the aid parties to learn about this illness. The aid parties will lack medical experience and I think the best way to avoid another severe outbreak is by sending our most experienced medical specialist." "But what if he dies from exposure before finding a cure?", the king asked. Timothy said, "It is possible, but the risk of him contracting the illness and it killing him in the several weeks it is anticipated that he would be away to try to discover a cure is one I believe you should take."

Phillip stood up slowly, to avoid spilling his chalice of wine, and said, "I appreciate your advice, as always, Timothy. Please speak with Jol and send him to my chambers after I have eaten lunch with my family. I will discuss this matter with him myself and you are welcome to be a part of this briefing too."

The king walked to the stairs leading to his grounds and proceeded up to his chambers. Phillip entered the royal dining room and his entire family was sitting at the table waiting for his arrival. His wife, Queen Tanya Denvion, could tell by his face that there was something uneasy about the king. Phillip had always known Tanya to be the sweetest woman and her genuine loving and caring personality was the reason he had married her. Tanya was five foot four, with straight brown hair, brown eyes, and a very thin body. Years earlier, Phillip's father pushed him to marry another woman, one his father emphasized was far more beautiful than Tanya and would produce attractive Denvion children who would be essential to their legacy. Phillip, unlike his brother and father, did not marry based on looks.

Tanya asked, "Has something happened, Phillip? You are hardly ever late to your own lunches." Phillip, grabbing his chair and sitting, said, "I just heard news that a sickness has started to spread in the towns between Torust and Gofon. I plan to help those infected while also trying to find a cure for it early on. I have closed the city gates, so no more adventuring for a while for you two", as he turned his head toward his son Kip and his daughter Fayna. The children were both in their teens with Kip being fifteen and Fayna thirteen.

Fayna had always been into the musical arts and would often travel to Torust to deepen her understanding of various instruments. Torust was known as the musical city and was home to the most well-respected musicians, who would often teach Fayna. She would be escorted to Torust with the soldiers of the king's army and would spend several weeks there at a time. Kip, on the other hand, was pursuing the path of combat just like his grandfather and uncle Kendrin. Under the protection of Gofon soldiers, he would travel to Tyrades and train for weeks to enhance his fighting skills under the guidance of various gladiators.

Fayna distraughtly exclaimed, "But father, I need to travel to Torust for my lessons. Learning musical instruments is the only thing I am good at. Please father, there has to be a different way of getting there." The king said, "I am sorry, but we cannot risk your life over music. Even if we tried getting you there with a different route, we do not know those territories well enough, so it would be too dangerous. You can learn with the musicians here in Gofon until this illness is taken care of."

Kip, who patiently waited and did not want to agitate his father, finally said, "How about me, father? I was about to leave for Tyrades in a few days and I know you do not want anyone stepping outside the city, but Tyrades is in the opposite direction. We are first hearing of the seriousness of this outbreak now, so there is little chance of it having spread to the southern towns by now. In fact, I believe I would be safer and better off settling in Tyrades until the sickness is taken care of. The kingdom is less populated and a few hundred miles further away from the outbreak." Phillip, looking down at his plate and listening intently, responded, "When you put it that way, I suppose you are right, my son. Change of arrangements though, you leave for Tyrades tomorrow morning. Please be careful on your journey, sicknesses are among the deadliest things for our royal family, for any family. All the gold in the bank cannot save us from dying if we do not have a cure, as the death of my brother, the king, clearly demonstrates. I have to leave to discuss these matters with Timothy, I will see you again before you depart." The king jabbed the last few pieces of salmon into his mouth and swallowed a mouthful of wine before he left the dining room.

Phillip walked to the balcony area of his chambers to provide some privacy for his meeting. He sat in a chair overlooking the gardens and his vineyard below as he waited and thought about what he would ask of Jol. He thought, 'The potions master was always good to the kings; he did not discover the cure in time to save Kendrin, but he did not have enough time.'

Moments later the knocking on the door that he expected came. "Gentlemen, come in and grab a seat", the king shouted out as he started adjusting his chair. Timothy Milton and Jol Parantis entered and sat at the king's request. The king, twiddling his fingers, said, "I am not sure if you are aware yet, Jol, but there have been reports of an outbreak of an illness that is spreading rapidly and has claimed its first deaths in the towns beyond our walls to the east. Jol, Timothy here has reminded me of the cure you discovered for the last sickness, what did you call it again?" Jol, with a grave face, said, "Skin Shorn, it caused the skin to deteriorate from the outside cutting in, layer by layer after eliminating the hair. Once there was little or no skin left the infected felt excruciating pain and would be prone to contract even more illnesses until the they died or committed suicide. That was by far the hardest time I ever had in finding a cure for an illness. The illness was so complex I cannot imagine that it would have originated from a natural cause, it was almost, well, it was as if it was somehow made intentionally.

The king said, "Yes, that was it. I still remember seeing my poor brother, the damn king, in his bed with his skin rotting away in his very last few moments." Timothy addressed the king, "I never asked you, being that you were the last one that spoke with him, what was the last thing he said?" Phillip hesitantly spoke, holding back his tears, "He told me I will make a good king and that he regretted not focusing on the illness earlier and as a result it took his kingship and life from him. The very last thing he said was that he accepted dying at that point because his face, skin, and image as a king would forever be tarnished from his monstrous appearance. At that moment, he said this is it brother, please kill me."

Phillip held his face in his hands as he said, "It's... it's been the hardest thing I've ever done and the most difficult thing I have had to live with." A single tear flashed down his face as he rapidly smacked it. Jol, in an attempt to comfort his king, said, "Don't let that bring you down, he would have died anyway and would have suffered more if you didn't take the action you did. I had to take many lives that very same way from patients who lost the will to live. I can tell that you are concerned about this new sickness and I know that you requested for me to come here so that I can help in some way. So, my king, how can I help you with this outbreak?"

The king responded, "I was speaking with Timothy about this matter earlier and he advised me to send you out with the aid party tomorrow morning because your experience and expertise can be our best chance at eradicating this illness. I would agree with Timothy that this is in the best interest of our kingdom, but it puts you at risk of contracting the illness yourself. You are already respected by Gofon and me, Jol, for saving thousands of lives close to two decades ago. If I wanted, I could choose to send you out without question, but that would not be the noble thing to do. All I can do is leave this choice in your hands."

Jol smiled and said, "Your reputation as a caring king clearly precedes you. I cannot thank you enough for offering me the choice of whether to go. But I really look at it as if you are giving me the opportunity to go. You see, my king, it is my purpose in life to save lives. Even if I had to sacrifice my life to try to find a cure, it would be a worthwhile sacrifice. Even if I perish, there are still several experienced alchemists who have years of training and I have full confidence that they can assume my responsibilities. I will be truly honored to aid the people and cure this illness for you, the king of Gofon."

The king confidently spoke, "Thank you, Jol. If you require any resources, let Timothy or me know. I am not certain what you will find in the lands beyond the gates, but we must do all we can to ensure the continued success and well-being of our kingdom. Now, Timothy and I must speak to the Gofon council to inform them of our plan. I wish you the best of luck on your journey, Jol. And I have great confidence in you." Jol responded, "Thank you, my king. I must go myself and prepare for my departure tomorrow morning."

Timothy and Phillip made their way out of the king's chambers and headed toward the council's meeting room. The king would need to explain how he intended to handle the illness, which was now spreading throughout the lands, to prevent it from reaching the center of Gofon. The council had always been subservient and complied with the king's wishes, but Phillip had recently started to sense some resistance. The king knew that his close to two decades of holding the kingship was more than enough to stir jealous competition. He knew that he now had to be careful with every decision he was to make as a single mistake would lead to harsh scrutiny and possibly challenge to his kingship by the council.

Phillip and Timothy walked into the council meeting room and greeted the council. Council representative Winston Caven said, "Thank you for meeting with us, my king. The reports of this illness are very concerning. What is your planned choice of action?" The king responded, "I am sending out aid parties to help relieve some of those in need, but I am also sending our head potions master, Jol Parantis, to study the epidemic and find a cure. Jol will accompany one of the aid parties. He is the man who cured the last illness, so Timothy and I believe this is a necessary action."

The councilmembers started whispering among themselves for a few moments before another council member, John Pittus, spoke out and said, "It is quite risky jeopardizing our most veteran potions master on an illness we know very little about. What if this illness is quite difficult to cure? These aid parties you are sending out are using resources that belong to the kingdom of Gofon, why are we wasting resources on infected that are going to die anyway. How long will this go on for before our city banks go broke?"

The king, now agitated, replied, "We have already spoken with the potions master, Jol, and he is honored and driven to find a cure. That is our best chance at fighting this terrible epidemic. Aiding these people when they are infected may help them survive for a few weeks, days, or even hours longer, which could possibly save their lives in the end if we find the cure. I am not concerned right now with the economic impact this will have when we can be saving lives. We are the most powerful kingdom and have trustworthy alliances. We will manage just fine."

"My king", Jack Haxon, a council member, called out, "For the record, I fully support your decision to send Jol and aid to the infected, you truly are a king of the people." The council members then spoke among themselves and then John Pittus said, "The council does not fully support, but acquiesces in, the king's decision." The king was relieved and said, "Excellent. We will talk more soon when we hear more news of the illness." As the king got up to leave, he whispered in Timothy's ear, "I forgot to mention it earlier, make sure Rus Trenode is watching over my son on his trip to Tyrades in the morning." With a quick nod from Timothy, the king turned and left for his chambers.

Phillip walked into his royal dining room and poured red wine into his chalice to the very top and he drank it all down with a single gulp. The day had been tremendously stressful, and the king realized it would change the city's mood for the next few months, at the very least. He filled up his chalice yet again and walked across the chambers to his son Kip's room.

Phillip knocked on his door a few times and entered to see his son gathering his belongings for the trip. Phillip said, "You will be in good hands on your journey, I am sending Rus Trenode and several other soldiers with you. I am glad to see you and your sister focusing on the things that make you happy and I can certainly tell that both of you are getting a lot better at what inspires you. I used to love what I did; now I do not have the time to craft creative stories. But if you keep practicing, you can become a better fighter than Kendrin and even your grandfather." Kip smiled and said, "Thank you, father. Because of you I can learn from the best. I get a small injury or a scar here and there, but it's okay, the girls seem to love it." They both chuckled as Phillip was amused by Kip talking about girls and he now realized that Kip, who was at the age when boys start to grow up. With a more serious face and voice Kip paused and said, "One day I want to become a Grand Gladiator."

Chapter Three: Snowstorm

Oakley Nodon, Sterafia - The sound of oak in the fireplace crackled on a chilly winter morning in the harsh terrain of Sterafia, a winter tundra to the west of all the other kingdoms. "I will get up out of this bed in ten minutes, I have to", Oakley Nodon told himself as he curled up in his bed content with the warmth of his leather hides. Oakley was almost eighteen years old and stood at five feet and eleven inches, with a very slim and athletic build. He had long brown hair that went down to his eyebrows, grey eyes, and a very pale body that was rarely exposed to sunlight.

As the only son of the chief military general of Sterafia, Damien Nodon, Oakley had a lot to live up to as high expectations were set for him by his father and the general population of Sterafia. Oakley's mother, Telessa Nodon, passed away giving birth to Oakley's sister, who also died in that tragic event. This traumatic void in Oakley's life took place when he was only nine. With his father busy with his military duties there was a lack of parental guidance when Oakley was growing up. Oakley had just now started to realize that he was struggling to discover what he wanted to do with his life.

Oakley, still sitting in bed, eyes locked on the source of warmth, tossed a leather hide off his shoulder and got out of bed. He gathered his warm clothing and did not even need to look outside to tell that it was going to be a bitter cold, frosty day. He put on his wool shirt and thick pants followed by his leather armor and his animal fur top layer cloak that covered his head, shoulders, and backside. He then slipped his feet into his thick winter leather boots. He went to the corner of the room and placed his quiver of arrows under his fur hide and threw his bow around his shoulder. As he was about to leave, he grabbed his slim fingerless gloves from his pockets and put them on to partially cover his hands. Lastly, he put on his warm leather gloves, which he wore when he was not in immediate need of his bow and arrows. As a hunter and bow wielder, the most precise shots came from the natural surface of the finger.

Instantly, the chilly wind swept against his face as he walked out the door. Large flakes of snow were descending from the white hazy sky. Oakley walked down the stairs of the residence and headed toward the training grounds. The echo of swords clanking against each other grew louder and louder as he got closer. Someone then shouted out in a familiar voice, "And look who it is, the head idler himself." Oakley stopped walking and turned his head to the right to face the person who was addressing him; his father, Damien Nodon, stood next to King Renga Khonzas. King Renga stood at six feet and two inches, he possessed dark skin with brown eyes, an athletic build, and a small ponytail of thin dreadlocks. He wore a thick brownish-black coat made from the fur of a full-grown bear he once killed on his own. King Renga had been the king for six years. Being in his early forties, it was widely believed that he likely had a few decades of kingship ahead.

The king smiled and said, "Strong winds today, should be a good challenge for your marksmanship." Oakley responded, "Just need to aim a bit to the right and should hit my target just fine. You used to use the bow a bit back in your youth, right my king?" Damien walked closer and set his hand on Oakley's shoulder as he said, "King Renga used to be excellent with the bow until he realized his potential with an axe and shield. Maybe one of these days you will leave the bow aside and try something a bit more exciting yourself. But, for now, just get out there and practice, you are doing quite well with the bow for your age." Damien launched his hand into Oakley's back pushing him forward to get started.

Oakley swiftly walked over to the archery range, knowing that both the king and Damien were watching him intently. Damien softly said, "That boy is lost, and I do not know how to help him. I try helping him with what I know and with what I found my purpose in life to be, but I can tell he is different and very much like his mother in many ways. I love him more than anything, the last of my blood still alive." The king told Damien, "We all get lost, there are times I try to understand the purpose of my kingship, but it takes time to figure out. I just try to keep the people of our kingdom safe from the many threats of Lodas. I still do not have a wife or a child, but I know I must find my own way. Give the boy time, I can tell he will bring pride to your legacy."

After taking off his outer gloves, Oakley took out his combat arrows and set them aside as he grabbed practice arrows for the training. He walked up to the shooting area of the range, planted his feet, faced the target, pulled his bow up, pulled back as he took a deep breath and released. The arrow made a few swivels through the harsh wind as it made a swishing sound. The impact of the arrow hitting half a foot below and to the left of the bullseye echoed back to Oakley.

Oakley readjusted his arm to the right a little more now, placed another arrow in his bow and pulled back, took another deep breath, and let the arrow go. His eyes precisely followed the shaft of the arrow as it maneuvered through the wind directly into the bullseye, as he hoped. He smiled and quickly readjusted for his next shot trying to execute it in half the time as practice for combat. The arrow landed a few inches high, then an inch and a half to the right, then in rapid progression he landed two back to back bullseyes and that was his sign that he was ready for a quick hunt. Oakley walked up to the arrows and pulled them out of the board before placing them back in the chest and grabbing his combat arrows for his quiver.

The royal gate was an entrance reserved only for the king and the military, but Oakley had a special privilege being the son of Damien. He was friendly with the gatekeepers as he often went alone to hunt for food, leather for hides and clothes, or just to practice and venture into the world outside of Sterafia. As he approached the royal gate the guard said, "It is a rough day to hunt, are you sure you want to be out there alone in this weather? I can sense a blizzard coming." Oakley replied, "Yes, I am not going far." The guard nodded and said, "Do not stay out long, the men would not appreciate it if your father sent us searching for you."

Outside the royal gate, all one could see in the distance was the vast white terrain with scattered trees. Despite its despairing and intimidating appearance, Oakley found solitude walking in the unknown and enjoying the peace and quiet of nature. As he continued walking south of the royal gate, he noticed the snow start to intensify just as the guard predicted. Oakley looked up and felt a few snowflakes land on his hairless cheeks. The snow did not bother him, but the strong wind blowing directly against him wore him down with each step he took. He kept walking until he arrived at a tree that overlooked a valley. He thought that it was an ideal spot to view any animals out in the open, so he sat down next to the tree and waited. All he could see past the heavy falling snow was open space and two large trees.

Suddenly, to Oakley's amazement, two enormous white tigers with long black stripes on their fur came running from the west heading east. They stood at least close to seven feet and had to weigh at least a thousand pounds, Oakley thought. He had heard stories about them being in this area but had never seen them himself. As they got closer, he noticed both were holding small white tiger cubs in their huge mouths. One of the tigers was running with two cubs in its mouth while the other was holding three. "What the hell is going on?", Oakley asked himself. He saw the tiger that was holding three cubs accidentally drop one of them next to one of the trees. For some reason, the tigers kept running. "Why aren't they going back?!", Oakley said with unease. He then suddenly heard howls of wolves, many of them.

Oakley turned his head and saw hundreds of wolves approximately one thousand meters west charging through the snow after their target. Oakley's mouth suddenly dropped, and he held his head in his hands for several seconds before he stood up, dropped his bow and quiver, and said, "This can't happen". He launched himself forward down a slope in the ground and with quick steps set off toward the tree where the cub was. The cub was only about fifty feet away, but each step felt like it took a year. As he approached the cub he looked to the right and saw the pack of wolves and what appeared to be people coming from only about three hundred feet away.

Oakley was ecstatic when he finally got to the cub. He could hear the desperate cries of the cub hoping its parents would return. Oakley went to pick up the cub, but it charged him at first. He took off his large animal fur cloak and threw it over the cub and tied the cloak up with a knot. Oakley slipped his arm through the hole of the cloak and started to ascend the large tree. As the march and howls of the wolves were growing fiercer and fiercer, he needed to lift himself up quickly. As Oakley placed his hands on the tree and used his legs to kick up, he felt the burden of the weight of the cub on his right side. The cub was heavier than he expected, and it was moving around frantically in a state of panic. Oakley managed to lift himself a few feet before he grabbed a dead branch from the tree that almost sent him falling. He felt around and grabbed ahold of a stronger branch that he used to pull up higher. Then he was able to grab the thicker, stronger branches of the tree.

Suddenly, some of the wolves arrived at the tree and started jumping at Oakley and the cub, but they could not reach them. Oakley peered down nervously and was astonished to see what appeared to be feral humans who were running among and just like the wolves. In fact, about one-third of the pack were feral humans who jumped at the tree just like the wolves. Oakley was thankful that the feral humans did not understand the concept of climbing. Oakley had never seen or heard of feral people roaming the wild with packs of wolves. It was just as frightening as it was surprising to him.

The rest of the pack went running past the tree in pursuit of the other tigers. Oakley was able to sit on a thick branch and slowly, with a tight grip on the cloak, open the knot so the cub could get some air. Oakley slowly moved his left hand in front of the cub to let it smell his scent. The cub went to gnaw at it, but Oakley slowly pulled it away and then again presented his hand in front of the cub's face. This time the cub smelled his hand and looked Oakley in his eyes.

Oakley felt great pride holding the cub in his arms, saving it from certain death. But none of this would matter if he did not get out of this himself. He knew he just needed to wait in the tree for the last of the pack to depart. Oakley reached into his pocket and took out a few pieces of jerky. After tossing one in his mouth he presented a small piece in front of the cub for it to eat. The cub reached its head forward and licked it off Oakley's fingers. Oakley swung the cub around in the cloak for about a half an hour before the pesky, ferocious wolves and feral humans left to find their pack. He waited another twenty minutes to be safe and closed the cloak again with the sleeping cub inside. Oakley slowly and carefully made his way down the tree. It was a lot easier going down as he was no longer in a state of panic.

Once he got to the bottom, he opened the knot of the cloak again and quickly walked toward his bow and quiver that he had earlier left behind. Oakley grabbed his gear and swiftly made his way back to Sterafia. As he approached the royal gate hours after Oakley was expected to be back, the guard exclaimed, "What took so long?! Is that your idea of a quick hunting trip?" Oakley, holding the resting cub in his cloak at his hip, smiled and said, "Hunting an animal takes patience and I needed a lot of it today". The guard shook his head and was clearly annoyed with Oakley showing up so late. Oakley smirked as the cub began to nip his finger through the cloak.

After walking through Sterafia back to his room in record time, Oakley opened the cloak and laid the cub onto his bed. The resting cub was majestic with soft white fur and black stripes lined across its body. He could see its chest contracting and expanding as it was breathing in and out with soft breaths. Oakley carelessly ran his fingers through the fur of the cub. Slowly the cub opened its eyes, stood up, and looked at Oakley. The cub had magnificent grey eyes just like him. Oakley held out his hand, but the cub backed up. As the cub paced back and forth on Oakley's bed Oakley said to himself, "What did I get myself into?" As Oakley again slowly reached his hand out to pet the cub, the cub hesitantly dropped its front legs, but then stood and ran its head under Oakley's hand. Oakley smiled and reflected on how he had saved this beautiful cub amid an intense storm of snow, wolves and feral people and said, "I am going to name you Snowstorm."

Chapter Four: The Halls of Absolute

Ria Falune, Torust – Queen Ria Falune stood on her balcony gazing down upon the majestic city of Torust, located in the heart of the desert near the Sahine Sea. She lived in a wide, cylinder-shaped sandstone building that stood out in the city at a few hundred feet high. This building was occupied by only Ria and her two siblings. The city of Torust was once the most powerful kingdom in Lodas. That changed several hundred years ago when Gofon's economy and military started to boom. Ria was the oldest of three children from the late King Tari Falune and Queen Jaci Falune. After Ria, the middle child was her brother Gardas Falune and her younger sister Natiana Falune. Torust was the only kingdom that allowed its kingship to be inherited by the eldest child instead of the eldest son. Ria liked being queen but made sure her siblings lived lavish lifestyles within Torust too.

Ria made her way back into her bedroom and slipped her clothes off till she was naked. Ria stood at five feet and seven inches tall, and had a slim, attractive body, tan skin, long brown hair, brown eyes, and was thirty-two years of age. She grabbed a red silk dress she would wear for the day and sat down and called in her handmaid, "I am ready for your service." The handmaid entered and said, "Quite a striking dress", as she started making the queen's hair straight. Ria smiled in approval and said, "Small braid on the side...and dark shading." The handmaid, with steady hands, made some of the hair on the right of Ria's head into a small, but appealing braid. She then opened a case and took out a tiny brush of horsehair and dipped the brush into a black substance. She lined the queen's eyes with the substance and asked, "Does this please you?" Ria stood up and said, "Truly a piece of art, as always."

The queen walked over to her dresser and took her golden bracelet and golden necklace with a giant ruby in it and put them on. She left the sandstone building and made her way to the Halls of Absolute, a place where only those deemed loyal to the queen were granted access. The halls were made with sand bricks over a thousand years ago and the ceiling was painted with ancient Torustian figures that had rubies as eyes. No one understood the significance of the rubies, but it was assumed that jewel trade was historically a key interest for the city.

As Ria entered past the guards, she saw her sister Natiana sitting with Torb Daxo, the archaeological master who also sold jewels. "You know I like Onyx", Natiana said as she giggled softly. Ria greeted them with a hand gesture as she kept walking further into the halls.

Deeper inside the halls, she walked over to Haigar Loseef, her military leader and personal advisor. He had served the family for close to fifteen years now. Haigar, with a serious face, said, "Word from Gofon is that an illness is spreading between that city and Torust. It appears to be located significantly closer to their city now. Our messenger confirmed these rumors this morning. I think we should stop all trading and visitors from the southern lands until a cure is found. What are your orders on addressing this issue?" Ria responded, "Do nothing to assist Gofon. Gofon has the power and resources to handle it themselves. There is no need to help them, especially if the illness is located within their kingdom. However, I do like your advice. Please close off the southern borders from trading and visitors at once."

Haigar said, "I will take care of it. But more bad news. The reports from Tyrades are that Peter Fardine made it to the final duel but was defeated by a fighter from Biros. The final blow was said to have been a potentially fatal strike. With the absence of Peter Fardine here in Torust, it is reasonable to assume that he passed away in Tyrades." The queen, with a frown, responded, "What a shame, he was the favorite to win. I grieve for his loss, but also for his life, he always fought to honor my family and me as queen. Please send flowers and our respects to his wife. Tell her she is welcome to speak with me whenever she would like." Haigar nodded and said, "Yes, my queen. We will continue training the finest warriors in all of the kingdoms so we can bring a gladiator to Torust under your leadership."

Torb Daxo swiftly approached the queen and said, "Greetings, my stunning queen." Ria exclaimed, "I am not easily flattered like my sister; I am the queen of Torust. Do not approach me like this again." With a now worrisome face, Torb replied, "My most sin... sincere apologies, my queen. I come to you now to serve you. I heard from one of my men that there is a cave possessing jewels to the northeast. Your sister also told me about your fascination with jewels, like myself. I was wondering if you would like to take a trip there, with your guards of course." Ria, smiling now, said, "I am slightly more flattered now than I was seconds ago, but I must serve the kingdom as queen and must refuse. Your services help this kingdom thrive as jewel trade is the main source of income and one of the most sought-after luxuries, so I wish you luck on your expedition. Bring me back some nice jewels if you get lucky."

Ria walked toward her sister in the other room and sat down next to her. With a smirk Ria said, "So Natiana, what is the next 'necessity' to reduce our gold supply?" Natiana, in a half-joking and half-serious manner, smiled and said, "I like my jewels, mother always told us to match your jewels with your clothes. If we represent the rulers of Torust we need to look the part, especially if we want to meet handsome men. Besides, what about all the money Gardas uses on women? And you, you... well you don't really spend a lot although you do dress very fancy."

Ria said, "I do not support his spending habits, but we are all entitled to a lavish lifestyle. In order to grow more powerful, you need the resources. And once you become more powerful you can keep gaining and gaining more wealth. I have no desire to waste it on lust or beauty. I want to make Torust the supreme kingdom of Lodas and I intend to use my wealth to accomplish that. Our people are what matter. I am not going to waste our resources supporting struggling foreigners because then we fall victim to other forces. Everything I do is for our people and for you, Gardas, and me. Father and mother led Torust with great care for our people and built strong relations with other kingdoms. However, in doing so, they did some things that they believed were necessary to support those kingdoms because of their alliances and the need to maintain good relations. I will not make the same mistake. I just heard Gofon will soon be facing a serious illness. I will make sure Torust will rule Lodas once again."

Chapter Five: The Stars in the Sky

Liava Pontas, Village of Staga – "Come Liava, sit by the fire with us", Liava's mother, Yana Pontas, shouted. Liava nodded and carefully walked her way to the fire, trying to avoid bumping into any of the dancers circling around the campfire. After letting a few dancers go past her, Liava proceeded walking to her mother and father by the fire where she sat down in between them. The village was very spirited with drums and flutes, dancers, and an abundance of drysium, a liquid substance believed to open the soul to the world and that helped the villagers of Staga see visions. The villagers of Staga had a unique connection with nature and had been using this mind-altering substance for many years as a tradition.

At the age of seventeen, Liava was still maturing and was not completely comfortable dancing in front of her parents and villagers. She had long brown hair, light skin, brown eyes and was five feet and six inches in height. To her right she saw her father, Bytal Pontas, take a bowl of drysium that another man had passed him. Bytal took a gulp, closed his eyes, and sprawled out on the ground in a relaxed position. Yana and Liava passed the bucket of drysium to the left as they were not at all interested.

Yana started braiding Liava's hair as she said, "Liava, my beautiful girl, in a few years you will marry a man and start a new path for your soul. You have always been a shy girl, but you need to get involved with the village more. There are plenty of young souls here just like you. I met your father when I was just a little older than you and it has been the greatest part of my journey in Lodas. Look at him, he was once a simple warrior, but now he has become a lot more aware of the world around him. Liava looked to her right and saw her father on his back with his body still and his eyes wide open staring at the stars in the dark, clear sky.

The humming of the chanter started to pick up as a lady proclaimed, "Drink up my brothers and sisters, look into the beauty of the world and the spirits around us. We share our existence with many living creatures, and we must continue to always protect them with our lives."

Yana pushed Liava's head into her lap and said, "Lie down my child, look into the stars. Our souls fuel the very light that fills the night sky. Every single star you see represents the souls of just one living species in this world. Whenever a soul passes away it becomes a part of the star for its species. The only way to keep a star going is to procreate. There are millions of species, many you have never seen before and many that need our help. If we fail to protect a species, then the star dies forever. My mother used to tell me that the night sky was filled with bright stars. Now there are much less, and we humans are the cause of this problem. You are never to kill an animal the way many humans do every day for food, fur, and trade. Our ancestors have been trying to understand the significance of the stars and what they do to us and to our world, but all we know is that we are meant to coexist and live among all creatures peacefully. We share a unique bond with all species. One day when you are ready you will drink the drysium and see it for yourself."

Yana took off her necklace with a silver star shaped pendant and put it over Liava's head and around her neck as she said, "My mother passed this down to me a long time ago. I want you to wear it so that you remember what our purpose is. The people of Staga are not kings and queens or city folk that only care about money and riches. We stand for just and selfless causes that protect the souls of all species. Pass the necklace down to your offspring when you are ready."

Liava stared at the sky with beaming eyes, searching and wondering about the other side of the world she never knew existed. For the first time in her life she felt like she understood the complexity of the world around her, and that it somehow understood her as well. Liava's eyes slowly closed until she fell asleep on her mother's lap. Later in the night, Bytal lifted and carried Liava back to her tent to sleep for the night. Liava shared a tent with her younger brother, Ryos Pontas, who was fourteen years of age. Ryos woke up and saw his father carefully place Liava down to sleep. Bytal hushed Ryos before he could speak and slowly backed out of the tent.

Once outside the tent, Bytal took a moment and looked up at the stars. Something big blocked out the stars from his sight as it moved in the sky. Bytal was unsure what it was, or even whether it was real or just the effects of the drysium, but he had no fear of what it could be as he was a protector of the wild.

Liava woke up at dawn, as did most of the villagers of Staga living out in nature. Ryos was standing outside the tent looking in the distance. Liava asked, "What is wrong?" Ryos, with a serious face, said, "Look", with his pointer finger aimed in the direction he was facing. Liava left the tent and looked in that direction and saw their father along with some other villagers of Staga holding weapons and talking to a group of men holding bows from another village.

The two groups of men faced each other standing ten feet apart. Bytal questioned the men, "What are you doing in the territory of Staga wielding bows?" One of the men said, "We come from the village of Tsirian to hunt on your land. There are many types of animals in your territory that are vast in numbers. Killing a few will have little impact. We desire their fur for warmth and meat for food. As our village continues to expand, we require more and more resources, as I am sure you can understand."

Bytal, with confidence, said, "We are the village of Staga, protectors of the wild. If you hunt and kill an animal in our territory, then you yourselves will be hunted and killed. The villagers of Posbor and Ranfet have come before trying to hunt but found that out the hard way. When you enter our territory, you must respect our rules." The hunters of Tsirian turned their backs as they grunted and whispered among themselves. As they walked off heading north, Bytal said, "They will be back."

Chapter Six: The Truth

Searleone Vallas, Skyrock – Searleone sat on the balcony of Skyrock, a sanctuary for mages that was on the highest point of a mountain. The mountain itself was so high that some clouds were below the view from the sanctuary of Skyrock. Voron Fastios, the mage who was second-in-charge after Searleone, the leader of the mages, approached the balcony that Searleone was meditating on. A dense cloud was passing through the balcony preventing Voron from seeing anything. Voron called out, "Searleone, it is time to meet in the sanctuary and teach the mages." Several seconds later Searleone emerged from the cloud in his black robe. Searleone was around the age of sixty and had a long black beard. With a long exhale his stomach expanded as he blew a moist mist out from his lungs.

"What will you be teaching today, my master?", Voron asked. Searleone replied, "Understanding the source of magic and developing it to master your potential." Searleone and Voron walked through the sanctuary of the mages, a high ceiling stone building with a round shape. The top of the building had some windows that allowed sunlight to beam through the sanctuary. The halls stored thousands of books on topics such as spells, the history of mages, and the nature of Lodas. The two mages entered the teaching halls, an open space with a table in the middle where Searleone sat. That table was surrounded by additional tables on different levels for the students. As Searleone walked toward the bottom level with the single table hundreds of mages sat at the surrounding tables quietly awaiting his first words of the lesson.

Searleone projected his voice as he called out, "I have had many of you recently ask me how I became the powerful mage I am so early in my life. It was around the age of thirty that I started to excel as a mage and understand matters that helped me develop my skills. At the age of forty-eight, I became the first and only head mage of Skyrock. I have always believed and explained that the fundamental concept behind magic is understanding its source, the world itself. You cannot and do not witness any evidence of magic in your dreams, and that is because dreams are fundamentally unique to Lodas itself. In order to utilize magic and expand your abilities you need to have good intent. If you wish to do good, then the world will grant you more potential."

A student called out and asked, "You have learned and understand the need for this good intent, but can you share with us how to better ourselves so that we too can share in this fundamental concept and become more powerful under your lead?" The head mage answered, "No, I cannot. Once this level of magic is reached, the mage cannot be weakened. If I share it with all of you, some of you might not agree with the truth and will rebel. Therefore, I can only leave it to those who are worthy to achieve this for themselves. Please start reflecting on what your purpose is as a mage of Skyrock. It is quite lonely not being able to discuss these ideas with any of you. Many of you see me mediate a few times a day, this is my favorite way of opening my mind to the world around us. That is the only advice I can provide. Use the dramatic scenery around us to your advantage."

Chapter Seven: The Path of Combat

Roy Syssian, Biros - The guards at the front gates of Biros appeared overly cautious, Roy thought to himself as he approached the gates on his white horse. When he left for the gladiator tournament not so long ago there were just six men at the front gates, but now there were close to fifteen. A guard stepped forward and said, "Halt!" Roy said, "I am Roy Syssian of Biros, and now known as Grand Gladiator. I have brought the gladiator title to our kingdom for the people and for the king." The guard stepped aside and softly spoke, "I hope it will serve as the source of a lot of pride because this city certainly needs it. Please make your way to the king's chambers and speak with Nollie Gent."

The white horse trotted forward past the gates into the city. With each step Roy felt the dismal mood of the city grow more palpable. With a long swing of his body he dismounted the horse and walked it to the stable in the city that held horses for his family. Roy quickly proceeded past the town marketplace where there was, uncharacteristically, a somber mood and no music. He had a very eerie feeling.

Once Roy arrived at the entrance of the king's chambers, he encountered several disgruntled guards who were visibly shaken and on high alert. Roy approached and said, "I am here to see the king and Nollie Gent, the guards at the front gates sent me." One of the guards agitatedly exclaimed, "The king is dead. His wife, daughter, little boy. All gone, all poisoned. The royal family is dead, and we must keep outsiders out of the chambers in this time of uncertainty."

Roy became nauseated and could not believe how this could have happened on his short trip to Tyrades. He had always liked the king, and the king even gave Roy a proper sendoff in his quest to win the gladiator tournament. But now Roy felt totally disgusted that the royal family had been murdered. Roy looked down with displeasure and happened to notice the gladiator pin on his chest. The pin, and being a gladiator, were still so new to him that he occasionally forgot the privileges that came with it. Roy looked up at the guards and said, "I am Roy Syssian, Grand Gladiator", as he pointed to his gladiator pin. The guard said, "Hmmmm, we have heard of you. Come this way, Nollie should still be up in the royal keep."

Roy walked to the stairs to the right of the guard and made his way up to the king's chambers. Roy entered the corridor leading to the royal bedrooms and followed the voices coming from the king's bedroom at the end of the hall. Roy peaked inside the bedroom and saw several men discussing the death of the king and his family members. Pushing the door aside Roy spoke, "I am Roy Syssian, Grand Gladiator. I was sent here to speak with Nollie Gent." An older man in his late fifties with long hair and a bald spot on his head came forward and said, "I am Nollie Gent, the advisor to the king. I am sure you have heard the tragic news of the royal family by now." Roy nodded his head and softly said, "I am truly heartbroken to hear the news." Nollie said, "Follow me, let us talk in private somewhere else."

Nollie and Roy walked down the flight of stairs and into the council meeting hall. Nollie softly said, "Roy, I want to congratulate you on becoming a grand gladiator. It has been decades since the last gladiator from Biros honored us with this accomplishment. King Stewart Nare and his family would have been proud of you as well. The news of you becoming gladiator reached the council but has not officially gotten to the general population of Biros yet so the citizens are still mourning the loss of the royal family without anything to be joyous for.

Still visibly bothered by the passing of the royal family, Roy asked, "Who did it, or rather who do you think did it?" Nollie answered, "We are still questioning the chefs and staff and investigating, but I have no idea, only time will tell. It could have been an internal move or perhaps the actions of another kingdom. One thing is for certain, trust is extremely low among the council and the city at this time. Many of the guards are starting to question us, the very council of the kingdom. I have already had numerous discussions with the council regarding the well-being and future of our kingdom and we strongly believe that you are the best candidate to become king of Biros. There are no true heirs to the kingship here anymore with the passing of Stewart's children. Your commitment, actions, and success of bringing Biros a gladiator title will be very influential with the citizens of Biros. The Syssian name also has a long and impressive legacy in Biros and your father was very well respected by the king and the population. You will not just bring pride and hope to a mourning kingdom, but you will also be the perfect king to lead Biros. What say you?"

Roy, who was now perplexed, said, "I was just named Grand Gladiator, now I am to be a king? I have spent years of my life training to become a gladiator, but I am not sure I deserve or am ready to be a king. I have not worked for it at all." Nollie smiled as he said, "Acquiring kingship can happen in unique ways, but I assure you that all the work you put into becoming a gladiator was also meant for you to become king, you just didn't know it at the time. I know you are probably a little worried about being murdered as king, but I can say with confidence that the council and the guards of Biros will have incredibly strict and elaborate security protocols going forward." Roy grabbed his right fist as he thought for a moment and said, "That does not worry me. I truly would be honored to serve as king of Biros if the council believes I am the best fit to lead our kingdom. I will always consult with you as advisor to serve not just our own interests, but also those of the people of Biros. Out there in our kingdom there are families that will need me to provide them with the resources to help benefit our kingdom."

Nollie stood and said, "When you are ready, I will be the one responsible for anointing you king. The council will then instruct the guards to blow horns and you will stand from the King's Eye to greet the citizens of the city. I need you to release all of the emotions you have built up over these past few days and reassure and motivate these people." Roy, nodding to himself, knew what he would be expected to say to the people. Nollie continued, "Stay here for a moment and let me inform the council and the guards." Roy sat for a few moments, his heart and mind racing from the turn of events and the endless potential that had come his way in such a short period of time. He had not even begun to consider how he would utilize his influence as king, naturally a much more powerful rank in Biros than gladiator.

Nollie returned and asked, "This is your last moment before you accept the kingship, is there anything you want to leave behind you?" Roy shook his head, no, confidently, as he waited to be seated in the anointment throne, the seat within the council hall reserved only for the king.

After the other council members and a group of guards entered the room, Nollie said, "Please sit, sense my sword and hear what the core of kingship in Biros is." As he pointed his sword at Roy's feet, he exclaimed, "Use your feet to walk and follow your path, but do not run. Lead your kingdom in the path of righteousness and justice and accomplish feats of pride for your people." Nollie lifted his sword to Roy's hands and said, "Empower your hands to feel the best of what life brings and try to use these things as king of your land to help and support your people. Embrace your queen's body and comfort her in life. Grab hold of the spear of combat, direct your army and strike down any evil that seeks to conquer the kingdom of Biros in the honor of a king."

With a final adjustment of the sword the point shifted to Roy's head, as Nollie said, "Think in the ways of our former kings and make decisions in the best interests of our kingdom. Be wise and never treat combat with jest." The sword quickly swung back to Nollie's hip as he said, "From this moment on you, Roy Syssian, are regarded as the king of Biros."

As Roy stood up, he never felt as empowered in all his life. Roy proudly said, "Thank you, Nollie, council members and royal guards. I will try my best to bring pride to the prior family of kings, the council, the royal guards and the entire kingdom." Nollie nodded with approval as he said, "Out of all the paths to fulfill kingship, the path of combat is the bravest and proudest. Use this to your advantage, but only when necessary. Make the men of your army powerful and never let anyone try to intimidate you. You must find yourself a queen who can connect with the women of the kingdom. Take the time to find the one who you deem fit for yourself and the queen of Biros."

As word spread, horns within Biros started to project throughout the city and hundreds gathered in front of the king's halls to see the new king and be part of the ceremony. Nollie went to crown Roy with the king's crown of Biros. Roy put out his hand to push it away and said, "Not now, I do not want them to see me as royalty just yet. They need to see the Roy that was a fighter and just a man of Biros." "As you wish, my king", Nollie responded. Nollie spoke to the guards, "Go ahead, spread the curtain."

Roy proceeded to walk past the curtain and up a few stairs to a flat level called the King's Eye. From there he could see the distant mountains, a magnificent sight he thought. Roy took another few steps until he now saw thousands of citizens anxiously and curiously looking up at him. Roy placed his weapon on a table next to him and looked into the crowd before beginning to speak.

Roy said, "My name is Roy Syssian. I became a Grand Gladiator several days ago and king of Biros today, but I grew up alongside all of you here in the city as a citizen. In this time of mourning, let us reflect on all the prosperity that the Nare family has brought us over the years. I hope to sustain that success and peace throughout the kingdom and all kingdoms as I serve as your king. With every strong kingdom, there is confidence and optimism. Right now, all the kingdoms are looking at Biros not only as a nation that lost their king, but also as the kingdom that won the gladiator tournament and that produces the fiercest warriors. I ask you all to celebrate our kingdom's accomplishment in the tournament and the life of the royal family tonight. Leave all of your sorrows behind you so that we can continue to function as the prosperous kingdom we have always been."

Roy grabbed his weapon with his right hand and aimed it high in the air as he shouted, "To the future of Biros!" The crowd erupted with exhilaration as they chanted, "Roy! Roy! Roy! Roy!" Roy took a few moments to face all angles of the crowd and let himself be seen by all the people.

The king turned around and walked into the halls as he asked, "How was that for a morale booster?" Nollie smirked and said, "You are a natural with words, I see. It will be very helpful for speeches and kingdom relations." The king sat down on his throne and said, "I am already on good terms with the king of Tyrades. His daughter is very beautiful and would make a suitable queen. I intend on talking with her more when I head back to Tyrades in a few weeks." Nollie, with hesitation, said, "My king, I must say I do not believe that would be a wise path for you to pursue in searching for a queen." The king smiled for a moment and then replied, "The path of combat led me to become a gladiator, a king, and to meet her. It is funny how things work out."

Chapter Eight: A Spark of the Wildfire

Jol Parantis, Path Toward the Contaminated Towns – "Trees, trees, and more trees, that's all there is out here", one of the young soldiers said with a bored attitude. Another soldier snapped back at him, "We have not even eaten lunch yet and you are already moaning. Jol here is a bright guy, perhaps you can speak with him and learn a thing or two on our trip." The younger soldier responded, "I have always wanted to save people's lives. I attempted potion mastery as a child and unfortunately combined ingredients that are not meant to be mixed. I concluded that I am not meant for alchemy. But I knew I could become a soldier and save people's lives by the blade." The older soldier laughed and said, "You moron, if I have to save you from the angry mob of citizens up ahead, I will not let you, the soldiers, or even Jol forget about it, ha!"

Jol and the large group of fifteen soldiers rode swiftly ahead on their horses. Jol calmly said, "It is not the healthy citizens that we have to be as worried about, but we still must keep our distance when possible to be safe. Hopefully, they will appreciate our aid, and let us all hope the illness has not already spread too rapidly." The older guard asked, "What the hell could be in that big sack of yours, Jol? You do realize that we are the ones doing the fighting, right?" Jol agitatedly responded, "The items that will hopefully save our lives, and theirs, from this sickness."

The aid group continued heading north until a little after midday when one of the soldiers called out, "Up ahead!" Jol kicked his horse to go closer. He had hardly been on a horse in recent years, but he had experience riding from when he was younger. As Jol got closer he finally pulled on the reins and commanded his horse to stop. The horse quickly stopped and Jol leaned to the side and looked down upon three dead corpses. Jol called out, "Everyone stay back, let me inspect." After dismounting from his horse, Jol stood over what appeared to be burned bodies. Jol whispered to himself,

"They are burning the bodies without even knowing anything about the disease." He called out, "Proceed with caution", as he mounted his horse.

As the group slowly made their way closer to the town, Jol noticed that wildlife was still thriving. He saw what appeared to be healthy deer, rabbits, and foxes roaming and eating without any signs of distress. Jol instantly recalled the last illness, another plague where only humans suffered from the symptoms. This finding was somewhat unsettling for Jol as he hoped this sickness did not relate to the last one.

Upon entering the town, there was little sign of human activity. Only a few citizens roamed around with pieces of cloth covering their mouths. Jol reached into his bag and snagged a bunch of face cloths for all the members of the group. "Put these on now!", Jol commanded his group. Jol looked around and again noticed no signs of struggle from the animals. Cows, horses, and other farm animals all looked healthy.

Jol dismounted from his horse and walked closer to the main set of buildings in the town as he spoke to the group, "A few of you come with me." A few of the soldiers walked with Jol into what appeared to be a tavern. Only three men were in the tavern and no one was talking; they just sat there and sipped their ale.

Jol asked one man sitting at a table, "What is going on here?" The man looked at Jol and said, "People are starting to get sick and die. I have the early symptoms of the illness. You probably shouldn't get too close." Jol asked, "What are the symptoms?" The man said, "It starts with a deep, dark cough, severe fever, and".

One of the other men in the tavern dropped his ale on the ground and started shaking as he grabbed his head. The man started screaming, "No, no, no, no, this can't be it! Someone please help me!" His body started shaking more violently and in an instant his body burst into flames. The soldiers grabbed all the water they could get their hands on to douse the fire, but it did not go out. The man rolled around burning until his body abruptly stopped, and the flames started to slowly reside. The other man, with an emotionless face, continued, "And that. Should be another week or so until it consumes me too."

Jol said, "I am here to help, and I will try my hardest to save you if I can find a cure, but I have never seen anything like that. The body getting so warm that it ignites itself on fire? I would be considered mad if I tried to describe this back in the city. Have most of the people of the town died yet?" The man had a drink of his ale and said, "No, not yet, only those who were exposed first. Most are staying quarantined in their homes trying to evade the illness. The sick stay home so they can die in peace. My wife died a few nights ago, I do not need your cure. I want this to be my end."

The man leaned to his right and coughed a few times. A dark mist of black ash came out with each cough. One of the guards said, "Once the town dies won't the illness die with them?" The man responded, "No, this is just a spark of the wildfire. The illness started in the town next to us named Federeck. You must head east of here to get there. I hope you find a way to end this, no one deserves to meet their fate this way." Jol said, "We will head there and try to get to the root of the problem. Thank you for your help. I will find a cure and avenge your wife." The man said, "And likely me."

Chapter Nine: A Summons from a King and an Invitation from a Princess

Kip Denvion, Path to Tyrades – Kip slowly dozed off after a long day riding to Tyrades. He was not used to waking up before dawn and riding in the sun for a full day. Right as he started to tilt over on his horse, Rus Trenode grabbed his arm and said, "Keep yourself awake, we are only a short distance away from arriving in Tyrades." Kip said, "I am sorry, this sun is really wearing me down", as he grabbed his canteen from his bag and started to drink some water.

Kip looked at Rus and asked, "Are you guys going to stay the night in Tyrades?" Rus responded, "You will see me sleeping in the wild before you see me spend a night in that ridiculous city. Fighters from all around Lodas go to that city just to become a gladiator, like it means something. All that happens is they become King Hasting's bitch. The only king I will ever respect is the king of Gofon, especially King Phillip Denvion and the Denvion family. Kendrin and I grew up together as close friends. We trained together all of the time and, although I was better than him, I could tell he was a good man who was much more fit to be a king." Kip responded, "My father always said you were not just an amazing fighter, but also most loyal to the Denvion family."

As they kept riding toward Tyrades Rus said, "I know that the attractions of Tyrades appeal to you, the fighting, gladiators and fame, but I must warn you, never let serving a different king come before the interests of your own kingdom. Do not forget, you will become the next king of Gofon. You have nothing to prove by becoming a gladiator. I could have entered and won that stupid tournament years ago, but I do not care about having pretty looking armor that matches my weapon."

Kip said, "I understand why you do not like Tyrades. I will make sure it has no influence on the decisions I make. It is a shame you will not be staying tonight as I was hoping we could play some Borsty on the unique marble playing boards they have." Rus said, "You will have to practice and train at Borsty for your entire stay in Tyrades to have a chance at beating me. Besides, you should be spending your free time in Tyrades with some women your age. Tyrades is home to some of the most beautiful women in all the kingdoms." Kip smiled and said, "I do know some girls there from my last visit, they all realize who I am, and they want to be a queen someday. Some of them younger, some older, and they try to impress me with their beauty. I will keep them hoping for it until I finally decide to marry one, which I do not plan on any time soon." Rus looked at Kip in awe and said, "You lucky boy, it must be nice."

In the distance Kip could see the high walls of Tyrades and knew that they were very close to arriving at their destination. Half a year had passed since his last visit and he was eager to start training again. He was going to miss his family a lot, as he always did, especially because this time there was so much uncertainty around their well-being. As Kip, Rus, and the group of soldiers approached the gates, Rus whispered to Kip, "Send a message to one of the Gofon traders if you need anything. Hopefully, everything will be better in several weeks so you can come back home."

They all stopped in front of the gates of Tyrades as they now faced the guards. Rus shouted, "We are here to drop off Kip Denvion, the son of King Denvion of Gofon." The guards nodded and said, "Welcome back" to Kip as he came closer. As Kip proceeded past the guards, he went straight to the king's chambers to greet the king of Tyrades. One of the guards said to Kip, "Please wait here for a moment." The guard entered the king's chambers and called out to the king, "My king, Kip Denvion is here to speak with you." The king waved his hand at himself beckoning that Kip be allowed to enter and said, "Let him in."

The guard went back and signaled for Kip to walk ahead. Kip walked into the room and looked at King Hasting as he said, "Greetings, King Hasting. I am glad to be back in Tyrades and learn some new fighting techniques." The king said, "Kip, it is great to have you back here. You are like a second son to me. Please stay as long as you desire, you know the gladiators will train with you whenever you would like."

James Farenter entered and saw that Kip was in the room with the king. James said, "Back so soon, warrior?", with a smile on his face. Kip responded, "Yes, I have continued training with my sword and buckler, I think you will be impressed." James said, "I am sure I will be. We shall start training tomorrow morning, so get some rest, I have a few moves to teach you." Kip smiled with excitement and he started to leave the room and said, "I will be there. See you soon and thank you for having me King Hasting."

As the door closed behind Kip, James walked closer to King Hasting. He leaned down to King Hasting, who was sitting, and whispered, "The spy in Biros was successful. The royal family of Biros is dead, and Biros has crowned Roy Syssian to be king just as we had hoped." The king smirked and said, "The royal summons has already gone out, but have Leora write a letter to Roy that she looks forward to seeing him when he comes for his gladiator ceremony, which will be in three fortnights. She has already asked about him, so I am sure she will be happy to write to him and it will be more reason for Roy to look forward to arriving." James said, "I will go and speak with her now." As he turned to leave the room, the king said, "And James, we are slowly gaining more control over all of the kingdoms. Soon Tyrades and the gladiators will rule all the lands."

James left the king and walked outside to the gardens where Leora and a few of her friends were conversing. Leora and the group of girls, all mature daughters of nobles in Tyrades, were sipping wine on an enjoyable sunny day. James called out, "Leora, can I have a word with you?" Leora walked over to James and asked, "How can I help you?" James held out a blank scroll and said, "Your father has asked that you write to Roy Syssian and tell him that you will give him a royal welcome when he arrives for his gladiator ceremony in three fortnights." Leora smiled and said, "Yes, of course, I will go write a letter to Roy right now." James said, "I can tell Roy enjoyed talking to you when you met him." Leora responded, "Really?" James nodded with confirmation and said "Absolutely," as he turned and headed back to the royal chambers.

Leora headed back to her room in the royal chambers and laid out the scroll while she prepared her quill and ink. She sat and paused for a moment as she thought about what to say and how to start her letter. She finally let the tip of the quill hit the scroll and started writing:

Respected King and Grand Gladiator Roy Syssian,

As you are by now very likely aware, the king of Tyrades, my father, Lance Hasting, has summoned you to the city of Tyrades for your gladiator ceremony in three fortnights from today, the tenth day of the fourth month. I have heard that the blacksmith is hard at work on your equipment, so the equipment and your ceremony should be very exciting. Every day I think about ideas to help you make your kingdom a better place, which I can share with you when you return to Tyrades. You will need to tell me more about your kingdom and your people so I can continue to brainstorm and try to help you. Until then, I will look forward to your return.

Wholeheartedly, your friend in Tyrades,

Leora Hasting

Leora rolled up and sealed the scroll with her custom circular seal in red ink and marked, 'Leora Hasting', with rotating outside letters saying, 'Tyrades'. She brought the letter to her father and said, "The letter for Roy that James asked of me." King Hasting said, "Thank you, my daughter. Your writing has always been more pleasant than mine."

A few buildings away, Kip was setting up his gear and clothing for the next morning. Kip heard a knock on the door and opened it. His old friend, Julia Trove, was standing at the door and greeted him, "Welcome back to Tyrades, I heard you arrived this morning," as she gave him a kiss on the cheek. Julia was seventeen years old with brown hair, light skin, and light green eyes. Kip was happy to see her and said, "Thanks, I am glad to be back. I will be training again for a few weeks, at the very least. The spread of an illness to the northeast by Gofon might keep me here longer. What do you say we go grab some food and play some Borsty like we used to?" Julia smiled and said, "I was about to ask you the same."

Chapter Ten: The Boy's Purpose

Oakley Nodon, Sterafia - The sound of Snowstorm's footsteps woke Oakley every morning before dawn, including this particular morning. Oakley tried to keep still, hoping he would not alert the growing cub that he was now awake. In the wild, tigers rise early every morning to start hunting. Oakley himself started to realize this as he was getting less and less sleep since adopting the cub. Snowstorm grew more impatient as he started running across the floor. Oakley lifted his body and said, "Okay, I am up."

The cub jumped at Oakley's thigh in a playful manner, slightly scratching his leg. Oakley and Snowstorm were bonding quickly after several weeks, but Oakley found it increasingly difficult to balance his life and keep the growing cub a secret. Oakley could tell Snowstorm needed more time outdoors. Oakley took Snowstorm out late in the night and early in the morning to let the cub pee and poop if the cub had not already done so in Oakley's room. Oakley opened the door to let Snowstorm out to do his business while he grabbed a handful of jerky for the cub. Snowstorm sniffed his way back in after peeing outside. After the cub ate all the jerky out of his hand, Oakley struggled to lift the cub onto his bed to go back to sleep. Oakley whispered, "You are growing so fast; I can't believe it. You are already more than twice the size from when I found you." Oakley slid into bed and managed to cuddle the cub back to sleep.

A couple of hours passed, and Oakley awoke to Snowstorm licking his hand. Oakley sat up and noticed the light from the outdoors. "How did I sleep this long?", he asked himself. He quickly gathered his clothes and got changed, grabbed his equipment, petted Snowstorm, and left his room. Oakley knew he was late for the training grounds. His participation had only gotten worse since taking care of Snowstorm. As he approached the training grounds he walked straight past his father and the king to get to the archery range. The two men noticed that Oakley did not seem himself, a common occurrence of late, but they did not say anything to him.

King Renga said to Damien, "Oakley has been late quite often recently. Do you think he is alright?" Damien, scratching his cheek, responded, "I am not sure, but I feel like he is hiding something. I know him well enough to see that something does not seem right with him. Interestingly, two days ago I was talking to him in the dining halls and I noticed a few scratches on his shoulder and arm. There could have been more, but I could not see through his shirt. I am under the impression he has found a close friend." King Renga and Damien laughed together until Damien said, "Let's go find out."

The king and Damien approached Oakley and Damien said, "We have noticed your lack of effort in training recently. What is going on?" Oakley, with a straight face, said, "Nothing, just feeling tired recently." King Renga asked, "Have you found yourself a woman? Your father was telling me about the scratch marks, we won't tell anyone." Oakley stared at the ground for a moment and said, "Come with me, I know I should have told you earlier." Oakley led the king and Damien to the outside of his room. Oakley paused and said, "Please let me explain when we get inside."

Oakley opened the door and the king and Damien entered behind him. In the left corner of the room, Snowstorm stood, his head tilted to one side, and looked at all of them in confusion. The sight of two men next to his master felt unusual. King Renga and Damien stared with shock at this magnificent cub with white fur and black stripes.

Oakley said, "This is Snowstorm. I went hunting a few weeks ago and witnessed two adult tigers running with several cubs in their mouths. One of them dropped him as it was running from hundreds of wolves and feral humans who ran just like wolves. I ran to save him, and I was fortunate to grab him and climb a tree in time saving both of us. I have had him a few weeks now and I have felt guilty about not telling you, but I was worried something would happen to him. He means too much to me after I saved him."

King Renga smiled and said, "The boy has found a purpose. Oakley, you are granted permission to raise this tiger throughout Sterafia. It can roam the city at your side if it does not attack our people or our horses. I am impressed that you have managed to domesticate it and it appears that you have built a strong bond with Snowstorm."

Damien said, "For a moment, I thought we were about to witness the first brothel in Sterafia. You can tell me anything, son. I want you to trust me so I can help you in these situations." Oakley nodded as Damien continued, "He truly is a beautiful creature." Oakley went to the corner and picked up Snowstorm so that the king and Damien could pet him. The king said,

"Although he is cute now, in a few months he will be a massive tiger. Train him wisely. Now can you please elaborate on the wolf pack."

Oakley said, "I will, king Renga. The wolf pack was huge, I would say there were several hundred of them. And for every two wolves, there was one feral human. I know we do not really send troops to the south much anymore, but I did not think the land would be so hostile. Tigers are usually the predators in that territory, not wolf packs." Damien softly responded, "Wolf litters can have several pups at a time. And who knows what is going on with the feral people. I think this is a serious issue that will only become more problematic for us the longer we wait. We cannot send men through the royal gate unless it is a large military force. We may have to put down this wolf pack. I can prepare the army at your command, my king."

King Renga thought for a moment and responded, "We have little knowledge of the southern territory; it has always been an uncivilized and uninhabitable land for humans. We always assumed it was only inhabited by wildlife. We cannot send any troops to combat the problem without knowing where the pack or the den is. The weather conditions have been rough this winter and the land is quite large. We need to scout out the land, as safely as possible, to find some relevant information before we can attack. If we do not make this our main priority, the size of this wolf pack and feral people could devastate the civilians of Sterafia if we are exposed in any way. Damien, let us plan this out with some of your men as we consider our course of action." Damien nodded with approval as he thought about the issue himself. Oakley walked out the door with Snowstorm at his side and said, "I am going to go introduce Snowstorm to Sterafia."

As Oakley walked closer to the shops in Sterafia, people stared at him and Snowstorm with shocked faces. Oakley reassured them that Snowstorm was still young and would not harm them. Snowstorm, not surprisingly, was most interested in the food cart and its pleasant aroma.

The vendor asked, with a smile, "What would the cub like to eat?" Oakley responded, "Can I get a few slabs of rabbit meat, please?" The vendor handed it to Oakley and excitedly said, "This meal is for free, I want to see the beast grow just as much as you do. You know these streets have been having some pesky rats go after our food recently. You think you can help us out?" Oakley smiled and said, "That would make for a good hunting experience for Snowstorm, and a good meal too." Oakley pulled up a chair to sit next to the food cart.

The vendor said, "My name is Ralph Torron. I am curious how you managed to obtain and domesticate a tiger cub." Oakley said, "It is quite the story, but I have already shared it enough today. I will tell you another time if that is alright with you." Ralph said, "Okay, please share it soon." Oakley asked, "How long have you been selling meats here?" Ralph responded, "My family and I hunt these meats ourselves. It has been a little over two decades now." Oakley asked, "How often do you go hunting in the land to the south of Sterafia?" Ralph said, "Not too often anymore. All the good meats that sell, like rabbit and deer, are hard to find. It used to be my favorite spot, but I have changed my hunting location to the northern land now."

A rat slowly approached the food cart from the opposite side and within seconds Oakley and Ralph heard a scuffle. By the time they looked over Snowstorm held a rat in his mouth and looked at Oakley for a sign of his appreciation.

Chapter Eleven: The Inscription

Ria Falune, Torust - Ria held her gold necklace with the ruby pendant as she was about to wear it around her neck. She stopped halfway and brought it back down to her dresser to take a closer look at it. Her recent conversations with her sister and Torb had made her more interested in jewels and her necklace. The necklace had always been worn by the ruler of Torust instead of the traditional crown most kingdoms used to honor their kings and queens. In fact, the necklace had been passed down by the rulers of Torust for almost a millennium. On the inner side of the gold that touched her skin there were inscribed words of an unknown language.

Ria tried to decipher the words, any word, but none of the letters were in Torustian, the native language of Torust. Ria's father left her this necklace when he passed away, but he never mentioned anything about its meaning. Ria felt the inscribed letters with her thumb as if it helped her understand what it meant in some way. As she placed it around her neck, she told herself she would make it her goal to find out its meaning.

Ria made her way to the Halls of Absolute, where she sat as a performer played pleasant melodies on a flute. Being a talented musician was highly respected in Torust, but Ria and her family never had much interest in learning an instrument as they were more concerned with being powerful and respected rulers. Ria did, however, admire and enjoy the talents of the top musical artists in Torust.

Ria sat and enjoyed her breakfast by herself until Haigar entered the Halls of Absolute. Ria called him over to join her and asked if she could have a word with him. Haigar responded, "Of course, my queen. How can I help?" The queen responded, "My father left me this necklace, which the rulers of Torust have worn for several centuries, but its significance and meaning are unknown." As Ria took off the necklace, she handed it to Haigar and said, "The lettering on the back, I want to find out what it means." Haigar held the necklace in his large hands and said, "Let us ask Halon Tracher, the master of languages here in Torust. Stay here and I will go speak with him and get him to come examine the necklace."

Ria sat and inspected the necklace again as she waited for Haigar to return with Halon. She looked around the room as she wondered what the necklace could mean. Ria looked up and gazed at all the rubies scattered across the ceiling. The rubies were used as eyes in the old Torustian figures. She measured the ruby in her necklace to have a diameter of about two inches, which appeared to be the same size as the ruby eyes of the figures on the ceiling.

Haigar and Halon soon arrived and sat at the table with the queen. Halon spoke, "Greetings my splendid queen. Haigar has informed me that there is something you need my expertise for." Ria nodded and said, "Yes, I want to know what the inscription on this necklace means. My understanding is that my father and the rulers before him ignored it for centuries but let us just say that I am more curious than they were. Take a look."

Ria then handed the necklace to Halon. The master of languages closely inspected the ruby and the inscribed letters on the back. Halon looked at the inscription for a moment and said, "It appears to be an ancient dialect of Torustian. I apologize as even I do not understand what it means. I never had the opportunity to learn this dialect and its purposes, but I would have pursued it if it were ever possible. I have heard rumors in the past that there are elders in one of the outposts northwest of here that still understand this ancient dialect."

Haigar faced Ria and said, "We would have to cross the Tazir Desert to get there. I have been through the desert a bunch of times and the sandstorms can get really harsh." Ria said, "The sand does not bother me. We are all native to the desert, so we will be fine. We leave tomorrow at dawn, so prepare and dress accordingly. Both of you will accompany me. Haigar, please gather fifty of your soldiers to come with us. Halon, please coordinate with the troops to ensure we are heading to the outpost you speak of. I have a feeling the meaning of this necklace will help me become a better leader for the kingdom of Torust."

Chapter Twelve: The Cave of Jewels

Torb Daxo, Sahine Sea – "Onward, men. Keep the ship stable!", Torb shouted. He continued, "The waters are starting to intensify!" Torb and several of his workers were crossing the Sahine Sea as it was required to get to the cave one of the workers had discovered. Torb encouraged the workers and said, "A cave of promising fortunes awaits us men. Each of you will be paid according to your efforts."

The waves grew larger and the powerful forces of water smacked against the side of the ship the men were navigating. One of the men threw up over the side of the ship from sea sickness as Torb grabbed the worker's hips so that he would not fall overboard. Torb said, "First time at sea, I can tell", as he laughed. The worker turned around, sat down, and said, "Thank you, master", as he wiped his mouth with his sleeve. Torb shouted, "I can see land, just a bit longer!"

As the ship came closer to land, the strength of the current and waves started to subside, and the sailing became smooth. Once the ship came close enough to the shore Torb said, "Alright men, we are here. Grab your equipment and bags. The journey to the cave should take several hours, but we should arrive by nightfall." Torb pointed to the seasick worker and said, "You will stay here and take care of the ship." The worker said, "I'd do anything to get off this rotten ship, master." Torb smiled and said, "I bet you would, I want you to spend some time with the ship, get to know her and hopefully by the time we return to sail back you will be close friends." The other workers laughed in amusement at Torb's words.

Torb and the workers boarded some smaller boats and paddled their way toward land. The seasick sailor was soon left all alone. The men steadily stroked their oars through the water and were coming closer and closer to land. Along the way, Torb dunked his hat under water and then set it back on top of his head to block out the sunlight and keep cool. Torb said, "Stay hydrated, but conserve your water. We still need enough water to make it back if there are no water streams along the way. It may rain, but I doubt it will."

Once on land, Torb said to the worker who had already been to the cave, "You lead the way." The worker nodded and said, "We must continue to the northeast." After a few hours of walking under the scorching sun, one of the workers said, "If only we had camels, this journey would be much more tolerable." Torb smirked as he responded, "I know, this is why I have avoided crossing the Sahine Sea for years. However, if this cave is as promising as I have been told, I can ask the queen for aid on a return trip. At the very least, she can lend us larger ships so that we can board camels with us." The worker leading the way said, "Just up ahead through that passage in the distance."

As the sun started to set, the men began walking into a narrow passageway that led up a mountain. After several minutes of walking through the passageway, the men came across a massive cave opening. Torb said to his workers, "Set up camp and a fire here." Torb went to the man leading the way and said, "Go light your torch, you and I are going inside." In a moment, the worker entered the cave with a lit torch and Torb by his side. The worker whispered, "I have only made it into this large opening ahead, which is only the beginning of this cave. I did not want to venture further without a group. But I have never seen anything like this before. It is a cave of jewels", the worker said as he handed the torch to Torb.

Torb grabbed the torch with his left hand to guide the way since his right hand was his dominant hand if needed for self-defense. As an adventurer, he never feared the unknown or the darkness. The thrill of the reward was always in the back of his mind. The opening was totally dark. The light of the torch he held was the only reason that they could maneuver. With small deliberate steps they made it to the entrance of the big opening. The light of Torb's torch extended a couple of feet beyond his body. Torb's walk through the aperture was filled with excitement, anxiousness, and the thrill of adventuring into the unknown. He always relished those emotions in search to discovering ancient treasures and relics for Torust and, of course, himself.

With a bend of his neck, Torb proceeded through the entranceway and entered the large opening. He walked to the right side of the path, the side he always started with. The light from his torch slowly started to bring the elements of the surroundings to life. First, he saw the darkness fade, then a few sparkles, then more shininess, and finally the bedazzling colors of copious emeralds. His mouth was open as he stared at the beauty of the cave. A single tear ran down his cheek as his heart was filled with exuberance and excitement. He continued to walk along, letting the torch and the emeralds lead the way. The wall was covered with what seemed to be endless emeralds. Suddenly, the jewels started blending darker. The wall became filled with Onyx. Torb smiled at the aesthetic diversity of his surroundings. He kept walking following the wall until he arrived at the aperture he came from. He turned to face the room again, completely dark now. Torb smiled and said, "It truly is the cave of jewels."

Chapter Thirteen: The Fall of a Lifetime

Liava Pontas, Village of Staga - The scream of an adult woman awoke Liava from her sleep. Liava thought to herself, 'What is going on, I hope that was not my mother.' She looked next to her, but Ryos was gone. She heard more screams. She looked at the small opening of her tent and saw people running past. Liava grabbed her small knife and placed it in her pocket as she got up and quickly ran out of the tent. She looked around and could see the villagers of Staga in panic. The women and children tried to run behind the men of Staga who made a last-ditch effort to fend off the villagers of Posbor, Ranfet, and Tsirian. Liava realized that it was a unified attack against Staga. In the past, Staga successfully prevented individual villages from hunting on its land, but this unified attack would be a more formidable challenge.

In the heart of the village, Liava watched in horror as her father, Bytal, was stabbed by a few different enemies. The first stab stunned him, but the next ones sent him to his knees before he fell over to die. Liava's mother, Yana, was right behind Bytal and managed to stab one of the attackers before she was cut and stabbed. Yana fell right beside Bytal who was at the forefront of the Staga defense. The two were now facing each other in their dying moments. Yana whispered, "See you in the stars, beautiful soul." Despite the loud echoes of war surrounding them, her words were the only thing Bytal internalized before he smiled and passed on.

Liava was panicking and in shock as she saw her parents murdered right before her eyes. She was crying uncontrollably and was not sure what to do or where to go. Nowhere seemed safe. There was no sign of Ryos. As she watched her village fall, she turned toward the woods and started running as fast as she ever had. Branches hit her in the face and thorns of bushes cut her arms and legs. She tripped over a rock and went tumbling, but then was able to get up and keep running deeper and deeper into the forest.

As she continued to run, she was not afraid of the unknown, but was hopeful that there would be something that could keep her and her people going. The tears blurred her vision. She saw smudges of trees and objects around her. When she was not using her hands to push branches out of the way, she was trying to wipe her eyes and face from the vast tears streaming down her face. She kept telling herself that she was strong enough to make it out of this. Liava finally grew more confident in her escape and started running even faster.

Suddenly, Liava ran straight off a cliff and, as she did so, her feet were still running in the air. Liava was overcome with fear as she realized she was falling. She looked down and saw what she thought was a fatal drop into a large lake. Liava thought to herself, 'I should have known this was here. It really doesn't matter, I guess.' She fell for what felt like a lifetime. She closed her eyes and braced for the imminent impact.

The plash of the impact echoed across the lake. The sound reverberated within the immediate surroundings. Just a short distance away, a large, green dragon was standing on the shore drinking water from the lake. The dragon witnessed the girl, the fall, and the impact. As the events progressed, the dragon lifted its head up higher with curiosity to see the girl falling. The dragon had never encountered a situation like this in its lifetime, but instinctually it felt like saving the girl was the correct response.

The legs of the dragon dipped lower to the ground as its wide wings started to open. With a hard thrust, the dragon shot straight up into the air and within seconds dove straight down into the water toward Liava. The dragon grabbed the unconscious body of the girl and shot straight up out of the lake. The dragon flew higher and south of their location and the Village of Staga.

A loud screech of the dragon filled the sky and awoke Liava who opened her eyes and noticed that she was somehow in the air and, incredibly, a green dragon was the reason. Liava looked down and realized that the dragon had her gripped around her waist. She was frightened but knew that the dragon had saved her from drowning.

Liava squirmed as the impact of her fall made her stomach quite sore. The dragon clenched its grip slightly tighter so that the girl would not fall. Liava wondered where this enormous creature might be headed, but it did not matter to her; her home was destroyed, her people were gone, and the vision of her people changing Lodas had painfully disappeared. To try to distract her from her emotional turmoil, and the anger and bewilderment she felt from her current situation, Liava tried to concentrate on the sensational view from the sky.

From the corner of her eye, Liava spotted another mature dragon with navy coloring and a juvenile dragon with red coloring resting near what appeared to be a dragon lair overlooking a valley. The dragon lair was a very large area lying on higher ground, which gave the dragons strategic vision around them. The flapping of the wings of the flying dragon started to become slower as it prepared to land and lower Liava to the ground.

The other adult dragon opened a single eye to see what was happening and a moment later shut the eye as it continued with its rest. The younger dragon awoke and, with more curiosity, walked slowly toward Liava with its nose leading the way. The dragon had never encountered a person before and did not want to intimidate the guest the older dragon had just brought to the lair. Something about Liava seemed to comfort all the dragons, which came as a surprise to Liava and the dragons themselves.

The red dragon proceeded to slowly and curiously sniff the girl as Liava extended her hand to greet the young dragon. The dragon did not hesitate to let her feel the side of his thick-skinned neck. The two found happiness and comfort in each other, both teens and both completely perplexed by how the world was flipped on them this day. The green dragon looked on with pleasure as the red dragon and Liava appreciated each other's company. Liava turned toward the green dragon and whispered, "Thank you", as she cried tears of joy and sorrow. As she lost her family to humans, nature and the wild somehow found a way to provide her with a new one on the same day. A family of dragons no less.

Liava thought to herself, 'Mother and father were right, the good in this world is being destroyed by our own kind. One day, if I can, I will change that.' The deep emotions of the day exhausted Liava and she found herself falling asleep on the hard surface of the ground. Several seconds later, the red dragon circled around her and plopped on the ground next to her. The dragon extended its wing for a moment and pulled it back inward so that it covered Liava and provided warmth. After a long, hostile morning, Liava surprisingly found comfort and security in the wilderness amid the company of dragons. 'I cannot believe this', she thought. 'I am even sleeping at noon, just like them.'

Chapter Fourteen: The Shifting of Loyalty

Ryos Pontas, Village of Tsirian - Ryos stood among the remaining villagers of Staga, all children and young teens, in the conquering Village of Tsirian. The group of children and teens were twenty in total and they were standing in rows of two, as directed. The rest of their fellow villagers had been killed during the invasion of Staga the previous day. The boy next to Ryos was shaking immensely as he asked Ryos, "What are they going to do with us?" Ryos, who was also extremely nervous, tried to control himself and said, "I do not know, but don't be afraid, okay? My father always told me that."

A villager of Tsirian called out, "Welcome to Tsirian. My name is Edgar Haurok and I am the leader of the village. Here we do things much differently than in your native village. When we need food, we hunt for meat. When we need warmth, we hunt for the hides and fur of animals. Otherwise, we would not be able to survive. Becoming a member of our village is not granted freely, especially to the offspring of the villagers we just killed. There will be challenges that few of you will be capable of accomplishing. I want all of you to step aside from the boy standing next to you." As each boy started to walk several feet apart from the boy to has side, Edgar continued, "I like to call this the shifting of loyalty. The best proof of your loyalty to join us is through betrayal of your own kind. You must take the life of the boy standing across from you in any way necessary. I do not care how, but if neither of you die then your loyalties will clearly stand with the fallen of Staga and both you will be executed immediately."

Each boy instantly looked into the eyes of his counterpart trying to determine his loyalty and intent. Two of the younger boys instantly ran for the woods as their parents had taught them. Beyond the surrounding trees emerged villagers of Tsirian ready to stop and kill any runners. The men emerged and ran toward the escaping boys who were still so young that they ran at half speed. As the villagers caught up with the boys, they hacked them to death with their axes.

One set of two teenage boys who were close friends decided to give their loyalty to Staga. They walked up to each other and gave the other a deep, long hug. It was an embrace that they wished could have been for their families, but instead served to promote the legacy of Staga and demonstrate their friendship. They then stood side by side and stared up to the sky looking for stars. As they stood waiting to be executed, they knew that they would shortly also be up among the stars with their families. One boy asked, "Which one do you think will be us?" The other boy smiled as he pointed to the sky and said, "That one, it always shined bright, but tonight it is even more illuminating." The loud and frightening steps of villagers closed in on them as they closed their eyes for the last time.

One of the boys next to Ryos charged another boy with a rock in his hand. The target was kneeling on the ground showing little fear. He kneeled for several seconds as the enemy charged him until he shot up at the last moment and thrust a dagger that he hid behind his back deep into his opponent's stomach. As he thrusted it another few times, he said, "I would have died alongside you."

Ryos felt his back pocket and noticed that he still had the dagger his father had always advised him to carry for self-defense. The boy across from him was indecisive at this point as well, but Ryos looked around and saw most of the boys starting to attack their opponents with daggers, rocks, or even their fists. Ryos held the dagger in his right hand as he looked at it. He looked up at the boy and back down to his dagger another few times before he remorsefully called out, "I'm sorry!".

As Ryos walked closer to the boy, the boy said, "Please, please, please, please! I don't want to get hurt!" Tears started to erupt from the boy's eyes as Ryos looked straight ahead and was not deterred. A tear came down from Ryos's right eye, but he used his forearm to wipe it away as he proceeded closer. The boy slowly started to back up as he continued, "You are my friend! That is going to hurt me!" The mortified boy struggled to pronounce the simple words boys at his age spoke.

Ryos charged forward and aimed directly for the boy's heart. The dagger pieced the boy's chest missing the heart. Ryos quickly pulled the dagger out and thrusted it into the boy's heart. Ryos held the gentle body of the dying boy as he laid him down slowly. All Ryos could think to say was, "It's okay, you will be okay. I am doing this for our people." The boy made eye contact with Ryos as he struggled to speak another word. His eyes shifted to the ground as he breathed his final breath.

Ryos stood above the body of the boy and looked down with misery at what he had just done. As he backed up a few steps, Edgar shouted, "All of you, come forward!" The remaining eight boys all came closer to Edgar. "You have completed the shifting of loyalty from Staga to Tsirian. Now that you are villagers of Tsirian, I intend to make all of you stronger and tougher. You will reside in the room next to the armory and always be ready for combat whenever called upon. Now that you are all one of us, you will contribute to the village just like us. Later this week, we will be taking some of you hunting. And, when we do, you better have the will to kill what we find." Edgar turned his back and walked away from the boys.

Chapter Fifteen: The Passageway

Searleone Vallas, Skyrock - Searleone was on the balcony of the sanctuary of Skyrock, pacing back and forth while he was looking down upon the passageway leading up to Skyrock. Voron walked out onto the balcony and asked, "Are you expecting someone?" Searleone said, "No, looking down below our sanctuary is great for meditation. I picture a world where we can embrace all the lands below us. It is this kind of meditation that has helped me grow." Voron thought for a moment and asked, "Grow with ideas that support your views?" Searleone walked past Voron into the sanctuary of the mages and said, "Yes."

Once he entered the sanctuary, Searleone headed to his potion's lab. Voron still stood in the same spot on the balcony reflecting on what Searleone had just shared with him. Voron asked himself, 'What did he mean? Does he think that coexisting with the rest of Lodas is the answer and the truth? If that is so, I am right in supporting him.' He walked closer to the edge of the balcony and peered down at the same passageway that Searleone was looking at earlier. Voron said, "I can see it too", as he smiled at the image.

Once Searleone walked into the potions lab he picked up his black mixing goggles. The goggles strapped around the back of his head and had extra strong glass lenses to protect his eyes in the front. The potions lab was his for personal use and he spent many late nights experimenting and with different concoctions. All the practice and experimenting allowed him to become the most talented alchemist within Skyrock and all of Lodas.

As Searleone prepared his experimentation table, he paced around the room looking for various ingredients to try. It was his lab and he could make whatever he wanted, even if it served no purpose. He opened a jar of mushroom fungus and scattered some onto a plate. "Mmm", he murmured to himself. Next, he walked over to the minerals section of the lab and tossed a few small minerals onto the plate. Next came some wild berries. Lastly,

Searleone walked to the flammable section. He took a few looks around and decided to grab some flour and cinnamon. He brought the plate back over to his workstation and poured the ingredients into a funnel that led into a glass tube. He used a small burner to heat up his flask as he inspected how the ingredients were being transformed from the heat. The mushroom fungus burnt out quickly and Searleone said to himself, "A bit too much flammable ingredients, could be. Possibly need more ingredients to mask the intensity of the heat. We will see."

Searleone spent hours and hours looking around the lab, mixing the same ingredients in different amounts, mixing the ingredients with other ingredients, trying different levels of heat and even no heat, and then finally started to tire. He stood up and removed his goggles and looked down at his final experiment for the night. He murmured, "Could be something." He wrote in a scroll the ingredients he used, how much of each, how he prepared them, what level of heat he used, how long the heat lasted for, and the result, which wasn't quite what he was looking for, but showed potential.

Searleone then left his lab, closing the door behind him, and walked into the main part of the sanctuary. In the late hours of the night, only a dozen of mages remained in the main halls. Those who were still around were tirelessly studying from various books while a few sat at the tables resting. Some had nodded off. Searleone walked past them all, not caring to see what was going on. He walked straight to the balcony and looked down at the passageway leading to Skyrock as he said to himself, "Where are you, already?"

Chapter Sixteen: A King's Desires

Roy Syssian, Gates of Tyrades - "We will be back for you in a few days my king. Are you sure you will be okay?", a guard asked. Roy answered, "I am a gladiator; they love me here. Soon they will love Biros too." Roy Syssian and forty of his guards approached the gates of Tyrades on horseback. Roy dismounted his white horse and told one of the guards, "Please take care of him for me." The guard nodded and said, "Yes, my king." Roy placed his hands on his horse's neck and felt the animal one last time. As he turned to walk toward the guards of Tyrades, the horse whinnied. The guards stood aside and said, "Welcome back, your honor." Roy nodded and asked, "Where did King Hasting want me to meet him?" One of the guards said, "King's chambers, sir."

Roy slowly walked through the city, satisfied with the change of scenery after being in Biros for a while. As he approached the marketplace of the city, a teenage boy approached him. The boy, with a spirited smile, asked, "Is it you, the gladiator from Biros?" Roy responded, "Yes, it is quite unusual to be recognized as a gladiator instead of a king."

The boy bowed and said, "It is an honor to meet you, the gladiators here have told me all about you. They are training me as I hope to one day become a gladiator just like you."

Roy then asked the boy, "And who may you be?" The boy said, "My name is Kip Denvion. I am the son of King Phillip Denvion of Gofon." Roy smiled and laughingly said, "What are you doing bowing to me, I thought you were one of the peasants here." They both laughed in amusement as Roy continued, "You are royal blood of one of the kingdoms, there is no need to bow to me in the future." Kip nodded and said, "I will never bow again, well, of course, unless the situation calls for it."

"I am here for a few days, perhaps we can do a little training together if you would like", Roy said. Kip responded, "Yes, if you have time that would be great and quite the honor for me. After all, you are the most recently crowned gladiator. I wish I could have been here to see the fight myself. Have you met my father yet?" Roy said, "It was quite a fight. No, I have not met your father although I do intend to meet him soon and get to know him so that our kingdoms can continue to maintain friendly and prosperous relations. But I am glad to have had the opportunity to meet you before him. I must go meet with King Hasting for matters of the gladiator council. Keep training and one day hopefully you will be a part of it." Kip said, "I hope I can succeed; can we train tomorrow morning?" Roy said, "I will meet you at the training grounds."

Roy proceeded to walk through the city until he arrived at the king's chambers. Roy flashed his gladiator pin at the guards and walked into the king's chambers.

King Lance Hasting was sitting on his balcony with his back turned to Roy. Roy called out, "Greetings, King Hasting." Lance turned his head and said, "Oh, splendid to see you again, king. I believe that is how I should address you now. I heard the news about the royal family, truly terrible to hear." Roy responded, "I got back to Biros shortly after becoming gladiator, and I was named king, the most life changing few days of my life. As king of Biros I am sure together we can bring our kingdoms closer as allies." Lance smiled and said, "There is more to being a king and gladiator than you have learned in the short time. As you start to understand the gladiator council more, the more our kingdoms will be able to aid each other. But yes, Biros remains a trustworthy kingdom to us." Roy nodded and said, "Anything I can do, always let me know."

Lance asked, "So, are you ready for the ceremony later?" Roy nodded and said, "I have longed for this moment for months now, even more so once I received the letter from your daughter, Leora." Lance pointed at Leora in the garden below as he said, "She is outside in the garden; you should go greet her. She has asked about you a few times recently. The gladiator ceremony is at the gladiator chambers at sundown, show up early." Roy responded, "I will go speak with her now. I will see you in a few hours, Lance."

Roy left the king's chambers and thought about what he would say to Leora as he walked to the garden. Roy thought to himself, 'I shouldn't worry, she seems just as interested in me. Her father seems to accept our friendship, perhaps because I am a king now.' Roy walked out into the garden, proceeding closer to Leora who sat at a table with her back to Roy. Roy called out, "It is beautiful out here; may I accompany you?" Leora turned around and stood at the sight of Roy. She responded, "Certainly, it is great to see you again. She walked up to Roy and gave him a big, tight hug. Roy said, "Thank you for your letter, I have been anxious to come here for the gladiator ceremony and to receive my gladiator gear, and to see you. I brought you a gift."

Roy took a small bag out of his pocket and handed it to Leora. Leora anxiously, but slowly, opened the bag and took out a gold and red bracelet that Roy placed around her wrist. She said, "It is magnificent, I cannot thank you enough King Syssian." Roy responded, "I am honored that you like it. The ceremony is tonight, and I will be receiving my gladiator gear with matching colors. I want the gift to be a sign of our friendship." Leora beamed with happiness as she smiled and grabbed Roy's hand. Leora softly said, "A sign of our friendship." The two leaned in closer until their lips kissed for the first time. Leora said, "I knew from the first time I met you that you saw something in me. Well, I saw something in you as well, Roy Syssian."

Roy said, "I am a king now; you should be with me. You can help me more than ever. Come spend some time in Biros with me. You can help me take care of my people." Leora said, "I really want to; I wonder what my father will say." Roy said, "He just told me to come out and speak with you, it seems he approves. Have you ever been to Biros?" Leora, with a slightly embarrassed face, responded, "I have never left the kingdom of Tyrades." Roy said, "It will be a new journey for you. My men are coming back to get me in a few days, you can ride back with us." Leora said, "I will go with you, Roy", as she kissed him on the cheek. Roy said, "Great, I think you will really like where I come from. I have to go get ready for the gladiator ceremony tonight, I will talk to you again soon." Leora said, "Good luck, I know you must be excited." Roy nodded as he started to leave and said, "More than you know."

Roy walked back to his room and dressed in clothes proper for the ceremony. After Roy was finished with all his preparations, he became filled with mixed emotions for his ceremony. 'Who will be there?', he thought. 'Did they perfect my gladiator gear? What will Leora think? Will she be proud of me? Time to go find out', Roy thought to himself as he left for the gladiators' chambers.

Roy looked up at the descending sun in the sky. 'Sundown has not arrived yet, I am early', he told himself. He waited and sat by the entrance of the gladiators' chambers for several minutes until the thick metal door opened. Roy looked ahead at the dark opening and slowly walked closer. One by one, he saw the flames of torches become lit. "Come forward, Roy", someone called out. Roy walked ahead still unsure of who the speaker was. In an instant, the man's face was exposed by the illumination of the torch he was holding. It was James Farenter, his fellow gladiator and friend. He was wearing a white tunic.

Roy looked around and noticed all the other gladiators in both corners of the room next to the entrance. The gladiators were wearing white tunics as well and stood silently. By the light of the torches on the wall ahead, Roy was able to see the armor, sword, and shield of a late gladiator. Standing a few feet in front of the wall were two guards of Tyrades. James pointed to the wall and said, "Please stand next to the wall, behind the guards." Roy nodded and he continued walking to the wall. Roy stood with his back facing the wall, in between the armor on one side of the wall and the sword and shield on the other side. James said, "After your astonishing performance in the gladiator tournament, you deserve the finest equipment a fighter can have. Tyrades and the gladiator council are honored to arm you as one of us. Guards, please bring him his jaxion steel gear."

The guards both walked over to a wooden table in the corner of the room and gathered Roy's leg plates, plate boots, and chest plate armor. They carried them to Roy and helped him maneuver his way into the armor. The guards walked back to the table and came back with a helmet and finally the two-handed weapon Roy mastered. All the equipment glistened with gold and red detailing just as Roy desired. Roy grabbed the helmet with his left hand and the weapon his right hand as he stood as one impressive force.

James commanded the guards, "Bow before the gladiator as Tyrades has always done." The two guards both stood in front of Roy, knelt, and bowed as they faced each other and whispered, "The fight for dominance, the way of Tyrades." Roy, now full of adrenaline, held his weapon high in the air, empowered by his dual role of being the gladiator king.

Chapter Seventeen: The Entertainer of the Square

Phillip Denvion, Gofon – The hymns from the plucking of harp strings filled the dining halls as Fayna played for her father and his company. Being kept away from her training lessons in Torust meant she had to practice more on her own at home. Although there were gifted teachers in Gofon, Fayna believed that if she was not being taught by her favorite instructors in Torust then the lessons were just going to be a waste of time. Although the dining halls were filled with men eating and conversing, the only thing on Fayna's mind were her fingers and the strings that filled the halls with a harmonic ambience. Dressed in a long white dress, she sat on a stool by the harp. Fayna always enjoyed matching the mood of her music with her fashion.

King Phillip and his advisor, Timothy Milton, sat together eating chicken and bread. Timothy was called out for official business so he wiped his cheek and said, "I will be back, my king". After he returned, Timothy informed the king, "Sir, the first message from the aid party reached Gofon just moments ago." The two men stared at each other for a few seconds. "And?", the king asked. "Not good", Timothy responded. He continued, "The infected, their bodies are getting overheated and are bursting into flames. Water cannot even help counter this fatal symptom." The king, visibly disturbed, murmured, "It's worse than we expected..." Timothy said, "I know. Luckily, the aid party has learned where the infection originated. It started in a neighboring town from where they last made contact. They are currently in route or possibly already at that town."

The king asked, "Can we send more supplies to help the citizens in the towns plagued by the disease?" Timothy responded, "Yes, the choice is yours. You can expect some resistance from the council, but I know you and I know why you want to help." The king said, "Thank you, I always knew you had my back on these types of difficult matters. By the way, has Torust responded to our request to aid the infected?" Timothy said, "No response, sir. The king asked, "Did the message mention anything on the status of the aid party members, and in particular Jol?" "Yes, all are currently healthy", Timothy replied. The king said, "Without Jol, this whole kingdom is hopeless. It is hard to fathom how the most powerful kingdom with the most very timely resources, and the most powerful military, can have little chance of survival without potions masters like Jol. He is the only man who can save us now."

Both men binged on the lunch feast until they were stuffed and fatigued from overeating. The king said, "Let us take a walk." Timothy said, "It would be a pleasure, my king. She plays beautifully by the way, your daughter. She might just become the next greatest musical talent out of Gofon." The king placed his hand on Timothy's shoulder and said, "Thanks, she is a bit upset that she cannot travel to Torust and practice there, but I constantly reassure her that she is getting better. When you get the chance, tell her yourself. It will bring her great joy."

The king and Timothy left the dining halls and made their way out toward the city streets. As they walked out, six guards followed behind them for protection. The city looked full of life as the king said, "This is why I have always loved this kingdom, and this is the best city of them all. In uncertain times, people do not get afraid. They go on with their lives and push any fears aside." Timothy said, "You are correct as usual, my king. The city was the same way during the last sickness, and I have heard the citizens were strong during the wars many years ago."

The sound of laughter and excitement could be heard in the main square at the heart of the city. Many citizens went to the square for food or just to let the kids play and roam around. The king and Timothy approached the square and saw a jester entertaining the crowd of kids and their mothers. The jester wore patterned clothing covering its whole body except for its face. Its face was covered in white oil and it wore a hat that covered its hair. In one of its hands it held a cane that had a bell on the top that made a ringing noise when it was shaken. Bright blue, yellow and red were striped across the outfit of its costume. 'Extremely exquisite attire,' the king thought.

The jester danced around to the music being played in the square in an entertaining manner. The jester was swimming higher in the air like he was flying away until he was left standing on the tiptoes of just one foot. As planned, the jester fell over on the ground in amusing fashion and much to the delight of the laughing kids. The jester rose back to his feet and jumped straight up in the air. As his feet hit the ground again, he wobbled from side to side until he was jumping from his left foot to his right foot and back and forth. He shook his cane as he wobbled from side to side.

The jester stopped wobbling as he noticed the king spectating within the crowd. The jester took a few steps closer to the king and started to dramatically bow to the king. As he bowed, his left arm and hand led, then his right side, then his left, over and over. The kids found the jester's overly dramatic and submissive orientation to the king quite funny and they showed their appreciation with their claps and giggles.

The king finally spoke publicly to the jester, "Your gratitude and performance have been well-received", as he smiled and waved at the rest of the crowd. The jester nodded his head with approval as he proceeded to dance to the side a few times and maneuver his body in amusing ways. As the king and Timothy started to leave the square Timothy said, "I never cared much for town entertainers." Phillip responded, "I have always appreciated them since I grew up loving the arts and acting. It takes talent and a unique mind to stand in public trying to make random people laugh, young kids in particular. We often forget what it is like to be so genuine and just laugh at something that is meaningless, but enjoyable. As adults, we want bawdy jokes, or we just get drunk to be entertained."

Timothy said, "Not much to lose if you hide your identity though. I even wonder if the jester is a male or a female." The king responded, "I am not sure, but it does not matter. Even with your identity hidden, it takes some degree of courage to put yourself out there like that. And the potential humiliation can be excruciating. I have been there before. The toughest part of my life was failing time and time again as an actor. As the son of the king I got every opportunity possible, but I lacked the natural talent. Instead, I became a writer for the plays." Timothy said, "I remember, you did very well writing some of the plays." The king smiled and said, "Thank you, I do miss those days. Maybe once we find a way to resolve this illness and get things back to normal, I will spend some time writing again." Timothy said, "You should, my king. You need to find ways to enjoy your interests and relieve your stress. It is not easy being the king."

The king and Timothy approached the blacksmith who was standing and talking with Rus Trenode. The king called out, "Greetings, Rus. Thank you for accompanying Kip on the trip to Tyrades a few weeks back." Rus turned to the king and said, "Greetings, my king. I will always be at your command whenever you need me." The king nodded and said, "What brings you to the blacksmith?" Rus responded, "I like to have my equipment checked and my blade sharpened often. The blacksmith and I have been friends for years now." The king said, "He does produce some great gear. The king handed a small bag of coins to the blacksmith and said, "Let this visit for his gear be on me." The blacksmith nodded as Rus said, "Thank you, you did not have to do that." The king looked at Rus and said, "When you are ready for new gear, make sure you come to me first."

Chapter Eighteen: The Robed Guest

Jol Parantis, Town of Federeck - One of the soldiers called ahead to Jol, "Wait, Wait! The soldiers back here are struggling to keep up." The aid party had just made their entrance into the Town of Federeck. Jol instructed the soldiers standing next to him, "Wait here."

Jol walked back and found two fatigued soldiers. These soldiers were clearly weak and exhausted. For some reason, they dismounted their horses and attempted to walk. Jol asked the two men, "What is wrong? Are you guys thirsty?" As both men stopped and stumbled, one of them said, "Yes, I... I just feel a bit out of it. I need to sit down; my head has a lot of pressure." Jol said, "Both of you just sit here and relax for a bit. We are going to go talk to some of the townspeople. As both men plopped down on the ground one of them nodded as the other said, "Thank you."

Jol walked back to the rest of the soldiers and said, "They will stay behind for now, all of you come with me." The group of men walked ahead until they arrived at the center of the town. As they walked, they were disturbed by what they were witnessing. The town appeared to be abandoned. Burnt corpses were scattered throughout the town. The devastation here was much more apparent than in any of the previous towns.

Jol shouted, "We are here to help! If anyone can hear us, please come out!" After waiting a few moments, one of the soldiers whispered to Jol, "I think it is just us, sir." Jol looked around and noticed the remnants of what appeared to be a celebration still scattered throughout the town center. Jol inspected the surroundings more as he said, "They were celebrating something here and it appears that the citizens did not have time to clean up the mess. Whatever happened here, it must have started during the celebration."

One of the guards noticed a big cauldron and walked up to it. Jol asked him from several feet away, "What is in that?" The guard picked up a giant ladle and moved the substance around and replied, "It appears to be some sort of soup or something liquid with chunky bits in it." A man standing at the entrance to a nearby shop called out, "You should stop messing around with that." The guard dropped the giant scooper back into the cauldron and stepped away from it. The man walked closer to Jol and said, "That is where the illness emanated from." Jol asked the man, "What is your name? My name is Jol Parantis and I am a potions master, I have come to help find a cure." The man responded, "Ked Larone. I was here the night of the feast. It was our annual celebration; we always celebrate the prosperity of our townspeople and the kingdom of Gofon. We all contribute and gather whatever food and drinks we can to allow everyone to appreciate the holiday."

Jol, listening intently, asked, "So what is it that is in the cauldron?" Ked replied, "No one knows, but a visiting guest came and provided what he said was soup as a gift for the celebration. We are all genuine and trustworthy people here, but perhaps too much so. An hour into the feast everyone that ate the soup started to hurl and become ill. By that time, the damn man was long gone." Jol asked, "Did anyone know or recognize the man? What was the man wearing and what did he look like?" Ked replied, "No, he was a total stranger. He was a younger looking man dressed in a brown robe. It was uncommon, I thought, but he mentioned he grew up in Federeck so everyone treated him like one of us. Looking back, I realize that it was very strange that none of the townspeople recognized him or knew of his family. We were obviously too trustworthy, but even if he hadn't claimed he was a local, we still would have welcomed him with open arms."

Jol asked, "What happened after the feast?" "Within days, those who ate the soup were being burnt alive. Those who got infected through others suffered the same symptoms, but they progressed much slower", Ked responded.

Jol asked, "Is it just you here?" Ked said, "No, there are a few others, but almost all of the townspeople are dead. Some people fled town, which I worry will be very bad for the surrounding towns. I stayed because I wanted to help those in need. I supported many of the infected until their last few moments. I do not have any kin, other than my brother and his family, and they all perished from this, so I do not care about surviving."

Jol thought for a moment and asked, "How... how haven't you gotten ill yet?" Ked shook his head a few times and replied, "I am unsure myself, but I know it would be absurd to say I am just lucky. For the past few weeks, I have interacted with numerous infected townspeople and I have had to watch them look back at me with jealous eyes; jealous of what I do not even wish to have, life itself."

Jol said, "I am sorry for what happened to you, your brother and his family, and your town. First, I will study the mysterious substance that caused this illness. Once I have a better understanding of this sickness, I will need to talk with you further. You might, even unknowingly, be more helpful in our quest to find a cure than you realize." Ked said, "If I can help in any way, you can find me by my home across this field right here." Jol looked at the house across the field and said, "Thank you, we will come and find you soon, Ked."

One of the soldiers said, "We better go and check on the others." Jol said, "Yes, there is something disturbing about how out of sorts those two soldiers felt." Jol and the group of soldiers walked back to the two soldiers who were lying motionless on the ground. Jol went up to them and asked, "How are you guys feeling?" One of the soldiers did not respond as he appeared to be napping. The other soldier sat up and said, "I don't think I will make it back, nor will he." The unconscious soldier then started coughing up black ash with each cough. Although they had been journeying for a few weeks, the intensity of the sickness had suddenly erupted.

Jol told the group, "We must care for these soldiers while we look for a cure. Everyone gather the supplies from the horses and make camp. I must study this illness immediately."

Chapter Nineteen: The First Love

Kip Denvion, Tyrades - Kip woke up, fully clothed, as his friend Julia was fast asleep in his arms. Kip tried to slowly slip his arm from underneath her as he tried to get up. Julia awoke and turned to Kip and said, "I can lie here and sleep in with you all morning. Must you go?" Kip, who still had pink oil remnants from Julia's lips on his neck, pushed his hair to the side as he said, "Yes, I am training today with a gladiator, who also actually happens to be a king. I am surprised he still wants to train with me as, he must be extremely busy with his new responsibilities."

Kip grabbed his plate armor from the corner of his room. He sat on the bed and as he started slipping his armor on, Julia seductively said, "You look so alluring in your armor. Let me ask you something." Kip sat up straighter on the bed and slightly turned to face Julia. As their eyes met and locked, Julia continued, "Would you fight for me someday?" Kip firmly said, "I would", as he reflected on how their friendship had as of late turned into his first love.

Kip went in for a kiss and they both passionately locked lips for a short moment. Kip stood up and said, "I would fight with everything I have. I have never felt this way about a girl before. I do not know if this is a familiar thing for you, but the feelings I have felt recently, the moments we have shared, I want them too last longer." Julia smiled and said, "I hope they do, Kip. We can make it happen." Kip grabbed the remainder of his gear and replied, "We can", as he smiled for a quick moment and walked out of his room.

Kip strolled through the town until he arrived at the arena gates. Kip said to the guard, "Morning, sir." The guard said, "Morning, go on ahead. Roy is waiting for you." Kip entered the arena where a few men were already sparring and training since the early morning. Kip saw Roy swinging his long two-handed weapon with various techniques as he was getting warmed up. The sunlight illuminated the shiny gold and red armor that Roy had just received and was wearing. Compared to the rest of the men in the arena, Roy stood out visually from his armor and by his fighting skills.

Roy noticed Kip enter the arena and went to greet him. Roy said, "I am glad we found time to make this happen before I left." As he came closer, he noticed the pink lip marks on Kip's neck and smirked as he asked, "Did you rest well? Are you feeling invigorated?" As Kip responded, "Yes, actually, what is so funny?", Roy tapped the weapon in his hand. Roy replied, "Based on the love marks on your neck, it appears you have made a friend."

After reflecting for a moment, Roy said, "I must say, there is one thing you should know." Kip smiled, as he asked, "What is that?" Roy said, "Do not have a child before you try to become a gladiator. If that is something you strongly wish to pursue, do it, but forget about becoming a gladiator. Having a child, a wife or even a lover will make you weaker. You will become a softer fighter and will become more vulnerable to others." Kip replied, "After all this time, you still do not have a wife or a child?" Roy said, "That is correct, it was something I set aside till after I became gladiator. Now that I have accomplished it, I am ready to start a family. But it would not have been right to start a family and focus on training instead of raising kids properly. Having a family around takes the toughness out of us, we become too caring. Take it how you will." Kip said, "Thank you, I will reflect on your advice."

Kip was uncertain how to absorb Roy's advice. From one perspective, his new relationship with Julia was harmless and inspired him emotionally. But, from another perspective, it could pose a distraction to Kip's goal of becoming a gladiator.

Roy said, "Good. Now, let us train our techniques at half-speed." Kip asked, "Is that jaxion steel?" Roy said, "Yes, I just received this armor and weapon recently. I must be careful, I do not want to accidentally break any of your gear, I know how powerful this steel can be".

Roy then asked, "So I am assuming you specialize in the sword and shield?" Kip replied, "Yes, it will be difficult against your weapon. I have never seen someone use something like that." Roy said, "I understand what you mean, but you should just look at the weapon closely. The first thing I do when I am fighting an opponent is, I analyze the weapon they are wielding. Does it swing harder and do more damage than my weapon, is it heavier and harder to swing, how far it can reach, is there a weak point I can hit to disable the weapon? These are just a few questions that go into the process."

Roy then asked, "So, Kip, when you look at my weapon and compare it to yours what comes to your mind?" Kip took a moment to look at Roy's weapon and his own and said, "Your weapon clearly has more range. It looks heavier, but you are using both arms with it so I am unsure about how fast you can swing it. Based on the quality of steel and your strength over mine, it will hit harder. The pole of the weapon is steel, so there really are not any weak points. How did I do?" Roy replied, "Good observations, you did well. Just get in the habit of practicing this before all your fights. Are you ready to practice?" Kip nodded and they both stood ten feet apart and readied their weapons.

With slower and softer than usual strikes, they both swung their weapons, which clanked against each other as they met. Kip took a step back and tried to swing at Roy, but it was blocked by the pole of Roy's weapon. As Kip tried to get back, Roy thrust his blade straight ahead as it flashed past the sword and shield of Kip's defenses. It clanked against the chest plate of Kip who sighed and removed his headpiece.

Roy removed his headpiece and asked, "With a shorter-range weapon, where should you be fighting me? Kip said, "Close range, I suppose." Roy nodded and said, "That is right, you must get up close and stay within close range. For the entire time you cannot reach me, I have a significant advantage to strike you down."

Watching from the balcony of the royal chambers was King Lance Hasting and James Farenter. The long view made it difficult for them to determine the identity of the men practicing afar in the arena. "Are you sure that is Roy down there?", the king asked. James responded, "It has to be, I can tell by the gold and red colors he is wearing." The king said, "Yes, I am sure he was quite eager to try out the new armor." James laughed and said, "I am confident I did the same thing when I became a gladiator. My ceremony was in the morning, so I went straight to the arena though."

The king laughed for a moment and said in a more serious tone, "Listen, Leora came to me asking for my blessing for her to travel to Biros with the gladiator king." James looked at Lance, uncertain of the implication. "What did you tell her?", James asked. The king said, "I allowed it. They seem to have feelings for another. What father would not let his daughter travel with a king? Besides, when the time comes for Roy and me to speak about the future our of kingdoms, I will have more leverage, won't I?", Lance said as he smirked.

James asked, "Is there something I should know about?" The king said, "Yes, but not yet. At the next gladiator meeting in a few weeks I will inform you and the others of the plan. Roy will not be invited to the meeting so do not tell the others just yet." James asked, "One question, is this the first major action after the killing of the royal family?" The king answered, "Precisely. We must carefully plan every step. One small error and we could start a war."

Chapter Twenty: The Blood-Stained Fur

Oakley Nodon, Sterafia - "Come here, Oakley", Damien called out. Oakley turned around and started walking closer to his father in the training grounds as he whistled for Snowstorm to follow. Snowstorm was developing rapidly, as demonstrated by his increasing speed and strength. He now weighed over a hundred pounds and had grown another foot long. Oakley enjoyed Snowstorm's boundless energy and athleticism. With long strides, the tiger came charging to Damien ahead of Oakley. It did not matter where the two were heading, you could always count on Snowstorm to beat Oakley to the target.

The tiger charged up to Damien and ran around him a couple of times until Damien grabbed ahold of Snowstorm and stroked his hands through the tiger's lush, dense fur. The tiger stood there enjoying the moment until it ran up to Oakley and sought the same treatment from him. Oakley knelt on a knee and faced the tiger as he rubbed its head with both hands. Snowstorm chuffed at all the attention he was receiving from Oakley and Damien.

Damien said, "You better not be heading out through the royal gate." Oakley looked up at his father and said, "You know I wouldn't be that stupid. Snowstorm would not be safe down there in the south." Damien said, "It isn't all about the tiger. I know you care a lot about him, but you must watch out for yourself too. You are all I have left, Oakley." Oakley stood and gave his father a deep hug and said, "I will be wiser, I am starting to understand things." Snowstorm stood and circled both of them as they hugged. Snowstorm proceeded to hug Oakley's leg as he impatiently waited.

Oakley and his father stood apart as Oakley said, "We are going to go hunting to the north. Hopefully, we can manage to get some meat to feed him." Damien said, "Are you sure it is safe to go alone again?" Oakley replied, "I need Snowstorm to learn how to hunt and fight properly. Together we will be alright." Damien said, "Head to the paths if you find yourself needing help." Oakley said, "Okay, are you and the king planning anything to fight the wolf pack in the south?" Damien said, "Between you and me, we are planning to send a scouting party soon. I am not sure who will be part of the party, but I might be one of them." Oakley, with a serious face, said, "Let me know." Damien nodded with approval as he turned around and walked away.

Oakley took a moment and watched his father walk away before he turned and walked ahead, clapping his hands for Snowstorm to follow. The two jogged ahead to the northern gates of the city and walked past the guards. As they left the city gates, Snowstorm jumped around Oakley joyously. Oakley, with a flat hand, signaled for the tiger to sit still and be calm. Oakley bent over and said, "We are in the wild now, your home. We must be on alert for predators and prey." Oakley, noticing that the tiger had become somewhat calmer, stood, and started to walk. Snowstorm again anxiously charged ahead of Oakley and looked at him with a mischievous face. Oakley, with another flat hand signal and a displeased face, said, "Settle down." Snowstorm, ever eager to please his master, now understood how Oakley wanted him to behave.

Snowstorm and Oakley continued to walk the snowy hills on the outskirts of Sterafia. Oakley thought to himself, 'I wonder if Snowstorm's parents and siblings are still alive. If Snowstorm saw them again, would he recognize them?' As the two were walking, Snowstorm paused for a moment and let his nostrils sniff the air. Oakley knew he was onto something. Snowstorm slowly started to stroll to the west with his nose leading the way. Once they got to the top of a small overlook, Oakley and Snowstorm spotted a winter fox a few hundred feet below them. Snowstorm anxiously wanted to charge ahead, but Oakley commanded the tiger to lay on the ground in a prone position. Oakley signaled with his hands for the tiger to stay put as he showed a flat hand. Oakley crept to the left side of the overlook and slowly made his way down so that he could quietly sneak up on the roaming fox.

Oakley thought, 'I have to get this just right.' He peeked out from the side to see where the fox was and where he thought he left Snowstorm. The tiger was hard to notice as his fur blended in with the surroundings. He finally spotted Snowstorm and saw him quickly and nervously licking his paw. 'Just a bit more to the side', Oakley thought. He moved a bit more to the north until the fox was perfectly in between the tiger and himself. With an instant burst of speed, Oakley ran in the direction of the fox and continued to give chase so that the fox would run toward Snowstorm. Oakley held his bow in hand, but intentionally did not shoot at the fox since he wanted Snowstorm to have the natural hunting experience. The fox charged up the hill in an attempt to escape, but as the fox got closer to the top, Snowstorm pounced from a few feet away and tackled and snagged the fox with its long claws.

Snowstorm instinctively widened his mouth as his jaws started to extend. With a fierce bite, Snowstorm tore into the back of the fox's neck. He continued to rip and tear the flesh of the fox to totally incapacitate it and eat the valuable meat that served as his nutrition and reward. Snowstorm took his time eating the now motionless fox. Oakley stood a few feet back watching Snowstorm devour the meat of the fox. He smiled with excitement as he realized Snowstorm was growing and learning quickly; Snowstorm was starting to learn the essentials of hunting.

Snowstorm finished eating and walked over to Oakley with joy. Oakley smiled as he said, "Hold still, Snowy. I need to clean you up." Oakley bent over to the ground and picked up some snow that he wiped against the bloody cheeks of Snowstorm. His usually white with black striped face was blood-stained from his meal. He cleaned his face all he could, but the red marks on the white fur would be difficult to remove entirely. Oakley proceeded to recover whatever fur he could obtain from the fox's corpse to sell at the marketplace back in Sterafia. Oakley started walking back to the city with Snowstorm. As he stroked the top of his head, Oakley looked down at Snowstorm with a deep smile and said, "This is just the beginning."

Chapter Twenty-One: The Caller

Ria Falune, Tazir Desert - Even though her kingdom was located in the heart of a desert, being surrounded by only sand was an uncommon situation for the queen. She had not traveled far outside the city in years and had never ventured across the Tazir Desert. Her body slowly swayed a bit from side to side as her camel took slow, but heavy, strides. Ria turned her head as far as she could to the right. She could see Torust afar in the distance, now just a tiny figure sticking out of the sand.

Ria said, "One day, I want all of Lodas to see us. Many cities spread across all of the landscapes, all under Torust creation and rule." Haigar replied, "I will help you get there, slowly but surely. How are you holding up so far?" Ria responded, "Fine, the sand does not bother me. Although, I am getting quite hungry." Haigar snapped his fingers twice and one of his soldiers rode up ahead on a camel and handed Ria a bag filled with an assortment of fresh fruit.

Ria, Haigar, Halon, and thirty soldiers of Torust all rode on camels equipped for combat and the desert conditions. Ria tossed a berry into her mouth and bit into it, savoring the sweet taste of the fruit she loved so much. She tapped the shoulder of Haigar, who was riding directly side by side with her. He turned his head and Ria held out a handful of fruit she generously shared. Haigar cupped the fruit with his big hand as he said, "Much appreciated, Ria." With a single toss, the handful of fruit was tossed into his mouth as he chewed and started to swallow it all down.

Haigar started to cough a few times after he swallowed the fruit. Ria said, "Everything okay, Haigar?" Haigar started to clear his throat as he spit out a big splash of saliva and sand. Haigar said, "Yes, the winds are starting to pick up and some sand got caught in my mouth." Haigar looked at Halon who was riding in front of him and asked, "How are you holding up, Halon?" Halon turned his face a little and responded, "I am doing well, it has been a while since I ventured through the desert. There rarely is a purpose for me to come through here, but I am glad to accompany you and the queen on the quest to understand the meaning of the inscription."

Haigar asked, "I do not intend to offend you, but what made you want to specialize in languages? What interested you to do that with your life in Torust?" Halon replied, "No worries, I understand why you ask, you are certainly not the first. Without people like me, there would be wars. Without interpreters and proper translations, it is hard for two kingdoms with different languages to build friendships. Without people like me, everyone that speaks a foreign tongue is a mysterious threat. In the same way an adventurer discovers treasures, I seek to uncover the meaning of words that someone at some point wanted to share, regardless of their importance." Haigar smirked and said, "Maybe next time you can uncover the meaning of the inscription without us having to trek through the desert." Halon, with a humorous tone, said, "Maybe if it isn't thousands of years old."

Ria intervened and said, "Both of you contribute greatly to Torust and my interests. Halon is leading us to people who can translate the inscription, so it is as if he is doing it himself." Halon quietly said, "People I believe can translate it." Haigar said, "Would you make up your mind. If we are traveling all the way across the desert for nothing my men and I are going to be irate."

One of the soldiers in the front started calling out, "It's getting bad, I can see it up ahead!" "What's going on?", Ria asked. Haigar replied, "I am not sure, but let me check." Haigar commanded his camel to ride ahead of the others. Within a short moment, Haigar shouted, "There is a sandstorm coming, we must cover our faces with scarves and get to high ground." Halon said, "I guess we are going into the storm then." Ria said, "It looks like you are right. We are still heading toward it." Halon said, "If we can get up that hill before the storm hits it will make it a lot less dangerous and difficult."

Ria and the others started to cover their faces the best they could as the thick cloud of sand was speedily approaching them from ahead. The group started to ascend the hill as the storm was just moments away. Ria and Halon anxiously sped up their camels to reach high ground and attempt to summit before the storm hit. As they both made it to the top of the hill, the sandstorm had already blown in and covered the soldiers leading the group.

Halon shouted, "Here it comes!" The sand cloud expanded as it came closer and blocked all the vision of more and more of the group. Ria and Halon started to dismount as they only had a few seconds remaining. Halon stepped off his camel and looked to the side to see if Ria was off of hers. As she was stepping off, one of her feet became entangled in the camel's saddle and she started to panic. She exclaimed, "I cannot get off!" Halon looked to his side to see the impending storm about to hit and he quickly took a few steps closer to Ria. The storm smacked against Ria, Halon, and their camels, sending Ria falling backward. Halon, who stood beneath Ria, caught her in his skinny arms saving her from plunging to the bottom of the hill.

"I got you!", Halon shouted. "Grab onto the camel and hold on till the storm ends", he yelled. Ria hugged her camel closely to protect her face from the harsh, sandy wind. Ria closed her eyes as she held onto the large, gentle creature that blocked much of the wind. She tried to imagine something else to pass the time as her lack of control of the situation was an unpleasant feeling for the queen.

Ria reflected on a moment from her childhood. A time when she was no more than the daughter of the king and queen. Ria was playing with a friend in the outskirts of Torust when she picked up a rock and got stung by the stinger of a poisonous scorpion. Ria lay motionless in the sand, completely vulnerable to nature. Somehow, Ria's small body managed to overcome the toxins that flowed through her veins. However, the experience was the most memorable and frightening one of her life.

In an attempt to mentally escape the sandstorm, ironically her mind wandered to this painful memory. Although the memory made her feel uneasy, the fact that she overcame the poison made her realize she would overcome the storm too. Halon shouted to Ria, "Just a little longer, the winds are dying down."

Ria thought back to her memory. One of the Torust guards carried her powerless body toward the city to get help. Ria was placed on her bed and left to fight the toxins on her own. The city had no cure to save those stung by these poisonous scorpions. Ria's parents looked down at her suffering and squirming. Ria's mother grabbed her hand and said, "Be strong, for us, for Torust. One day, you will rule just like us."

Ria felt a hand grab her shoulder as she opened her eyes and heard, "We can go now." Halon helped Ria to get her balance as he helped brush the sand off her. Ria looked at Halon and said, "Thank you for saving me back there. I really owe you." Halon said, "I would do anything for my queen. I am glad you are safe now."

Haigar came back and said, "I am sorry my queen, I was in the front of the group and had little time to get back here. And I could not see." Ria replied, "Halon here saved me from falling off my camel and down the hill. If he did not have your respect before, maybe he should have it now." Haigar said, "You have proven yourself, Halon. I respect the bravery you displayed to save the queen during the storm. If any of the soldiers give you any kind of hassle, let me know." Halon nodded and said, "Thank you. We should keep moving, we want to get as far as possible before nightfall. The desert will start to get quite cold."

As everyone started to mount their camels, Ria took the scarf off her face and started to shake the sand out from her hair. Halon was intrigued by Ria's long, beautiful hair and looked at her as she shook the sand out. She looked over at Halon and said, "What?" Halon jokingly said, "Are you done getting the sand out?" They both laughed as Haigar called out, "Everyone proceed ahead."

Hours and hours of riding had passed as sundown approached. Haigar noticed a desert town a few miles out and asked Halon, "Do you think that town could be the one we are looking for?" Halon nodded and said, "Yes, the people of Daraz have a unique culture. This community once was the central hub of jewel mining and trade with Torust. The structures of their community are still the same as they have been for thousands of years. You see the large buildings closest to the mountain? Those used to store the vast jewels that were mined."

Ria asked, "What happened to this community? How did it fall apart, or rather, lose its energy?" Halon replied, "All of the jewels that were discovered were mined and the vast presence of jewel traders disappeared from Daraz once all the jewels were depleted. This town served as one of the primary trade channels that helped make Torust the most powerful kingdom at that time. In addition to discovering the meaning of the inscription, visiting this place is worth the journey for historical reasons." Ria said, "Interesting, I will have to talk to Torb about it when we get back."

The desert became increasingly dark as the queen and the group of men approached Daraz. Haigar lit a torch and led the way to show the townspeople that they were approaching. Two guards came forward and asked, "Are you all from Torust?" Haigar replied, "Yes, I am the leader of the military. The queen of our kingdom is with us as well." Ria came forward and said, "I am pleased to see this historic outlet of Torust for the first time. I come seeking the meaning of an inscription that appears to be of an ancient dialect and I hope you can lead me to someone who can help." The guards bowed and said, "It is our honor to welcome you to the town of Daraz. Please stay for as long as you need. Follow us and we can bring you to the people who might be able to help."

Ria, Haigar, Halon, and several of the soldiers followed the guards to what appeared to be a cave in the mountain that was developed into a living space. The guards said, "The men in the cave are the sages of Daraz. Whenever we have a question about history, life, or anything of purpose we come to them." Ria, Haigar, and Halon walked ahead into the cave entrance. There were torches, chairs, tables, food, books, and most of all silence. Ria called out, "Greetings. We come from Torust seeking your expertise."

An old tan man with no hair on his head came forward and said, "My name is Yaako Lator and I am one of two of the remaining sages of Daraz. Who may you all be?" Ria said, "I am Ria Falune, the queen of Torust. Next to me is Haigar, my adviser, and Halon, the Master of Languages in Torust." Yaako bowed and said, "It is an honor to meet you, the queen of our land. How may we help you?" Ria took the necklace off of her neck and handed it to the sage. She said, "The inscription, do you know what it means?" The sage looked very closely at the inscription for a moment. He looked up and said, "It is an ancient dialect of Torustian. It was used for a mysterious purpose; one we still do not know. However, we do understand the meaning of the language. The inscription translates into 'The Caller.'"

Chapter Twenty-Two: The Yearning Desert

Torb Daxo, The Cave of Jewels - "Mine everything you can, no one leaves without a full sack of jewels", Torb shouted. The workers ferociously smacked their pickaxes against the chunks of emerald and onyx that clung to the walls of the Cave of Jewels. The lighting of several torches kept the room lit for the workers to see where their strikes were needed. Torb held a torch in his hand watching the efforts of each individual worker, something Torb would remember when the time came to reward each man for his work. Watching the beauty of the cave lose itself to the pickaxes bothered Torb in a way. As an adventurer, there was something about an untouched piece of nature that represented an ideal image of beauty. However, Torb knew that the cave and the jewels presented a once in a millennium opportunity and were needed for his success and his job as a jewel trader in Torust.

Chunks of large emerald and onyx jewels flew from the walls of the cave. One worker had the job of picking up all the pieces and placing them in bags scattered throughout the cave. This worker anxiously ran around picking up various jewels before they were accidentally stepped on. Torb asked the worker picking up the jewels, "How much space do we have left?" The man replied, "They are filling up, only three bags have space left in them." Torb nodded and called out, "We are almost done here. Once all the bags are filled take a few minutes to relax and gather your things, then we will be heading back to the ship before it gets too late." Torb could sense the relief the men felt as their efforts, which had lasted for hours, were finally coming to an end.

After some time, the worker picking up the jewels noticed the last bag had been filled and told Torb, "The bags are all filled." Torb called out, "Everyone stop mining, go drink some water and gather your belongings, we will leave here in twenty minutes. You do not need to take the pickaxes and other tools with you since we will return here soon." Torb looked around in satisfaction as many bags were filled to the brim with jewels; this represented the equivalent of many lifetimes' worth of work for him. This was by far the biggest score of his life as an adventurer and far exceeded his wildest imagination. One thing was for sure, he would return to the Cave of Jewels in force as there was still plenty of jewels left to be mined.

As Torb and his men started their descent down the pathway, Torb shouted, "I know the bags are quite heavy, but if you men take breaks and try to take turns holding the bags as a group, we will be more likely to get to the ship easier and faster." The men grunted and sweated excessively with each careful footstep they took down the narrow pathway. Once they all regrouped at the bottom, Torb said, "Alright men, just a few miles walking through the desert and we will be back at the ship and our fellow seasick voyager. I know you guys want to see how he is doing just as much as I do." Before they left, Torb marked the entrance of the pathway by sticking his unlit torch in the ground.

The group of men walked through the desert in unusually cloudy conditions, all hoping for a few drops of rain to cool them off. Torb could feel the coarse sand against his body; the desert was yearning for a rainstorm just as much as the men. Torb called out, "Let's try walking a bit south to see if we can spot any water pools."

The group of men all took step after step awaiting the moment of fulfillment of being back on the sea and the ship, and even more so being back in Torust with their reward of gold. One worker dropped his bag for a moment to catch his breath and said, "One moment, I...I just need a minute." As the man stood hunched over, Torb patted him on the back and said, "No problem, I do not punish those who are punishing themselves for me. I saw how tirelessly all of you worked and it will not go unrewarded. All of you who made this first and most difficult trek to the Cave of Jewels will be rewarded even more on the next trip, if you choose to come again." The hunched over man said, "Thank you, master. You are too kind to us." He lifted his bag and with a nod signaled he was ready to proceed to the ship.

The skies grew darker as Torb felt a cool, moist wind blow against his face. Torb called out, "I think we are in great luck men, hopefully we will all get what we deserve soon." One of the workers asked, "What are you talking about?" Torb said, "You will see, just keep moving ahead." The men anxiously walked ahead hoping for something immediate that would make their journey and excruciating efforts worth the struggle. Something that would satisfy thirst and bodily needs, something that jewels could not do for them in the desert. Another worker dropped his bag and said, "I need a minute too." Torb said, "Take your time, we are making progress."

One of the workers felt a thick, cool raindrop on his right arm. The man excitedly shouted, "Rain, rain, I felt it!" Torb stood waiting to confirm if the man was telling the truth. A refreshing raindrop hit Torb on his left cheek and he smiled and called out, "Rainstorm! Everyone open your water jugs!" To the men's delight, the raindrops started to appear in great quantity and speed. Torb smiled and said to himself, "The beauty of rain."

The men dropped their bags and opened their water jugs, which they stuck straight up in the sand. The workers danced around and looked straight up in the air with their mouths open. The euphoria of realizing there was a rainstorm was almost as rewarding as the sight within the Cave of Jewels.

After a moment, Torb called out, "Gather your bags and your jugs, let's keep moving while the rain is supporting us." The men happily picked up their stuff and started to walk on for the final push to the ship. At this point, the sight of the sea and the ship was in each man's head. Eventually, after pushing on a little further, the sight of the ship in the distance was a reality. Torb shouted, "Last push, the end is almost here." The men marched ahead with confidence that they had enough energy to get to the ship. They imagined that the ship awaited them just like some of their wives back in Torust.

The men closed in on the ship and Torb was relieved that at least the ship had not been stolen. The workers speedily made their way to the small boats, and, with their last burst of energy, paddled with complete bliss. The man on the ship helped all the workers and Torb board the ship, together with the bags of jewels. Torb asked, "How have you been holding up?" The worker on the ship said, "I thought you guys weren't coming back, but I spent so long on here I am ready to sail the damn ship back to Torust myself!" The men chuckled and laughed as they got ready to set sail across the Sahine Sea.

Torb shouted, "Smooth sailing ahead, let us embark while the sea is calm." The workers lifted the anchors and maneuvered the ship in the correct direction toward Torust. Torb sat on the ship relaxing and envisioning the sight of a happy Queen Ria Falune impressed by the plentiful jewels he would present to her. Torb thought to himself, 'What should I gift her? How much will it take for her to support my return trip to the Cave of Jewels? Will she be so impressed she might want to come herself?' Many ideas flew through his mind as he suddenly dozed off into a peaceful rest that was sustained by the refreshing cool winds of the sea breeze.

Before long, one of Torb's workers rung the bell alerting the Torust sea harbor of their arrival. Torb awoke and said, "Smooth sailing, I see you men did not need my help." The man who was seasick on the first leg of the trip spoke out, "No need to awake the master." Torb looked back and noticed he was the worker sailing the ship. Torb laughed and said, "You have proven yourself just as much as the others who hauled the bags to the ship."

The ship docked in the harbor of Torust and Torb said, "I need you men to carry the bags of jewels to my residence, I will meet you back there shortly with your gold payouts." The men lifted the bags again and made their way to his residence.

Torb walked to the harbor guards and said, "Do you know where the queen is?" They responded and said, "She has left the city recently for a short trip to the north." Torb nodded and made his way to follow the workers who were heading to his residence.

Once Torb and the workers arrived at Torb's residence, Torb said, "You all displayed exceptional effort so you all will receive your fair share of pay. I hope you will join me on the return trip to the Cave of Jewels after I speak to the queen about getting appropriate resources to make the trip more efficient." The men all individually thanked Torb for the opportunity and the pay they received. Once everyone left his residence he sat alone and looked around surrounded by a lifetime of jewels. Torb said, "What a trip, what a cave."

Chapter Twenty-Three: The Bed of Flowers

Peter Fardine, Outskirts of Torust - The bandage around Peter's neck started to grow itchier and more irritating. 'I cannot wait to take this damn thing off', Peter thought to himself as he scratched over the bandage trying to ease his discomfort. After spending months in Tyrades recovering from the life-threatening injury he suffered against Roy in the final gladiator battle, he was finally fit to return to his home city. Peter's friends, who had accompanied him from Torust left him for dead in Tyrades presuming he was not going to recover.

Peter had a lot going through his mind recently. The failure of reaching gladiator and his serious injuries had left him trying to get his life back together. He felt weaker than he was months earlier, before the fight, and was eager to return to his wife, Vasa, and son, Cazier, who was twenty years old. As Peter rode his horse onto the final sandy pathway near Torust he recalled the fateful blow delivered by Roy, the thrust that sent Peter to the ground and into months of agony. Peter thought to himself, 'I must have misjudged Roy. But that is all behind me now.'

Peter rode for a few moments on what appeared to him to be an unusually quiet path to the main gate of Torust. Once he got to the main gate, the guards came forward and said, "No one can enter the city." Peter said, "Back off, I am Peter Fardine. I want to see my family." The guards looked at each other in shock and one of them said to the other, "I thought he was dead." The other guard nodded in agreement and said, "We are glad to see you are alive, Peter. Rumors have spread over the past few months that you were killed during the final gladiator battle. You should get word to the queen and let her know that you are still alive." Peter, visibly displeased, replied, "Well, I was recovering for months, but here I am. My immediate intention is to see my family. I will concern myself with the queen after I get settled in."

Peter walked very quickly through Torust toward his residence trying to go unnoticed by anyone. The city looked the same way as it was when he departed months earlier. Peter walked past the core of the city and eventually onto the pathway that led to his residence. He thought about the improvement he had made as he was able to walk up the stairs leading to his home without any pain, something he struggled to do until recently. He thought, 'Almost there, I can just about see them already.' A single tear of happiness rolled down his cheek as he anxiously walked closer and closer to his home.

The sight of the front door came as a shock to Peter. A bed of flowers lined the doorway of his residence. Peter took a moment and gazed at the bed of flowers in front of the door and said, "This whole time these people thought I was dead, complete nonsense." Peter knocked on the door a few times waiting to see the bright smiles on the faces of his wife and his son. 'Who would be the first?', Peter thought.

With harder and more frustrated determination, Peter knocked on the door a few more times. He could hear someone moving around inside. 'Yes, someone is home', he thought with a smile. The sound of the slow, but promising, footsteps grew louder. Suddenly, the door swung open and it was his son Cazier. Peter's smile quickly turned to a more puzzled look as his son seemed to be very unstable. Peter stepped closer and grabbed his son who almost fell over. Peter placed his arm under Cazier's shoulder to help him stand. Peter asked, "What is going on? Aren't you happy to see that I am still alive?" Cazier reeked of alcohol and was attempting to speak as he mumbled his words, "I...ahhh...I am not happy to be here."

Peter noticed his son was completely drunk and said, "Why are you so drunk? Where is your mother?" Cazier looked at his father as his eyes started to tear up. Cazier said, "I thought you were dead father. We all did." Cazier came closer and gave his father a tight hug as the tears started to flow. Peter replied, "I am fine, I am still here. Where is your mother? I want to see her too." Cazier mumbled, "The flowers, didn't you see." Peter asked with trepidation, "What about the flowers?" Cazier, with a serious face, looked directly into Peter's eyes and whispered, "The flowers, they are for her. She killed herself last week."

"The flowers were for her", Peter whispered to himself. His body simultaneously became filled with anger and sadness. Peter, with the last ounce of self-control, asked, "What made her do it?" Cazier said, "Everyone believed you were dead. Weeks passed, months passed, she could not continue without you. And all I was to her was a useless homosexual son, a complete monster. Her life was meaningless in the end. She stabbed herself in the heart with a knife."

Peter yelled, "Rhaaaaaa!", as he smacked his hand onto a table sending everything flying. "I was so close, so close to being back in time to save all of us", Peter said. He continued, "But you, my son. You will always be just like me. I want you to be yourself until the end of your life. Do not be afraid of being the person who you want to be, who you really are. I was always rooting for you and I will continue to support you until my dying breath. The thought of having grandchildren and keeping the family bloodline thriving was always exciting for me, but you can adopt, you can keep the Fardine name alive in different ways. How does that sound, Cazier?" Cazier, with endless tears, nodded and hugged his father. He said to his father, "You keep me going, dad." Peter said, "Take a seat, let me get you some water. Take a break from the alcohol; it will only make things worse for you."

Chapter Twenty-Four: The Melody of Flames

Liava Pontas, Dragon Lair - Liava carefully made her way down from the high overlook. The dragons had already left to roam and eat, and this was usually a very boring period of the day for Liava. She was starting to learn that she needed to find ways to entertain herself. Liava slowly stepped down to the bottom and then walked toward several trees. She looked around for possible branches that she could use. Liava lifted one and said, "Too thin." She continued to walk around searching for thick branches. As she picked up another, she said, "Looks rotten." She found a branch that was more appealing to her at the base of one of the trees and she walked over and picked it up. Liava murmured to herself, "Just right."

Liava carried the branch to the hill where she sat and took out the blade that she had carried with her since she escaped from the village. She slowly started to carve the branch as she had done many times before. Her flute had to be crafted to meet all her preferences, which was the reason she never had anyone else make her flutes for her. Liava held the branch with her left hand and slowly used the blade in her right hand to slice pieces of wood off from the branch. Once the branch was thinned out, she cut down the height of the branch to be roughly a foot tall. She took her blade and slowly twirled it around to cut out the inside of the branch to make an opening that would allow the air pressure to flow through the flute. Lastly, she cut seven holes toward the top allowing her to control the sounds emitted by covering the holes in various ways. Crafting the flute had taken Liava hours and she sat anxiously waiting to try out her freshly carved instrument.

Liava said to herself, 'Let me get back to the top first and then I will play my new flute.' She took small footsteps while she used her hands to maneuver her way up the rocky hill to the top where she felt safer. Near the top of the hill Liava turned around and saw the intense drop below her.

Although it appeared intimidating at first, Liava said, "If I managed to survive the drop from the cliff, I should not fear any heights."

Liava proceeded up the hill until she summited to safe ground and walked over to a spot that overlooked the surroundings. She sat on the rocky surface as she pulled the flute out of her pocket and looked at the beautiful scenery around her. She held the flute up to her lips and, with a promising breath, exhaled into the flute. The pressure of the air working its way through the wooden flute and out of the holes and other end was to her liking and she grinned from ear to ear. Liava continued to play while holding down various holes just as she used to.

From the distance, Liava heard a screech of one of the dragons. Something upset it. 'Are they okay?', Liava thought for a moment while she sat still waiting patiently for another sign. The sound of flapping wings grew louder as one of the dragons was flying closer. Suddenly, the red dragon came flying across the sky above Liava. Liava turned her head around and directly upwards to watch the red dragon fly into the lair. The dragon made eye contact with Liava to ensure her safety. The thud of the dragon landing gave the ground around Liava a slight shake. The face of the dragon shifted side to side investigating the source of the mysterious noise. The dragon started walking to the side of Liava as it began circling her for protection; its head perched up in the air listening intently.

Liava placed her hand on the dragon's cheek to try to calm it down. She grabbed the flute with her other hand and put it in front of the dragon's face to show it what made the noise. The dragon looked at the piece of wood for a second but did not show any interest. Liava took a few steps in front of the dragon and brought the wooden flute to her mouth. She then took a deep breath and exhaled into the flute producing a pleasant sound. The uneasy expression of the dragon eased as its face transitioned to a puzzled look. Liava continued blowing into the flute while adjusting her fingers along its holes emitting an array of sounds and rhythms. Although perplexed, the dragon trusted Liava and found comfort in the soothing sounds Liava was somehow creating.

The dragon sprawled out on the rocky ground and faced Liava who continued to sooth the dragon with her favorite musical instrument. She played for the dragon with great enthusiasm, as if her entire village was listening to her perform. Back in Staga, Liava was just an average flute performer, but to this teenage dragon her abilities with the flute represented something far bolder. The dragon listened intently as Liava serenaded him continuously. Eventually, Liava could hear flaps of larger wings in the distance. Liava said, "That must be them", as she took a moment to catch her breath from playing so vigorously. Liava looked far in the distance and saw the navy and green adult dragons flying toward the lair. As they arrived, Liava noticed they were both carrying large berry bushes. Liava turned her head for a moment to see if the red dragon saw them coming, but the red dragon was fast asleep as she heard the snores of the snoozing dragon.

The thud of the returning dragons hitting the ground awoke the younger dragon who opened just one eye to gaze at them. Liava walked over to the bushes of berries the dragons brought back. She slowly started to pick the berries while trying to avoid any prickly thorns. After throwing several into her mouth, she carried a handful over to the napping dragon and tapped its arm. Once the dragon opened its eyes, Liava placed the berries on the ground in front of the dragon. The red dragon leaned forward and swallowed all the berries in a single gulp. The navy and green dragons must have eaten before they returned as they did not appear to be hungry.

Liava grabbed the flute out of her pocket and held it in her hands as she wondered how the older dragons would react to her melodies. Liava held it up and blew into the flute. Within a few seconds, the older dragons came charging over to Liava. She did not know how this would end so she stopped playing and stood completely still. The dragons stopped in front of her and inspected her and the wooden stick she was holding. Liava lifted her hand allowing them to smell and look at the flute. 'The dragons must think it is magic or something', Liava thought to herself. She left it in front of them for a moment before she slowly returned it to her face and started playing again. Liava noticed how the eyes of the dragons became more sensitive as she played her calming melody. The dragons looked around as if they had seen the world in a new way. Liava thought to herself, 'They have never heard music before. This must be so beautiful to them.'

Liava could still hear the memorable melodies from her village in her head. A chaotic and stormy melody popped into her head; it was the one that was her father's favorite. Liava remembered seeing him dance around in complete ecstasy and joy. Liava started playing this melody as the sounds of the flute became darker, louder, and faster. The sleepy red dragon opened its eyes and was now standing, as if it were disturbed by the melody. Liava played the melody as she thought to herself, 'This is for you mother and father.' She closed her eyes for a moment as she got carried away performing the melody. Liava, even with her eyes closed, felt the distinct movements of the dragons around her. 'Sounds like they enjoy this melody too', she thought. Liava took a deep breath before she engaged in the climactic ending of the melody.

Then, suddenly, the air went hot as Liava's arms, legs, and face felt the heat within the air. Liava opened her eyes in an instant and saw the older dragons exhaling fire all over the forest landscape below. Liava stopped playing the flute, but the dragons continued to breathe fire carelessly into the distance. For the first time, Liava witnessed the aggressive nature of these mystical creatures. Liava wondered what it was about the melody that caused this violent and aggressive display. Liava started playing the flute calmly to return the dragons to their soothing state. As she played her flute she wondered, 'This might be the way of communicating with them that I have been looking for.'

Chapter Twenty-Five: The Decaying Hope

Ryos Pontas, Village of Tsirian - Ryos and the remaining surviving teenagers of Staga heard knocking on the door of their barracks. After a moment, the door swung open and Edgar entered with a few other men behind him. Edgar said, "Get up and get your stuff together. This morning I will present all of you with another obstacle. These past few days you all ate the meat of the animals you were brought up protecting. Some of you struggled, but that is understandable. Soon, you all will grow stronger from eating animal meat. In order to feed the village and your mouths, the undesirable job of hunting animals is necessary. No one enjoys killing, but it is something that must be done. It makes us stronger mentally and physically. This morning we are going to go hunt and bring back meat to supply this village. I do not expect all of you to have the opportunity to kill an animal today, but I expect all of you to be ready and willing to do so. Meet us outside in ten minutes and we will leave."

Ryos grabbed his gear as he thought about what he was going to have to do. 'Killing another person was bad enough, but now we have to continue the onslaught by killing animals? It is bad enough that we were already forced to eat them.', Ryos said to himself. The taste of meat freaked him out along with some of the other villagers from Staga. Ryos and the other boys took a moment to get ready and then met Edgar and his hunting party outside the barracks. The sky was still dark as the sun had not yet shown itself. The fog of the morning made the climate a bit more chilly than usual.

Edgar faced the boys and said, "I hope you boys are ready and have your minds wrapped around the task at hand. We will head southeast and hunt some animals. Some of you will use bows while some of you will use blades to kill them up close." Ryos realized that this meant that he would have to fight the animals by hand since he had more experience using his blade.

Edgar continued, "Fill your jugs with water before we depart. The trip could be several miles." Ryos and the other did as they were told.

Along the way a boy walking next to Ryos said, "Hey, my name is Hyfor." Ryos replied, "I am Ryos, I remember seeing you around Staga. It is nice to officially meet." Hyfor said, "Likewise. I am not really sure how I am going to manage to kill an animal that we grew up admiring. They usually sense us as friendly. It feels like we are betraying them." Ryos said, "I know, but we must do whatever they tell us. It is the only way we will be able to keep ourselves alive."

Edgar continued to lead the boys and his fellow villagers southeast to start the journey. The group walked quietly as they did not want to alert any potential prey. Edgar stopped and looked around him as he said, "The skill of hunting takes time to develop. It takes more effort to kill the animal than it takes for it to escape. You must rely on your senses to provide an advantage over them. Use your eyes to uncover what does not belong with the surroundings. Use your ears to listen and hear where the movements are coming from and to tell you the size of the animal. Use your nose to try to sniff out any unusual scents."

After walking a short distance further one of the villagers quickly pulled up his bow, steadied his aim, and released an arrow that went directly into a rabbit killing it instantly. Ryos and Hyfor stood watching in shock at how quickly the kill shot was taken. The man who killed the rabbit walked over to the body, pulled out the arrow, and threw the dead rabbit into his bag. Edgar looked at the man and said, "Stellar accuracy, well done."

After walking for close to five miles, Edgar said, "We are not having very good luck today. Now that we can cross safely into the old Staga territory we can venture further and see what the hunting is like down here." The group crossed a water stream and walked next to a lush grassland to avoid walking out in the open and allowing them to be easily spotted by the prey. In the distance, they could hear the calls of wild boars. Edgar called out, "Quickly, let's move!" The group started running toward the unsettling calls of the boars. Ryos could feel his heart rapidly beating as he ran closer to another traumatizing moment.

As he ran ahead with the group, Ryos wondered whether his parents or his sister would have made it this far in the village of Tsirian or would they have submitted to a different fate. He also wondered why his sister was not with the group that was rounded up at the end. The villagers of Tsirian killed all the women and girls of Staga, but Liava was not with them. Ryos thought, 'Regardless of how she died, I am glad it was not something I had to witness.'

Suddenly, several boars came charging at the group. The sight caught everyone off guard. The boars were not attacking, but rather seemed to be fleeing from the hill above. The villagers all prepared their weapons to pick off any of the boars they could manage to bring down. Hyfor pulled back on his bow and shot a boar in its back-left leg.

Ryos saw these events rapidly unfolding and knew he had to strike immediately to prove he had a place within Tsirian. Ryos shouted with anger at the world as he pulled out his blade and moved sideways to pick off a desperate boar fleeing for its life. Ryos jumped forward as he pulled his blade from the right side to the left and cut a large opening in the side of the boar. The boar only made it a few feet further before it fell to the ground incapacitated. Ryos wanted to cry but held back his tears for the sake of looking strong. The remaining, but decaying, hope of Staga officially died within him.

Only three other boars, besides the one that Ryos took down, were killed during the commotion as several got away. The men started to grab the boars to carry them away. Edgar called out, "Impressive effort, all of you. That attack took some courage, Ryos. You could have been killed if the boar got you with one of its tusks. This should be sufficient meat for now. We will return to this location to hunt more soon."

As the group started to walk back to the village, Edgar tapped Ryos on the shoulder and said, "You stand out from the others, I see more potential in you." Ryos replied, "Thank you, it all happened so fast, I did not want to miss my chance to show my place in Tsirian." Edgar said, "Your actions today displayed a lot of courage, keep it up. There will be more opportunities soon. This area is filled with a vast array of creatures that were kept away from us for years. We were in the territory of Staga for a few minutes and easily found prey. Those boars were not attacking us, they were running from something. We will have to find out what was scaring them so much. Us Tsirians love decorating the village with trophy kills."

Chapter Twenty-Six: The Boulder of Fire

Searleone Vallas, Skyrock - Searleone stood on the balcony of the sanctuary teaching several younger mages of Skyrock how to master the craft of creating fireballs. Searleone said, "Palm both hands together and let the friction of your skin build from palm to palm. Maneuver your hands as if you are shaping a well-balanced clay ball." As he was demonstrating this, Searleone's hands created a burst of hot energy. He slowly started to move his hands apart and craft the fireball. Searleone continued instructing and demonstrating, "Bring your hands apart, but continue to craft all around the dimensions of the fireball to round it out." The mages watched as Searleone proceeded to craft a growing fireball that was now bigger than his head.

Searleone said, "You can go slowly or quickly as long as you manage to keep the ball well-balanced." One of the mages asked, "What happens if it is not well-balanced in a round ball?" Searleone chuckled as he responded, "It does not need to be perfectly round. But it should still resemble a round, well-balanced ball. If not, when you release the fireball it will not project where you want it to go. Instead of going straight it could go in various directions, so I strongly recommend that you do not launch unbalanced fireballs."

By now, the fireball in between Searleone's hands had grown larger than his upper body. Searleone said, "I would not go this large. Make sure that you keep it to a smaller, safer limit, which will be a better starting point for you beginners. Once you have more years of experience like me, you can take it a step further." Searleone lifted the massive fireball above his head as he started shifting it in the air. The younger mages now stared in amazement at the fireball, which was now the size of a large boulder, and Searleone's ability to handle it with such little effort.

Searleone told the mages, "Come closer, but stand a few feet to the side of me." As the mages walked closer to the edge of the balcony overlooking the terrain below Searleone turned around to face the surroundings as well. Searleone said, "Watch the colossal power of the impact." He leaned his arms back a little and heaved the boulder-sized fireball out and downward into an empty dirt section of the ground hundreds of feet away. The massive fireball seemed to defy gravity as it traveled exactly to the spot where Searleone projected it. The group of mages looked on in excitement as they awaited the impact of the boulder-sized fireball. Suddenly, the ground shook in the distance as the large fireball hit its target. Large sparks of fire flew through the air from the impact. The other mages were visibly impressed by the fiery spectacle.

A young mage walked onto the balcony from the sanctuary. He appeared to have been away for a while since he had dirt scattered and embedded on his robe and on his hands and cheeks. Searleone noticed him walking closer as the young mage said, "Sorry for my late appearance." Searleone immediately called out, "With that display of the crafting of a fireball, I leave you all to spend some time trying it for yourselves. Please head to the training room to practice." The mages eagerly complied and left for the training room of the sanctuary.

The young mage walked closer to Searleone. Searleone said, "How was the expedition, Rinci." The young mage responded, "I went to the town that you instructed me to go to and I shared the soup with them as requested. I left after thirty minutes as instructed. On the journey back, I got lost a little. That is why I haven't returned sooner." Searleone said, "Sounds like it was a successful journey, I appreciate your display of loyalty."

Rinci asked, "If you grew up in that town, why didn't you want to attend the celebration with them? They seemed friendly; they welcomed me as one of their own." Searleone replied, "I haven't left Skyrock in decades, I have no desire to leave this sanctuary. It means everything to me." Rinci continued, "The whole thing seemed a bit mysterious. How come I couldn't stay for the celebration, the journey was so long." Searleone said, "I sent you there on a personal request and I did not want you to assimilate too much with the regulars of the world. You should not be distracted by the outside world; you are meant to be here learning. I am sorry that I took some of that valuable time to send you away." Rinci replied, "I understand, but I will always be happy to help you when needed.

As he was about to depart, Rinci decided to ask Searleone to help him craft a fireball. "Can you show me how to craft a fireball since I missed it, it is the most exciting thing we are learning in some time." Searleone said, "Yes, of course. But you should understand that although everything is not equally exciting, sometimes the most boring studies are the most important." Rinci nodded and said, "You are right, I will remember and share this knowledge with the others during our studies." Searleone stepped closer to the balcony edge and started crafting a fireball in his hands as they were held together. Searleone said, "The fireball starts with the friction of your hands. Put your mind in a good place and begin."

Chapter Twenty-Seven: The Enticing Storm

Roy Syssian, Outskirts of Biros - Leora squeezed Roy's waist tighter as the horse they were riding accelerated for a moment. Roy said, "You will get used to it, soon you will be riding on your own." Leora said, "It might take longer than you think. But I am willing to learn so we can travel more easily together." Roy smiled and flirtingly said, "You are too kind, it must be because I am a king. You do not need to obey my every command." Leora smirked and said, "I liked you before you were a king." Roy said, "I was a gladiator, you must have felt intimidated." Leora said, "Yes, being in the presence of the most powerful fighter in Lodas is more exhilarating than being with a king. You still haven't told me about your fighting experiences." Roy said, "It can't be more interesting than growing up as the daughter of the king of Gofon." Leora said, "It has been amazing, but only in the local royal traditions. I still have not traveled at all. And I really want to with you, Roy."

Leora saw a city with white walls close by and asked, "Is that Biros?" Roy replied, "Yes, the finest city of them all", as he jokingly laughed. He continued, "Looks like it is going to storm, we should hurry into the city." Roy sped up his horse and signaled to his men to do the same to beat the approaching storm. Roy and his men galloped past the guards into the city as the rain began to pour down. Leora jokingly slapped Roy's shoulder, "We are going to get dirty and soaked. You must go faster." Roy rode ahead of his men toward the stables to drop off his horse. Once they arrived, Roy dismounted his white horse and helped Leora off as well. Roy and Leora happily held hands as they ran through the rain.

Once they got into the royal chambers Roy and Leora were totally soaked and they stopped for a moment to catch their breath. They both laughed to hide their nervous emotions. After looking at each other for a few seconds, Roy felt the same loving affection from Leora and went forward to kiss her.

Leora smiled and kissed him back as they both held each other's wet-clothed bodies in the middle of a torch lit corridor.

Roy and Leora separated for a moment and Roy said, "Let's go get changed into more comfortable, dry clothes." Leora nodded as they began walking. She smiled at the thought of what he might have been maneuvering toward, but then thought that maybe he was just taking care or her; either way Leora felt very attracted to Roy. They both walked through the corridors, not saying a word to each other or the guards they passed along the way. Once they entered the king's bedroom, Roy said, "Wait here, I will grab you some of my clothes to wear while I get a proper dress for you from my maids." Roy went into a cabinet and tossed various night clothes on the bed for Leora to wear. Roy said, "Be right back." Roy left, making sure to close the door behind him.

Leora stood in the room alone, contemplating what to wear from the options that were on the bed. She picked them up and placed them on a dresser next to the bed. She undid her wet clothes until her body was bare naked. Leora lifted the bed sheets and laid on the bed before covering her body with the sheets. Leora had always been reserved when it came to men, but now she found herself overwhelmingly enticed by the moment she shared with Roy running through the storm. She stayed in bed waiting for Roy to return.

After a few minutes, Leora heard footsteps coming closer to the door. Leora gripped the bed sheet with nervousness as the door swung open. Roy walked in as he said, "I brought you this dress for dinner later." It took a moment for Roy to realize that she was not wearing any clothes from the look of her bare shoulders. Leora smiled and stood up out of the bed. Roy stared directly at her naked body, which he was now expecting to see. He noticed the delicate curves around her hips and breasts. Roy slowly walked closer, gazing upon her beauty. Roy said, "You have an astonishing body." Leora grabbed Roy's hands and whispered in his ear, "You can touch it", as she placed his hands upon her breasts.

Roy and Leora locked lips as Roy continued to gently caress her soft body. They stopped for a moment as Leora helped undress Roy. Roy grabbed for his bottoms as Leora assisted with his top. Once they both stood face to face completely naked Leora grabbed his hand and pulled him into the bed behind her. They felt each other's body, discovering the unknown for the first time before engaging in sensual love. As they shared this beautiful moment, the flashes of lightning and calls of thunder struck throughout the sky.

After sharing their intimate love together, Roy and Leora stayed in bed listening to the roar of the thunder. Leora said, "I am starting to really like being with you. I hope the women in Biros won't be jealous of me." Roy replied, "Me too, and who cares if they will be. I will make sure you are treated with the same respect as when you are in your home city." Leora said, "Thank you", as she kissed him on the cheek. She continued, "My mother and father really like you as well." Roy said, "I can tell. Lance has welcomed me as a gladiator quite warmly. Speaking of family, my parents will be at the dinner tonight. I hope you are okay with going, they wanted to have this banquet dinner upon my return to the city." Leora said, "I can't imagine a better first night here." Roy said, "I usually do not drink much, but, for some reason, I feel like enjoying some wine." Leora said, "I am in a wonderful mood too." They came closer in bed and kissed.

After some time passed, Roy said, "I think it is time for us to start getting ready." Leora said, "Okay, if we must." She sat up and got out of bed and lifted the dress that Roy had brought her. Leora inspected the dress for a moment and said, "I really like this dress, you did well." Roy said, "You can thank my maid. Besides, Biros has some of the best tailors, you might want to spend some time looking while you are here." Roy got out of the bed too and went to his cabinet to select some stylish clothes. As he slipped on his clothes, he opened the door leading to the corridor and called for a maid. Leora asked, "What is that for?" Roy replied, "To help you with your hair and dress, if you need it." Leora said, "Thanks, I probably will", as she ran her hands through her hair and felt a few knots.

Roy sat in his chair as the maid came into the room and helped straighten Leora's hair. The maid said to Leora, "Such lovely hair you have." Leora smiled as she replied, "So do you, I love your curls." Roy watched as the maid and Leora conversed with each other. Roy noticed how Leora did not act like royalty even though she grew up that way her whole life. She treated Roy's maid like an equal, and Roy mentally took note of it. He could feel in his royal and fierce heart that he was starting to love her.

Once the maid was done straightening her hair, Roy and Leora finished getting ready. Roy said, "We should head there now." Leora said, "I am ready when you are." They looked at each other and locked arms as they walked through the royal corridor heading for the royal banquet. Nollie Gent, who was roaming the halls, noticed Roy with his arm wrapped around Leora's. Nollie called out, "Roy, how great to see you again, my king." Roy responded, "Likewise, my adviser." Nollie walked closer to Roy and said, "I just need to tell you something quickly." Nollie and Roy took a couple of steps away from Leora and Nollie leaned into Roy's left ear as Roy maneuvered his body a few inches closer to Nollie. Nollie whispered, "Are you sure about this? If they see you this way with her, some women might begin to think you have chosen a queen." Roy replied, "So be it, I do not care", as he returned to Leora. They continued to walk with locked arms through the corridors as Nollie looked on with concern.

Leora asked Roy, "Is everything, ok?" "It is", Roy replied. Leora, with a wide smile, said, "This was a dream of mine when I was younger. Something just like this moment." Roy looked at Leora with a smile and said, "When fantasy becomes a reality." Roy noticed that they were approaching the entrance to the royal banquet dining hall and asked, "Are you ready?" Leora replied, "Ready as I ever will be." Without saying a word, Roy kept walking with Leora through the doorway and into the dining hall. Leora saw a large room filled with people, some still waiting to be seated for the meal. Roy said, "This is the royal table." Leora asked, "Who will be dining at this table with us?" Roy replied, "My parents and Nollie. Since I became king, I haven't had a lot of time to sit down and talk with my parents." Roy and Leora walked up to their table and sat down before Nollie and Roy's parents arrived.

Roy lifted a bottle of red wine from the table and poured some into Leora's cup before his own. Roy and Leora lifted their cup, and Roy said, "To your first time in Biros." They both sipped the wine as Roy noticed his father, Lucas, and his mother, Sathina, approaching the table. Roy stood up to greet his parents as he said, "This is my friend, Leora Hasting, the daughter of the king of Gofon." Leora stood up and Lucas and Sathina greeted her as Roy sat down and observed them converse. The night had totally gone Roy's way he thought, despite the concerns of his advisor, Nollie. Roy had noticed that he was starting to make his own decisions, when necessary.

The dining hall filled as people arrived to feast at the banquet. After a night that brought a messy, yet enticing, storm, Roy found himself poised for what he hoped to be an enjoyable and steady life.

Chapter Twenty-Eight: The Agreeable King

Phillip Denvion, Gofon – King Denvion sat outside in his vineyard enjoying a moment of isolation from all the problems his kingdom was facing. He drank his glass of red wine with large swallows. Timothy Milton, who noticed the king's rapid drinking, said, "You should slow down, my king. You are presenting to the council soon." King Phillip responded, "Wise man, one more glass and I will wait till later. That council annoys me, they are starting to really piss me off. They do not care about anyone outside the city. I say that, we are helping the citizens of our kingdom." Timothy said, "They are only interested in the security of our city and the longevity of our dominance. If you wish to continue spending resources on helping the ill, you should prepare for the anticipated grilling. They will ask you what your intentions are, and you have to be careful with every word."

Phillip said, "These stupid council meetings get me annoyed every time." Timothy asked, "You know what they want, don't you?" The king responded, "They want me to be removed from kingship, I can tell. The longer I have been king, the more they have grown defiant and jealous. I do not even care anymore, a few more years filled with quality time with my wife and family would be worth being removed. Besides, they are just an "advisory" council." Timothy replied, "An "advisory" council that can be very powerful and effective in helping to overthrow a king or at the very least dividing his kingdom and sending it into turmoil." Phillip lifted his cup and finished drinking the wine. Phillip said, "Let's take a walk before the council meeting."

Both men stood up and started walking toward the royal chambers. Timothy said, "If it means anything to you, you are the last king I wish to serve. If something were to happen, I want my assistance to end on a high." The king said, "You can be done whenever you please, you have done so much for my family over the years. I will make sure you are well-taken care of." Timothy said, "Thank you, my king."

Phillip said, "I am disappointed with Torust. I will tell the council that I decided to fund the relief aid thinking that Torust would contribute in some way. I will keep this in mind the next time they need us." Timothy said, "Your brother always found them hard to trust. They are just not like us; they have different motives." Phillip said, "The king of Torust used to visit Gofon often. Now, Queen Ria Falune still has not made one visit. I find it quite insulting considering I have made it to Torust several times over the years."

Timothy and Phillip entered the royal chambers and started to walk toward the council room. Timothy said, "We will be there early if we get in now." The king said, "Good, it will give them less time to prepare." The king stopped in front of the council door and thought to himself, 'I know what they want, I will put on a show.' A guard opened the door and the king and Timothy entered. The council members stopped their conversing and looked at the men as they entered.

Council representative John Pittus called out, "Welcome, we have much to discuss. You can be seated if you would like." The king stood and walked around anxiously as he said, "Please, proceed with your concerns, I am fine standing." John continued, "For some time now you have ordered resources to be sent to the ill in towns within Gofon to the east. This has cost the kingdom resources that we need for security and for our economy. We are here to help guide the kingdom and to help you make rational decisions just like Timothy here. Sometimes the right decisions are not the moral ones, but rather the ones that keep our kingdom secure from future issues, problems and threats. We believe this is one such example."

The king smiled on the inside as he pranced around and said, "Tomorrow, I plan on sending out what I intend to be the last aid party for the towns. I believe many of the towns have already received aid and this could save thousands of lives if we discover the cure soon. And that, my dear council, could help the kingdom prosper more in the future. As such, I want to give all the towns a fighting chance and, in order to do so, we must aid every single one."

Winston Caven spoke out at the king and said, "My king, we do not have the resources to aid every town. It is necessary that we cut these expenses quickly." The king said, "I hear your concern, I assure you that I will work with you and your associates and cut down after tomorrow." Jack Haxon said, "I believe you, all we ask is that you keep your word." The other council representatives nodded and murmured their agreement to Jack's words.

John Pittus asked, "Is there something you are hiding, Phillip?" The king showed that he was dismayed by the question and snapped back in response, "I would not lie to you, the esteemed council." John said, "If that is the case, that is all we need here today. Thank you for your time, my king." The king, with a contrived smile, said, "My pleasure, see you all soon." The king started to leave with Timothy at his side. The council representatives rejoiced over the positive discussion they had had with the king.

Once the king and Timothy exited the council meeting room, Phillip whispered in Timothy's ear, "For the aid party going out tomorrow, make sure they send three times more resources than usual so that we can supply more towns." Timothy smiled as he said, "Now everything makes sense, I will make it happen, my king." Timothy started rapidly walking away to put the king's command into effect. The king reflected on his meeting with the council members and thought to himself, 'I might have been a terrible theatre actor, but when it comes to acting in real situations, I excel.' The king walked back toward his vineyard where he intended to stay for the remainder of the afternoon.

Chapter Twenty-Nine: The Minty Grove

Jol Parantis, Federeck - Jol woke up feeling miserable after a terrible night of sleep. In the middle of the night, one of the two soldiers who had been infected erupted in flames and met his end. Jol reflected on the heartbreaking and frightening experience all the men had to face seeing one of their own burn to death.

To make matters even worse, there was still no hope of a cure. After weeks and weeks of trying to develop a cure, every attempt ended in failure. Jol would concoct potential cures from various mixes of ingredients that he had the infected soldiers drink, rub, or sniff, but nothing was successful. Jol sat up and wondered, 'How the hell am I going to fix this.' He felt slight discomfort in his stomach as he let out a few dark coughs. Jol realized that he had contracted the illness a few days before and now was on borrowed time just like everyone else who was infected with the disease. Jol, for the first time in his life, had failed to find a cure. Jol stood up and noticed he was the first one at the camp to be awake.

Jol had grown so desperate that he knew it was time to speak with Ked Larone again. Jol started walking into the town and into the field to get to Ked's residence. Along the way, Jol had to stop twice as his lungs were now far weaker than they usually were. By the time Jol made his way through the field, he realized just how tough it was going to be to get around while sick. He took the last steps and knocked on the door of Ked Larone's home.

After a few seconds, Ked opened the door and, with a disappointed face, said, "I am assuming you have failed." Jol said, "Unfortunately, yes. These damn sicknesses keep getting more difficult to cure for some reason. The first soldier in our group to be infected died when he burst into flames last night. I knew it was time to come to you. You are right, there has to be something about you that can stop the illness. I am not sure if it is something in your blood or something else, but I need you to tell me everything. I want to know what your life is like, what you do, what you eat and drink, where you go?"

Ked said, "I notice you are sick yourself." Jol nodded and said, "I can leave if you are worried." Ked said, "I should be fine if I have made it this long. Grab a seat and let us talk. So, where do I begin. I live a life of solitude, usually isolated from others, although I do not believe that is why I have not been infected. As you have seen, most of the townspeople live on the other side of the field. I always preferred it out here much more. I eat mostly meat and vegetables and drink water like the rest of the town. We can only afford the simple meals; extravagant celebrations like the one that you heard about are rare, but very enjoyable. As for what I do, that is where I would say I am different from the rest of the townspeople. I would work in the fields for food during the days helping to supply the town. I would occasionally spend time with my brother and his family. In my free time, though, I am an adventurer and enjoy roaming the woods to the east. There is a lot of beauty to see there."

Jol asked, "Do any of the other members of the town go with you?" Ked said, "No, I always go alone. It is nice to feel like I am the only one in the woods and maybe even the first and only person to see some of nature's beauty there." Jol asked, "Can you share with me the most notable scenes or objects that you encountered out there?" Ked replied, "Sure, if you go northeast from here there are a few apple trees where I get my apples. To the east, there is a great pathway up the mountain that I enjoy trekking. From the top, you have a great view all around the mountain. To the southeast, there is a grove that is filled with blue flowers that smell of mint, I like to call it the Minty Grove. Tons of hummingbirds fly around enjoying the flowers themselves. It is my favorite spot to go to."

Jol sat there for a moment and said, "Minty blue flowers? I have never heard of that. Can you take me there?" Ked said, "Yes, of course. It is many miles away, are you good to walk?" Jol said, "I am going to have to be." Ked said, "Okay, I can help you too. Let us leave now and get an early start." Jol and Ked both stood up and Jol walked over to the door as Ked grabbed a few things for the journey. Jol pushed the door open as they left Ked's home. Ked said, "Just follow me and let me know when you need a break. I brought some water for us to drink too, but not much since we will come across water streams during the trip."

Both men started walking into the woods as Ked curiously asked, "So tell me what life is like in the city of Gofon." Jol said, "It is constantly busy, every day you have something to do. People are wiser in some ways, but also less trustworthy. I have always favored nature like you. I ended up in the city because I can have more of an impact on the world being able to teach younger alchemists. I really hate to see what happened in your town, it seemed like a great place to live." Ked said, "I never made it out to Gofon, but I have always been curious. I remember I planned on visiting in hopes of meeting a woman, but someone told me that they would never settle for townsfolk like us."

Jol said, "Wait a second", as he stopped and hunched over as he started coughing up black mist. Ked asked, "How many days has it been?" Jol said, "Just two, but it already has weakened me so much. Okay, let us continue." Ked said, "Hang in there, there is a fighting spirit in you." Jol said, "Thanks, so tell me more about this man who came to the village on that fateful night." Ked said, "He was wearing a robe, he came from the east, he looked rather young with a face clean of any facial hair. What stood out to me the most was how intrigued he was with the town, almost like he had not seen one before, as hard as that may seem." Jol thought for a moment and said, "Interesting, it sounds like he was a mage from Skyrock." Ked asked, "What is that?" Jol replied, "They live in Skyrock, a sanctuary in the mountains far to the east. They work on alchemy quite a bit and wear robes." Ked said, "I have never heard of these mages before."

Ked asked, "Do they care about us?" Jol replied, "Who?" Ked said, "The king, the city of Gofon. We are part of the kingdom." Jol responded, "Definitely, but not all of them. The king is a very caring man. He fought for me to come out here looking for a cure and to send aid for your town and many others." Ked said, "That is very nice to hear, I can tell you are like that too.

After walking for a long time and taking many breaks, Ked asked, "Do you see all of the trees up ahead?" Jol said, "Yes, is that the Minty Grove?" Ked replied, "Yes, we are almost there. The swarms of hummingbirds are so majestic." Jol asked, "Did you ever tell anyone about this place?" Ked said, "No, if I did, I would risk losing my favorite hideout. If the townspeople knew of this place they would come and make it their own and probably pull all the flowers out of the ground. This is what I live for." Jol responded, "I understand. I think I can already smell the mint in the air." Ked said, "It is so invigorating, right? Jol said, "More than I would have thought, it is very relaxing."

Jol and Ked walked closer to the source of the pleasant scent until they could see the flowers. Jol looked between two trees in astonishment at the flowers that stood about a foot tall with white stems and fluorescent light blue petals at the top of the flowers. Ked said, "Look, the glow comes from the inside", as he carefully pulled a few petals apart to display the glowing essence of the flower. Jol slowly walked closer as he stared in bliss at the deeply beautiful flower. As Jol slowly came forward, Ked leaned over and gave the flower a deep inhale, which produced a big smile on his face. Jol, with a sense of hope, leaned over and inhaled the flower as he closed his eyes.

Jol felt the soothing rush of mint flow through his nose and into his lungs. Within a few seconds, something had changed. Within a few minutes, he felt alive again and healthier than ever. Jol looked at Ked in shock. Jol said, "This is it! This is the cure! You did it!" Ked asked, "Are you sure?" Jol said, "I can sense it, I am no longer ill. Look I can run around!" Jol started happily running through the grove as he ran his fingers through the flowers.

After a moment of running, Jol said, "We need to pick a lot of these. I know it is what you feared, Ked, but we will make sure we keep some planted and replenished for the future. Okay?" Ked said, "If this is the cure, I understand." Jol said, "They will be named "Ked's Gift", as you not only led me to the Minty Grove and showed me the flowers, but also discovered the cure." Ked said, "They are not mine to give, they belong to nature." Jol said, "Regardless, please accept the recognition." Jol started picking a few flowers out of the ground and said, "This should be enough to help the soldiers back at town. Grab some to hand out to the town's citizens. I am going to come back with the soldiers to get more to try to cure all the citizens and then we will head to Gofon to inform the king. You should come, this will change your life." Ked said, "You know what, I do want to be a part of that. Let us head back, every second matters to save as many lives as possible." With hands filled with Ked's Gift, Ked and Jol started on their return journey, a healthier one for Jol, back to the town to save the lives of a few, and in the near future, thousands.

Chapter Thirty: The Hourglass of Time

Lance Hasting, Tyrades - The view from the king's room grew more monotonous and it frustrated Lance. After years of ruling Tyrades, Lance was focused on how he would be remembered as a king, not for the world, but for his kingdom. From his balcony he could oversee much of the city of Tyrades. Lance could recall a time when there were difficulties for the kingdom. He peered down at his hands, which were starting to show signs of age. Lance got up and walked into the room toward his table and flipped his hourglass. As the soft sand started to flow down, Lance mentally emulated the hourglass through the frame of his kingship. He was now in his sixties and he knew that his kingship would not last forever.

Lance curiously peered at the hourglass thinking that nothing significant would change this time. But as he stared at the sand sliding down the glass, he started to contemplate it in a far more meaningful way. Lance spoke to himself as his eyes gazed into the hourglass, "Am I going to let my time as king plod along to its inevitable end or am I going to make it mean something more than just a passage of time?" Lance suddenly became invigorated and with a burst of energy slammed the table and shouted, "Tyrades will rule all!" The hourglass violently fell over and broke on his table. Lance knew that his vision to control the world was something that made him different than the previous kings of Tyrades. Lance considered the breaking of the hourglass, which his father had given to him, to be symbolic of an eventful remainder to his kingship.

Lance marched out of his royal chambers and walked toward the arena for the gladiator council meeting, which he was eagerly awaiting. A few guards left the royal chambers with the king to escort him to the arena safely. From the distance, the echo of steel could be heard. Lance said to himself, "They better not keep me waiting."

Lance walked through the arena gates and sat in the audience to observe what was happening below. Lance saw two men still practicing. After studying them for a moment, Lance noticed the two men were James Farenter and Kip Denvion. Sitting alone in the audience was an attractive, younger woman. Lance approached her and asked, "What brings you out here? This is an uncommon place for a young woman to be." The woman happily said, "My name is Julia, I am here to watch Kip train. It is an honor to meet you, my king." King Hasting replied, "Kip is a wonderful boy, I recommend you win over his affection before another woman does. He will be the king of Gofon one day and that could make you a queen." Julia said, "It is every girl's dream, but do not worry, I will treat him wonderfully while he is here visiting." The king said, "That is what I like to hear."

Lance turned toward the skirmishing men below and shouted, "James, it is almost time." James took a final step and smacked Kip's sword out of his hand with ease. James smiled at Kip and said, "Till next time." Kip reclaimed his weapon and said, "Thank you, gladiator." James looked up at the king and nodded as he hurried off to prepare for the meeting. Kip looked up at Julia and smiled as he called out, "Wait just a moment, I will come to you." Lance turned back at Julia and said, "I will see you around, Julia." Julia replied, "I would be honored, my king!" Lance left to meet the gladiators in their chambers.

Kip came up through a side entrance and walked up to Julia. He kissed her on the cheek and said, "I am surprised you find this entertaining." Julia replied, "I usually don't, but I know you really like it and spend so much time practicing so I had to see it for myself." Kip asked, "So, what did you think?" Julia said, "It looks like you know a lot of impressive moves; it is tough to tell because the other man is a gladiator." Kip said, "Thanks, let's go get some food, I am starving."

James entered the gladiators' chambers below and said, "My apologies for keeping you all waiting, I must have lost track of the time." The king said, "No problem, I see you have been spending much time with the boy. Keep it up, he appears to find comfort in being here. I am assuming many of you are wondering about the purpose of the gladiator council meeting today, especially with keeping Roy in the dark. Well, it is about time that I take a major risk in the interests of Tyrades and the gladiators. I have decided that I will inform our spy in Biros to kill the king's advisor, Nollie Gent. Roy will be quite vulnerable and easy to influence without the expertise of a knowledgeable and wise advisor."

Lemit Osrone asked, "Will he suspect us in any way?" Lance replied, "Highly doubtful, he has been spending time with my daughter and so far, has no reason not to trust us. I want to capitalize on my relationship with him while he is still a new king. But do not mistake me, gladiators, he is one of us and deserves to be treated, at least for appearance sake, as one of us." Lance then smirked and laughed.

James asked, "How do you plan on influencing Roy?" Lance replied, "Tyrades has existed as an inferior power to Torust and Gofon for centuries now. If I can unite Tyrades and Biros in some way, we will be able to grow more powerful. I want to enhance the army and economy of Tyrades through this enhanced strategic alliance."

Chapter Thirty-One: The Echo of Howls

Damien Nodon, Sterafia - Damien sat by the fire pit of the barracks, letting the heat of the flames warm his hands. The danger of the mission made him anxious and he had awoken before dawn, as he always had when his job kept him on edge. Damien stood up and walked to his son's residence without displaying any emotions. The cool wind blew against the side of his face, but he hardly felt anything anymore. Damien's cheeks had become so tough and resilient to the cold that only extreme weather conditions had an impact on his face.

Damien knocked firmly on Oakley's door knowing that there was no chance he would be awake at that hour. On most days, Oakley would be grumpy at this early hour, but today the reason for his pre-dawn greeting would be justified. A short moment later, Damien heard scratching coming from the other side of the door. Damien said to himself, "That makes one of them awake." Damien knocked slightly harder to wake Oakley without scaring him. Damien heard a thud and footsteps approaching the door as Oakley softly said, "Watch out, Snowstorm." A moment later, the door swung open and Oakley faced his father and asked, "What is it?", as he rubbed his eyes and yawned tiredly. Damien said, "I am sorry for waking you, but I had to see you before I left. I am going out with ten other soldiers today to venture south toward the wolf pack you came across."

Oakley's eyes were now wide open, and he was wide awake. He replied, "You can't, there are too many. You need your entire military to face them." Damien said, "Before we are ready to face them in battle, we need to identify where they are so we can properly prepare our men for combat. The wolf den could be a few days away to the south, if we sent our entire military without knowing where to go, we could have too little resources to supply the men." Oakley said, "I understand, but there has to be another way father, you do not need to go with them, you are more valuable here and alive." Damien said, "I am the head of the military and I must fulfill my duty leading them today. I will be by the barracks for a bit if you want to talk further." Oakley, feeling uneasy, said, "Okay, I will talk to you in a bit."

As Damien proceeded back to the barracks, he thought, 'I won't let him be left alone. I must quickly go and come back once we have what we need.' By the time he returned to the fire pit, a few of the other soldiers who would accompany him on the scouting group had arrived and were sitting by the fire. Damien could tell by their faces that they shared the same uneasy mood about the scouting trip. Damien thought to himself, 'Hundreds of wolves and feral humans running around like wolves, I can hardly blame them.' Damien sat next to one of the soldiers and patted him on the shoulder and said, "We will be on horses, we will return once we identify where the den is." The soldier said, "Sounds good, I am a bit nervous, but I am trained to obey your command. Sir, behind you, the king is approaching."

Damien stood and faced King Renga as he said, "Good morning, my king." The king motioned for Damien to walk closer. Once Damien came by his side, the king whispered in his ear, "Are you sure you want to go with the soldiers? As king, I am saying you do not need go, but I will never tell you what to do unless absolutely necessary. So, the choice is yours, Damien." Damien replied, "I have confidence in my men, but I feel as though I can lead them safely through the wild better than anyone else." The king asked, "Have you spoken with your son yet?" Damien said, "Yes, briefly this morning and I will possibly talk to him more before I depart. If anything happens to me out there, please watch over him for me." King Renga placed his hand on Damien's shoulder and said, "I always will, I see greatness in that boy just like I have always seen in you." Damien said, "Thank you, once the soldiers and I return we can start planning the attack on the wolf pack." The king said, "I agree, I will provide whatever resources are necessary, but focus on finding the den for now."

Damien turned around and signaled for one of the soldiers to prepare the meat on the fire. Damien called out, "Men, we will eat our morning meal and then equip our gear. In approximately an hour, we will be passing the royal gates to the south." King Renga went closer to Damien and gave him a handshake as he said, "Good luck out there." Damien nodded at the king and turned back to observe his men preparing as he instructed them.

After a while, Damien and the soldiers started to eat the cooked meat, which they hoped would provide them with the plentiful energy needed to last the day. Damien called out, "Eat up, we are only taking a limited amount of food supply for the trip. This could be your last meal in several hours or even a few days." As the men finished eating and started equipping their gear, Oakley and Snowstorm looked on from a balcony overhead. Oakley said, "Let's go, Snowstorm." They quickly walked toward the barracks and came up to Damien who had just finished putting on his armor. Damien grabbed Oakley and said, "I love you son, I will see you in a few hours." The two hugged before Damien mounted his horse. The other soldiers quickly tried to keep up with Damien as they finished putting on their gear. Oakley said, "Me too, I would go with you if I could." Damien said, "One day we will journey together."

The last of the soldiers mounted their horses and Damien called out, "On behalf of the military of Sterafia, it is our duty to pinpoint the threat of the growing wolf pack. Keep your eyes open and hopefully we can achieve the objective without any conflict or confrontation. Let us move out." The ground shook a little as all eleven horses started moving at once through the royal gates into the winter wasteland.

As the men departed, Snowstorm let out an anxious roar as he witnessed the march through the gates. Oakley, in disbelief, started to pet Snowstorm as he said, "What is wrong, Snowstorm? I have never heard you roar before." As his hands flowed through the soft coat of the tiger, Snowstorm did not move at all. The tiger's gaze was locked onto the march of the scouting party. Oakley looked again at the men leaving and the realization of Snowstorm's concern caught Oakley by surprise. Oakley said, "I cannot believe it, you do remember that day, don't you Snowstorm. One day we will find your family too." As Oakley pet Snowstorm, the tiger rubbed up against Oakley's stomach and moaned sensitively. Oakley said "Come on, Snowstorm. Let us go find something to do." Oakley slowly turned and walked into the marketplace of Sterafia with Snowstorm by his side.

Damien and the soldiers rode quietly to the south as dawn broke and the sun beamed over the hills. Damien finally broke the silence and said, "My son informed me as to where he saw them, we will ride to that location and beyond, if necessary. The terrain will become hillier, but I will try to stick to flat land whenever possible." One of the soldiers asked, "Do you believe him?" Damien replied, "Of course I do, why wouldn't I?" The soldier said, "He needed a reason to come home with a tiger. If he did not have a story, he wouldn't have been able to keep it." Damien said, "I can see why you might think that way, but knowing my son, I know he is telling the truth. He would not have let this idea of a massive wolf pack continue otherwise. He journeys into the wild a lot more than any of us."

After riding for a few hours, the men started to notice the lack of wildlife. One of the soldiers said, "Is it me or are there far less animals out here. I haven't seen a single animal in almost an hour." Damien nodded and said, "I agree, that must mean we are getting closer." After riding for a bit longer the scouting party came across some deer bones that had been stripped of every piece of meat. Damien said, "Hungry predators it looks like. Not enough meat to fill their stomachs." As the scouting party rode deeper into what became a snow-covered forest, the amount of animal bones grew. Damien and the men stopped inspecting each set of bones; the hostile and tense atmosphere kept all the soldiers on edge.

The sun was now high in the sky, but only a few beams of light could creep through the vast trees covering the snowy terrain. Suddenly, the echo of howls projected throughout the cold air. At that moment, the soldiers all faced each other, the look on their faces confirming that Oakley was telling the truth and that they had gotten close enough to the threat to become worried and fearful.

The howls were sustained as one of the soldiers said, "The den is somewhere over there, we can go back now, right?" Damien said, "It is tough to tell, just because that is where the howls are coming from, it does not mean it is their den. They might just be out hunting." Damien took a moment and thought to himself as he dismounted his horse and pointed to five other soldiers and said, "You guys, off your horses and come up this hill with me. We need to observe from high ground." The men nervously dismounted their horses and carefully climbed up the hill with Damien. The howls slowly started to fade as the men stopped climbing. After a moment, Damien said, "We are almost there, let's just go up and see." Damien got to the top and provided his hand to help the others up. Damien and the soldiers all crouched down low and peeked out onto the terrain below. In the distance, they could see close to fifty wolves and feral humans lounging around what appeared to be a den. Damien said, "That looks like the den, I can see wolf pups."

Howls from both sides of the hill behind the trees started to echo through the air again. Suddenly, mobs of wolves came running at them from both sides. Damien shouted, "They see us! Quick, get to the bottom!" The men rapidly tried to race down the hill without taking the time to take careful steps. One of the soldiers slipped and tumbled at the top knocking down all the men trying to reach the bottom. Their bodies bounced off the tough hill until they hit the bottom with force. The men on the horses shouted, "Hurry, they are coming down fast!" One of the soldiers stood back up on his feet and ran over to a horse. A couple of the soldiers had trouble walking and could only move at half the speed they wanted.

Damien blacked out for a few seconds after hitting his head hard on the ground. When he came to his senses, Damien joined the others trying to get back to the horses. The men on the horses started to command their horses to flee while Damien ran for his horse. Behind him he could hear the struggling soldiers getting picked off one by one. Damien ran as fast as he could trying to reach his horse before it was too late. Suddenly, the sharp pain of a wolf bite in his calf knocked him down. Damien watched as his horse ran off behind all the others to escape. The wolf came closer to Damien and he waited for the animal to finish him off with a lethal bite. Instead, inexplicably, the wolf ran after the fleeing soldiers. Damien was lying on his back in the snow facing the sky as he said, "I am sorry, Oakley."

Damien sat up for a moment and noticed the wolves were not eating the other soldiers. The wolves appeared to be scouting the area looking for any other deserters. Suddenly, Damien felt an intense twitch in the side of his left shoulder. Then he felt another twitch in his calf that was bitten. Another forceful twitch shot across his right forearm. Damien was now lying on the ground completely clueless about what was happening to his body as it was not the death he had expected. The twitches grew more rapid and severe as Damien started to lose control of his own body. His face started to twitch, and Damien suspected this would be his last moment. As his whole body started to twitch all together, the last image in his mind was Oakley standing next to a full-grown Snowstorm. Once his mind went blank and he could no longer process a thought, his body shot up on all fours and he began walking around on his hands and feet like the other feral humans and the four soldiers who had been bitten moments earlier.

A short distance away, the fleeing soldiers and the uncontrolled horses continued their fast retreat to Sterafia. One of the men shouted, "We lost Damien! I cannot believe it, they all died!" Another soldier shouted, "We will avenge them now that we know where the den is. We will strike with force and kill every last one of them."

Back in Sterafia, Oakley bought several pounds of meat for Snowstorm and himself to eat. Ralph, the food vendor, said, "He is growing so fast, how have you been managing?" Oakley said, "I am excited to see him grow, but some things, especially, feeding him, have become more difficult." Ralph said, "I am sure, here is another piece on me", as he handed Oakley another pound of meat. Oakley said, "Thanks, if you ever need us for anything, we will be happy to help." As Oakley held another pound of meat in his hand, Snowstorm chuffed at him and sat hoping for an extended meal. Oakley said, "Wait, let me take a few bites. As Oakley chewed on the thick meat, Snowstorm impatiently pawed at Oakley as if he were asking for more.

Oakley said, "Fine, you beggar", as he tossed Snowstorm the rest of the meat. Ralph and Oakley chuckled as Snowstorm devoured the last few pieces. Oakley said, "See you soon, Ralph. Be well." Ralph replied, "You too, come back soon."

Oakley and Snowstorm strolled back to Oakley's room as Oakley wondered about his father's well-being. Once Oakley opened his door, Snowstorm squeezed past him into the room first. Oakley noticed how Snowstorm was growing rapidly and soon would not be able to fit comfortably in the room. All the anxiety stressed Oakley out and he jumped on his bed to relax for a while. Snowstorm swiftly jumped onto the bed next to Oakley. Oakley put his arm around Snowstorm and dosed off for a nap.

The sound of a blasting horn alarmed the city and Oakley and Snowstorm woke up from their nap. Oakley said, "They are back", as he scrambled to put his boots on. Oakley ran outside with Snowstorm following him. A moment later, Oakley and Snowstorm were waiting by the royal gates as the scouting party started to pass through the entrance. Oakley looked at each passing man and noticed a few empty horses and asked one of the soldiers, "Where is Damien?" The soldier said, "The wolves, they got him." Oakley ran back to his room as tears started to pour down his face. Back in his room, Oakley cried for hours. Snowstorm moaned in sadness with Oakley as he sensed Oakley's raw, sad emotions.

Chapter Thirty-Two: The Re-Emerging Warrior

Ria Falune, Torust - Ria sat down in the Halls of Absolute alongside Haigar and Halon after a long trip back from their trip to the north. Ria asked, "What could the significance of 'The Caller' mean?" Haigar said, "My queen, it is probably just a riddle. I do not think you should concern yourself too much with this necklace, although I think you should continue wearing it, it does look very nice." Ria said, "Thank you, but I must know. Halon, I want you to search all your work and see if you can find anything that may help us." Halon said, "I am happy to serve you, my queen."

Ria asked, "Haigar, how has Gofon coped with the illness since we were away?" Haigar replied, "Based on the report my men have provided to me, the illness is spreading across the towns and Gofon is spending vast resources trying to aid them. There are mass casualties and the problem seems to be growing." Ria smiled and said, "Excellent, the weaker they become, the more powerful we are."

From across the Halls of Absolute, Ria noticed a tall and bulky man who looked familiar. After looking at the man for a moment, Ria alarmingly asked the others, "Is that Peter Fardine?" Haigar said, "Yes, I cannot believe it, the finest warrior of Torust has reemerged. He is supposed to be dead." Haigar called out, "Peter!" Peter Fardine looked from across the halls and saw the three of them sitting at the table. Peter walked over with a surprisingly unfriendly face.

Ria said, "It is great to see you, Peter. We all thought you were dead. Can you share what happened?" Peter said, "As you know, I lost the final fight against Roy Syssian of Biros. His blade caught the back of my neck and almost paralyzed me. I was in bed for months and in a coma for much of the time. Once I came to, I was committed to making a complete recovery. Eventually, I was able to walk on my own and made steady progress from there. I rode back to Torust a few days ago. My wife had just killed herself a couple of weeks prior to my return and my son is not well, so if you do not mind I need a little time before I can get involved in the city again." Haigar said, "I am so sorry, I was the one that had to tell her. She was heartbroken from the news. From then on, she looked deeply saddened every time we saw her."

Peter shouted at them, "Why did you tell her I was dead?! Why didn't any of you comfort her when she was depressed?!" Ria said, "I am sorry too, Peter, but we tried. Nothing else mattered to her beside you." Ria stood and hugged Peter and said, "Take all the time you need, I am here for you if you want to talk about things." Peter said, "I am sorry I lost my temper with you all, it is these times that most warriors struggle with; the emotions of love that all the power and dominance in the world cannot conquer." Ria said, "That was deep and beautiful, Peter."

Peter excused himself as he walked away from the others. Ria said, "Peter is totally devastated, and rightfully so. Let him take as much time as he needs. He will come to us when he is ready. And once he is ready, he will be very valuable for us." Haigar said, "I agree, he is the best fighter in Torust." Ria said, "His son's name is Cazier, right?" Haigar replied, "That is correct, I have met him before." Ria said, "Go summon my brother Gardas, I need his help with getting Cazier back to normal." Haigar said, "I will do that now, my queen", as he got up to go summon Gardas.

Ria told Halon, "I am going to set Cazier up with a woman from the brothel. You saved me on the journey, I would be happy to arrange for a few visits for you too if you are interested in visiting the brothel. My brother is a regular there, unfortunately." Halon replied, "I appreciate your offer, but I do not partake in that type of artificial love. I always prefer the real thing." Ria said, "I understand, I am the same way."

Torb Daxo approached the table and said, "Welcome back, my queen." The queen turned toward Torb and said, "Hello Torb, how was your journey to that cave you were speaking of?" Torb, with a big smile, replied, "Very, very well. The cave was filled with emeralds and onyx and that was only the surface. I am calling it the Cave of Jewels because that is what it is." Torb then held up a sack of jewels that was filled to the top and closed shut. Torb handed the sack to Ria and said, "This is my gift to you, my lovely queen."

Ria curiously opened the sack and held it upside down. A few handfuls of emeralds and onyx gems came flowing out of the sack onto the table. Ria, with a stunned look, said, "Thank you! You said you only saw part of the cave?" Torb said, "Yes, I had all of my men carry bags filled with the gems, but there is still plenty in the top level of the cave where we were. There was also an opening leading to a lower level, and while we did not venture into it, we could tell that there were gems there as well from what we saw in the pathway. I want to ask you, my queen, if you can please assist me by supplying a larger ship so that I can bring camels and more men. You can bring some workers of your own as well, but I would definitely split the gems with you for helping me. And just like I invited you last time, it would be a pleasure if you would accompany me." The queen replied, "I would be happy to supply you with whatever you need, and I think I will go with you this time. It would be a very rewarding trip and could help me take my mind off a more recent personal matter." Torb said, "Excellent, let me know when you are ready." Ria said, "I will, and excellent find Torb, you are one of a kind at what you do."

Haigar returned to the table with Gardas by his side. Gardas said, "Greetings, sister. I haven't seen you in a while." Ria said, "Yea, because you live in a whorehouse." Gardas smirked and said, "That is true, you lose track of things when you are there all of the time. Anyway, what can I of all people help the queen with? I really am curious to know." The queen said, "I need you to provide...one of the women to sexually provide for Peter Fardine's son." Haigar said, "Is this what we really needed him for?" Gardas happily said, "Oh, this is going to be good. I would ask why, but I really do not care enough to know. I would rather see this happen. I know the perfect woman for a young man his age." Ria said, "Good, do not make this a mistake for me." Gardas said, "Do not worry, the boy will be more than happy afterward."

Chapter Thirty-Three: The Physical Gift

Cazier Fardine, Torust - "I miss the way things were", Cazier said to himself as he thought of memories from his childhood with his mother and father. Unlike his father, Cazier had struggled to get out of the house since the passing of his mother, Vasa. Just then, Cazier could hear the laughter of a man coming closer to the door. The sound of laughter was almost new to Cazier after being secluded for so long. Cazier wondered who this man was, what he looked like, and why he seemed so happy.

Suddenly, the laughter paused as the man started knocking on the door. Cazier approached the door curiously, but cautiously, and opened it. The man said, "Hello, my name is Gardas Falune. I am the brother of the queen. You must be Cazier Fardine, right?" Cazier, with a confused look, said, "Yes, that is me. What do you need?" Gardas smiled and said, "I do not need anything, the rulers of Torust are not that cruel. The queen has asked me to assist you in...how do you say...in receiving a special gift." Cazier said, "Well, where is the gift, can you just hand it to me?" Gardas said, "It is not a physical gift, well, actually, it really is, but not in the way you are thinking. Just come with me, you will not be disappointed."

Cazier looked behind him at the empty house where he had just spent weeks mourning and said, "Might as well, nothing is going on here." Gardas said, "That is the spirit. You are the son of Peter Fardine, are you trying to become a great fighter like him?" Cazier said, "No, not particularly." Gardas said, "Oh, that is a shame, seeing genetic talent on display is quite satisfying." Cazier asked, "Why were you sent to walk me to the gift instead of one of the queen's guards?" Gardas turned and faced Cazier. He smirked and said, "I see the beauty and talent in this particular art." They then left Cazier's home.

Gardas said, "Here we are, just inside. Follow me." Cazier followed Gardas into a building he had never been in before. From the entrance,

Cazier heard the sound of distant moans coming from a room further in the building. Cazier nervously asked, "Where are we?" Gardas said, "The brothel, I still remember my first time here, I was just as nervous as you are now. Wait here."

As Gardas walked off into another room, Cazier thought to himself, 'How am I going to be able to explain this?' A short moment later Gardas reentered the room with a beautiful young woman around the same age as Cazier who was wearing garments that revealed a lot of her beauty. Gardas said, "This is Nera, I thought she would be a good choice for you as she is around your age." Cazier nervously nodded and said, "That she is", as Nera walked closer and started to seductively touch Cazier's chest. Cazier said, "Can I have a quick word with you, Gardas?" Gardas said, "Yes, Nera can you please wait in the other room for a moment." Nera nodded and smiled back at Cazier with excitement.

Gardas walked closer to Cazier and asked, "Is she not a good fit? Damn, I thought she would have been a good one. If you want to have someone else, she won't be upset." Cazier said, "That is not it. If I tell you, I hope you can keep a secret." Gardas said, "I promised the queen I would help you and I do promise to keep a secret confidential. What is it?" Cazier said, "I am sexually attracted to the opposite gender, I mean the same gender as me." Gardas replied, "Ohh, now I understand. So, I assume the brothel serves no service to you then?" Cazier replied, "Well, I did have an idea, but it is not a regular request." Gardas curiously said, "Go on." Cazier said, "My mother just passed away and my father helped me find my purpose again. I know how important family legacies can be and I will never have the opportunity to give him a child. I want to make my father happy in some way and I feel like having a child will make him happy. I know this is asking too much, but, if it is possible, I want to use my gift to impregnate a woman and have her bear my child. I would always be there for them, but I do not have the resources right now to support them."

Gardas thought for a moment and said, "It could take a bunch of attempts you know?" Cazier nodded and said, "I do realize that." Gardas said, "Let me go ask Nera, it is about time we create a more positive atmosphere around here."

Gardas walked into the room with Nera and spoke with her for a short moment before returning to Cazier. Gardas smiled and said, "She will be the one." Cazier walked up to Gardas and hugged him as he said, "I cannot thank you enough." Gardas replied, "I am happy to help. I admire your desire and will to please your father, I always loved mine as well. I was a different person before he passed away. Not the type to be found around here. Go on, enjoy yourself. I knew it would be a physical gift, but I did not expect it to be a baby."

Cazier walked into the other room and Nera grabbed his hand and led him into a bedroom. Cazier said, "Tell me about yourself, I want to know a little about my child's mother." Nera sat on the bed and said, "I am beautiful, and I enjoy using my body for this profession. When Gardas told me your request, I thought he was joking, but when he explained why you want to have a child, I decided to help. The money he is going to give me is very generous as well."

Nera stood up and undid her clothes revealing her bare body, as she asked, "What made you want to have a child with one of us here in the brothel?" Cazier said, "Out there, you cannot hide secrets. Here, I can have the child I desire without any attachments, although I do intend on being there for you along the way." Nera pushed Cazier back onto the bed and started to take off his pants, as she said, "Now, for the most enjoyable part."

Chapter Thirty-Four: The Horn of Danger

Liava Pontas, Dragon Lair - Liava jokingly tugged on the young dragon's tail hoping to convince it to stay in the lair with her. The red dragon turned around and looked Liava in her eyes trying to communicate a sense of trust and loyalty. Liava let go of the tail and mumbled, "Go on, it is okay." The red dragon turned around and took off into the sky to keep up with the other dragons.

Liava looked down and noticed her wooden bowl was empty. Before it got too warm outside, Liava knew she had to fill it up with some water for the day. She grabbed her wooden flute and a ram's horn that she recently found. The horn was intact, and she was able to modify it so that it produced a unique sound when she blew into it. Liava recently taught the dragons that the sound of the horn meant that she was in danger.

Liava had spent the past few weeks learning to communicate with the dragons using various methods of sounds and expressions. When Liava wanted to teach them the meaning of the horn, she ran around blowing the horn while making faces of distress and frantic gestures. The dragons quickly came flying toward her in a protective manner as they associated the noise, facial expressions and gestures with danger. This method also had come in handy for basic communication. Liava let out moans of hunger when she wanted them to know she needed food. In the beginning, she moaned and rubbed her stomach. By now, though, the dragons knew what Liava wanted just from the sounds she made whether vocal or through the flute and horn. Aside from the music, her flute and horn now served a more important purpose, that of survival.

Liava walked into the upper forest surrounding the lair to retrieve some water from a nearby lake. During her time with the dragons, she found great appreciation for the lake. She would cleanse herself with the water and relax to the pleasant sound of the flowing water. There was even a small waterfall that she enjoyed. Today, Liava decided to walk along the lake since she was up earlier than usual. As Liava walked along the water's edge she picked up branches and twigs and tossed them into her bag so that she could start a fire later that night. Liava walked and walked uncovering the lush forest filled with wildlife that her people strived to protect.

Liava set her stuff down on the ground and kneeled closer to the lake. She cupped water in both of her hands and started to drink a few handfuls of water. She then extended her face closer to the water and started to wash it, scrubbing away the dirt that had built up as a result of her living in the dragons' lair. Liava ran her hands against her face, using the reflection of the water as a mirror.

Liava then noticed something moving on the other side of the lake. Whatever it was quickly moved behind a bush and she could no longer see it. Liava stood up and slowly started to back up. Suddenly, a large mountain lion emerged from the bush and launched itself as far as possible across the lake. The mountain lion made it almost halfway across and started to quickly swim closer to Liava's side aided by the water current that started to shift in its favor. Liava rapidly ran over to her items and picked up her flute and horn. As she started running back to the lair, she strongly exhaled a deep breath into her horn of danger. A loud blast projected throughout the sky. The mountain lion made its way to Liava's side of the lake and immediately set after her. The mountain lion was running at a far faster speed than Liava. Liava ran ahead while occasionally looking back and blowing the horn.

The mountain lion was quickly gaining ground, shortening the distance between himself and Liava. In desperation, Liava pulled out her blade. This would be the moment her father prepared her for. Killing a predator animal out of self-defense; something the people of Staga hated but knew was sometimes necessary.

Suddenly, to Liava's delight, the red dragon emerged from the sky and started to fly in circles around Liava creating a slight spiral of wind before landing. The mountain lion abruptly stopped its hunt and gazed at the menacing dragon that saved Liava. Liava held her flute in her hands and lifted it up to her mouth. She thought to herself, 'This creature should die, it was going to kill me!' Anger and the thought of revenge filled her mind and she was ready to play the melody of flames. She suddenly pulled the flute away from her lips and placed it back in her pocket. She remembered what she was taught and said to the mountain lion, "You are no longer a threat." The mountain lion understood the threat that the dragon presented and fled into the forest. Liava walked up to the dragon and placed her arms around its neck as she hugged it firmly. She said, "Next time, I am going with you."

Chapter Thirty-Five: The Reward for Suffering

Ryos Pontas, Village of Tsirian - Ryos sat by the firepit in the center of the village slicing up pieces of meat with his blade. One by one he tossed thick, juicy pieces of dense meat into his mouth. Ryos and the other surviving teenage boys of Staga had come to believe that the meat of animals would, in fact, make them strong like the villagers that defeated their parents. Ryos looked into the fire and, for a moment, thought back to the times his family used to enjoy dancing around the fire and gazing at the stars, sans the meat, of course.

Ryos smiled in envy at the life he used to have. His smile quickly turned into a childish frown as he realized that this was the first time in weeks that he had thought of his old life. Although Ryos was learning and adapting to the new way of life, he still thought of the past as a much better time.

From across the fire, he spotted a young teenage girl smiling at him while talking to a girl who was sitting next to her. Ryos smiled back as he wondered if they were talking about him. As a new villager, he did not know how to react, so he waited passively.

The two girls stood up and walked to both sides of him before sitting. A girl with light red hair said, "Hi, my name is Gibia." The other girl, with dark brown hair, tapped his right arm and said, "And my name is Dasina." Ryos, feeling somewhat overwhelmed by their eagerness, replied, "My name is Ryos, it is nice to meet you both."

Gibia said, "We noticed that you were the first of the newcomers to be welcomed as a villager. You must have done something impressive." Ryos said, "I guess so, I did somewhat surprise myself." Dasina excitedly said, "Well, tell us, tell us!" Ryos said, "Well, as Edgar tells it, I charged headfirst at a full-sized boar and gutted it open, allowing our village the opportunity to eat and survive." The two girls looked at Ryos in awe and Gibia said, "That is so brave for a young warrior like yourself."

Dasina felt the muscle on Ryos's arm as she asked, "Flex, I want to feel your strength." Ryos said, "I am not that strong, I am just quick, but I will do it anyway." As he flexed his arm, he could feel Dasina gripping his muscle tighter. Dasina said, "Has anyone told you about life here at the village, family life that is." Ryos replied, "No, they have not. It seems like people here get married at a younger age than in my old village." Dasina said, "We are a year or two away from the age of marriage and the wise girls pursue the strongest boys. We want our children to be strong too."

Ryos asked, "How come some men walk around with two women as if they are both his wives?" Gibia said, "Here in Tsirian, some men can have two wives. There are many men that die in combat or of illness, so the women here heavily outnumber the men." Ryos said, "So that is why they killed all the women from my village?" Gibia said, "Unfortunately, I would assume so."

Gibia continued, "Dasina and I have been close friends since birth. We are both interested in you as you are brave and strong. Do you find us pretty?" Ryos confidently smiled and said, "Yes, very much so. I would dream of having one of you by my side in life, but to have both of you is unreal. In my old village, I was quiet and did not talk to many girls, but I am happy to have met both of you here now." Dasina said, "We will help you get accustomed to things here, but we are looking forward to the great things that you will do for the village and us." Both girls kissed him on the cheek and excused themselves for lunch. Ryos thought to himself, 'Life here is not too bad, two girls for marriage, this is the reward for suffering.'

Chapter Thirty-Six: The Cloud of Vision

Searleone Vallas, Skyrock - Searleone opened his eyes as he finished his meditation. The moist air of the clouds left his robe damp. Searleone placed his hands on his chest and pulled the wet particles out of his robe as he said, "Steroy Oust." Searleone heard a chorus in his mind singing to him and he felt inclined to join in. Searleone stroked his beard as he sung out loud to himself, "The soft lands of Lodas, a majestic place to be. The wildlife run free, free from the threat of a man. A threat to all, a menace to a life we need be. Through substance, through fire, a dream can be a dream for Lodas and all creatures who can be. Sanctify Lodas and set it free, a new world awaits, a place for them and me."

Searleone continued humming to himself as he walked around the balcony and looked out onto the surrounding mountains. Voron approached Searleone from the sanctuary and said, "It sounds like a pleasant melody. Which one is it?" Searleone said, "I can't remember, sometimes I just make some up in my head while I am meditating. How are the young mages doing with their fireball training?" Voron said, "Very well, and I am assisting them with their studies for hours every day. They continue to get better and better." Searleone said, "Excellent, I have a vision and the young mages play a role in the future just like us." Voron asked, "What do you see them using the fire for?" Searleone said, "Some battles are necessary to make the world a better place, we will see in time." Voron replied, "I trust your word, I will do what you wish to improve our world, like the others."

Searleone said, "Excuse me for a moment, I feel the need to meditate." Searleone sat down on the balcony and closed his eyes as his mind started to focus. After a moment, his mind transferred to a part of his soul that he left behind in a passing cloud moments earlier. Searleone could see the world through the vision of the cloud. Just as he had expected, the cloud was overlooking some of the towns east of Gofon. These towns appeared desolate and void of any form of human life. Some of the other towns in his vision seemed more active but were still suffering the effects of the illness.

Searleone waited patiently as the cloud of vision extended into some forestry to the west where Searleone could see animals and wildlife starting to prosper with the absence of human interference. Searleone started to release his soul from the cloud; returning it to his body along with the vision that now accompanied his soul. Searleone focused on the surroundings as that part of his soul now rapidly traveled from the cloud back to his meditating body. Searleone stood up and shed a tear at the beautiful sight of the thriving wildlife, the result of his doing.

Chapter Thirty-Seven: Dunlow Bridge

Roy Syssian, Biros - Roy slowly and quietly snuck out of bed, trying not to wake Leora. He carefully walked a few steps to his dresser and opened the top drawer. He felt around for the bag he needed as there was little lighting in the room for him to be able to see. Once the tip of his fingers touched the bag, he grabbed it and tossed it in his pants pocket as he heard Leora roll over and ask, "What are you doing up so early?" Roy said, "I got restless, I am going to go get some food for us before our trip." Leora said, "What trip? You didn't mention anything to me about a trip." Roy said, "I want to take you someplace special; I can't tell you where, I just want you to see it." Leora said, "Okay, let me sleep a little more." Roy said, "I am going to walk around a little and then I will come back with some food."

As Roy left his bedroom, he greeted the guard in the hallway and walked toward the royal dining halls. Roy nervously touched the bag in his pocket and felt around for the item he had put in the bag. Roy could tell that it was still in there. Roy entered the dining halls before dawn and sat at his table. Only a few others were in the dining halls at that time. Roy rarely showed up before sunrise, but today was one of those times. One of the servants asked Roy, "Can I get you some eggs and steak my king?" Roy nodded and said, "Certainly, that sounds great. And some food for the lady."

Roy sat alone and thought to himself, 'Is this the right decision? Will I be happy?' Roy's mind started to roam to different thoughts as he sat considering what he was going to do with his future. He could tell that his gut was telling him to go ahead with his plan. Roy thought about how he usually did well when he trusted his instincts.

After eating his meal alone, Roy walked back to his room with the servant who was carrying the food for Leora. Roy took the plate of food and said, "I have it from here, thanks." Roy placed the food on his dresser and sat on the bed to wake Leora. Roy said, "I have some food here for you. Eat and then get ready to leave." Leora sat up and said, "Okay, just give me a moment, I never wake up this early." Roy laughed and said, "You really are royalty. They say the royal families never rise before the sun." Leora yawned and said, "I never intend to. Can you pass me the food?" Roy handed Leora the food and started to get changed for the day. As he changed his pants, he slyly exchanged the bag into the pants he put on. Leora finished her food and prepared for the trip as well. Moments later, Leora said, "Okay, I am ready. Where are you taking me, I want to know?" Roy said, "It is called Dunlow Bridge, it is a relaxing spot, you will see."

Roy and Leora left the royal chambers and headed a few minutes north until they arrived at the royal stables of the city. Leora asked, "Is it safe for us to leave the city alone?" Roy said, "It is only a short journey from here, we will be fine. When I was growing up, I spent a lot of time there. And taking these horses from the stables and riding there will be fun too."

Roy walked up to the stables and approached his white horse. Leora said, "Such a beautiful horse, I can tell he is your favorite." Roy said, "He is my loyal boy." Leora said, "Seems like it, the two of you seem to have a great bond." Roy walked a beautiful black horse out of the stables and helped Leora onto it before mounting his own horse. The horses maintained a steady trot as they passed the northern gates of Biros. Leora said, "This is the first time I have left the city since we arrived. It feels strange, Biros almost feels like home already." Roy said, "Home does not need to be where you grew up or where your family resides. Home can be wherever you want to spend the next portion of your life, whether it is years or even months. Your home is only good until you find your next home. More importantly, you want your home to be with the right person." Leora smiled and said, "If that is so, maybe Biros will be my home."

The horses continued to trot further north as Leora and Roy relaxed and enjoyed the scenic surroundings. In the distance, Leora noticed a small stone bridge above a calm lake. Leora asked, "Is that Dunlow Bridge?" Roy replied, "Yes, there is something about this place that brings me back in time. I have many wonderful memories of this place from when I was younger, and I always wanted to share them with my love one day."

Roy dismounted his horse and carefully helped Leora off her horse before they walked closer to the lake and sat down. Roy asked, "Have you ever wondered what life would be like if we met as normal people? With no royal background or fighting expertise, just regular citizens of this world?" Leora said, "No, I have not, although I know I still would feel the same was about you." Roy said, "Well, I brought you out here to show you what that would be like. I want to show you how life can be when we remove all the artificial titles and luxuries we possess. I was not meant to be a king. I am still a citizen at heart, and I can tell deep down you are looking for someone who wants more out of life than just ruling over others and fighting all of the time. Someone who wants peace and wants to do good for others. I hope you want something deeper, like I hope for."

Roy took the bag out of his pocket and reached inside. His cupped hand slid out of the bag and he opened his hand revealing a golden marriage bracelet. Roy asked, "Would you want me for life; and the many homes we shall share?" Leora started crying as her face blossomed red with the most genuine smile. Leora nodded several times and lifted her left arm forward. Roy, smiling back at Leora, opened the bracelet and placed it on her wrist before closing and locking it shut. Roy said, "With that, I extend my love to you for eternity." Leora said, "My love is all yours" as she came closer and kissed Roy. Leora said, "Excellent setting for this moment, I must say." Roy nodded and said, "I know, Dunlow Bridge will always be special to both of us now." Leora looked down at her gold bracelet and said, "This is the moment I have dreamt of, only better."

Roy and Leora spent their time relaxing, napping, laughing, and talking about what their future together would be like. Hours went by and the two knew that they had to return to Biros. As they stood up and started to walk toward their horses, Leora asked, "Does anyone else know about this yet?" Roy said, "No, only you. However, once we return, I am going to tell the others that we will be celebrating with an extravagant feast tonight." Leora said, "I cannot wait! I must say, you really love making these feasts happen and I cannot complain." Roy said, "Yes, that is perhaps the one thing I have taken advantage of during my kingship."

Roy and Leora mounted the horses and rode back to Biros where they stopped at the stables to drop them off. From there, Roy and Leora went into the royal chambers and found Nollie Gent. Roy said, "Nollie, good to see you. I have news for you." Nollie curiously looked at Roy and asked, "What is it?" Roy lifted Leora's arm revealing the golden marriage bracelet and said, "We are going to be married soon, I need you to organize a celebratory feast this evening." Nollie smiled and said, "Congratulations, I will get it prepared. Many celebratory drinks to be consumed."

Roy and Leora went back to their residence and changed into their more formal clothing for the feast. Roy said, "This is a very important night for both of us, let's have an exciting time." Leora nodded and said, "Are you going to have to speak?" Roy said, "Yes, but only a little." Leora said, "I might have a little something to say." Roy asked, "Is that so?" Leora nodded and came closer to Roy and kissed him.

Roy said, "It is time", as he held out his hand. Leora grabbed his hand and they walked off toward the royal dining halls. Once they entered the dining halls, it was still somewhat empty. Roy said, "I wanted to get here before everyone else." Roy called over a servant and said, "Some wine." The servant nodded and said, "Yes, my king." A moment later, the servant arrived with the wine and poured it into two cups for Roy and Leora. Roy lifted his cup and said, "To us." Leora smiled and clanked her cup against his before they both had their first sip of red wine. Leora and Roy kept drinking and joking around as the dining halls filled up with the attendees of the celebration.

Roy whispered to Leora, "I need to slow down, I still have a speech to give." Leora nodded and said, "Yes, just get it over with." Roy said, "In a bit, give people a chance to eat, and me too." Roy picked up a piece of chicken and ate it with his hands. Leora took a moment before picking up some bread and eating. Suddenly, one of the attendees shouted out, "Cheers, to the king and his new queen to be!" Everyone in the dining hall lifted their cups and took a drink.

As the dining halls were now full, Roy seized the moment and stood and looked around at all the faces, except this time he was in a tipsy daze. Roy called out, "Listen, this woman right here... not many of you have met her, but she is the perfect woman. Beautiful, loving, and fit to lead as the queen of Biros. She is a firm believer in supporting all residents of the kingdom. I cannot tell you enough how..."

Roy paused as his vision locked onto something to his right. Sitting a few seats over, Nollie Gent was listening to Roy speak. Nollie nodded at Roy encouraging him to continue speaking. Roy saw Nollie's entire body turn gold. About twenty feet away, a man was carrying a cup filled with a liquid that Roy saw turning bright red, much brighter than ordinary red wine. The man was slowly walking closer to the front of the room where Nollie was sitting.

Roy continued to speak, "Excuse me, I am just so excited that I lost my words." Roy peered anxiously at the visions that kept switching on and off. Nollie kept turning gold and the cup the man was holding kept turning bright red. Roy was confused, perhaps because he had a few drinks of wine, and did not know what to make of the situation.

As the man approached Nollie, he slipped some of the liquid into Nollie's cup as Nollie was looking at Roy. Roy angrily shouted, "Guards, seize that man! Nollie, do not drink from your cup!" As the man tried running off, sounds of panic could be heard from the crowd. A guard stopped the fleeing man and grabbed him by the arm. Another guard kicked the back of his knee, forcing him to kneel.

Roy, now in a mildly drunken rage, said, "What did you put in his drink?!" The man said, "Nothing, I did no such thing." Roy said, "I hope you are thirsty then, because I am nice enough to offer you his drink." One guard held the man's arms as another guard kept the man's face from moving.

Nollie said, "No, Roy, we need to ask him questions." Roy said, "He tried to kill you, I owe him no pity." Roy lifted Nollie's cup with the unknown liquid and held it high for all to see. As Roy brought it closer to the man's face, the man started squirming, but the guard resisted his movement. The man started yelling, "No, don't do it! It was not me! No!"

Roy, Nollie, and the guards tried to convince the man to talk, but to no avail. He would not divulge who sent him. At Roy's instruction, the guard forced the man's mouth open and Roy started pouring the liquid making sure that each drop found its targeted point of entry. Once the entire cup was emptied, the guard held the man's mouth shut and forced him to swallow the drink. Everyone anxiously looked to see what would happen. The man very quickly started to cough profusely. The man fell over onto the ground and started to cough up blood, as Nollie said, "He tried to kill me. Roy, how did you know?" Roy, with a look of disdain at the suffering man, said, "I saw it happen." The man continued to suffer until he coughed up blood one last time.

Roy shouted, "The night has not been ruined, Nollie is alive, and the celebration will continue." Roy walked toward Leora and then sat with her; he was disappointed with the way the night turned out, but grateful for his vision.

Chapter Thirty-Eight: The Unjust Orders

Phillip Denvion, Gofon - Timothy quickly opened the door, interrupting Phillip's meal with his wife. After he managed to catch his breath, Timothy exclaimed, "I bring wonderful news, my king. Jol has returned with the cure!" Phillip stood up and asked, "How do we know?" Timothy said, "He is sure, you can ask him for yourself, he is outside waiting to come in." Phillip dispatched a guard to summon Jol to quickly come in. Phillip said, "If this is the cure, our plan will be a huge success. We will be able to tell the council just how right we were in our plans. Most importantly, we will be able to save lives and the kingdom." Timothy said, "I agree with you, my king."

Jol entered with another man. Phillip, unphased by the appearance of another man with Jol, asked, "Is it true? A cure is known?" Jol said, "Yes, thanks to Ked Larone here." Jol then held up some flowers and said, "I plan on conjuring up these flowers that we brought back into efficient oils that many people can inhale and be cured." The king asked, "What type of flower is it?" Jol replied, "A new one that we have never seen before. I named it Ked's Gift after Ked showed me the origin of the flowers that we used for the cure."

The king looked at Ked and said, "It is quite something to be responsible for curing thousands of people, you should be honored. We are very proud of you." Ked replied, "I never thought I would have such a positive impact on our world. I am honored to have helped our great kingdom of Gofon in some way."

The king asked, "What is it that you want, Ked? You name it and I have it for you." Ked said, "I need to start fresh; I want a new home so hopefully I can start a family here." The king nodded and said, "A home with a scenic view overlooking the square; a historic residence I give you, Ked Larone, discoverer of Ked's Gift." Ked said, "Thank you my king, I will have to fill the home with happiness."

The king asked Jol, "When can we start sending out the cure to the towns in need?" Jol replied, "Tomorrow, just give me the night to create the oils efficiently so we do not run out of the short supply we have." The king said, "Of course, may I smell it?" Jol held out the flower and the king leaned over until his nose was a few inches away. The king inhaled and with a very relaxed facial expression said, "Very refreshing, a powerful hint of mint. After the cure, I think we may have found a new fragrance too." Jol and Ked laughed in agreement.

The king said, "Jol, you will be handsomely rewarded too. I am proud of both of you, I will check in with you later." Jol said, "Before you leave, you must know something that I have not shared yet. It was the mages of Skyrock who did this." The king asked, "Who did what?" Jol said, "They somehow created this illness and knew that it would spread. A mage brought a soup to the town of Federeck, which caused the onset of the sickness. They must be dealt with for all who perished." The king said, "Something will be done."

As Jol and Ked left, Timothy said, "You must be relieved, my king. All the months of worrying will come to an immediate end once we get the cure to the towns." The king said, "I have been thinking about what I would do for weeks now if we discovered the cure, and somehow it has happened, the cure has been found." Timothy asked, "What have you been thinking?" The king said, "Torust did not help us for a reason. They are tired of being weaker than us and jealous of how powerful we have become. If they want us to be weak, I think we should want the same of them. I am not going to deliver the cure to every town." Timothy said, "What do you mean, you sent resources to a lot of the towns, why would you now let some of them suffer intentionally?"

The king responded, "I hate to say it, but I will not provide the cure to the towns that are within the kingdom of Torust. The illness must rapidly spread into Torust and weaken them just as it has us. Otherwise, they will seek to overthrow us as the dominant kingdom." Timothy said, "My king, you are talking about letting thousands of citizens die. This is not like you." The king said, "It is a very difficult decision, but I know it must be done to preserve our people. That greedy bitch to the north has been scheming something, I can tell. Leading a kingdom has changed me. Decades ago, I never would have done this. However, I refuse to be seen as the leader that let Torust replace us. As unjust as this is, it must be done." Timothy said, "Jol will not be happy if he hears about this you know." The king said, "He will not hear about it. I want you to give the orders to my top advisors but inform them that it is confidential and Jol must not know." Timothy uneasily nodded and said, "I honor your orders, my king. Through thick and thin, your word is my direction."

Phillip walked up to Timothy and he said, "Now, as for Skyrock, those sly sorcerers. What do you think should be done?" Timothy said, "Well, it is clear they are up to no good. I have known for some time that they have great respect for their leader, Searleone. I have no doubt that he is the one who gave the orders. They see him as not just a leader, but also as a teacher and guide." The king asked, "Teacher and guide of what?" Timothy replied, "That I am not sure. Teacher of spirituality of Lodas, perhaps. He is at the root of the problem. If we can eliminate him, then maybe the mages will proceed in a new direction." The king said, "You seem like you know a lot about them. I think we should take a couple of our spies, provide them the proper mage attire, and send them in to kill him and end this." Timothy said, "I am certain the council will support this decision. I will go speak with them and get the proper men for the task." The king said, "Excellent, we must make them pay for their treacherous acts."

Chapter Thirty-Nine: The Extended Stay

Kip Denvion, Tyrades - Kip eagerly looked around the marketplace searching for Julia. Kip looked by the food market but could not spot the beautiful girl. He walked further into the marketplace until he noticed Julia and her girlfriends, who were Julia's age and a little older than Kip. Kip called out, "There you are, Julia." Julia, who was holding a dress in her hands, turned to Kip, and said, "One moment." Julia paid the merchant with some silver pieces and excused herself from her friends as she walked toward Kip.

Julia said, "I bought a new dress, do you like it?" Kip replied, "Yes, but I haven't seen it on you." Julia said, "Let us go relax at my home. I have been wanting wine all day." As they started walking back, Julia asked, "Why are you so quiet today? Is something wrong?" Kip replied, "No, nothing really." Julia said, "You didn't look at me, I know something is wrong." Kip said, "Fine, I will tell you. I received a letter from my father in Gofon. It appears that a cure for the illness has been discovered." Julia excitedly said, "That is stunning news, you must be very pleased!" Kip said, "I am, but I am not ready to leave Tyrades yet. I am very happy being here with you." Julia opened her door and grabbed Kip's hand, pulling him inside. Julia said, "The longer you stay, the better", before kissing him on the cheek. Julia turned around and said, "Help me take off this dress."

Kip stood nervously as slowly slipped his hands underneath the straps of her dress. She maneuvered her shoulders until the dress slipped off to her feet. Julia then turned around to face Kip and said, "If this is going to be our last moment together, I want it to be a special one", as she grabbed Kip's hands and placed them upon her breasts. Kip looked at her breasts as he felt them. He looked up at Julia and said, "I wish for the same." The two came closer for a long kiss. Kip started to take off his clothes as Julia laid on the bed naked. Kip took a few deep breaths before he came in contact with

Julia's beautiful naked body. In his mind he thought, 'Compose yourself, this needs to last. Life is much better here in Tyrades.' Kip said, "You look better without a dress. And no, I am not going to leave. I will extend my stay longer."

Across the city, King Lance Hasting sat and read a letter from Biros. "What is the message?", James asked. Lance peered down at the letter from Biros and murmured, "Hold on." James, who sat across from the king impatiently, looked at the King's eyes moving from side to side as he read the letter. As Lance finished reading the letter it fell from his hands. He looked at the letter on the table with uncertainty. James asked, "What is it?" The king replied, "A royal invitation from Roy Syssian and Leora for their wedding to be held in Biros. The Sunlit Gardens of Biros is the location it says here. All of the gladiators are invited as well."

James asked with uncertainty, "What do you make of this?" Lance smiled to himself and said, "My first child is getting married. I cannot hold back my complete happiness." James stood up and said, "You know what this means, right?" Lance nodded and smirked, "It presents us with a second chance. I still cannot believe they caught the last spy and executed him. When I see Leora I will coyly ask her how things have been, and I am certain she will tell me." James asked, "What shall we do then?" The king said, "I will speak with Roy. No need to kill anyone. He is marrying my daughter and I think he will be very accommodating." James asked, "What do we do if he does not conform to your expectations?" The king said, "Divide and manipulate Leora, she cannot face upsetting me and losing the family." James said, "I know, but she is becoming a queen, let us hope that you are right."

Chapter Forty: New Beginnings

Renga Khonzas, Sterafia - The king stood tall on the platform and faced his army as he called out, "The greatest threat to our people lives, breathes, and roams just outside our walls. Although we have lost our military general and other soldiers, we were successful in locating the den, the heart of the threat. I have ramped up the production of military equipment for a large battle aimed at eradicating these wolves from the face of Lodas. Despite the fierceness of these beasts, we outnumber them and have sufficient armor and weapons to defeat them. However, we do not dare underestimate their slyness and cleverness, especially around their den, where they are the most dangerous. We should view them as the equivalent of a small-sized military of a few hundred strong. In a few weeks, you all will embark on the southern frozen wasteland and I expect complete victory. We will achieve success and bring peace to Sterafia and its wildlife yet again! Let us avenge Damien Nodon and the fallen soldiers who did not return!"

The king stared out into the crowd as the soldiers started clanking their weapons against their shields, fueled by the vision of bringing peace to their lands. Standing on a hill in the distance overlooking the site of the speech was Oakley with Snowstorm by his side. The king noticed him and gave him a confident nod seeking Oakley's approval. Oakley nodded back at the king and turned around to leave with the tiger. The king walked off and headed for Oakley's room where he hoped to meet with Oakley. As he walked there, he wondered to himself if he had made a mistake allowing Damien to go with the scouting party. The king said to himself, "That boy is ruined, he should be very upset with me."

After a short moment, the king knocked on Oakley's door and said, "It is King Renga, may I speak with you?" Oakley opened the door and said, "Sure, what is it my king?" The king asked, "How have you been holding up, Oakley?" Oakley said, "Better, I have been thinking a lot, probably too much, but Snowstorm helps keep my mind off things." The king asked,

"What have you been thinking about?" Oakley replied, "Our purpose here. Why am I alive in the current generation? What am I capable of accomplishing? Stuff like that. I do not want to pursue a wife and a family like the others just yet. I want to go out there in the world and see things. I want to understand what I can do, and new adventures will help understand that."

The king said, "The world can be harsh, I do not think you are safe to travel alone." Oakley said, "I am a fine marksman with the bow and Snowstorm has grown large enough to easily kill a grown man. My father would not have liked the idea, but he would have understood." The king said, "If that is your wish, let me know what I can do for you. I can help provide you with the resources you need. Also, I noticed Snowstorm indeed is quite large, but still has not grown fully. I want you to take your father's home. It usually belongs to members of the military, but I have assigned it to you, if you will have it." Oakley replied, "Gladly, thank you, my king. I was starting to worry about fitting Snowstorm in here with me, but he should have plenty of space in the new place."

The king asked, "So, where do you plan on traveling to?" Oakley replied, "East and eventually south maybe. I was looking at a map and there is little known about that area. I want to be the first to see it and that way I can contribute to Sterafia in some way." The king said, "That is generous of you, who knows what you might find." Oakley said, "Yeah, and with Damien being gone I need to get away from all of this for a while." Renga said, "Anything you need, let me know. Please excuse me, I must be somewhere else now."

Oakley and Snowstorm walked outside and headed to a highpoint in Sterafia that overlooked the surroundings of the city. The king started walking toward the blacksmiths' shops next to the training grounds of the city. From the distance, he could hear the clanking of metal. Once he could see the sparks of the liquid metal projecting through the air he stopped and watched. His eyes locked onto several different blacksmiths who were producing military equipment with untiring effort.

Oakley stood at the hill near the southeastern gates of the city and pointed in the distance as he said, "Look Snowstorm, we are heading that way." Snowstorm jumped up in the air at Oakley, showing he shared Oakley's excitement. He came down and landed on all fours before rubbing his head against Oakley's side. Oakley ran his hand through Snowstorm's head of fur as he said, "It is just you and me in this world, Snowstorm. Our parents are gone. Time for us to grow up and start a new life, a new beginning."

Chapter Forty-One: The Enigmatic Treasure

Ria Falune, Sahine Sea - Ria curiously looked out in the distance from the ship. She had never crossed the Sahine Sea before. Torb said, "I cannot thank you enough, my queen. This ship allows us to take these camels with us along with more men. I understand you recently went on a journey through the desert to the north. How was that for you?" Ria replied, "A bit rough, but I managed. I am excited to see this cave you speak so highly of." Torb said, "The Cave of Jewels is unlike anything I have ever seen before. Once we get to land it will be a few hours before we get to the cave, but it is well worth the trip. Besides, there is still much more to the cave that has not been explored or discovered. I think we were just at the tip of the iceberg on our last trip."

Ria asked, "What are you expecting to find deeper in the cave?" Torb said, "I am guessing more emeralds, onyx, or even other jewels. There could be more, could be less, or even nothing at all in some places. But the cave is huge, and we just do not know. That is the thrill of exploration. The most rewarding experience for me is venturing into the unknown for the first time. You do not know what you will find. You do not know if the area has been discovered before. You do not know if it is safe. Sometimes it is very dark, and you must hold a torch with you at all times. That is like the cave and there still is so much to see for the first time. Next time it could be in the desert under the burning sun. The experience is a feeling unlike any other. I am glad you came along. You can be the first one to venture deeper into the cave with me if you are looking for more of a thrill."

The ferocious wind of the sea blew Ria's hair around her face. Ria grabbed her hair and pulled out a band from her pocket that she slid on top of her head to keep her hair still. Ria replied, "Maybe, let me think about it. I am going to nap before we get to land." Torb nodded and said, "Rest easy, my queen."

Torb sat down on the upper deck of the large ship and looked ahead in the distance. The captain of the ship asked, "About how much longer do you think?" Torb replied, "About an hour, calm waters, you shouldn't have any trouble getting there." Torb sat back and looked up at the sky. As the wind calmed down, he enjoyed the feeling of it blowing against his face. It did not take long for Torb to fall asleep.

After a while, the captain of the ship called to Torb and said, "Torb, we are about to arrive." Torb opened his eyes and slowly stood up stretching out his arms. The captain asked, "Is that where you want me to anchor?" Torb nodded and said, "That will do just fine. Get as close as you can."

Torb started walking to the lower deck to wake the queen, but he saw her standing with a few guards who were already helping her get ready for the trip. Torb walked up to Ria and said, "We will take the smaller boats to land. It may be a bit choppy." Ria replied, "I figured, it is fine. It wouldn't be an adventure without getting a little wet and dirty."

Torb waited until the ship steadied and then instructed the men to board the smaller boats. Some of the men helped the camels onto the smaller boats Once everyone made it to shore, Torb said to Ria, "There are several camels, but most of the men will have to travel on foot." Ria said, "That is fine, my men can switch off so that a couple of yours can ride too."

Ria mounted the camel as she nodded to Torb who was already on his. Torb called out, "Onwards! The Cave of Jewels awaits our return." The group rode for hours under the blazing desert sun. Torb said to Ria, "Having these camels carry water for us is a lifesaver, I owe you enormously, my queen. Half of what we find in the cave is yours." Ria smiled and said, "I like the sound of that." Torb said, "This is by far the biggest discovery I have ever made; it should propel our economy. What do you plan on doing with the jewels?" Ria said, "Sell them and use the resources for our military. I want Torust to become very powerful, just like old times." Torb nodded and said, "Interesting, well this should help you with that."

By nightfall, the group arrived at the pathway leading to the cave. Torb called out, "Everyone off your camels, they must stay down here. The pathways are too narrow, only two people at most side by side." Torb led the way as the group carefully walked up the pathway. Ria asked Torb, "How come only some of your men are holding mining equipment?" Torb said, "I ordered some of them to leave theirs by the cave last time, I knew we would be back." Ria said, "Wise man, I can tell you love what you do. I am glad you are helping Torust with your adventures." Torb smiled and said, "My beloved kingdom, there will never be any place like Torust."

After walking for a while longer, the group reached the top and were at the entrance of the dark and intimidating cave. The workers' equipment was still on the ground, untouched from where they left it on the prior excursion. Torb called out, "We will begin work at dawn, but for now I will venture into the cave. A few of you are welcome to explore with me." Torb looked at Ria and asked, "Would you like to lead with me?" Ria hesitated for a moment. Then she nodded and said, "Yes, you made it seem very thrilling." Torb smiled and said, "It certainly is", as he lit a torch for himself and lit another torch that he held out to give Ria. Ria took the torch and looked behind her as her guards stood ready to protect her, if need be.

Torb and Ria walked into the cave. Their torches only projected enough light to see the immediate surroundings. Torb asked, "Are you ready for it?" Ria replied, "I am", as Torb was pointing to the opening ahead of them. Ria held out her torch and walked ahead following Torb into the opening. Ria looked to her right and saw a wall covered in emeralds. Part of the wall was missing from the mining the workers performed during their last visit. Torb said, "Beautiful, isn't it? Come to this side." Ria walked over to Torb and looked at the wall covered in Onyx, which also had some parts missing. Ria asked, "The missing sections, is that from your workers?" Torb replied, "Yes, it is a shame that we had to do it, but that is the sad reality of doing this for a living. And, after all, we wanted the jewels then, just as we want them now. In my memory, I can see it, how it was, but reality projects a far less beautiful image. Now, for the unknown."

Ria followed Torb to the next opening and stopped by the entrance. Torb said, "You can go first if you want." Ria said, "You do the honors, the cave is your finding." Torb said, "Thank you, follow my lead." Torb walked ahead into a tighter gap that led deeper underground in the cave. Torb said, "It looks like someone had mined their way to the next level." Torb carefully stepped down through a gap, took a few steps on pieces of rock, and landed on both feet at the next level. Torb held out his hand open so that Ria could grab it for support on her way down. Ria landed on the bottom with him and asked, "Do you see anything yet?" Torb said, "No, but I am going to go look around."

Torb walked over to the left allowing the light from his torch to lead the way. As he continued to walk, the light from the torch started to illuminate some sparkles. Torb said, "I think we got some", as he walked closer. Ria was walking to the other side of the cave as Torb called out, "The entire side over here is covered in Onyx!" Some of the guards had reached the bottom and rushed over to Ria.

Ria walked until the light from her torch uncovered a skeleton still dressed in clothes. A startled Ria exclaimed, "I found a skeleton over here." Torb said, "Careful, we do not know what lurks in this cave." Ria noticed a bag sitting next to the man and carefully picked it up. She walked a few steps away before carefully dumping the contents of the bag onto the floor of the cave. Out came a few coins, a ring with a ruby gem, and a scroll.

Ria kneeled and picked up one of the coins. She carefully maneuvered her torch closer to the coin to get a better look. She noticed that the coin was very old, and she did not recognize it. She picked up the ring and started to examine it. She was aghast as she saw that the back of the ring had the inscription of the 'The Caller' engraved in ancient Torustian. The inscription was identical to the one on her necklace.

Ria tried to steady her shaky hands as she picked up the scroll and opened it. The lettering on the scroll appeared to be the same ancient Torustian that was on her necklace and the newly discovered ring. Torb walked over and asked, "What did you find?" Ria said, "A few old coins, a ring, and a scroll written in ancient Torustian. I am going to have them examined. Let us keep looking around the cave." Torb said, "Yes, interestingly, it is much, much bigger down here than the cave area up top." Ria took the items and placed them back into the bag before closing it. She held the bag herself, refusing the offers of her guards.

Torb said, "The other side is covered in onyx. Same side as up top, so if the cave is similar then this side should be emerald. Ria walked closer to that side and saw green gems sparkling before her eyes. The green side started to increasingly illuminate as she approached the jewels. She said, "Yes! I have never seen these many jewels in one place before." Torb said, "Tomorrow will be a very busy day for the workers." Ria said, "Should be."

The cave was nothing like anything Ria had ever seen before. But as thrilling of an experience as it was for her, and as excited as she was to see the jewels, she could not help but think that it was the contents of the bag, the enigmatic treasure, that was going to be the most rewarding experience of the adventure of the Cave of Jewels. She could not help but to continue to focus on how the mystery would be unveiled.

Chapter Forty-Two: The Relationship Progresses

Cazier Fardine, Torust - "I see you have gotten back to being yourself again. You have made me happy, my son. I have recovered a bit too, but not completely. Things will never be the same, but it is up to us to make things better", Peter said. Cazier responded, "I have moved on and I am trying to make things better for us, you will see." Cazier walked to the front door of the home and slipped on his sandals. Peter asked, "Where are you going for the day?" Cazier said, "I am going to spend some time with my friends. I lost touch with them after mother passed away, but things are getting back to normal now." Peter said, "Excellent, eventually we should spend some time together for a few days." Cazier opened the front door to leave as he said, "Sure, sometime soon father."

Cazier walked quickly through town trying to meet Nera without breaking into a sweat in the process. He had made frequent visits to Nera's home as the goal of impregnating her had carried on longer than he had anticipated. Cazier approached her home and stopped before he entered. He looked behind him carefully to be certain no one was watching him. After seeing that the coast was clear, he walked up to her door and knocked.

Nera approached the door and opened it for him. Nera said, "Hello, come in Cazier." Cazier entered and asked, "How have you been?" Nera said, "Good, life outside of the brothel is not terrible. Besides, I have good news, I think." Cazier anxiously asked, "What is it?" Nera smiled and said, "I threw up this morning and I have missed my period. I am confident that I am pregnant." Cazier placed one hand on Nera's stomach and said, "That is wonderful, I couldn't wait for this moment."

Nera and Cazier sat down at a table together and Cazier continued to speak, "Nera, I need you to do all you can to take care of yourself during the pregnancy. I will do everything to help you. This is the only chance I will get at having a child. I will stay here with you some nights to help assist you if that is okay." Nera said, "That is really sweet of you, and, honestly, that would be helpful. I have never been pregnant before, so I have no idea of what to expect." Cazier said, "I know, but that is okay. Just do not tell anyone that I am the father, no one can know." Nera said, "You do not have to worry about that, aside from two girls in the brothel no one will know." Surprised, Cazier asked, "You told two of the girls in the brothel?!" Nera replied, "I had to, otherwise how would they understand that I am taking almost a year off from working there?" Cazier asked, "Will they stay quiet?" Nera said, "Yes. They are my friends. I also referred my clients to them. I am confident that they will cover up for me while I am gone. So what good would it serve them to gossip?" Cazier nodded at Nera in agreement and said, "You are right, I guess."

Cazier continued, "Oh, before I forget, I brought you this silk hair scarf as a gift." Nera took the scarf from Cazier's hands and looked at it for a moment. She said, "It is so beautiful, I love the designs on it. How were you able to afford this?" Cazier said, "Don't worry about it, I want to take care of you, Nera. Go on, try it on." Nera tied her hair in a ponytail as Cazier watched her put on the scarf. Cazier said, "I knew it would look great on you." Nera replied, "Cazier, I am confused. How are you able to do all of this, who exactly are you? I only ask because no one has treated me this way before." Cazier said, "It really does not matter, but I am glad I picked you then. You are a sweet person and you deserve a better life."

Nera asked, "What is your last name?" Cazier paused for a moment. Nera continued, "I am having your child, you can trust me." Cazier said, "Fardine." Nera, with a shocked look, said, "You are the son of Peter Fardine?" Cazier nodded and said, "Yes, I am." Nera said, "I have heard he is the greatest fighter in the kingdom. If you do not mind me asking, is he okay with who you are?" Cazier said, "Yes, my admiration for him goes beyond his fighting capacity. My mother was not accepting of me though." Nera said, "I know it is tough, when all of this is done, I will continue to support you as a friend, if you still intend to continue our friendship." Cazier nodded and said, "I am liking you more and more and of course I want to stay friends with the mother of my child. Our friendship is progressing deeply."

Chapter Forty-Three: The Hemp Harness

Liava Pontas, Dragon Lair - Liava ran her hands through the two ropes of hemp she was smoothing. The ropes would need to be strong and long enough to fit around a dragon's stomach and neck and extend around to Liava's hands. Liava held the ropes about two feet apart and tugged to make sure they were sturdy. She did this for the entire length of the ropes to ensure that there were no weak spots and that it could sustain a tight grip. Liava learned how to craft ropes of hemp in her village when she was younger. The ropes were primarily used for lifting water buckets but served other important purposes as well.

After months of staying behind by herself at the dragon lair when the dragons flew away on their trips, Liava now was making an attempt to join them. Liava thought to herself, 'I wonder who I should ride on. I think all of them would allow me to ride on them, but the red dragon is probably the best choice. I spend the most time with him and he is the smallest of the three.' Looking at her ropes, Liava thought that they definitely would reach all the way around the red dragon, but she was uncertain about the others. The last major consideration was that the red dragon was the slowest of the three, which also would make him the best choice as she was all set to embark on her mission to learn to fly a dragon.

The sun was first rising above the hills and Liava had planned on finishing her project before the dragons awoke for their daily morning flight. Liava sat down with the ropes in her hands as she waited for the dragons to wake up. Liava was literally shaking from her nervousness and she wondered, 'What if I fall off the dragon?' As nervous as she was, she knew deep down that the dragons would protect her.

The sunrise over the hills was quite a beautiful view for Liava, but her eyes started to close as she had been up very early preparing the ropes. The serene and quiet setting was relaxing. Her eyes flickered shut and open and shut. Her eyes stayed shut for a short time until she was awakened by the shuffling of one of the dragons. As the sun slowly peaked higher, the dragons were now awake. They slowly arose and grunted as they tiredly moved around. It did not matter how much they slept, when they arose in the mornings, they made it seem like they could never get enough sleep.

Liava, with sudden excitement, stood and held the ropes in the air. The dragons observed the ropes with curiosity, just as Liava had expected. Liava walked up to greet the red dragon who was still half asleep. She moved her hand around the side of the dragon to comfort it for a minute or so before she swung the rope around the dragon's stomach. She took a deep breath and then whistled a tune as she slowly pulled her way up onto the red dragon who was, to Liava's delight, carefully staying still allowing her to mount properly and safely.

Once Liava got onto the dragon, she tied the first rope around the dragon's stomach. She then took the other rope and swung it around the dragon's neck. Once she tied that rope too, she grabbed hold of the higher rope with her hands. She then tucked her legs underneath the rope that went around the dragon's stomach. Once she felt that she was securely mounted, she took a deep breath and tapped the dragon's neck with both of her hands twice. With a sudden outburst, the dragon took a few steps forward aiming toward the side of the hill. As it got to the edge, the dragon took one deep lunge into the sky and started thrusting its wings intensely as it needed to adapt to the additional weight of flying with Liava on its back. After a few seconds, Liava felt the air become cooler as the dragon flew higher and higher. Liava closed her eyes for a few seconds to adjust to this new sensational experience. When she opened them, she started smiling as the ground was moving further and further away. Liava recalled how she fell off the cliff months prior and thought how much better it was to soar through the sky on a dragon.

Liava slowly peered over her right shoulder at the ground below. The lair that she spent the past few months residing in gradually disappeared from her sight. She slowly maneuvered her way around, trying to look over her left shoulder this time. Liava noticed the dragons were flying to the east. She expected that the east was where they ate since they always came from that direction when they returned home with food. Ahead of the red dragon Liava saw the older dragons flying gracefully. Liava thought to herself, 'I can go anywhere I wish from now on.' The rising sun started to extend higher in the sky as sunlight pressed against the side of Liava's face. Liava pressed her head against the thick scales of the dragon as she waited for the dragon to descend to the food source.

After a short time, the red dragon tucked its wings inside for a few seconds as it peaked its head downward. Liava felt the speed intensify for a few seconds before the dragon spread its wings and started to glide through the sky toward the ground. Liava gripped the ropes tightly as she felt slightly anxious and tried to adjust to the intense speed. A few seconds later, as Liava felt a slight thud, the dragon softly landed on the ground.

Liava waited until the dragon stopped moving before letting go of the ropes. She untucked her hands and legs from beneath the ropes and sat up on the dragon. She looked around and noticed vast vegetation spread throughout a forest. The red dragon hunched over allowing Liava to step off. She got off the dragon and immediately checked her pockets for her flute and horn. She was relieved when she felt that both of the instruments were still in her pockets. As the tension left her body and she was more at ease, Liava lovingly caressed the red dragon.

The red dragon stood up and walked over to the other dragons who were already eating from the apple trees. Liava walked around to inspect the surroundings. She noticed large bushes of berries. Liava walked up to one of the berry bushes and said, "This must be where they get all of the berries. My village would have loved this place if they knew about it." Liava plucked a small berry from a bush and tossed it into her mouth. She bit into it and swallowed the sweet juice. She proceeded to pluck several more berries and put them into her mouth as well.

Liava walked over to the dragons but could not reach the apples hanging from the high trees. Liava tapped the green dragon and pointed to a big apple hanging in the tree. The green dragon pulled the apple off the tree with its mouth and leaned down toward Liava to give her the apple. Liava took the apple and bit into it. The apple was amazingly fresh, Liava thought. She looked up and noticed the dragons feasting on tons of apples.

In the months Liava had spent with the dragons, she had bonded with them in various ways, but she often thought about how the dragons obtained their food. Liava knew she could trust each of them and thought that they felt the same about her. Liava watched as the dragons continued to eat the bushes of berries whole. She thought to herself, 'My parents would be amazed with how my life is going, probably proud too.'

As she continued to observe the dragons, Liava wondered, 'Would these dragons fight for me? Would they help me avenge my family and my people?' Liava had a good feeling about the way things were progressing with the dragons but realized she would need more flying experience before she could use them to strike the villages that eradicated her people and village.

Once the dragons finished eating, they moved into position to fly north. Liava walked close to the red dragon and whistled. The red dragon leaned down and used its leg as a foot stand to help Liava onto its back. Just as she had done earlier, Liava placed her hands and legs under the ropes and held on. She tapped the dragon on the neck and within a second the dragon was charging forward toward flight. Liava, with more confidence than earlier, leaned up a little. She looked toward the sky and said to the dragon, "If only we could fly away and leave this world behind."

As the dragons flew further north, Liava noticed vast wildlife roaming free. She looked down and smiled as she said, "The animals, they still prosper." The animals were protected by her village and their efforts had apparently left a lasting impact. In the back of her mind, Liava knew why the villages came to attack her village. She remembered what they wanted. They wanted the animals that Liava was looking down upon and she was the only one remaining who could protect them. She boldly envisioned herself doing so.

Chapter Forty-Four: The Mysterious Creature

Ryos Pontas, Village of Tsirian - Ryos gripped the handle of the axe and swung it smoothly into the side of the tree. He shook his axe a few times as he tried to pull it out from the tree. Once he got it out, he grabbed the handle and prepared to swing it again just how he had been instructed. He stopped and used his forearm to wipe the sweat from his forehead as he looked around at some of his fellow villagers striking other trees. Ryos had learned that the wood from the trees served many important functions for the village. It allowed them to craft weapons such as spears and arrows. The wood also allowed them to build sturdy habitable structures that were superior to the tents of his old village, especially when the seasons became cold.

As Ryos continued his short break, he thought to himself, 'I used to do nothing all day. Now, in Tsirian, I contribute to the village and make a difference.' He was really starting to see the good in his new surroundings and way of life. Ryos grabbed the handle and smacked the axe hard into the side of the tree. This time the tree started to shake; Ryos could sense it was almost ready to fall. He freed the axe from the tree and with a strong thrust again smacked it against the opening in the side of the tree. Ryos immediately started to back up as the tree started to fall in his direction. He quickly jumped to his right as his instincts managed to take over.

Ryos moved closer to the downed tree and started striking it until the whole tree was transformed into split logs. He lifted some of the logs and, making several trips, walked them back to the village. Ryos noticed some of the older men carrying more logs than him, but he knew that he still had a lot of growing to do before his muscles could carry the additional weight.

Back in the village, Edgar walked up to Ryos, who was still carrying his logs, and said, "Once you are done making your drop offs, get your hunting gear on. Our food supply has been used up quite a bit recently and we need to stock up." Ryos replied, "Will do, Edgar." Ryos went back and forth to the tree and carried back the remainder of the logs to the village. Once there, he filled up a bucket of water and sat for a moment to drink. He was tired and thirsty after hours of draining work. After having a few chugs from the bucket, he took the rest of the bucket and dumped it over his head to cool off.

Ryos walked back to his cabin to retrieve his trusty dagger that he had made when he had lived in the village of Staga. This dagger was the one thing that reminded him of his past. After losing his mother, father, and sister, his life had been reborn. Ryos looked down at his dagger and saw contradicting aspects of his life. How odd, he thought, that in the past, he used the dagger in his old village to protect the animals from hunters, hunters like himself. In the present, this dagger was used to hunt animals for survival. Ryos looked at the dagger for another moment and then slipped it into a dagger holder that he placed on his side.

Ryos proceeded to walk to the center of the village by the big campfire to wait for the rest of the hunting party. Hyfor approached Ryos and asked, "I assume you will take part in the hunt as well?" Ryos said, "Yes, and it is good to see you. Last time we went hunting together was our first hunt with the villagers. I have gained more experience since then." Hyfor said, "Same with me, my archery is developing nicely as I hunt more. I am learning what parts of the body of the animals I should be targeting. You must have been honored to have been the first one brought to live in the village out of all of us who came from Staga. I also noticed you have two girls that it looks like you will marry in time to come." Ryos said, "Thank you, it was a good feeling and yes, they are great. I plan on going forward with both of them in my life. Have you met any of the girls here?" Hyfor said, "Yes, one, her name is Yraza. I will have to introduce you to her soon. Just one woman for me though." Ryos said, "I am glad you have found some happiness being here too."

Edgar called out, "It looks like all seven of you are here. We are heading out to the lands northeast of the former village of Staga. Last time we were there we hunted some boar. A few former villagers of Staga were selected for this hunt as they may have more expertise navigating if we delve deep into the territory. Let us get to hunting!"

Ryos, Hyfor, and the rest of the hunting party started to embark on the hunting trip. Ryos stayed quiet, as did many of the others. His only satisfaction from these trips came from knowing that the animals that they killed were used for necessary supplies for the village. Since becoming a villager of Tsirian, Ryos had seen the hunting party hunt rabbit, boar, deer, fox, and a few other animals that he had learned to acquire a taste for.

After walking for a few uneventful hours, the hunting party crossed a water stream into the territory of Staga where they had killed the boars months earlier. Ryos signaled to the group to be on alert since he remembered the events of the last hunt in Staga. The hunting party slowly crept their way up the snowy hillside into unseen territory. A very loud grunt echoed from a few hundred feet further into the hills near the mountainside. The group of startled villagers looked at each other in confusion. Edgar quietly said, "Sounds like a bear, it would make for a great feast. You two sneak up the right side." Hyfor and another villager with a spear quietly made their way up to the right side to meet at the top.

Ryos remembered that the only time in his life that he had seen a bear before was when he had ventured into the woods with his father at a young age. His father told him not to move and just let the bear pass. His father had always taught him to see the good in animals. He told Ryos that the bear, although intimidating, only strives to survive off food it needs just like the rest of the animals in nature. Only if you threaten it or its cubs, or compete for its food, will it strike, he remembered his father telling him. Ryos had an unsettling feeling that the encounter with the "bear" the hunting party was looking for was going to be a less pleasant encounter.

Once at the top of the mountainside, the members of the hunting party noticed a cave. On the opposite side of the cave, roughly a hundred feet away, were the other two hunters of the party. Edgar signaled for one of the men with him to use his spear to try to lure out whatever was in the dark cave. The man with the spear nervously walked closer to the cave and was unsure what to do. He noticed a rock on the ground and picked it up and threw it into the dark cave to spark the encounter. From the cave, an angry, distinct growl projected loudly to the outside. The man with the spear waited for whatever it was to appear from the cave. However, it did not show itself. It appeared as though the hunting party would need to make the first move.

Edgar again signaled for the man with the spear to do something. The man, trying not to do anything too risky, picked up another rock and tossed it firmly into the cave as he had just done. To their surprise, this time there was no clinking of the rock in the cave. From the darkness of the cave a giant white roaring yeti came charging toward the man. The yeti was about thirty feet tall and had excessively large features compared to all the men. The man tried to back up and hold out his spear, but the speed and intensity of the yeti caught him off guard and he tripped backward over a rock and onto the ground. The yeti lifted the man up in the air with his giant hands and ripped the man's body in half. Hyfor aimed his arrow and released it directly into the yeti's shoulder.

Ryos went ahead to try to attack and help Hyfor, but Edgar held him back and said, "There is nothing we can do here." The angry yeti charged toward Hyfor and smacked him into the side of the mountain where he fell to the ground unconscious. Edgar said to his men, "Retreat, we need to leave now!" The yeti looked at the hunting party as if it were going to chase them but stopped once the men started running.

The hunting party ran back toward the water stream where they could regroup and take a breath. Ryos, who was deeply disturbed, exclaimed, "I can't believe Hyfor is dead. Why did he shoot the yeti?" Edgar said, "I am not sure. We need to do some hunting before we head back to the village but let us put some more distance between us and the yeti. We will return in a few weeks to avenge our fallen villagers and remove that evil creature from this world."

Chapter Forty-Five: Ice and Skin

Searleone Vallas, Skyrock - Searleone looked around the sanctuary halls and observed some of the mages studying scrolls. Other mages were with their families and some young children were listening to a fable of a mystical beast. Searleone thought back to his childhood when he heard these same stories for the first time. As a child, nothing was more thrilling than imagining what these powerful and unpredictable creatures might look like and how they might behave. As an adult, however, he knew what to expect from such creatures. It was from his fellow humans, though, that he still never knew what to expect.

Seeing the young children and parents in the halls made him happy, but Searleone knew he made the right decision in not having a family of his own. Searleone reflected on a time when he was younger and had looked forward to having a family, like many other mages. He remembered feeling this way for years until he had started to see the visions. In his visions, Searleone saw the world that he desired, a world free of people. Searleone clearly saw the steps he would need to take as a mage and a leader to accomplish this and having a family surely had no place in this world. Early on, Searleone learned how to clear his mind and absolve himself of any wrongdoing or immoral or unethical thoughts or actions. Slowly, over time, Searleone noticed that he was beginning to think less and less about how other people felt and his thoughts and actions no longer felt wrong, immoral or unethical.

Searleone stood up and started to walk toward the outside balcony. He had started growing different types of plants in a section of the balcony that was closed off to the other mages. The plants were being used for medicinal studies, according to Searleone, and could hopefully serve the well-being of animals in the wild. Searleone walked up to the garden and inspected many of the plants closely. "Hmmm, coming along nicely", Searleone murmured to himself. Searleone started to wiggle his fingers around until drops of water started to pour out over the plants throughout the garden.

As Searleone was still watering the plants, he heard a mage shout, "Searleone, watch out! They are coming for you!" Searleone, who was hunched over, tilted his head sideways to see what was going on. From the entrance of the balcony, Searleone saw several men dressed as mages with swords running toward him. Searleone instantly extended his hands firmly and used them to start to craft frost. His hands began to move rapidly as he maneuvered them together crafting a round, icy ball. The men continued to run toward Searleone intending to kill him. Searleone readied the ice ball in his hands as the men got closer and closer. Once they were several feet away, Searleone waved the ice ball rapidly in front of him. A mist from the ice ball spread onto the men and blurred much of their vision. After about fifteen seconds of waving the ice ball, the men stood completely frozen in place in blocks of ice.

One of the mages came running over and said, "I am sorry, Searleone, they were dressed up just like us. Once we tried to inspect them at the entrance to the sanctuary halls, they stabbed one of the mages and ran down the halls looking for you here." Searleone said, "It is fine, we will learn the meaning of this." Searleone slowly walked in a circle around the several men who were frozen in ice blocks. He walked closer to them, not necessarily trying to distill fear, but rather trying to look for clues of where they had come from.

Once an audience of mages made their way onto the balcony of the sanctuary, Searleone created a ball of fire within his hands. Searleone took the ball and held it up against the top of one of the ice blocks. As the ice slowly started to melt, the eyes of the man in the block started to nervously move around. Once the top of the ice block melted and the man's face was freed, the man took several deep breaths of air before Searleone asked, "Why are you here?" The man replied, "To kill you." Searleone said, "Why try to kill a man who does not present evil to this world?" The man said, "You sent the mage to poison the whole world, didn't you? I was told you were behind it." Searleone asked, "What mage do you speak of? What does he look like?" The man said, "He was a young male wearing a brown robe, he poisoned the town of Federeck and created an illness that spread to thousands of people. And you ask why we are here to kill you."

Searleone thought intently for a moment and said, "I do recall a young mage being away from Skyrock a few weeks ago. Hold on." Searleone called out, "Bring me Rinci." Searleone took the fireball in his hand and used it to free the faces of the other men submerged in the ice blocks as they waited for Rinci to arrive.

Rinci walked out onto the balcony and approached Searleone. Rinci said, "I heard you were looking for me." The man frozen in the ice block started saying, "He was wearing the same brown robe from how it was described to me." Rinci said, "Searleone gave me this robe as a gift. He said it helped him learn as a young mage". Searleone then suddenly plunged the fireball he was holding deep into Rinci's skull. Rinci's body plummeted to the ground as his lifeless body was completely still. Searleone called out, "Anyone who commits such acts behind the backs of our society is of no use anymore. Let this be a lesson to you all not to act on your own, ever."

The mages stood around in shock and none of them spoke a word. Searleone continued, "And for those who attempt to come into our sanctuary and murder without reason, we will treat them no differently." Searleone signaled for the mages to cast fireballs on the defenseless men as he turned his back and started walking into the sanctuary. The disturbing cries of pain could be heard as fire sizzled against ice and skin.

Chapter Forty-Six: The Love of Two Kingdoms

Roy Syssian, Biros - "The king of Tyrades has just arrived, my king", Nollie said. Roy said, "Excellent, please make the royal family feel at home here in Biros. They treated me with honor and respect when I was in Tyrades as a gladiator and then again when I was both gladiator and king of Biros." Nollie asked, "Where is Leora?" Roy said, "She went to take a walk and get some fresh air. She is a little nervous, and I can't lie, I am a bit myself." Nollie said, "I understand, a wedding is a major, life-changing event. It does not matter what title one has; it brings out the deepest emotions in all of us. If you need anything, I will be around. Just ask." The king said, "Thanks, I will let you know."

Roy closed the door and turned toward the inside of his bedroom. The bed was messy and undone. It would usually have bothered Roy, but it was his formal attire for the wedding hanging in the corner of the room that held his focus. Roy walked over to the clothes and started to put them on, as Leora walked into the room. Leora said, "Wait up, I still need to get ready too." Roy said, "You don't need to rush, I will wait for you. I will have to if I want to get married anyway." Leora walked over to her clothes on the other side of the room and said, "I can't argue with that." Roy said, "I just heard that your family has arrived." Leora said, "I can't wait to see them, it has been months." Roy said, "Let me go greet them while you get ready." Leora said, "Fine, I will be a while."

Roy finished dressing in his wedding attire and left to meet Leora's family. As he walked out of his palace toward the gates of Biros, Roy noticed a large gathering of people from Tyrades who had just entered the city. Roy walked closer and noticed the royal family. Roy called out, "King Hasting, over here!" Lance waved to Roy and started to ride over on his horse as his family followed. Lance said, "Great to see you, Roy. What are you doing here, the wedding is in a few hours, don't you have other things to take care of?" Roy said, "Making sure the royal family is welcome properly and settled in is also very important." Lance said, "We appreciate it, go prepare, we can catch up later." Lance walked his horse closer to Roy and whispered, "We have some talking to do later too." Roy nodded and said, "Of course, I will talk with you later."

Roy walked back to the bedroom where Leora was still getting ready. Roy said, "They seem excited, it was good to see them." A few bangs on the front door echoed through the bedroom. Roy opened the door and was greeted by a few servants. A servant said, "We are here to assist Leora with her wedding preparations." Roy said, "Go ahead, the wedding is in two hours so do not take too long." Roy called out in the corridor, "Can we get some wine?" Roy sat on the bed fidgeting until a servant brought him some wine. Roy drank the wine as he passed the time, anxiously waiting for his wedding.

A while later, Roy and Leora left for the wedding ceremony. Roy said, "This is the day we have been waiting for. Are you ready to become the queen of Biros?" Leora said, "I think I am just about ready, but I will have to learn a thing or two from my mother first." The two arrived at the outdoor wedding reception and sat at the main table surrounded by all the guests. A wedding crier sang out, "The love of a man finding and returning the love of a woman. Two special people of utmost respected royalty, bringing together two kingdoms in unity. Let us rejoice at the marriage of these two and invite good fortune for Biros and Tyrades. Love of two people and the love of two kingdoms." Everyone raised their glasses to toast and then drank their wine.

Joyful, uplifting tunes and melodies filled the air as people cheerfully drank their wine and ate their dinner. Roy went through his wine in no time before requesting more. Since becoming the king of Biros, he had acquired a taste for wine and gotten accustomed to drinking at dinner when the setting was right, and it usually was. Roy filled up his chalice and continued to drink as Leora and he sat and looked around before smiling at each other. Roy and Lance then delivered their speeches. Roy, who was feeling more relaxed and very cheerful at this point, got up and asked Leora to dance with him. Leora happily nodded and grabbed Roy's hands. The two started slowly dancing as other guests followed their lead. They looked around as the guests started to join them to dance. Roy nodded at his parents who were dancing. He also noticed Leora's parents and gave them a nod as well.

Roy whispered to Leora, "This is the best moment of my life. Becoming gladiator and then becoming king were special, but this is where my visions led me, to this moment." Leora replied, "I agree, I wish this moment could last forever." Roy said, "It can if we do good for the people and the future of our world. Then people will always look at us in awe just as they are now, but only for the right reasons." Leora smiled and said, "You are right, you have a wonderful heart and your priorities are in order. Deep down in my heart I have a feeling that you will be a better king than my father. Just don't tell him I said that." Leora winked at Roy. Roy said, "He is very well-respected, so I do not know about that, but every king leads in his own unique way. The same could be said about queens. I am eager to see how you will lead." The song ended as Roy and Leora came together for a kiss. The guests all showed appreciation for the two by clapping.

As the night went on, and the wine flowed and flowed, the melodies became more robust and the party livelier. Despite the cultural differences between Biros and Tyrades, the one thing they both could truly appreciate was excessive drinking during formal events. As Roy and Leora were walking through the crowd of dancing guests, Roy bumped into King Hasting. Lance took a step back as Roy sincerely apologized to him. Lance noticed that Roy's gladiator pin fell off so he picked it up off the ground and said, "I think you just dropped this, you will be needing it." Roy, somewhat surprised, replied "Thank you, and I suppose I will."

Lance then asked Roy, "I know this is a big night for you and you are very busy, but I was wondering if you had a quick moment to discuss something as kings?" Roy said, "Sure, let us step inside and let me know what is on your mind." Lance followed Roy into a room inside where the noise was much lower. Lance said, "Roy, I am getting to the point in my life that I am starting to reflect on what I have done as king. I like to think that I have contributed to Tyrades and the world in positive ways, but what I have accomplished is not enough. I need to make the kingdoms better and safer places, for both of us. We must eliminate the threats that steadily grow more powerful in terms of military, trade, alchemy, you name it. In short, I am asking if you will back me in a war, as a king and as a kingdom."

Roy thought to himself for a moment, 'How can he ask me this on my wedding night?' Roy knew that he had to make a quick decision. His mind instantly reflected on the matters that were relevant to help him make the right decision. Lance was a powerful king. It was important to have him as an ally. The gladiators treated him with great respect from the beginning. That helped him to become king. Lastly, this was the father of his new wife. Saying no would be a significant insult. Roy nodded and placed his right hand over Lance's shoulder as he spoke, "I support you." Lance smiled and said, "That is great to hear Roy. We have taken our kingdoms' alliance to the next stage. Together, we will influence the world, not follow it. Are you ready?" Roy said, "Yes, I am." Lance said, "I am happy for you and Leora. I could not have picked a better man than you for my daughter. I would tell you to take care of her, but I can already tell you will go beyond my expectations. As always, if you need anything from me or the gladiators, we support you."

Roy and Lance walked back outside into the dining area where Leora walked up to them. Leora said, "I was looking for you both." Lance said, "We had some talking to do, nothing to worry about. Just making sure you return to Tyrades to visit your family." Leora smiled and said, "Stop, I do miss home, and I will make visits often, right Roy." Roy firmly nodded and said, "When possible, we will. Absolutely."

Chapter Forty-Seven: The Stare of Illusions

Jol Parantis, Gofon - Jol knocked on the king's door a couple of times before the king shouted, "Come in." Jol opened the door as Phillip said, "Take a seat, Jol. I have good news." Jol sat down and Phillip said, "The mint oil that you prepared was delivered to the infected towns and has successfully changed the lives of thousands. People are recovering and many are starting to feel completely healthy already. Jol, you have helped this kingdom multiple times now from deadly epidemics, but nothing quite as severe as this. You are the true hero that Lodas has given to us."

Jol said, "Thank you, having fought it myself, I must say that this time the illness proved more challenging. In the end, my most important discovery was of another person who helped give me the insight that I needed to find the cure. I have been wanting to ask you, have you done anything to get back at the mages yet?" The king, with a disappointed look on his face, said, "We sent a few men to try to kill their leader, but they failed. They were somehow caught and killed, and they never returned." Jol said, "That is a real shame, I was hoping we could get some revenge." Phillip said, "In time, I am keeping my eye more on Torust now. Recent events have escalated tensions between us, so we do not want to start a war with the mages if we have not done so already."

Jol stood up and said, "I understand. I am going to go take a walk through town, care to join me?" The king said, "I am meeting with my family for lunch soon, next time." Jol walked out the door and past the royal dining halls. Jol heard someone call out, "Jol, wait up." A man approached him and said, "My name is Rus Trenode. I heard about the great work you did in finding a cure. I wanted to thank you for what you have done. I am a fighter, but my skills serve no purpose when it comes to epidemics." Jol said, "Thank you, sir. I am going to spend some time with the younger alchemists in the next few months to ensure they can follow in my footsteps." Rus said, "Bright plan, I will let you be on your way. I just wanted to show my appreciation." Jol nodded and said, "Stop by the potions lab anytime."

Jol was grateful to be able to enjoy walking outdoors again and feel the sunshine on the city. Jol felt great comfort in being back in the city and to his normal routine. Jol walked up to his favorite fruit vendor and bought a sour green apple. As he walked toward the center of the city, he bit and chewed on his favorite type of apple.

Jol heard laughs and giggles coming from the central square of the city. The square was always a pleasant place to relax, Jol had recalled. Jol walked into the square to join the audience, which was observing something, but he could not tell what it was. Just then, the bright flashy colors of the jester caught Jol's eyes. Jol had seen the jester a couple of times before in the square. Jol stood and watched the jester dance and entertain for a couple of minutes before walking past a couple of spectators.

Jol, who was walking with his back turned to the jester, heard excitement from the crowd. Jol turned around and noticed the jester was slyly walking toward him. Jol thought to himself, 'Is he coming toward me?' The crowd watched with excitement as the jester was about to interact with someone in the audience. Jol turned and continued to walk away until a cane with a jester head blocked his path. Jol looked up and the jester, who was holding out his cane, prevented Jol from walking away.

Jol nervously asked the jester, "What do you want?" The jester just stared at him with an intense smile. The jester lifted his cane and started shaking it, creating a ringing noise. Jol slowly started walking away now that the path was clear, but the jester quickly maneuvered and was again in the way. Jol was becoming agitated, but, for the sake of the children and their parents, he tried not to act out. Jol had always been very mature and able to control his temper. The jester started dancing around hopping from one leg to the other as he shook his cane.

Jol looked around for a moment as the spectators were laughing with amusement. He looked at the jester's movements before lifting his head and making eye contact with the smiling jester. Jol felt that there was something very dark and eerie about this jester. Jol continued to stare at the jester; he did not want to look away. The jester kept staring him in the eyes as his body shifted as he kept dancing. Jol noticed the jester's pupils starting to enlarge. Jol could not do anything but look as he was now in a trance. The jester's pupils kept expanding until his eyes were completely black. Jol's facial appearance went from being disturbed to being completely calm. In an instant, the pupils of the jester's eyes became entirely white until they went back to normal again.

The jester then went side-stepping back closer to the other side as the spectators started clapping. Jol felt shaken up as his head now felt light. Jol carefully stepped away from the crowd and sat down near the marketplace. He could tell something was wrong. His thoughts were not processing as clearly through his brilliant mind.

Jol took a few minutes to catch his breath before he stood up and made his way back to his home. Jol drank some water and sat down as he reflected on what he saw in the jester. Jol asked himself, "How did his eyes change like that? What was he trying to do to me? Why was he doing something to me?" Jol tried to put some ideas together to help understand the events that transpired, but it was nothing like he had ever seen before.

Suddenly, Jol saw a small jester, about two feet tall, appear in the corner of his room. The jester started dancing before it laughed and then disappeared before Jol's eyes. Jol stood up and started panicking. He quickly went to the other room to get his oil that cured the recent illness. Jol took a deep inhale of the oil hoping it could somehow help his condition. 'Was it real or just an illusion?', Jol wondered.

After a while, Jol left his home and went to meet with the king again. This time, he did not intend on going through the square. Jol arrived at the royal chambers and told the guards, "I need to speak with the king, immediately." One of the guards replied, "Follow us, Jol." Jol quickly walked toward the king's chambers with the guards. The guards knocked on the king's door for Jol as the king called out, "Yes?" The guard loudly said, "Jol is here to speak with you again. Shall we let him in?" The king replied, "Yes, proceed." The guard opened the door and Jol rapidly walked inside and sat down in front of the king.

The king asked, "Everything okay, Jol? I just saw you about two hours ago." Jol look puzzled and said, "Has it been that long already?" The king looked perplexed and asked, "Since what?" Jol firmly replied, "After I left here earlier, I went for a walk. As I was going through the square the jester approached me and stared at me intensely for a moment. Somehow, he did something to me and when I returned home, I saw a small jester appear in my room. He was only there for a moment before he vanished. We need to do something right away. We need to go capture the jester and figure out what he has done to me!" The king said, "Settle down, Jol. Based on what you have told me, he just stared at you. How can he possibly have done something to harm you from just doing that? I have been to the square plenty of times before and I have seen the jester entertain the spectators. Maybe he was just trying to get you involved." Jol replied, "My king, it was not like that. Whatever he may have done to me, I do not believe I have the expertise to fix. Please, send some men and see what is going on with the jester."

The king thought for a moment and said, "Based on the facts, normally this would be ignored, but I can't even begin to describe how indebted I am to you, Jol. As you wish." The king called out, "Timothy!" They both sat there for a moment until one of the guards entered and said "Timothy is not here at the moment. What do you need, my king?" The king said, "Jol here claims the jester in the square did something to him. Can you walk to the square with him and bring the jester back here for questioning?" The guard nodded and welcomed Jol to walk with him.

As the two started walking to the square the guard asked Jol, "What exactly happened?" Jol replied, "If I told you, you wouldn't believe me. Hell, the king does not even believe me, he is just doing this because of who I am. But I want answers from whoever the jester is."

As the guard and Jol got closer to the square, Jol noticed there were far less people than earlier. He started looking all around him and said, "It looks like the jester is not here anymore." The guard said, "Appears that is the case. I am sorry, but I do not think we can do anything now." The guard then started walking back to the royal chambers.

Jol continued to desperately look around for the jester. Just then, about ten feet away, the small jester reappeared. Jol asked a lady nearby, "Do you see the small jester?! Right there!", as he pointed at the little dancing jester he saw. The lady shook her head and said, "No, I am sorry. But now I have to go."

Jol, accepting that it was only visible to him, stared back at the jester. Somehow, he thought, maybe he could beat it with his confidence and intimidate it by staring back. The jester extended its arm back and heaved its cane at Jol. Jol lifted his arms to block the incoming cane, but he never felt it hit his arm. The cane and the jester had vanished again. The illusions were playing tricks on Jol, something jesters were known for. Jol knew his field of expertise would not help him against this kind of threat. He would have to do some research and read some history books if he wanted to overcome this new menace. Jol thought, 'Just like fatal illnesses, these illusions felt like a ticking time bomb, and if he ignored them, his mental health would surely turn against him.

Chapter Forty-Eight: The Blue Flame of Sterafia

Renga Khonzas, Sterafia - "So that is where the den was located?", Renga asked. Renga and some of the survivors from the first expedition to the den of the wolf pack stood in the military planning room devising and configuring a strategy for their attack. One of the soldiers said, "Yes, we got to the top of the hill overlooking the den, but then got flanked on both sides." The king said, "We must avoid the hill then. If we swing to the right where it is flat ground, we will be better off." One of the soldiers said, "It is filled with trees though. It might limit the abilities of our archers." The king said, "I see, we can try going to the left." The soldiers nodded in agreement and one said, "That land is flat and there are not as many trees." The king continued, "If we can get that far we will set up a hard defense with swords and spears with the archers in the back. We have to let the archers rain down arrows on them, but we need to emphasize the defensive flank position since that is what they did to us last time."

As the king and the soldiers left the room to go prepare for battle, one of the soldiers asked the king, "Are you going to be leading us?" The king said, "Yes, our military advisor died out there for us and I want to be there when we avenge him and the other soldiers we lost."

The king went to his chambers to get his armor and weapon for the battle. The king felt confident about the attack and how it would turn out, but the idea of feral humans was unsettling to him. The king thought, 'How do they attack us? Do they actually bite us like the wolves or stab us? We just cannot let them get close enough to find out.' Renga dressed in his armor and clipped his thick bear fur coat over it. Lastly, he lifted his shield and battleaxe. The king walked down to the gates to meet up with all the soldiers who were preparing for the journey. The king shouted, "Bring food and warm clothes, it is going to be a long day."

With the time to embark for battle near, Renga addressed his troops who were now all gathered on their horses by the gates, "The archers need to stay in the back, we need a sufficient number of fighters ready to cover their flanks. We will strike from low ground in the open. Everyone prepare to leave for battle. I am ready to kill and I would like to be back to celebrate!" The men, already mounted on their horses, let out a loud battle cry. The king rode his horse to the front of the troops and then led them out of the city. The soldiers separated into three formations. The entire military was about two thousand strong and all three groups were given soldiers with spears, swords, and archers.

The three formations led by the king, made their advance to the south just as they had the last time. This time, the weather was not as harsh and the snow on the ground was not as deep. As the king rode on his horse, he could not help but realize that it had been months since he had left the city on horseback. The king thought to himself that somewhere out in the east Oakley was traveling on his own with Snowstorm. The king envisioned Oakley riding a mature Snowstorm and murmured to himself, "One day he will ride." The idea excited the king. He was thinking of ways it would work. The king thought of a leather saddle that could go around the tiger's back and have foot holds similar to horse saddles. In the rear, there could be a large piece of leather that would protect Oakley from falling back off Snowstorm. It could also allow him to stand up and shoot arrows from the tiger. The king smiled at the vision and said to one of the soldiers next to him, "When we get back to Sterafia, remind me about a saddle I am thinking about." The soldier nodded and said, "Of course, my king."

The king said, "It is funny, I have spent much of my life fighting by the blade, but today will be my first significant battle as the king." The soldier said, "I will protect you with my life." The king said, "Thank you, take care of yourself too. I still have so much I can do for Sterafia, it would be a shame if my life and rule were cut short, but it is still a risk I am willing to take." The soldier said, "I know my opinion is of little value, but I do respect that in you. I can say with certainty that most kings would choose to avoid the battle." The king said, "That is true. The thing is that in order to rule as a king you demand a lot from your people. In order to gain the respect, trust, and loyalty from everyone, a good king must lead by example. I need to be out here alongside all of you. Put all the titles aside and the only thing you would have is some men stronger than others, some more experienced in combat, and some lucky. I am a combination of all of those things, so why should I not be here today."

The three separate military formations rode for hours following the same path the first group of soldiers had been on. The king asked the soldier, "What is your name?" The soldier replied, "Arthur Trast." The king said, "I remember exploring this region when I was young. It is a shame what it has become. There is something not right here. The lands of our kingdom have grown dark." Arthur asked, "Can you tell me the story about the bear?" The king laughed and said, "Not at the moment, I need to focus on the battle. I shouldn't be thinking of stuff like that." Arthur asked, "Can you tell me when we get back to Sterafia, it would be a pleasure to hear it from the king himself." The king nodded and then said, "Vast forestry, you see that in the distance, right?" Arthur said, "It does appear to be that." The front group of soldiers stopped riding and waited for orders from the king.

One of the soldiers rode up to the king and said, "All the way over there, that is where the den is. Are we ready for the final part of the trip?" As they were still far enough away from the den, the king shouted, "The den is up ahead! Everyone focus, think of your families, think of the soldier at your side, think of your very own life!" The king pointed toward the location of the den and made sure that word of the location of the den was passed back to the troops as the groups continued their journey. The king felt his blood start to rush as his body was preparing itself for combat. Despite there being no overt physical changes to the body, the mind had its very own funny way of knowing what was ahead in these situations and affected the body accordingly.

The ride for the final portion of the trip was a very quiet, but tense, one for the soldiers. The three formations steered a bit to the left of the hill and dismounted apart from each other but close to where they anticipated the fighting would break out. The king and some soldiers started commanding the men, "Get ready!" The men with spears and swords set up mostly in the front and middle of each formation with their shields held up. The archers were in the rear with a small group of soldiers ready to protect them. The king stood in back of the soldiers, but in front of the archers. As the soldiers continued to prepare themselves in this new formation, the sound of howls could be heard from the location of the den. The king said to the men around him, "They know we are here; they may have known for a while now. They did not flee, which means they are ready for us too."

The large military group started marching toward the wolf den. The king kept looking around him for signs of incoming attacks. The group continued to march through the field toward the opening in the hill. One of the soldiers called out, "On the left!" The king looked to the left side and saw the wolves and feral humans charging at full force at the group. Most of the front forces were already past the hill. Soldiers started calling out for them to run back and defend from the flank. The king called out, "Fighters, get in position. Archers, fire away!" More and more enemies appeared from the side of the hill. By now, most of the wolf pack was heading toward them. The king estimated that there were about seven hundred or so wolves and feral humans.

The men with shields started to build a wall on the left flank while the archers readied their arrows and released them firmly. In the distance, several wolves and feral humans were hit by arrows. Some fell from injury, while some maintained their charge. The front of the wolf pack was charging the wall of shields, which the men held firmly. The king yelled, "Attack!" Close to fifty wolves came charging into the shields, some even managed to jump over them. The spears and blades of the men cut and slashed into the flesh of some of the wolves, while other wolves managed to viciously bite into the arms and legs of some men. The king realized that they were quickly being overwhelmed so he commanded the archers to retreat and the other fighters to cover their ground. The king, alongside the soldiers, tried to cover their retreat.

The soldier next to the king thrust his sword deep into the stomach of a wolf. A feral human jumped on the soldier and started biting into his neck. The king went to attack but paused out of shock. The feral person was Damien Nodon. The king said, "What has happened to you Damien!" Damien stopped biting the soldier and looked up at the king. The king saw the anger in his eyes. It no longer seemed like it was Damien anymore. Damien started growling as the king came forward and hacked his axe into Damien's neck. The king pulled out his axe and said "Sorry, old friend, but it is for the best", before he continued to run along and protect the archers.

Some of the fighters were able to assist the front lines and help them push back the advancing wolves. There were about a hundred wolves that were now surrounded by the king's military. The king commanded the archers to come to a halt and fire. He also commanded the fighters to kill the surrounded enemies. The archers fired at them before the soldiers advanced and started to slaughter the enemies. The king paused for a moment and noticed the battle was starting to turn in their favor. The king then commanded the archers to fire further into the distance at the remaining enemies. The king noticed that the man he saw get bitten by Damien was starting to twitch. He looked up and saw a few of his soldiers starting to rise on all fours just like the feral people. The twitching soldier rolled over on his side slowly and started to stand on all fours.

The king shouted, "Kill all of our soldiers that were bitten! If you see them twitching, execute them!" A couple of these new feral people started to attack the rear of the front lines. Some soldiers turned and killed the attackers before they started to kill the twitching soldiers on the ground. The king lifted his axe and struck it hard into the back of a feral soldier's neck. The king shouted, "Finish off the bitten ones, then push onward to victory!" The men charged toward the last one-third of the enemy and started to carefully attack the wolves while trying to avoid being bitten at all costs. The king commanded the archers to stop firing and to move closer to the enemies. The few hundred men on the front lines killed the remaining forces one by one as the whimpers of the wolves filled the air. The last whimpers were heard more distinctly as the battlefield became less noisy.

The king ran up to the front of the group and shouted, "Great fighting men, make sure all of the bitten soldiers are killed. Now we must march onto the den and make sure none remain." The group turned around and started walking back toward the hill they originally set out for. One of the soldiers asked the king, "Are we going to skin the wolves?" The king said, "No, they clearly had some infection that we do not want to contract. Otherwise, I would be up for it." As the group came closer to the den, they could hear innocent wolf pup whimpers. The group walked into the wolf den and saw animal bones scattered in the open. Inside a small cave opening the men noticed a little under a hundred younger wolf pups waiting for their parents to return.

One of the men asked the king, "What are we to do with the pups?" The king looked inside the cave for a moment and said, "They cannot be allowed to live. They are just like the other wolves only younger. As they grow, they will create the same problem and we will be faced with the threat again." The soldier asked, "Shall we go kill them?" The king said, "No, it will not be necessary. Pick up the rocks and block the entrance of the cave. I will not have our men shed any more blood, the wolves will starve in the days to come. It will be safer for our troops this way." The men picked up the rocks and started stacking them at the entrance of the cave.

The king called out, "Bring me the flag and pole." One of the men brought the flag of Sterafia while another soldier carried over a wooden pole. The king tightened the flag around the pole and firmly stuck the pole in the ground. The king backed up and watched as the flag waved in the wind. The blue fire from a campfire was the symbol of Sterafia and that was displayed on the white background of the flag. As the king backed up, the blue fire looked more alive. The king called out, "The blue flame of Sterafia refuses to extinguish, when tested by the elements the fire prospers and turns blue in the midst of winter. It does not weaken, it only spreads." All the men watched and bowed at the flag as the king sincerely bowed.

The king rose up and called out, "We are done here. Victory has been achieved. You all have been blessed by Sterafia and in turn have blessed the fortune of Sterafia. Upon our arrival to Sterafia, we will celebrate into the late hours. Let us return home and regroup in the next few hours." The men followed the king back past the hill as they walked by the battlefield. One of the soldiers asked the king, "How many do you think we have lost?" The king looked around and said, "It looks like somewhere around one hundred. One bite meant a sure death otherwise there would be far less deaths."

The king kept walking until he stopped at the sight of the familiar face of a man. It was Arthur Trast, the same man he had conversed with earlier on the trip. The king bent over and whispered to the corpse of Arthur, "The tiger saddle, thank you, Arthur. I hope you find peace." The king stood up and walked over to the horses with his men.

The king and his men rode back to Sterafia for hours after their hard-fought victory. The men celebrated for the remainder of the night. Drinking for victory, for their lives, for Sterafia, and to forget the cruelties of war that they had to witness and perform. The king brought celebrations to the kingdom and had cleansed the lands of Sterafia from the plague that darkened its horizons. Now the future again looked pleasant and promising for the people of Sterafia who favored seclusion from the other kingdoms and from war.

Chapter Forty-Nine: The Lost Settlement

Oakley Nodon, Southeast of Sterafia - Oakley awoke from his night of sleep with his head on Snowstorm's stomach. Oakley could tell the tiger was asleep from Snowstorm's slow, deep breaths. Had the tiger been awake, he would be full of energy and would have already been tugging on Oakley. After traveling through the hills for several days, Oakley had not discovered much other than the open land he was traversing, but he was driven to keep going.

Oakley sat up and looked at the sky to determine what time it was. The sun had just come up and the beaming light had awoken him. The tiger was quick to follow his lead as he also woke up and instantly smelled Oakley's presence. The tiger yawned and sat up to look for Oakley. Snowstorm noticed Oakley standing a few feet away and let out another yawn. Oakley walked over to Snowstorm and pet him on the head as he said, "Tired today I see. Time to get up." Oakley signaled for the tiger to get up and follow. Snowstorm obeyed the command and stood on all fours as he started to follow Oakley's lead.

The two walked for a couple of miles before they came across a small winter settlement. Oakley saw igloos in the distance constructed of ice. Oakley stopped and thought for a moment about whether he should approach the settlement. His whole journey traveling alone was a risk and he realized he had to be cautious along the way. Oakley then started walking to the settlement with Snowstorm at his side.

Once Oakley and Snowstorm got within a few hundred feet of the entrance of the settlement, several men came running over with bows. Oakley stood still and signaled for Snowstorm to not move. The men came closer to surround the unknown visitors. Oakley noticed the men wearing fur clothing all over their body. They did not have armor like the men in Sterafia, but rather wore clothing made of fur to protect themselves from the elements.

Oakley spoke in the common language of Lodas, but the men did not understand what he was saying. Oakley remembered most of the Sterafian language that he learned when he was younger. Using what he remembered he said, "I come from Sterafia, I come in peace." The men nodded and lowered their bows. One of them spoke back to Oakley in Sterafian and said, "Welcome traveler, we have been waiting for one of you to return." Oakley replied, "My tiger is not a threat, he will not attack without my order. What exactly have you been waiting for?" The man said, "Follow me."

As they walked, the man continued, "A couple of centuries ago around a hundred people native to Sterafia set out to explore and build a new outpost and this is where they settled. We had always been allies to Sterafia, but we knew they had forgotten about us. A couple of decades ago we sent a couple of men to find Sterafia to make contact and renew our alliance, but the men never returned. We did not know if they died in the wild or were killed in Sterafia. It is not too bad being unknown in this world though. In fact, you are one of the few men who have come across our settlement."

Oakley said, "I cannot believe that you all descend from Sterafia as well. I set out here to find meaning in my life and it led me to this place. What is it called?" The man replied, "Katorian. The settlement lost from the world. What is your name?" Oakley replied, "My name is Oakley Nodon and my tiger is called Snowstorm. What is your name?" The man said, "Hexes Torlian. So, you have come as a traveler seeking out the world?" Oakley and Snowstorm continued to follow the man into the settlement as Oakley said, "That is exactly what I am doing. My father just passed away and I want to find meaning in the enormous world we live in. We spend months and even years of our lives, and sometimes our entire lives, in the same small area. The truth is by the end of our lives we are not wise because we have not even seen a small portion of the world, only a spec." Hexes said, "That is very interesting. You may make yourself at home here as long as you would like. You may get funny looks, but just tell people where you come from and they will be amazed."

Oakley asked, "Will it be an issue having my tiger here?" Hexes said, "If anyone asks just tell them Hexes has allowed it. I am in charge of protecting the gates here and seeing that you are the first visitor in quite a while, I have no issues with you or your loyal friend here. You can sleep in this igloo right here, the owner just recently passed away, so it is open for you and your tiger to use." Oakley replied, "Thank you, I am very impressed with how you built these structures from ice." Oakley walked inside the igloo with Snowstorm following him. Oakley dropped his belongings on the inside and walked out with Snowstorm. Oakley said, "It will do just fine. I think we will explore the settlement if that is okay."

Hexes said, "Please do, I will leave you to explore on your own and make new friends. If you need me just ask around or you can find me by the gate." As Oakley and Snowstorm walked through the settlement, Oakley noticed that the natives all wore the same fur clothing that Hexes had worn. He also noticed various natives giving him curious looks.

Oakley came across a group of teenagers around his age. Oakley said, "Hello", to the teenage boy and girls. The boy in the group said, "Welcome, what is your name and where are you from?" Oakley said, "My name is Oakley Nodon and I am from Sterafia. It is a several days' trip from here. I was hoping to make some friends while I am staying here." The boy said, "My name is Ged Erdor, this is Swida Vorvaz, and this is Rika Pesgo." Oakley said, "It is nice to meet you all. This here with me is Snowstorm. You can pet him if you would like." The three natives came closer and pet the tiger in awe. Oakley said, "I was hoping someone could show me around." Ged said, "Rika and I have to go somewhere now, but what about you Swida?" Swida smiled and said, "I can help the visitor. Follow me Oakley Nodon." Oakley started following Swida through the settlement as she asked, "Beautiful tiger you have, how did you end up with him?" Oakley said, "That is a story I will have to tell some other time, it is a long one."

Oakley looked at Swida with curiosity and a new type of interest. Underneath all the fur he saw her natural beauty. She had pale skin with brown hair and light eyes. She was short and seemed to be very fit. Oakley asked, "How often do you get to leave the settlement?" Swida replied, "Whenever we would like, but usually when we hunt for food." Oakley said, "You hunt too? It is one of my favorite things to do. I grab my bow, Snowstorm here, and a few belongings and I go out into the wild for hours." Swida said, "I do not use the bow." Oakley with a surprised look asked, "Well, how do you hunt then?" She reached into the bag she was holding and pulled out a large net. Swida said, "I set up this net along the ground and lure animals into it with food. When they apply pressure to the net it triggers the pull and usually captures the animal in the net." Oakley said, "That is wise, I have never learned about that before. I am already learning so much from you." Swida asked, "Do you want to see my favorite spot outside the settlement?" Oakley replied, "Yes, please take me there." Swida said, "Once we get outside of the gates it is only a two-mile walk." Oakley said, "I have been walking for days, but a couple of more miles can't hurt."

The two made their way south toward the coast as Snowstorm followed Oakley and Swida. Swida said, "This is the coast of the ocean up ahead." Oakley asked, "What is an ocean?" Swida laughed and said, "A huge body of water, much larger than a lake." As they approached the coast Oakley was amazed by the sight of the ocean. Oakley stared out in the distance and said, "There is water beyond what the eye can see." Swida said, "Yes, it is very relaxing to look at and listen to. Take a seat."

Oakley sat down and stared out into the distance with Swida and Snowstorm who sat next to him. Oakley said, "I can't wait to tell the people back in Sterafia about what I have seen here." Swida asked, "Are you going back soon?" Oakley replied, "No, I do not intend to. I know we have certain differences, but I heard how your people are of the same roots as mine. It is interesting how some things remain the same and some things change over time."

Oakley looked into Swida's pretty eyes and she looked back at him with admiration. Oakley thought to himself, 'Is this the moment? Should I kiss her?' Before he could make his decision, he saw something moving in the distance over her right shoulder. It was several slim bluish figures that did not look human.

Oakley quickly stood up and said, "What are those blue people over there?" Snowstorm rapidly stood up as Oakley's quick movements surprised him. Swida said, "We do not know. I have only seen them a couple of times, but they do not bother us, and we do not bother them."

Oakley said, "I want to go meet them." Oakley started running in the direction of the figures as Snowstorm started to chase. Swida said, "No, stay here! Do not go!" Oakley ignored her and ran off in the distance. After he ran for a short moment, the blue figures saw him coming and started to run back toward the cliff. Oakley called out and said, "Do not go, I come as a friend!" The blue figures did not turn around as they continued their run toward the cliff. Oakley kept running ahead as he saw the blue figures dive off the cliff into the ocean below. Oakley arrived at the edge of the cliff and looked down below at the ocean. Oakley said, "That drop is too high, why did they jump?" Swida ran over and said, "Why did you run to them?" Oakley said, "I had to get a closer look, who are they?" Swida said, "We call them the people of the sea, but we do not know much about them. They live in the ocean and come to land from time to time. I do not know why." Oakley said, "They are probably curious, like me. We will meet them when they are ready."

Chapter Fifty: The Scroll of Awakening

Ria Falune, Desert Town of Daraz - The feeling of being back in Daraz excited Ria. She had returned with questions regarding the items she recently discovered in the Cave of Jewels. Ria, Haigar, and around thirty guards entered the town and were greeted by the guards of Daraz. A guard called out, "Welcome back, Queen Falune. Roam the town as you desire." The queen smiled at the guards and continued riding her camel into the town. Haigar asked the queen, "Where would you like to go first?" The queen replied, "Directly to the sages, the purpose of my visit. I remember where they are, just follow me."

The queen and Haigar rode toward the cave in the mountain. After they dismounted and approached the cave by foot, an older man said, "You must be the queen. My name is Begra Vanno and I am the sage you did not meet last time. Yaako told me all about the necklace called, The Caller. Quite fascinating. What brings you back to us? There must be something new." The queen responded, "Nice to meet you Begra. I have in fact brought with me something I found not too long ago. Perhaps, we should step inside the cave so you can take a closer look?" Begra said, "Yes, please follow me."

The queen and Haigar followed the sage into the cave where candles lit its natural darkness. The sage sat down and said, "Have a seat, and show me what it is you would like me to look at." After sitting, Haigar handed Ria the bag of belongings from the Cave of Jewels. As Ria opened the bag she said, "There are two items, both of which I discovered in a cave recently."

Ria pulled out the ring with the ruby and handed it to Begra. Ria said, "I noticed it had the same lettering as my necklace, which says, The Caller." The sage inspected the ring closely and said, "That is correct. By the look of it, it was made to match your necklace as a set. Have you tried it on with your necklace already?" The queen replied, "Yes," and added that, "the second item is a scroll which looks to be written in ancient Torustian as well." Ria carefully took the scroll from the bag and handed it to the sage.

Begra carefully opened the scroll and started reading it quietly as his mouth moved with each word. The sage stopped moving his lips and looked at the scroll in shock. The sage said, "My queen, you have come across something very serious." The queen asked, "What is it?" The sage said, "Please, give me just a moment. I want to finish reading it." As the sage kept reading the scroll, Ria stared at Haigar with a look of hope.

After a short moment, the sage looked up at the queen and said, "This is the scroll that tells you how you can bring the dead of Torust back to life." Ria was ecstatic as she had found the meaning and purpose of all her recent efforts. On the inside, all the worries she had bottled up inside her throughout her life now suddenly became irrelevant. No kingdom or animal, not even the scorpion that once stung her, could amount to any type of threat to her based upon the power she would soon possess.

The queen, who at first lost her words, said, "Read me the entire scroll, word for word." The sage looked back at the scroll and read, "The Scroll of Awakening: Those that yearn for the love and power that has been lost, I call upon you. With the proper luxuries of gold and jewels, you may possess the true blend of ruby polluted by the Torustian blood of sorrow and power. With the necklace and the ring, you shall be The Caller. The dead of Torust will rise together despite being lost by separate deaths. Just as the blood pollutes the ruby, the ruby pollutes the blood of the being. The arisen will look on with a red glare. They will speak the natural language of Torustian. They will be arisen, but not rejuvenated with their previous lives. Recite the following in the royal burial grounds of the Halls of Absolute: 'I call out to all the souls of Torust. Hear my words, find your way back to my calling. I promise to bring you back to this world. Come bring glory to Torust and fight for the blood of our kind. Come now and find your bodies, awaken to rejoin Torust!'"

Ria said, "This is exactly what I needed. Gofon has cured the illness for their own but left our kingdom to struggle. Our kingdom is suffering, and this is what we will need to overcome them in time. I want to spend some time here in Daraz and learn the language from you and Yaako. Will that be okay?" Begra replied, "Yes, you will need to be fluent in the language if you wish to speak with the arisen and command them. You should be aware that illnesses do not affect those that rise."

Ria asked, "Will I be able to speak with my parents again?" Begra replied, "Yes, they will arise. You just have to learn the language." Ria said, "I will stay here until you think I am ready." Haigar asked, "Are you going to be okay here on your own Ria? I do not think it is a good idea for you to stay here without any guards. Or do you want me to stay here with you?" Ria replied, "I trust them like one our own. I will send a letter to you when I am ready to be picked up."

Begra asked, "Are you ready to live the life of a sage? It requires extensive studying and long hours. You will be here in the cave most hours of every day studying and sleeping. It will be tough, but worth it once you are ready, which should be in a couple of months." Ria nodded and asked, "When do we begin?" Begra said, "Tomorrow morning, you will sleep over there in the corner with those blankets." Ria said, "Perfect. Haigar, while I am learning ancient Torustian I need you to prepare the military. Get the men ready as we could be at war in a few months." Haigar nodded and said, "It will be taken care of, my queen. With our military and the arisen Torustians, we will be able to conquer all of the kingdoms if we so choose." Ria said, "One step at a time, but for now we will take Gofon."

Ria looked down at the scroll and envisioned how mighty her military would soon be. She saw a massive army with her powerful troops being led by Haigar and Peter Fardine with thousands of risen men and women marching on Gofon. She reflected on the ceilings of the Halls of Absolute and how the red eyes of the illustrations were just like those that the arisen will have. She thought to herself, 'How did I not realize this? It was right there in front of me all along.' The necklace was more important than she had expected. What started as a personal curiosity now led her to believe that she would soon be summoning the largest and most powerful military to ever assemble under one kingdom.

Chapter Fifty-One: A Justice Beyond Comparison

Peter Fardine, Torust – Peter decided to mix things up a bit and sat in the market, to eat his lunch. He looked down at his arm absorbing the light of the warm sun. His brown-haired forearm revealed the unexpected. As he moved his forearm slowly, he saw that the hair appeared reddish under the sunlight, the color of his late wife's hair. Peter moved his forearm around again and again as he murmured, "I miss you, every day." Peter continued to look down at his arm until he heard a familiar voice. He looked up and saw his son Cazier with a young woman who appeared to be pregnant. Peter stood up and said, "Cazier, over here!"

Cazier and Nera approached Peter as Peter asked, "What brings you here?" Cazier said, "We are just roaming the marketplace. This is my friend Nera, by the way." Peter faced Nera who was smiling at him. Peter said, "Nice to meet you. Cazier, can I have a word with you."

Peter walked a few feet away as Cazier followed and asked, "What is it, father?" Peter said in a low voice, "You ought to be careful mingling with pregnant women. It can attract unwanted attention, especially from their partners. I know you don't have bad intentions, but you still should know." Cazier replied, "Nera and I have been friends for years, it is fine." Peter said, "Okay, I just wanted to warn you."

Cazier asked, "What are you doing today?" Peter said, "I have been doing a lot of thinking. My body is ready, I am going to start fighting again. I have not had any fighting practice since the day of my defeat, but it is time to start practicing again. After that injury, I expected my fighting days to be over." Cazier said, "Good luck and start slow, we don't want anyone getting hurt."

Cazier walked back to Nera as she asked, "Is that your father? Is that the great fighter of our kingdom?" Cazier said, "Yes, he is going to return to training today, actually. He has been recovering from a bad injury he sustained in the final battle to become a gladiator." Nera asked, "How come you do not practice like him?" Cazier said, "It used to be an interest, but not anymore."

Peter, with firm steps and a confident mind, walked back to his home. At home, he grabbed his armor and weapon and started to dress in his gear. As he picked up his chestplate, he noticed the scratch in the back where Roy's blade initially met his armor before skidding into his neck. Peter ran his thumb into the mark and felt the indentation of the blade in the armor. In his mind, he relived the exact moment of agony. Anger overcame him as he rapidly finished putting on his armor and made his way to the Torust military grounds. As he approached, he could hear Haigar's voice from a distance. Haigar was teaching fighting techniques to a large group of fighters. Peter walked closer and quietly stood at the back of the group.

Haigar paused for a moment at the sight of Peter and gave him an accepting nod. Haigar's voice boomed, "When the day of battle comes, many of you will be strong, many will be wise in combat, but the one thing that most fighters cannot prepare is their instincts. Whether you are defending your back, your side, or your ally's shoulder, you need to know how to move your blade without thinking about it. I want all of you to get in a straight line and stand about five feet apart."

As the men started getting in formation, Haigar walked to the center to face them all. Haigar called out, "Look how I maneuver my blade." He held out his sword and shifted it to the left above his shoulder. He then shifted it to the bottom right, then top right over his shoulder, and, lastly, around his back with one arm facing the bottom left. Haigar repeated the movements once more and continued to speak, "I want you all to practice these movements. Start slowly and then pick up the pace. When you are all ready, we will perform the movements with rapid speed and with the confidence that you will not accidentally strike yourselves or your neighbors.

Peter started the movements along with all the soldiers. Peter went through the movements a few times and noticed his strikes were right on the mark, but he lacked the speed and strength he used to possess. Haigar observed and corrected the soldiers as he walked along the line. When he got to Peter, he said, "Great to see you back, Peter. A few weeks and you will be fresh again."

As Peter continued moving through the motions, he envisioned his fight with Roy. The clanking of the blades and the rough body to body contacts that were exchanged were in his mind. Peter could feel his body beginning to reignite with power as he grew angered by the fight that caused so many problems in his life. Despite taking months to adjust to his new situation, it only took a brief moment of training to set Peter on a track that would allow him to pursue a justice beyond comparison.

Chapter Fifty-Two: The Search for Power

Liava Pontas, Lake by the Dragon Lair - Liava swam around in the lake cleansing her body of all the dirt that had built up over time. As she rubbed her body, she dunked her head under the water and came up with a mouth full of water, which she swallowed. Since the attack of the mountain lion she took the red dragon with her to the lake every time.

The red dragon sat closely by, watching Liava relax and frolic in the water. Liava signaled for the dragon to come closer to the water. The red dragon curiously stepped closer until Liava shot a mouth full of water at the dragon's foot as she laughed. The water did not bother the dragon as it bent over and started drinking from the lake.

Liava floated on her back for a moment and looked up at the early morning sky. The stars were dimming as the sun was about to make its appearance. Liava wondered which star represented the dragons. She knew that one of the brightest stars was for the humans, but she did not know if the dragon species was struggling or thriving. The three dragons she had befriended were the only ones she had seen aside from a large white dragon and a grey one she had seen years ago. Liava knew there were more dragons in the world but had no idea how many or if any other dragons were as tame as hers. Liava knew that if any other dragons saw her riding on one of her dragons, their curiosity would be piqued.

In her mind's eye, she could envision these interactions. She could see the other dragons uniting with her dragons and, as a result of these bonds, she could grow more powerful. Liava felt her star-shaped pendant necklace and was confident that her purpose in life was starting for take form. Liava looked at the red dragon and said, "We must venture further into this world and find more like you." Liava knew her words were not understood by the dragons, but she believed speaking to them helped unite them.

After cleansing the rest of her body, Liava stepped out of the water. The warmer weather made bathing in the lake enjoyable; in the previous months, the weather was too cold for her to get her whole body in the water. Liava dried her body off and put on her clothes before walking back to the other dragons who also were close by.

The red dragon followed Liava and noticed that she had grabbed the hemp harness. After several recent flights with Liava on its back, the dragon had learned that it meant that it was time to travel. The red dragon went and rubbed its head against the side of the other dragons. The dragons slowly moved around before being ready for flight. Liava walked closer to the red dragon and whistled to let the dragon know she was ready to mount. Liava prepared the harness and mounted the dragon as each had grown accustomed to.

The red dragon ran toward the edge of the cliff of the mountain and flew upward into the sky. The other dragons noticed the red dragon and Liava departing and started to fly into the sky alongside them. The dragons were heading northeast, in the direction close to Liava's old village of Staga. In recent weeks, Liava had learned to maneuver the red dragon's direction using her harness.

The dragons continued to soar through the sky flying toward the great unknown. After riding for half an hour, Liava heard an angry roar from below. She tipped her head carefully over the side of the red dragon to look around for the source of the loud noise. Hundreds of feet below a giant white yeti on a hill near a cave was trying to intimidate something.

Liava looked at the beast in amazement; it had to be the largest and most powerful creature, other than the dragons, she had ever seen. Its thick white fur gave it a majestic look. Just as Liava adored her dragons, she immediately felt a strong admiration for this beast. As the dragons kept flying ahead, Liava saw what had caught the yeti's attention. A threat all too familiar to Liava; a pack of about twenty to thirty men marching to end this beast's life just as savages had done to Liava's village. From above Liava could not tell what village it was, but to her it did not matter as she now viewed them all as enemies. Soon she would have the confidence to fight and destroy the villagers to end their savagery. Until then, gaining fighting experience with the dragons and searching for more dragons in the world was her primary focus.

Chapter Fifty-Three: Yeti Hill

Ryos Pontas, Yeti Hill - Edgar shouted, "Yeti hill, up ahead!" Ryos and the villagers advanced closer to the yeti up the hill. Ryos was still staring at the three dragons that had just flown overhead in the sky. His father had told him stories about dragons, but Ryos, for the first time in his life, was able to witness the beauty of these majestic creatures. Ryos thought to himself, 'They seem so calm and peaceful as they effortlessly and gracefully flap their large wings in the sky.' If the group were not dealing with an imminent dangerous encounter, Ryos would have really enjoyed continuing to gaze up at them. The group of villagers walked further up the hill as the disgruntled yeti continued to roar at them. Although Ryos could not yet see the yeti, he could tell that it was not far from the summit of the hill. Ryos could feel his body start to shake as the nervousness and anxiety started to control him. Ryos knew that the yeti was incredibly fierce after he saw it kill the two villagers.

Suddenly, a large rock came shooting over Ryos' head. Ryos ducked at the last possible second and heard a loud thud behind him. Ryos, who was now kneeling, turned around and saw the villager behind him lying on the ground dead with his head half detached from his body. The villagers looked at the dead body in shock before they turned back to continue their charge up the hill.

Edgar shouted, "Shields up!" Another large rock came flying through the air as it clanked against the shield of one of the villagers; the force was so intense it knocked him to the ground. Edgar yelled, "We must surround and kill the yeti!" The villagers continued to rush up the hill until they neared the top. The first villager held his shield high and carefully peeked out onto the summit. A large rock smacked against his shield forcefully knocking him back into another villager who caught him in place.

The group of villagers started to split into two lines to meet on each side of the yeti. Ryos climbed the hill after the first several men and he saw the savage, yet beautiful, beast he had seen on their last encounter. The men were running to the sides of the yeti, making sure there was plenty of distance to avoid its strong strikes. Before the full circle was formed, the yeti stepped to the right side and struck his claws into the face of one villager, virtually taking it fully off. The villager fell over crying in excruciating pain. The villagers around him, visibly shaken, aimed their spears and thrust them into the forearm of the yeti who shrieked in pain as the spears pierced its skin. The yeti started to flail its arms around in anger. Ryos had to side-step to his left to avoid being struck by the claws of the beast.

By now, the full circle of villagers had formed around the yeti, all holding out their spears leaving the creature with no direction to move. Ryos held out his spear with the other villagers around him. This was his first time using this weapon. Back in Staga, he was always too young to use anything other than a small dagger. He suddenly had a flashback of him and his friends tying their daggers to the ends of sticks in the woods when no one was watching. Ryos also remembered the way he tried to imitate his father's movements with the spear. His father used to practice with the spear and Ryos would mimic his father's spear movements with the impromptu stick spear he would make in the forest. 'Slash, slash, thrust', Ryos recalled.

Ryos' mind returned, somewhat reluctantly, to the immediate and real threat facing him, as he heard Edgar shout, "Spears firm, advance!" The villagers around Ryos started to step closer to the yeti and Ryos followed their lead. The yeti was facing the villagers in the opposite direction of Ryos and he could hear the sound of spears being snapped. Edgar shouted, "Quickly, thrust!" All the villagers came closer to the yeti and thrust their sharp weapons deep into its body from all angles.

In the fury of all the spears, Ryos dug his spear deep into the back of the yeti's leg. At that moment, the yeti became still. Everyone suspected the yeti was finished but backed up waiting to see him fall. The yeti, who had about fifteen spears dug into its body, fell directly over onto its front. Ryos watched as the once mighty and magnificent white yeti lay dead facing the ground. The thick white fur of the beast had now turned mostly red as the blood poured out from all parts of its body.

The men looked at the dead yeti in relief as they gratefully acknowledged to themselves that they would manage to live another day. Ryos asked Edgar, "What will we do now?" Edgar pulled out his sharp dagger and said, "We are going to skin it and bring the meat back for the village to eat. Why do you think we came all this way to fight the beast?" Ryos said, "I thought it was just to avenge our fallen?" Edgar replied, "Yes, but we will treat the beast the same way it treated ours; we will kill it and eat it."

Edgar called out, "Daggers out, time to skin it!" Ryos saw the villagers around him pulling out their daggers as they started to cut into the white and now red fur of the beast. Ryos forced himself to look away; something about bringing the white beast to bits and pieces disgusted him. Edgar said to Ryos, "It is okay, you will get used to it. If you want, take a quick walk." Ryos nodded and started to walk away.

Ryos walked closer to the cave and turned around noticing that he had company. Each person following Ryos was a former villager from Staga who, like Ryos, could not bring himself to skin the creature. Ryos slowly approached the cave and looked into it, but the darkness of the cave prevented him from seeing anything. He wanted to go inside but was not willing to face it alone. Edgar walked up to Ryos and said, "Here, a white fur hide from the yeti for your efforts." Edgar heaved a thick hide of the yeti over Ryos's left shoulder.

Edgar said, "It looks like you want to go in there." Ryos said, "Possibly, I am curious." Edgar said, "Another time, we should get back to the village, all the meat will be heavy to carry. Plus, we must take care of him." Ryos and Edgar looked at the unrecognizable man who was clawed by the yeti, sitting with multiple cloths and bandages wrapped all the way around his head. Ryos asked, "Will he survive?" Edgar said, "Hopefully, with our medical attention now we will be able to get him back to the village, but he will need plenty of care when we get back."

Edgar and Ryos walked back to the cut-up yeti. The creature did not appear like a yeti anymore or anything recognizable for that matter. Edgar called out, "Everyone squeeze the meat into your hides. We are bringing all the meat back to the village and we will supply the village for weeks!"

Ryos and all the villagers started grabbing the meat with their hands and stuffing it into their hides. Ryos asked the villager next to him, "How do we keep the hide together?" The villager handed him a small rope and said, "This should help keep it closed. Just give that back to me when we get back." Ryos nodded and started to wrap the rope around the hide. Ryos and the rest of the men walked back to the village and arrived a few hours before nightfall. Ryos dropped off his meat by the main campfire and went straight to his hut. He collapsed in bed from exhaustion, physical and mental, and thought to himself, 'That yeti was vicious, it would have killed me.' The yeti he had just encountered and killed was the opposite of what his parents had taught him about other species. Ryos realized that as he grew older, he was learning new things about life on his own; even things that contradicted his earlier beliefs.

Gibia and Dasina entered his hut and noticed him in bed. Dasina asked, "What is wrong? I heard the news of how you and the others slew the vicious beast, you should be proud." Ryos said, "I am glad we avenged our fallen, it is just now I know the flaws of my old village. The villagers of Staga were willing to protect beasts that would kill them in an instant. I feel like I am growing wiser and more knowledgeable about the world as a villager of Tsirian every day." Dasina and Gibia got into the bed alongside Ryos to comfort him. Gibia said, "We are glad you are smart enough to realize the flaws of your old life. It is very mature of you. The future of Tsirian might end up in your hands one day."

Chapter Fifty-Four: The Distant Rainbow

Searleone Vallas, Skyrock - Voron asked Searleone, "What did you know about the young mage, you know the one that you killed recently?" Searleone said, "He always had a sly and mischievous attitude. I could tell early on that he was a troublemaker. I just did not know he was capable of doing what he did. Why do you ask?" Voron replied, "I just never got that impression of him, but I guess I really didn't know him too well. You spent more time with him than I did." Searleone said, "Just a little, do not focus on the flaws of this mage. It is troubling, but what is important is the other bright minds that we have here with us in Skyrock. Excuse me for a moment." As Searleone walked away, Voron processed their conversation. He could always trust Searleone, but the actions of the young mage were very perplexing.

A part of Searleone's soul was still present in a passing cloud and he could sense something in the sky. Searleone sat down by his garden and closed his eyes as he started to meditate. Within a moment, his vision passed over to the part of his soul in the cloud a few miles away. The vision showed him something far beyond his childhood imaginations. Three dragons were flying in the sky through a rainbow. One of them had a teenage girl riding on its back who was twirling around the rainbow with laughter.

The vision was so incredible it brought a tear to Searleone's eye. He continued to watch from the passing cloud as the girl maneuvered the dragon through the rainbow again and again. For the first time in Searleone's life, he saw a human riding on the massive creature. Never in history had a human done this before, Searleone suspected. He watched until the dragons flew out far into the distance to the point where they appeared as just a spec in the sky.

Searleone released his vision and, in a sense, returned to his body. He opened his eyes intensely as if he had awoken from a fantastic and vivid dream. Searleone knew right away that whoever the girl was, he needed to meet her. She needed to see the world in the same perspective as he did. The power of having dragons on your side could go a long way in combat.

Searleone expected that the forces of Gofon would soon be back to seek revenge. Searleone wondered what he could do to get the attention of the girl and the dragons. The rainbow was unique enough to catch their attention; he would need to consider something just as appealing, but in a different way. The prosperity of the mages and Searleone seemed to depend on it.

Chapter Fifty-Five: The Shifting Relationship

Roy Syssian, Tyrades - Roy walked through the royal chambers to speak with Lance Hasting. The conversation he had with Lance on his wedding night had been on his mind for a few weeks now and Roy knew he had to correct his mistake. Roy thought to himself, 'I wonder how he is going to take this.'

Roy was stopped in front of the king's room by the king's guards. One of the guards asked, "What brings you here, King Syssian?" Roy said, "I need to speak with the king regarding personal matters." The guard opened the door and said, "Go ahead, sir." Roy entered and saw the king sitting on his balcony.

King Hasting said, "Welcome Roy. I am beginning to think you really love this city." Roy smiled and said, "My favorite after Biros." Lance smiled and asked, "So what brings you all the way here? You must be busy now that you are a married king." Roy replied, "Yes, I am, but I came here to follow up on a recent conversation of ours. When you came to me on the night of my wedding, I had a bit to drink and was not in my natural state of mind to handle matters as important as unconditional alliances. So now I want to be clear. We are allies and I hope our alliance remains strong, but I cannot put my kingdom in a war that we should not be involved in."

Lance said, "I wouldn't start a war and expect you to fight without having a just reason. Maybe we need to talk and be more aligned for what we can achieve together. What world we want for our future, and the future of your children and my grandchildren. If you are unsure, let me guide you because right now Gofon and Torust are pulling the strings in our world. They control more land, more resources, more towns. But together, we can make our kingdoms more powerful than they have ever been."

Roy said, "We don't want to be the aggressor, we never do. If they were to start a conflict with us or someone else, then we should have conversations, but for now it seems a bit excessive, too premature. The word is that tensions have arisen between Gofon and Torust already, perhaps they will weaken and hurt themselves without our involvement." Lance said, "That would be our perfect opportunity to strike. I am telling you, Roy, our legacies will be more than us being remembered as only kings of our kingdoms!" Roy said, "I am sorry, Lance, but for now I can't look to start a war. I wouldn't be the man your daughter married."

The kings exchanged farewells and Roy walked out of Lance's room and continued into the halls. King Hasting still sat at his table, silent and agitated. Despite the conversation with Roy not going the way he wanted, the news that Torust and Gofon were in conflict was a positive. Lance thought to himself, 'If they go to war and weaken each other, I may not even need the assistance of Biros.'

Once Roy walked out of the royal halls, he returned to his guards to make his way back to Biros. Just then, Roy heard a voice, "Roy, over here!" Roy turned his head and saw Kip Denvion standing next to a young woman. Roy walked over and said, "Nice to see you, Kip. I am surprised you are still here." Kip replied, "I was going to leave sooner, but things here are just too enjoyable. King Hasting takes great care of me and keeps telling me to stay longer so I can win gladiator in the future. This is my friend, Julia. She has made my time here amazing too. We just finished talking about how she will be going to Gofon with me in a few weeks. Tell her how great Gofon is." Roy said, "Gofon is a fine kingdom, I always enjoy my visits, although I still am yet to visit as king. Julia, you are going with Kip, you will certainly get the full experience of Gofon. I have heard that he is a promising fighter and is expected to be king one day. I think you should consider yourself fortunate that you captured his interests before another girl has."

Julia replied, "I am happy I have him every day. I am very much looking forward to my visit to Gofon." Roy, turning to Kip, said, "I know you will take good care of her. Maybe the next time we meet will be in Gofon. I am due to meet with your father soon." Kip said, "Certainly, I am looking forward to seeing my family again. It has been several months and this time they will get to meet Julia as well!" Roy said, "I know they must have missed you as well. Excuse me, I must be leaving for Biros."

After they exchanged their goodbyes, Roy walked toward his guards who were watching over him closely. A king always deserved to be protected, even a king as skilled in combat as Roy. Roy mounted his iconic white horse and started to ride with his squad of guards. Roy thought to himself, 'Looks like they are trying to influence Kip, just like Lance is trying to do with me. I must visit Gofon and warn the kingdom. Phillip will appreciate the tip.'

Despite informing Kip that they might meet next in Gofon, Roy had known he would have to make a visit much sooner before Kip would arrive there. Roy was seriously starting to question his alliance with his father-in-law, the king of Tyrades, and was coming to grips with the thought that he was going to be more of a problem.

Chapter Fifty-Six: The Illness Within

Jol Parantis, Gofon – Jol was in distress and he felt like his head was on fire. He lifted a cloth and padded his forehead, which was burning up and filled with sweat. As he sat in a chair in his potions room, Jol kept looking over his shoulder cautiously. Over the past several weeks, Jol had attempted to eradicate the jester from his mind many times, but his attempts always ended in disappointment. The jester had gotten the best of him and had spooked Jol to the point that he no longer remotely functioned as his old self. Day by day he grew mentally weaker; more afraid and fragile.

Jol started stirring a fresh batch of ingredients, which he hoped could be the remedy for his mental illusions. Jol's mind continued to race as he stirred the potions. His hands and legs trembled and shook from fatigue and anxiety. Jol could not tell what time of day it was or remember the last day he saw sunlight. A man as bright as him had been rendered hopeless in a very short time. Jol sought out help from the king a few times, but the king grew agitated with what seemed to be craziness on Jol's part. Jol was left to fend for and cure himself. Jol finished mixing the potion and quickly lifted it and chugged it down his mouth. He started pacing back and forth across the room waiting with uncertainty to see if it had worked as planned.

Suddenly, the small jester appeared on the table and was holding an empty glass up to his mouth to imitate Jol. The jester let out an unsettling laugh. Jol backed up into the corner of the room and started crying hysterically. The jester hopped off the table and bounced onto the ground. It slowly walked closer to Jol in the corner as it started shaking its small cane. After a moment of suspense, the jester stopped and stared at Jol. After a few seconds, it charged at him with the cane in hand ready to strike Jol. As the jester got within reach it vanished right before Jol's eyes.

Jol stood up and ran over to his table and grabbed something to write on. Jol grabbed his quill and started to draw a simple sketch of the jester that kept appearing to him. In his mind, he could still see the small jester vividly. Once

Jol finished, he dropped the quill and looked at the glass he had drank out of. Jol shamefully said to himself, "The illness within cannot be cured." Jol picked up the glass and smacked it against the table until there were shards of glass everywhere. Jol picked up some of the shards and slit both of his wrists. As blood started to pour out, he slit his throat with the limited power he had left. As he fell over on the ground and started to fade into death the small jester appeared on the table and tossed his cane respectfully onto Jol's body.

Hours later a young alchemist came to pay Jol a visit and ask him some questions to help with his research. He stood in shock at the sight of Jol's dead body. He immediately backed up and ran to the royal chambers. Once he approached, he said to the guards, "Jol Parantis is dead, please inform the king." The guard said, "Hold on." The guard entered the king's room and said, "My king, I have just been informed that Jol Parantis is dead, I do not know how he died. But the man who saw the body is just outside." The king said, "Send some men to investigate and clean up the scene. It is a shame, Jol did so much for our kingdom. It is terrible to hear this." The guard left the room and closed the door behind him.

Phillip sat down and thought to himself, 'Ever since he told me about what happened with the jester, he was never the same. Seeing all those people die on his journey must have really messed him up. Maybe the illness affected his mental health. Having the illness himself may have exposed his own vulnerability.'

Across the city, a man sat by himself at a table in his house. Spread across the table were various utensils, brushes, and face oils. The man lifted one of the brushes and dipped it into an oil before starting to layer it onto his face. The man started to hum to himself a pleasant tune. The feel of the soft and cool oil from the brush against his face was a soothing sensation for him. The man swiftly, but carefully, applied the oil to different parts of his face. The man lifted a bucket of water and placed it on the table in front of him. He stood up and leaned over the bucket to see his reflection in the water. The man looked at his reflection in the bucket and grinned as his face oil was coming along nicely.

The man continued applying the oils to his face until the process was complete. Jack Haxon smiled at the vibrant colors painted on his face. Doing work for the council was not nearly as entertaining as the time he spent as the jester. He stood up and grabbed the jester outfit and started to put it on. When he was done, he adjusted his hat until it sat firmly on his head, covering his hair. Lastly, he picked up his cane and looked at the small image of the jester on it and said, "I have a good feeling about today."

Chapter Fifty-Seven: A Fearless Taste of the Unknown

Oakley Nodon, Katorian Settlement - Oakley awoke to the sound of Snowstorm growling. Snowstorm was facing Swida, who had just entered the igloo. Oakley said, "Snowstorm, come here. It is okay, you should know Swida by now." Swida said, "It is okay, he is just being protective. It is good that he is that way. I have come to bring you and Snowstorm some fresh cooked meat. I added some extra spices to it as well, my own special recipe. Let me know what you think." Swida walked closer to Oakley and Snowstorm and handed Oakley a large pouch of meat. Oakley tossed some in his mouth and pulled a slab out of the bag that he tossed into Snowstorm's mouth.

Oakley said, "Tastes really good. It is delicious. I, ah we, really appreciate it." Swida said, "Thank you, what would you like to do today?" Oakley said, "I am planning on going to the cliffs again to try and meet the people of the sea." Swida disapprovingly said, "Not again, you have done that every day this week. They are very shy and will not speak with anyone." Oakley replied, "No one tries except me; I have to be the one to do something different and take a risk. How do you think I ended up here? I refused to live a standard life in Sterafia, I need to have a meaning for Snowstorm and myself. I never would have met you and who knows what can happen if these sea people choose to meet with me."

Swida paused for a moment before saying, "You seem very dedicated to meeting them, I must say. I hope it works out for you. I am not going again today, but you know I will be here in Katorian if you need me." Oakley said, "Thank you, Swida." Oakley stood up and gave Swida a big hug. Snowstorm stood up and came between their legs as he rubbed up against them. Swida said, "Is he fully grown?" Oakley said, "He has grown a lot, but he still has some more growing to do." Swida said, "I have never seen a domesticated animal this large before, you are a caring person, Oakley Nodon." Oakley smiled and said, "You are great too, I can tell he likes you. We will be back later."

Oakley and Snowstorm started walking past the settlement gates to the cliffs that they visited every day. Oakley walked through the uneven terrain and it reminded him of Sterafia. Although there were some differences, Oakley also noticed many similarities between his people and the people of Katorian.

After walking for a while, Oakley came across the sight he had seen every day. An ocean view from the cliff. Oakley promptly scanned the area and the water below for any signs of the sea people but did not see anything. Oakley looked down again from the cliff and decided to try to make his way down to the beach below. Oakley said to Snowstorm, "Let's try to get closer to the ocean." Oakley started walking toward the lower ground leading to the beach as Snowstorm followed closely behind. Oakley and Snowstorm started their descent by carefully placing their feet on the rocks on a sloping hill.

At the bottom of the hill, Oakley took a few steps and noticed the ground was different. It was soft like snow and his boot sunk a bit with each step. Oakley bent over and scooped some of it in his hand. It was dry and unlike anything he had seen before. Oakley walked closer to the ocean and looked as far as his eyes could see. He looked to his side and interestingly noticed Snowstorm doing the same. Oakley sat down in the sand and called Snowstorm over to sit next to him. Oakley kept his attention focused on the sea ahead of him. If there was any sign of the sea people, Oakley wanted to make sure he got their attention, if they had not already noticed him.

After sitting for a little over an hour, Oakley pulled out the pouch filled with the spiced meat that Swida gave him. He started to eat the meat and shared a lot of it with Snowstorm. As Snowstorm continued to grow, Oakley was realizing more and more of his food was being shared with the tiger as a result of its insatiable appetite.

As Oakley started to tie the pouch onto his side, the tide suddenly started to recede. This time it was receding in the shape of an inverted triangle. Oakley was alarmed and quickly stood up, as did Snowstorm. Oakley did not know much about the ocean, but he did realize that this seemed to be an unusual occurrence from the amount of time he spent by the water. The water kept receding until a tunnel of water started to emerge. Oakley thought to himself, 'Could this possibly be the people of the sea?!'.

The tunnel of water continued in its form until Oakley could see the tall, light blue figures walking toward the beach. Snowstorm stared at them with confusion and alarm. The tiger let out a growl, but Oakley called off Snowstorm's aggressive stance. The people of the sea appeared to have turquoise colored skin with a purple protrusion in their head and roundish ears. As they came closer, Oakley also noticed the scales all over their bodies and their long-webbed feet and hands.

All three of the people of the sea stepped onto the beach and slowly started to walk toward Oakley and Snowstorm. They all stopped and one of them called out, "Commoner of the land, what is your name?" Oakley responded, "My name is Oakley Nodon, from the kingdom of Sterafia. Master of Snowstorm the tiger and explorer of Lodas. Who are you all?" The same creature that spoke before said, "We are the Kulvani, and the sea is where we call home. You can call me Sefjan. Why have you waited for us day after day?" Oakley said, "I have developed a fearless taste of the unknown in this world. If you are what represents the good in this world, like me, I can learn a lot more from you than most other beings in Lodas." Sefjan said, "Well, if that is the case, we have a lot to learn from you as well, Oakley."

Snowstorm curiously walked closer to smell the Kulvani and Oakley asked, "Is it okay if he smells you?" Sefjan said, "No, please call him back. You and your tiger should not make any contact with us." Oakley called Snowstorm back to his side.

Oakley asked, "Why do you resist having any contact?" Sefjan said, "We do not want to spread any illnesses, nor contract any. We do admire your boldness and your unique relationship with such a magnificent animal. So much so that it brought us out from the depths of the sea. The Kulvani have not had any relations with the people of the land for close to a thousand years." Oakley asked, "Why is that?" Sefjan replied, "Evil emerged. Further north, in the kingdom of Torust, near the Sahine Sea, we learned of their hidden, ominous motive. They were the first land people who learned how to apply energy, but they used it for an evil, power-driven goal. They attempted to manipulate rubies to conjure up all the fallen of their kingdom and place them under their command. Their objective was to take over the world, but fortunately, they failed. The Kulvani retreated from the surface of this world and went into seclusion permanently. You have to understand that we are a peaceful species. Dealing with war and awoken dead is not something we ever want to face."

Oakley looked at the Kulvani in shock and awe and replied, "I have never heard any of that before or knew that it happened, but I now can understand why your people did not want to be here any longer." Sefjan said, "The calling of the dead never did happen, otherwise my ancestors would have witnessed it. But we still decided to remain in the sea."

Suddenly, an underwater noise started to project from the sea. Sefjan said, "I am sorry, but we must leave, Oakley. It was very nice to meet you. You are

our only friend on the surface. If you ever need us, use this to summon us."
One of the Kulvani handed Sefjan a horn that was carved from a large
seashell. Sefjan placed the horn in the sand and smiled at Oakley before
turning around and walking into the tunnel with the others. Oakley called out,
"Before we meet next, I will make things here better!" Oakley walked up to
the horn and lifted it; his first monumental achievement.

Simona Molino

Chapter Fifty-Eight: A Dream of Good Fortune

Ria Falune, Daraz - The night was quiet, and Ria roamed aimlessly through the Halls of Absolute. She did not know why, but she could sense something of importance was beckoning her. The Halls were unattended by the guards and there were no candles lighting the rooms. Ria quickly walked through the halls until she entered the Tomb of Kings and Queens, which was lit with torches. She saw a man and a woman standing across the room. Ria called out, "Hello!", but there was no response. Ria walked closer to them but could only see their backs. She came closer until she could tell that the man and woman looked a lot like her parents. Startled, Ria said, "Mother, father, is that you?" The two people turned around and Ria was amazed to see her parents looking back at her with glowing red eyes.

Ria jerked her body as she awoke from her dream; a dream of good fortune, Ria hoped. She stayed in bed and thought to herself, 'What does it mean? Am I going to see my parents again?' Ria peeked outside and saw that it was still pitch black. One of the sages was sitting outside the cave and said, "Up early today I see. We should get started. Rashine lo favan?" Ria responded, "The rubies of Torust. Before we start, I just had a dream I want to ask you about." Begra said, "What was it?" Ria said, "I was in the Halls of Absolute and roamed into the Tomb of Kings and Queens where I saw my parents with red eyes. Does this mean I will see them again?" Begra said, "If you successfully call on the dead, I believe you will be reunited with them again. But I should warn you, they will not be the same way that you always knew them. They will know who you are, but mentally there will be differences."

Ria said, "Thank you, I do hope I can see them again. I want them to be proud of my leadership more than anything. I want them to witness what I have done for the kingdom. Their legacy was more than just a sex addict and a jewel fanatic, like my siblings." The sage nodded and said, "We all will be proud of you. Our people were meant to rule, and you will lead us. But first, you must finish your studies." Ria asked, "How much longer do you expect that I will need to be here?" Begra tilted his head slightly from side to side with uncertainty and said, "About one month." Ria said, "One more thing before we begin. I need to write a message for Haigar in Torust." Begra said, "Go ahead, I will get us some breakfast and tea." Ria said, "Thank you", before picking up a quill and a piece of parchment. Ria knew exactly what she wanted to accomplish in the next few months. She started writing:

> *Greetings Haigar,*
>
> *I hope all preparations are going smoothly in Torust. I will be here for about another month, but I will write another message instructing you when to come for me. With my studies coming to a close, I will pursue the calling upon my return to Torust. In the meantime, I have some military plans I need you to act on. You must guide the military west and invade some towns outside our kingdom of Torust for their resources and numbers. Some of these men we will use in the fight against Gofon and they will not have a choice but to fight for us or die. In addition to our military, we will have these slave fighters and the awoken to fight against Gofon. Hopefully, we do not need to use our military extensively in case we get attacked from elsewhere. Please follow these instructions once you receive this and let me know what progress you make. Together, we can make Torust the powerful kingdom it should be.*
>
> *Sincerely, Your queen,*
>
> *Ria Falune*

Ria dropped the quill and sealed the parchment shut. She smiled and thought about how all her hard work studying and discovering the meaning of the jewels was going to transition into something no one could expect. Ria thought to herself, 'Call it luck, or call it success, but the whole world is not going to see this coming.'

Chapter Fifty-Nine: The Westward Expansion

Haigar Loseef, Torust - Haigar looked at his map with deep concentration until he heard Peter Fardine call out, "What is this I hear of you moving the military west?" Haigar looked up and saw Peter Fardine approaching him in the Halls of Absolute. Haigar said, "Orders of the queen. We are to siege and capture several towns outside our kingdom. No kingdom rules them today, so there will be no retaliation." Peter said, "You are preparing for battle and did not even want to mention this to me? I have been training with your men for weeks now." Haigar nodded and said, "They are required to fight, you are not. I would never ask you to fight for us after your recent injury." Peter said, "Everything I have done recently has been to prepare myself to return to combat. Now, will you let me join you later?" Haigar smiled and said, "Only if you fight as one of my most respected military leaders." Peter smiled back and said, "It would be my honor."

Haigar, with a serious look, said, "Before you take on this new role, I want to warn you. Full on war is ahead. What happens today is just the start. Be prepared for developments to escalate quickly. Next, we will be at war with Gofon." Peter said, "If war is ahead, so be it. I was born and raised as a fighter for Torust. What I will never understand is a man who refuses to push himself out of his comfort zone and into the realm of challenge. The military has now been adequately trained. I respect you as a military general and if war is coming, I know, that we are fully prepared. I will go get ready. When are we heading west?" Haigar replied, "Sundown. We will likely strike the towns around midnight when the people are asleep." Peter said, "Okay, I will meet you by the west gate. I am going to go speak with my son before we have to go."

Peter left the Halls of Absolute and made his way home. Peter called out, "Cazier, are you home?" There was silence as Peter went to his room. On a table, he noticed the necklace his wife wore for many years. Peter picked up the necklace and held it close to his heart. After holding it there for a moment, he tossed it over his head and wore it in honor of his late wife. Peter got into his bed and closed his eyes until he could envision his late wife in bed with him. Peter dosed off and fell asleep for an hour until he awoke to the sound of the opening of the front door. Peter sat up and called out, "Cazier?"

Cazier responded, "Are you upstairs, father?" Peter said, "Yes, I am coming down." Peter walked to the base level of the house and hugged his son. Peter said, "I am going to fight today as one of Haigar's leaders. I should be back by tomorrow." Cazier said, "Are you sure you are ready for this again, father? Last time you almost died. I don't want to be without you too." Peter said, "Do not worry, I am sharper than ever. I have been training for a while now with Haigar. I am not the least bit worried." Cazier asked, "Why will you be fighting?" Peter replied, "That does not concern you, but you should not worry. It is not war." Cazier said, "I noticed your armor on the table, how long have you been using that?" Peter said, "The queen gifted me that set about five years ago; it has been very reliable in combat. Anyway, I am going to try to fall back asleep for a while and then I will be on my way. I will see you soon, son." Cazier said, "You better be back here tomorrow, father." Peter said, "Do not worry, take care son."

Peter awoke from another nap and ate one last meal before dressing in his armor and heading out to meet up with the military units. Peter was used to being more of a duelist than a soldier in the military. He had competitive fights with the most talented in Torust under his belt, but he knew that the risks in battle were far more uncertain and not in his control. You could get blindsided by an enemy or even hit by an arrow from afar. But somehow Peter encouraged and emboldened himself to fight alongside Haigar in the upcoming battle.

Peter approached the west gate where a few hundred soldiers were preparing to depart. Peter walked up to Haigar and said, "I am going to need a horse." Haigar whistled and a stable master came walking over holding a rope with a horse. Haigar said, "I did not forget about you, that one is yours."

The horse whinnied as Peter hopped on its back. Peter sat on his horse alongside Haigar as they watched the rest of the men preparing for the trip. Haigar called out, "The sun is going to set soon, we must be on our way! Finish up your preparations!" The soldiers started to hasten their efforts.

Haigar leaned close to Peter and said, "The real loyalty will be revealed today, you realize that, right?" Peter, with a confused look, asked, "What do you mean?" Haigar said, "None of these fights will be fair. These towns will be outnumbered and overwhelmed, and many women and children will be in the way. Some of our men will not have it in them to cut them down if they do not surrender and swear loyalty to Torust. That is the thing with war, all your morals and values have to be left at home." Peter said, "You are right, many of these men will learn a lot about themselves today and will struggle with their own loyalties to Torust. They will learn how much they care for their wives and children. Despite most of their training efforts being based on combat, it remains to be seen how they will react in this situation."

After waiting a moment, Haigar rode through the gate with Peter and the few hundred men following his lead. The men rode west of Torust as the daylight started to dim. The men rode quietly; not all of them had rested as much as Peter and the darkness kept them on alert. The desert terrain slowly became grassier as they pushed farther west.

A few hours passed before they saw the torch flames at a town in the distance. Haigar commanded his men to split into two units and hit the town from different sides. Haigar led one unit to the left and Peter led the other soldiers to the right. After a brief moment, Haigar shouted, "All in, attack!" Both units swarmed the town from different sides. The few guards put up a futile defense as hundreds of soldiers came charging in.

Some men came out of their residences with weapons but were instantly struck down. Others came out with women and children and surrendered. Haigar yelled, "Bow and surrender before Torust if you wish to live!" Additional residents of the town started to come out and surrender. One man came out crying as he saw his family running in the distance toward the desert.

Haigar halted the fighting of his men as the townspeople had stopped any form of resistance. All of the town's residents were gathered together and Haigar called out, "The men will fight for us and the women and children will swear allegiance to us or you will all die here in your homeland tonight. We want your resources and your aid. In time, you will be a part of the greatest kingdom in Lodas. Until then, prove yourselves." Peter, unscathed from fighting, spectated as the hopeless men, women and children sat and listened on the ground. Peter did not have much sympathy, particularly for the men; he knew several more towns would face the same treatment that night.

Chapter Sixty: The Scales of Resistance

Liava Pontas, Dragon Lair - Liava stared in shock as the red dragon started shrieking and stretching its body until some of its scales started to tear off its body. She did not know what was going on nor what to do. The red dragon continued to flex its body as its expanding figure shed more of the scales. Some of the scales fell onto the ground and some hung from the side of the dragon. Liava walked over to the red dragon and touched its face, checking to make sure it was okay. The dragon appeared to be healthy and normal so Liava went around the dragon and pulled off any hanging scales. She gathered all the scales and put them into a pile. She looked back at the red dragon and noticed the areas where it no longer had any scales.

Liava realized that the dragon's shedding of its scales was due to the maturing of its body as the dragon was outgrowing the old scales from its juvenile years. Liava smiled as her favorite dragon was getting older, just like herself. Liava looked down at her own skin and noticed that it was getting rougher as she lived in the wild with the dragons. All the dirt and sleeping on rough surfaces allowed her body to adapt to the harsher conditions. Liava knew that she too was maturing. She could tell she was getting wiser and smarter as she could apply the foundational concepts she learned in her village to her present situation. She recalled shearing a sheep and using its wool to make a piece of warm clothing. Liava turned back to the pile of red dragon scales and knew that something could be done with them.

Liava slowly stepped closer to the pile of scales, her eyes locked on them the whole time. She bent over and picked one of them up. The scale felt very thick but was light in weight. As she was actively preparing herself mentally and physically for combat in the near future, she considered the potential benefits of using these scales as armor. Liava also thought, 'Wearing these scales would extend my bond with my dragon. We would share the same scales, and the dragon may never shed them again.'

After gathering some wood logs, Liava took out her flute and commanded the red dragon to use its fire to light the pile of wood. She held the scale over the fire for a moment. She then knelt and placed the scale closer to the flames. She looked in awe as the flames were bouncing off the scale to the sides. The scale was totally resistant to the flames.

Liava knew then and there that the scale's resistance to fire and other dangerous elements could help further her overall mission. Liava pulled the scale out of the flames and laid it down on the ground. She carefully placed two fingers on the scale. To her amazement, the scale was only slightly warm; not damaged nor scolding hot from the intense heat. Liava took her dagger and stabbed it into the scale to test the strength of the scale. To her surprise, the dagger barely pierced the scale. Liava grabbed her pile of hemp rope and cut it into thinner pieces.

Liava went over to the pile of dragon scales and began gathering the pieces she was going to use for armor. As she looked through the scales, she noticed one large scale that could be used to make a good piece of armor for her chest. She picked that scale up and placed it aside. She kept looking and noticed two long scales from the dragon's arms. Liava tilted her head and realized that these pieces could be used to make good leg pieces. She picked them up and placed them on the side next to the scale for the chest. Liava kept selecting scales until she had a piece for every part of her body, from head to toe.

Liava started working on the scale to use as a chest piece as she used her dagger to cut away any loose areas of the scale. She used her dagger and a sharp wooden stick to make holes for the rope to go through and then inserted the rope to tighten and tie the armor. Because of the strength of each scale, Liava spent hours working on them until she had completely constructed all the pieces of the dragon scale armor. She started putting on the armor one by one and used the ropes to tighten and tie the armor when necessary. After a short time, Liava was covered in red dragon scales all over her body.

Liava walked up to the dragons and could tell that they were intrigued by her new look. The dragons started smelling Liava as she said, "I am one of you now. She rubbed up against the red dragon and said, "Thank you for sharing." Liava walked away from the dragons who were still looking at her with excitement. She walked directly in front of the fire and paused. She nervously looked at the fire and said, "I must test the armor to be sure." She sighed and stepped into the fire. After a few seconds, she smiled and then laughed as she started dancing around in the flames. The dragon scale armor had resisted the flames just as she had hoped. Liava felt invincible as she looked at her dragons through the smoke of the flames. Beyond the smoke, she could envision many dragons. Not just three, not several, but a tribe of dragons.

Chapter Sixty-One: The Stealthful Aim

Searleone Vallas, Skyrock - Searleone walked around the relic room of the sanctuary in Skyrock. In the back of the room, he noticed a large sheet covering what he thought he was looking for.

Searleone walked up to the large object and lifted the sheet off of it. It was, in fact, the large bell he was looking for. Searleone ran his fingers against the sides of the sturdy bell. The bell was older than Searleone and he knew it came from a period that most of the mages at Skyrock were not familiar with. The bell was timeless and, like many of the items in the relic room, had been used across many generations. Searleone left the covering off the bell and walked out of the relic room. Searleone called over Voron who was reading on the other side of the sanctuary halls. Voron placed a feather in the book and walked over to Searleone.

Voron said, "How are you doing, Searleone?" Searleone replied, "Great, can you get some of the mages to set up the bell on the balcony outside?" Voron said, "Yes, of course. If I may ask, what is the new purpose of the bell?" Searleone said, "There is a girl riding around on a dragon in the skies. I want to meet her, and I believe ringing the bell throughout the sky is a good way of doing so." Voron said, "Interesting, I hope to see this for myself. I will get that set up for you before the end of the day." Searleone said, "I appreciate it, Voron."

Searleone walked off as Voron went to instruct the mages. Voron walked into a room with the younger mages and said, "I need four of you to assist me." Four of the young mages stood and started to follow Voron. Voron led the men into the relic room and told them to bring the bell to the balcony.

When the mages finished moving the bell to the balcony, Voron decided to go to his room as something had been on his mind. After returning to his room, Voron sat on his bed and started to think. Voron wondered, 'Did Rinci really commit the crimes that Searleone had accused him of or was Searleone framing him? What motive could Rinci have really had for infecting the town? Is it just a coincidence that Searleone gave the identified brown robe to Rinci?'

Voron knew things just did not seem to add up and no one else at the sanctuary knew how sly Searleone could be. As he was also the mage closest with him, Voron considered it his duty to bring justice to Skyrock if it was necessary. Voron thought, 'The motives of Searleone remain unclear; he offers little explanation for the direction he is taking the mages in and what he envisions for their future.' Voron was starting to come to the conclusion that the leadership of his people was possibly being corrupted and for once in his many years following Searleone, he would take some investigative measures. The key was investigating with a stealthful aim.

Chapter Sixty-Two: Power and Paranoia

Roy Syssian, Council Chambers of Gofon - "So, what brings you to Gofon to speak with us, King Syssian?", council member John Pittus asked. Roy stood up and said, "King Denvion, council of Gofon, thank you for welcoming me here today. I know this is our first meeting and I want to say that I hope our future together is bright as we strengthen our relations. Over these past several months, I have filled the roles of king and gladiator and there is no doubt that a large amount of power came along with that. With this power came paranoia. Not paranoia of being killed, but paranoia of who to trust. Some people look up to you as a role model and a leader, but others look at you as an opportunity, an opportunity to help themselves by taking advantage of you. The reason I am here today is because I have grown paranoid, or should I say, may have grown paranoid.

After marrying Leora a few months ago, her father, the king of Tyrades, has attempted to influence me to pursue his interests. I will not delve into what exactly that means, but I must warn you, you have left Kip Denvion there the better half of a year. I know because I have seen him there multiple times; I have even trained with him. I do not know what they are planning to do with him, but he seems like a good kid and the future king of Gofon. Therefore, I knew how important it is for me to come and bring you this information."

King Denvion said, "We must get Kip back here at once. He was supposed to be back already. Timothy, please get some men to retrieve him." Timothy nodded and said, "I will assemble a party immediately." John Pittus said, "Thank you, Roy. You have done well coming here to us with this information. Do we have to worry about King Hasting coming for us?" Roy replied, "No, I do not think so. He did not say he had any intentions of attacking Gofon, at this time anyway. Kip has been seeing a girl while he has been there too. Her name is Julia; that could also be the reason why he has stayed there longer."

Jack Haxon asked, "Is the king trying to motivate Kip to become a gladiator in the future?" Roy said, "Yes, that I know for sure." Jack asked, "If you had a son, would you trust leaving him in Tyrades with the king and the gladiators." Roy replied, "Probably not; too much influence." Jack said, "We must all keep an eye on the boy and Tyrades. They are trying to manipulate our potential future leader." King Denvion said, "Once he is back home, I will likely not let him return to Tyrades. I will handle Kip, do not worry."

King Denvion asked Roy, "Have you heard of the growing tension we have had with Torust?" Roy said, "I have heard rumors of it, but do you care to elaborate?" Phillip said, "When the illness broke out in our kingdom several months ago, Torust did not support us in any way; they did not even respond to our request to address the problem together. They were the only kingdom we contacted since the illness was only within the lands that affected our kingdoms. Then we heard reports of them strengthening their military. When the illness spread more to their side, we did not offer them the cure. Their towns are still suffering as we speak. You can call it immoral and that is fine, but I see it how I see it and they deserved it."

Roy said, "It is not my place to judge." Phillip continued, "Our latest reports say that they invaded a number of neutral towns out west in between Torust and Sterafia, but closer to Torust. Some of those citizens have turned up in some of the towns west of here already. It is clear that war is coming. We are relying on our brute force, resources, and allies to win the war. We hope that you and the other kingdoms see them as the aggressor and will form an alliance with us." Roy said, "It seems that way. I will definitely remember that when the time comes to make a decision, but, for now, you can expect to receive my support."

Phillip said, "Thank you, King Syssian. Together, we can maintain peace in the kingdoms of Lodas. In a few days, we are having our annual royal masquerade party to celebrate my anniversary as king of Gofon. You should stay a few days and attend; you can even have Leora come in to join you. It is my favorite event of the year." Roy said, "That does sound very appealing, but I have some things to attend to in Biros. Perhaps next year. I will save the date and do my best to make sure I do not have other things going on. I hope you all celebrate wonderfully. With all of the time you have been king you deserve to."

Jack Haxon walked over to Roy and said, "It is a shame you will miss it, the council and many of the king's friends and family will be there. But a king must do what is important for his kingdom. I hope to see you again soon,

Roy, and hopefully under better circumstances." Roy said, "I will be on my way, but send a letter or a messenger if you need me."

Chapter Sixty-Three: The Distraction of Love

Kip Denvion, Tyrades - Kip sat down on the ground on the side of the arena. He was catching his breath when James Farenter said, "You are getting better and more powerful, especially as you are getting older and are maturing." Kip said, "Thank you, it is a thrilling experience." James said, "You are going back to Gofon soon, right? We should train a couple of more times before you leave." Kip said, "Yes, I have about a week left, and gladly. I hope to continue training in Gofon when I get back." James said, "Keep at it, and remember, you are welcome back here whenever you want." Kip stood up to leave and said, "Thank you, I am going to go for now, see you soon."

Kip departed from the arena and walked into the marketplace to grab some fresh fruit. He took a big bite out of an apple and carried the rest of the fruit with him as he headed toward Julia's room to surprise her. Walking through the marketplace equipped with his armor was an empowering feeling for Kip. He always received lots of attention as it was rare to own expensive armor like his.

Once he got to Julia's front door, he took one last bite of the apple and heaved it off to the side. Kip knocked on the door and waited for her to greet him. Kip heard a subtle commotion and scuffling from her room. Kip walked over to the side window and could barely see past the curtain. Kip lifted his sword up and used it to push the curtain to the side. Kip's eyes shot wide open in disgust as he saw Julia and another man, both naked, attempting to quickly put their clothes back on. Kip turned around in disbelief; he could not believe what he had just seen. He felt crushed, embarrassed, and mostly angry.

Kip went back to the door and used his strong plate boot to kick it in. Julia shouted, "I am sorry, Kip. I screwed up." Kip said, "Damn well you did, both of you did", as he lifted his sword. The man said, "You will be hung if you kill me, I am a noble here, I support the king and the gladiators." Kip laughed and said, "Do you know who I am? I am the future king of Gofon, the future of Lodas. I am above whatever rules you might think exist here."

Kip menacingly stepped closer as the man picked up a vase and threw it at Kip. Kip leaned to the side and evaded the vase as it went flying over his shoulder crashing into the wall and shattering into many small pieces. Kip rushed forward and thrust his sword deep into the stomach of the man. Julia yelled as she backed up into the corner of the room. Kip released the sword and the man dropped to his knees as his hands desperately tried to cover the gaping wound.

The tears started to rush from Julia's face as Kip came closer to her. Kip said, "So, I guess you just like to use people it appears. The future king of Gofon, a noble with wealth; I wonder who else there might be." Julia shook her head and said, "No one, I swear. I love you, Kip. You have to trust me on that." Kip looked at the ground for a moment in disappointment and replied, "The king of Biros was right. At my age, in my current situation, love is nothing more than a distraction. Goodbye Julia." Kip thrust his sword into Julia's stomach before taking it out and doing it two more times. Julia gasped in pain as she looked at Kip in her last few moments. Kip ran his hand through her hair and shut her eyes. Kip said, "Thank you for teaching me the real meaning of love."

Kip took the bed sheet and wiped as much of the blood off his sword and armor as he could before leaving. Once he got outside, he made his way toward the stables by the city gates. Kip tossed the stable boy a small pouch of gold and said, "Give me the fastest horse in the stables." The boy said, "Are you sure you want to give this much gold for it?" Kip said, "Consider it a favor, but please be quick."

Within a moment, the boy came back with a large, muscular, brown horse with a white stripe down its head. Kip mounted the horse and looked down at the boy and asked, "What is your name?" The boy said, "Caden Bert." Kip said, "Thank you, Caden. I will not forget your help on this day." Kip rode off through the gates as he made his way for Gofon. Caden looked on as Kip sped off into the distance. He was not exactly sure why Kip rewarded him so handsomely, but he was happy to have the gold.

Chapter Sixty-Four: The King's Masquerade

Phillip Denvion, Gofon - "You look marvelous, Tanya", Phillip said. His wife replied, "Thank you, I see you finally got a new surcoat." Phillip said, "Yes, it took the tailor two whole months of work. I have always had a thing for exquisite costumes, especially after being able to wear them for acting. Most nobles prefer flashy designs and colors, but I do not believe that is what it should be about. When you wear clothing, you take on the personality of the attire; it is not just about standing out. I want my clothing to put me in a specific mood." Tanya asked, "So what mood are you going for with this outfit?" Phillip said, "Celebratory. This is the one day of the year that I reflect on my kingship and the progress and opportunity I have created for Gofon and Lodas. Keep in mind, you have had a huge influence on me, and I love you for that." Tanya came closer to Phillip and kissed him before saying, "Let's go, you need to set the mood for the party." Phillip placed his golden mask over his face and said, "Don't forget about your mask, darling. It is a masquerade party after all." The queen walked over to her dresser and picked up her red mask covered with black feathers and placed it around her face.

As the king and queen entered the royal dining room, Fayna started shaking some tambourines as a few other musicians played alongside her. All the attendees wore masks of their own and stood up from their tables and erupted with applause for the king and queen.

The king and queen walked further into the room and, after everyone sat down, the king said, "Thank you all for coming to celebrate my favorite festival of the year. Putting the celebration aside, I have made the well-being of our kingdom my life's purpose. Although my kingship started off unexpectedly, I have upheld my family's legacy of respect and care for our kingdom and its citizens. Over the past year, we have faced and handled a major conflict; the illness that took many lives. Thanks to the late Jol Parantis, we were able to find a cure. That was something that none of us were capable of. But even Jol himself would not have succeeded without the resources and support of our people, military, and kingdom. What I have learned over my time as king is that unity brings out the best in people, especially our people. Tonight, this week, and this year I ask you to unite with those around you and challenge each other to make Gofon stronger and bolder. And you can start by pouring those around you an ale!"

The attendees laughed and smiled as the music continued with an upbeat melody that started the dancing. The king walked over to his daughter, Fayna, and with a smile said, "I want to hear some of your new melodies tonight." Fayna said, "Sure, I liked your speech, father. Why isn't Kip here tonight?" Phillip said, "He was supposed to be, but I guess he stayed in Tyrades a bit longer. Hopefully, he will be home soon."

The king grabbed some red wine from a servant and walked over to Timothy Milton across the room. Timothy gave the king a hug and a pat on the shoulder and said, "Cheers to another successful year." The king said, "Thank you, I came to thank you for your service. Things would not be as smooth around here without you. I am proud to say that you are my best friend in addition to being my advisor." Timothy said, "True friendship and loyalty are hard to come by. With you, I always saw it as a mutual respect." Both men lifted their chalices and drank in unison.

Jack Haxon danced with a young woman as he twirled her around a few times and lifted his arms in the air with excitement. The woman smiled at Jack with joy despite not knowing the man behind the mask. Jack said, "Excuse me for a moment, charming lady." From the corner of his eye, Jack saw the king in the back of the room talking with Timothy. Jack subtly walked closer to the king. The king nodded to Timothy and started to walk in Jack's direction.

Once the king was within arm's reach, Jack turned around and said, "Hello, my king." Phillip turned and looked into the eyes of the masked man. He started to tremble with uneasiness as something behind Jack's eyes was unsettling. Jack said, "You did well. But your time as leader is no longer a reality." Jack's eyes gaped as he started to shake a bell from the inside of his top. The king felt nauseous and, as he attempted to get away from the unknown figure, he started to lose his balance with each step he took backward. The whole room heard the loud thud as the king fell over a wooden table.

Jack slipped away before anyone knew what had happened. Someone shouted, "The king, he has fallen!" All the guards came running over to assist and ensure the safety of the king. The first guard that got to the king knelt over him and said, "Are you alright, my king?" The king replied, "Yes, just a bit dizzy. There is a man here who stopped me and looked at me for a moment. He did something to me, but I am not sure what or how he did it. You must go find him, quickly."

Jack Haxon lifted a torch from behind the drapes in the corner of the room. He held the edge of it against a lit candle until the torch was emblazoned. He looked at the room one last time and smiled. He dropped the torch onto the drapes and ran toward the unguarded entranceway. The curtains were quickly engulfed with fire as Jack had previously covered them with flammable materials. Immediately, the fire spread across other curtains and to nearby tables Jack had also covered the legs of the tables with flammable materials.

Jack quickly ran out of the room and closed the door behind him. Just as he planned, no guards were there to stop him as they left the doors unattended to assist the fallen king. Jack lifted a heavy wooden plank and locked the door in place behind metal bindings. With that locked in, and the other door blocked off by the towering flames, no one was expected to get out. Jack took off his mask and walked out of the royal halls without being recognized.

On the inside of the royal dining hall, as the flames were quickly spreading, the attendees were in a state of panic. The guards lifted the king and attempted to get him to an exit. Some of the attendees looked for water, but there was only a small amount of it gathered for the party and was not enough to help in extinguishing the flames.

Fayna and Tanya ran over to Phillip and the guards desperately seeking help. Tanya said, "There has to be a way out of here, right?!" One of the guards said, "The main entrance is locked shut." Another guard said, "And we have no chance to get out through the other door. There is no way out." Fayna started crying as she began to understand the reality of the dire situation. Nothing her mother could tell her would settle her down after hearing the tragic news from the guard. The king watched as Rus Trenode kept desperately bashing his body into the main door that stood unshaken.

Phillip, who was still confused and fatigued, said, "Make my wife and daughter your priority. That is a direct order." A guard said, "Yes, my king. But I do not believe we will get out without someone opening the doors from the outside. We must move to the furthest corner where the flames will extend to last." The guards moved the royal family to the corner and waited in horror as the fire continued to fill the room. The screams of pain started to echo and overtake the screams of fear.

Before long, the fire had killed everyone in the room in front of the guards and royal family. A guard said, "I am sorry, my king. We have failed you." The king hugged his wife and daughter and said, "I love you both. I could have died alone of old age, but here I am dying with both of you in my arms." The fire finally covered the entire room as it engulfed the king and his family, mere mortals to the power of the flames.

Chapter Sixty-Five: The Guest from Savan

Renga Khonzas, Sterafia - The mist of the warm water and the cool air filled the hot spring. Renga breathed in and out as his breath also turned to mist. Renga had arranged it so that the hot spring was part of his official residence. It was a luxury he very much enjoyed. The only other people allowed there were those who he invited to use it. The king relaxed as the warm water seeped into his tense body. He looked up into the dark night sky and gazed at the bright stars shimmering from lifespans away. Renga could remember being a little kid and looking up at them, wondering what purpose they could serve in the vast and complex world he lived in.

Renga's brief moment of peace and seclusion was interrupted as one of his guards entered the outdoor corridor and said, "My king, a large group of outsiders has approached our northern gate. They come from various towns to the north, some very far away. The military of Torust came and raided their towns, taking their resources and men to use for battle. Should we let them into the city?" Renga replied, "Torust attacking neutral towns? That is unheard of. Yes, please let them in and hold them by the gate. Give them food and clothing. I will head over there myself shortly." The king stood up from the hot spring and quickly dried himself off to stay warm. The king walked back to his room and switched into his normal attire before leaving for the northern gate.

From a distance, the king could hear the guards questioning the large group of outsiders. The king walked up to some of his guards and said, "Be on high alert." The king walked up to a young, dark-skinned woman who was shaking from the cold. Renga could tell by her attire, a light top layer with thin pants and sandals, that she came from a town so far away that warm weather and sand were part of the natural environment. The king extended his greetings and then asked, "Can you explain to me what happened?" As she faced him, Renga was surprised by her genuine beauty. Despite trekking through the rigorous conditions over multiple days, Renga saw the exquisite beauty in her. The lady said, "The men of Torust, they came in the night and destroyed our towns like savages. I would have never expected that from the military of a kingdom. Now I do not have a home, none of us do. They killed my mother and now I have no family left."

The king could tell she was telling the truth and knew she was a strong-hearted woman. After losing her last family member, she journeyed through rough conditions just to live and start a new life. The king knew these people needed help and saw this as a new opportunity for Sterafia. The king looked over the woman's shoulder to get an idea of how many individuals had arrived. The king asked, "About how many of you are there?" The lady replied, "Roughly fifty if I had to guess." The king noticed she was still shaking from the cold and said, "Here, put this on", as he took off his large cape of bear fur. The king told the guards who were nearest to him, "Let them into the city, make them at home in the tents for now and make sure they are taken care of." The guards nodded and went to inform the gate guards.

The king turned to the lady and said, "I did not get to ask, what is your name?" The lady replied, "Sakia Habash, from the town of Savan. How about you?" The king said, "Renga Khonzas, I am the king of Sterafia. I invite you to dine with me tonight if you would like." Sakia, although greatly fatigued, replied, "That would be great." The king said, "Follow me, I will make sure you are able to clean up and get some proper clothing before then." Sakia followed the king into his royal keep and the king called over one of his servants. The servant asked, "What can I help you with, my king?" Renga said, "Take this woman and get her cleaned and clothed before dinner." The servant nodded and looked at Sakia to follow. Sakia took off the cloak and handed it to the king as she said, "Thank you, King Renga."

The king waited at the dinner table for over an hour wondering why Torust had attacked the towns to the north. The king heard a knock on the door and Sakia entered the room. She was completely clean with fresh clothes as the king instructed. Renga said, "Please, take a seat." Sakia sat down and said, "Thank you, for everything. I know I might be a bit dreary, but I just need time to recover from the recent horrific events." Renga said, "No issues from me, I hope I can help you move on from it for a short time. I want you to feel at home here in Sterafia where hopefully you can find that there still is some good in this world." Sakia said, "I can tell that you mean well, you and your kingdom." The servant brought out chicken soup to the table for Sakia and the king. The king said, "Please have some, you probably haven't had much to eat in days." Sakia said, "Only a couple bites."

Sakia took a couple of spoonfuls and said, "Can I ask you something, King Renga?" Renga said, "Sure, what is it?" Sakia said, "In a kingdom with mostly white-skinned natives, how did you become the king?" Renga placed his food down and said, "That is why I love this kingdom, they do not judge based on ethnicity or legacy, they look for true talent and leadership. The last king was dying and did not wish to pass the kingship down to his son because he believed the kingship should be earned not inherited. His son was our former military leader, Damien Nodon, who passed away a few months ago. He was a great man, one of my all-time favorite people. If it were not for me, he would have been king and alive right now. He did not even dislike or resent me for taking it from him."

Sakia asked, "How did you take it from him and become king?" Renga said, "The dying king held a competition in which all five invited contestants had to hunt an animal in the wild in the middle of winter. All we could use was a single arrow with a bow and a short weapon. I chose a small axe. In order to win, we had to kill the largest animal and present its hide to the king. The largest hide was the deciding factor and the winner would replace the king upon his death. Only one animal hide could be used. Two of the men died trying to kill wolves, another brought back a fox hide, and Damien brought back the hide with fur of the largest wolf I have ever seen. He even lost a finger and badly injured his arm during the fight. Although he did not win, everyone, including myself, had enormous respect and admiration for that brave man's efforts.

I found myself in the direst situation of my life. In the harsh winter conditions, I had ventured to parts of the northwest that most hunters would never dream of going. I knew I needed to do something bold, something daring to locate a winning prize. After traveling for a day and a half, I came across a massive black bear that was in the middle of eating its prey. I readied my bow and my only arrow and focused as I braced for the fight. I released the arrow and struck the beast right in its upper back and it roared in anger. It turned around and started to charge at me intending to make me its next prey. I pulled out my axe and waited as it came at me. The bear stood and swung its claws at me, but I ducked and swiped my axe into the bear's right hind leg. The bear turned around again, and I waited for it to attack before doing the same thing. My plan was to wear it down. When I tried to do it for the third time, the bear knocked me over and swiped its claws right into my bicep." Renga pulled up his sleeve and showed Sakia the large scars he had from the bear's claws.

Renga continued, "The bear tried to bite me, but I punched it in the nose with my other arm and quickly scrambled away. The nose is a very sensitive area and hitting it there saved my life. I tried to regain my composure as quickly as I could and decided to charge the bear before it could recover and attack again. I struck my axe into the side of its neck and that was enough to send the bear to the ground. I swung the axe into its neck a few more times until it lay dead in the snow. I skinned the beast and I knew I would be the next king if I could survive making it back to Sterafia. I wear the fur of the bear on my back every day as a reminder to myself of what I have accomplished and out of respect for the bear that I found myself having to kill. That is how I became the king of Sterafia."

Chapter Sixty-Six: The Welcome and the Goodbye

Oakley Nodon, Katorian Settlement - Oakley looked into Snowstorm's eyes and said, "I never knew you would be this loyal. You are my best friend." The tiger started to lick Oakley's hand as he went to pet it. Oakley started trying to pet the tiger without letting Snowstorm lick his hand and it turned into a friendly game between the two.

Swida entered the igloo and said, "Hello Oakley, I brought you a gift since it is your last day in Katorian and I really enjoyed spending time with you while you were here. I want to welcome you to Katorian as one of us as I say goodbye to you; you are welcome back any time." Oakley stood up and said, "What is it?" Swida revealed a large fur jacket with a hood that looked like the one the natives wore. Oakley said, "I love it, thank you, Swida. You have become very special to me."

Oakley started to try on the coat and felt the soft fur against his neck and face. Oakley asked, "What animal fur is this?" Swida said, "Rabbit, just like most of ours. I am glad you like it." Oakley pulled the hood over his head and bent over toward Snowstorm who started to sniff his new attire.

Swida asked, "Are you going to spend some time here today before you leave?" Oakley said, "Yes, I want to spend more time with you. He looked her into her eyes and came closer until their lips locked. Oakley said, "I should have done that sooner. Although I am leaving today, I will be back soon. I need to tell my people about the Kulvani and your people." Swida asked, "How do you know they will like us?" Oakley said, "I know the king on a personal level, and I know he will support me."

"Would you ever take a trip to Sterafia with me?", Oakley asked. Swida said, "Yes, but next time, I am not ready to leave Katorian yet." Oakley said, "Next time I return, I want to introduce you to the Kulvani. They are very passive and need allies like your people." Swida said, "We are not as adventurous as you, but if you want me to meet them, I will do it. What did you learn from them?" Oakley replied, "They live in seclusion, yet are interested in our people and environment. The people from the kingdom of Torust have a dark history that scared them off a long time ago." Swida asked, "Where is Torust?" Oakley said, "It is a kingdom northeast of Sterafia and here."

Snowstorm stood up and took up most of the space in the igloo. Swida said, "He is becoming gigantic, how will you manage?" Oakley said, "We have up until now and we will continue to be fine." Swida said, "It is amazing to see how you have domesticated Snowstorm. A few months ago, our people spotted a family of tigers with the same coloring as his passing by." Oakley, with a surprised look, asked, "The white fur with black stripes?!" Swida said, "Yes". Oakley asked, "How many were there? Can you give me all the details?" Swida said, "I did not see them myself, but the men by the gates saw several tigers passing by heading east. There were two larger tigers and a few young ones that appeared to be several months old." Oakley said, "I cannot believe it, that had to have been Snowstorm's family. They are alive! Next time I return I have to look for them. Snowstorm deserves the opportunity to live with them or at least be reunited, otherwise it would be very selfish on my part."

Swida said, "You never told me the story of how you got him." Oakley said, "Well, his family was being chased by a large pack of wolves and feral people that acted like wolves. One of his parents dropped him and did not have time to risk going back for him. I was hunting that day and happened to be there at that time. Thank goodness I was because I was able to run to him to try to save him before the wolves and the feral people got to him. I grabbed him and climbed up a tree to safety until they all moved on. I kept him a secret in Sterafia for a few weeks until I told my father and the king."

Swida said, "Wow, you both deserve each other for a lifetime. I wish I had a companion like him." Oakley said, "I want you to venture with me to the east when I return. I want you to be a part of the journey to find his family." Swida said, "They might be dangerous though." Oakley said, "Living life without fear has been the best thing I have done; I feel free. I can take you away from here and you can share the adventure." Swida said, "I want to be with you and make you happy. When will you return?" Oakley said, "Give me several weeks and I will be back." Swida kissed Oakley and said, "I will be ready."

Chapter Sixty-Seven: Torust Reborn

Ria Falune, Halls of Absolute - "So how was your first night of sleep back at home?", Haigar asked the queen. Ria replied, "Excellent, you do not truly appreciate the comfort of your own bed until you spend months on a cot in a cave." Haigar said, "I am sure you are glad to be back. I am still surprised you were willing to do that for so long, but it says a lot about your dedication for our kingdom. When are you going to perform the ritual? I see you are already wearing the necklace." Ria replied, "At sundown, I want to celebrate tonight as we welcome our ancestors back into our kingdom. At that time, I will put on the ring."

Haigar said, "More reports of the illness have reached the city, it is still spreading. It might delay our plans to attack Gofon." Ria said, "That is fine, we will use the time to strategize precisely how we will approach the war with Gofon. "Now leave me alone for a bit as I need to keep practicing to ensure I speak the summoning words correctly." Haigar said, "As you wish, let me know if I can help."

Ria looked back down at the scroll with the words written in ancient Torustian that she had been studying for the calling. She carefully chanted each word with emphasis on pronunciation. Her time with the sages had prepared her more than she expected. Ria read through the lines a couple of more times until she knew that she was sufficiently prepared. Ria tilted her head and looked above at the figures with red eyes on the ceiling. Ria wanted to unleash her excitement, but she knew she had to try to stay composed. Besides, as only a couple of others knew that she was going to bring the figures back to life later that night and she wanted to keep her secret concealed as much as possible.

Ria walked back to her residence and spent the remainder of the afternoon in seclusion. As much as Ria tried to stay calm, as the time of the calling was drawing near, she became increasingly nervous and the thoughts of bringing the dead back to life began to overwhelm her. Ria did not eat; she sat quietly until the time came to prepare for the ritual.

Ria left her room and walked back to the Halls of Absolute. Once inside, she entered the Tomb of Kings and Queens, just as she had in her dream not so long ago. Ria took a lit torch from the wall and used it to light candles throughout the rest of the Tomb. She walked up to the tombs where her parents were buried and placed her hand on their names. She shed a single tear and said, "This is for both of you; the inspiration of my dreams."

Ria walked to the center of the room and took out the scroll and ring from her bag. Ria placed the ring on her finger and took a deep breath and exhaled before she started to chant the calling words in ancient Torustian. As she spoke, she could hear her words echo throughout the quiet and lifeless surroundings. As she progressed through the calling, the red rubies in her necklace and ring started to shimmer. She could hear distant voices returning her call, "Where are you?" "We have yearned for this." "How long has it been?" Ria ignored the voices and continued to chant the calling words. Ria chanted the final sentences loud and firm as she waited with much anticipation. The rubies had become vibrant red and, seconds later, the entire Tomb started to shake around her.

Ria could hear the movement of structures within the Tomb. She looked all around as tombs started to crack and break. Suddenly, her eyes caught the first glimpse of red eyes. An old king kicked the side of his tomb open with unnatural strength and started to make his way out of the tomb. Ria heard another tomb shatter on her other side and instantly looked over to it. She looked at her parents' tombs with much anticipation. Just as she expected, their tombs had begun to crumble. Her father, Tari Falune, and her mother, Jaci Falune, destroyed the side of their tombs and they waited for each other. The other kings and queens had already walked over to Ria and started to kneel before her. Ria had hardly noticed as she excitedly watched her parents slowly but surely make their way closer to her.

After several seconds, her parents also kneeled in front of her to show respect. Ria spoke out in ancient Torustian, "I have uncovered the hidden meaning behind the Halls of Absolute and summoned you all back to Torust to recreate the sovereign rule of Torust in Lodas. All of you have been here and ruled at some point in time. Your knowledge and expertise will be vital. Torust has been reborn."

Ria looked around and noticed many red eyes looking directly at her. The eyes were glimmering with red just like her rubies. None of the former kings or queens said a single word. Ria walked up to her parents and said, "Mother, father, please stand." As her parents stood, Ria impatiently started to hug both of them. Tari said, "We acknowledge what you have done. Your efforts and accomplishments have surpassed ours. You have honored our name for Torust." Jaci said, "We are proud of you, my dear daughter." Ria said, "I missed you both so much. Everything I did for Torust was for you. I am glad you could be here now, the proudest moment of my life and hopefully not the peak."

Ria called out, "Past rulers of Torust, please follow me and enter your city. It may have changed since you last saw it, but it is as good now as it was then, and we are only going to make it better." Ria walked out of the Tomb of Kings and Queens, which was now filled with broken tombs, and entered the halls. Haigar, Peter, and the rest of the people in the Halls looked on in amazement at the former leaders of Torust who stood alongside their queen.

From the city, the sound of screams started to echo. Ria called out, "Inform the people of the city that all is well. The Arisen are our allies and are here to help. All of you, go now." Ria looked out over the side of the halls that overlooked part of the city. In the distance, she could see a large cemetery where people were rising from their graves. Her summoning had worked, and she was now the Caller; the redness of her rubies shined bright.

Chapter Sixty-Eight: The Dark Warning

Liava Pontas, Dragon Lair - Liava wrapped the hemp harness around the red dragon as she prepared to depart for the first feeding trip of the day. Moments later the dragons ascended into the sky and soared through the air. The sensation of cool air blowing against her cheeks was second nature to Liava after months of flying with the dragons every day. Her hands pressed against the back of the red dragon as she looked to the side. The hard scales of the dragon were the only physical contact she had with another living being since she escaped from the attack on her village.

In the distance, Liava could see a large herd of sheep fleeing from something. Liava maneuvered the harness so the dragon knew to fly in that direction. Once the red dragon changed paths, the other dragons swiftly turned and followed behind the red dragon. Liava's eyes were locked on the fleeing sheep below. After flying closer, Liava realized that the sheep were being chased by two villagers with bows. Liava pulled on the harness to let the red dragon know she wanted to land to interrupt the attack. The red dragon started to descend, and the other dragons followed. The villagers stopped their chase as they were stunned by the sight of the incoming dragons. The red dragon landed first, about fifty feet away from the villagers, followed by the other dragons.

Liava called out, "What are you doing?" One of the men said, "Hunting for food and warm clothing for our village. How did you...?" Liava interrupted the man and said, "What village do you come from?" One of the men said, "The village of Tsirian. Have you heard of it?" Liava said, "Yes, I know who you are. Your people came and decimated my village. Now I see that you hunt on the very land that we preserved. If your people had not done this, I never would have met these dragons. Once I am done with you, I will make sure the rest of your people burn."

The two men turned around and started to run away out of desperation. Liava took out her flute and played the melody of flames. The red dragon started to run forward and then flapped its wings. The red dragon lifted off the ground and shook its head slightly as it prepared itself. The fire rushed out from the red dragon's mouth and its flames engulfed the villagers. The other dragons flew over and inspected the scene to ensure there was no further sign of life.

Liava hopped off the red dragon and walked over to the fried corpses. Smoke was coming off their burnt bodies. The bows they carried, and their clothes had disintegrated from the vast heat of the flames. Liava felt slightly guilty as this was her first killings, but knew these men were at least partially responsible for the death of her family. She also knew that there would be more to come.

Liava mounted the red dragon and said, "No more hunting on our lands." By expelling the hunters Liava found that she could manage to protect the animals just as had been done in her old village. The dragons and Liava ascended into the sky again as Liava looked back at the dark circle in the ground. Liava could tell the corpses were noticeable, but that did not matter. Hopefully, it would send a dark warning to whoever discovered it.

Chapter Sixty-Nine: The Threat from The South

Ryos Pontas, Village of Tsirian - "Ryos, wake up", Dasina said as she shook Ryos. Ryos opened his eyes and said, "What is it, I just went to take a nap." Dasina said, "Edgar asked me to come get you; I think you need to go out into the forest with him for something." Ryos stood up and said, "Let me go see what he needs."

Ryos grabbed his weapon and headed out to meet with Edgar. Ryos saw Edgar in the center of the village by the campfire. Edgar called out, "Ryos, there you are." Ryos replied, "Yes, sorry, I was just napping for a little while. What do you need me for?" Edgar said, "Two days ago, Wext and Meeran went out for a hunt, but they never returned. I like to give them a day in case they just get lost, but once it becomes two days, I get concerned. You, Treb, and I are going to go search for them." Ryos asked, "Which direction did they go?" Treb said, "They went to the south to hunt. It was on the land of your old village." Edgar said, "Precisely, that is why we want you to join us. You should know your way around there much better than us." Ryos said, "I can assist with navigating. Let us head out before it gets dark."

The three villagers left the village and started walking south in search of the two missing men. Ryos tightened the rope around his shoulders and neck, that held his cloak of white yeti fur in place." Edgar said, "That was the most vicious animal I have taken down in my life." Ryos asked, "Which?" Edgar replied, "The yeti, and you were there for it. You helped defeat the creature." Ryos said, "I did my part as did every villager there."

"Would any of the other villages ever attack us?", Ryos asked. Edgar said, "No, we all have good relations. The unification against Staga actually helped boost the relations among us. I just want you to know, I did not want to kill your family. They resisted our hunting objective and we knew what had to be done." Ryos nodded his head and said, "I have moved on. That was my childhood, now I am becoming a man."

Edgar asked, "You are approaching marriage age, do you think you will be happy with both of the girls?" Ryos said, "Yes, they have helped me transition to become a member of our village. I am starting to love them both very much." Edgar said, "That is great, I am happy for you. We have had some unusual casualties recently. We need to explore this territory and find a safe way to hunt for our food and clothing." Ryos said, "These are not hostile grounds, my ancestors fostered an environment where animals only had to fear for their predators. They had adapted to us and understood we would not harm them. I suppose the men just got lost."

Treb said, "I think we should walk up that hill over there. Perhaps, we will be able to see more of our surroundings." Edgar nodded and said, "Sure, let's not lose track of where we came from." Once they arrived at the top, Treb asked, "Did either of you bring any water?" Edgar grabbed a canteen bottle from his bag and handed it to him as he said, "Here, next time do not forget."

The men and Ryos looked down on the open field below. Edgar said, "Do you see anything?" Ryos looked around until his eyes caught a glimpse of something dark in the field far out. Ryos said, "Do you guys see that out there?" Edgar asked, "What do you see?" Ryos replied, "A dark spot in the field. It has to be about twenty feet long." Edgar said, "I see it now, it looks out of the ordinary. Let us go see what it is." They carefully made their way down the hill and started to walk closer to investigate the dark spot in the field. Ryos said, "I have been to this field multiple times growing up and that dark spot was never there before."

After walking for a couple of minutes, they got closer to the mysterious sighting. Ryos said, "There it is!" They walked closer to the area until they stopped at the sight of two burnt corpses. Ryos asked, "Is that... is that them?" Edgar said, "I do not know, but it likely is them." Treb asked, "Who would have done this to them?" Edgar slowly stepped closer to the corpses and looked around. Edgar kneeled and felt the grass and inspected the corpses. Edgar said, "The flesh is nearly burnt off the bone and the grass is dead for at least fifteen feet around them. But there are no torches or any signs of weapons. Something is wrong here. We should head back to the village; it is not safe here without more support. I am not sure who or what is responsible for this, but there is a threat in these lands."

Chapter Seventy: The Sideways Book

Voron Fastios, Skyrock - "How much training have you had in alchemy?", Voron asked a young mage. The apprentice thought for a moment and replied, "Just a little in medicinal herbs; Searleone taught us two classes on conjuring up remedies to treat mild illnesses. That was a couple of months back." Voron asked, "Did you or any of the other mages in training learn about infectious alchemy?" The young mage said, "No, only medicinal studies. I would like to learn more though." Voron said, "I will see what I can do, thank you for your time."

Voron walked over to one of the bookcases and thought to himself, 'How could Rinci have infected the town if he had no training on the basics? It makes no sense.' Voron looked around for a general book on well-known mages that he thought could help him. He kept searching but could not find the type of book he was looking for. Voron thought, 'There has to be one here, something on this. I vaguely remember using it a few years ago.'

Voron noticed a couple of books that were sticking out about two inches further than the other books on one of the shelves. Voron pinched the books with his fingers and slowly pulled them from the shelf. Voron discovered a hidden book behind the front books, and it stood to the side unlike all the other books. Voron grabbed the book and looked at the title, which read, 'Encyclopedia of Respected Mages.' Voron could tell it was aged, but he knew it could contain what he was looking for.

Voron sat down at a table with the book and started looking in the back of it for references to Searleone Vallas. His name appeared with writing next to it which read 'Parchment 343.' Voron turned to Parchment 343 and saw Searleone's name as the heading of the page. Voron thought to himself, 'Well, this could clarify a lot.' The text read, 'Searleone Vallas, late-generation mage born in the town of Federeck. After leaving his town, he settled in Gofon where he became the most respected mage in the kingdom. Although mages were often looked down upon, his excellence in alchemy and the aid he gave to the alchemists of Gofon led to his renowned reputation among the city population, including the royals.' Voron sat in disbelief, 'Federeck was the town where the illness began', he thought. He slowly nodded his head to himself as he was starting to put the pieces together.

Searleone walked into the halls and noticed Voron reading in the corner. Searleone walked over to Voron and said, "I haven't seen you studying in quite some time, what are you looking at?" Voron replied, "Just the history of some mages from a few hundred years ago. I was curious." Searleone said, "Interesting, I have not seen that book around in a long time. Where did you find it?" Voron nervously pointed and said, "I found it on that bookcase over there, it caught my attention." Searleone said, "Very well, I will leave you to it."

Searleone walked out onto the balcony and began to ring the bell. He shook the rope a few times and looked out into the distance, but there were still no signs of any dragons. Searleone continued to shake the bell for a couple of minutes until he stopped to catch his breath as sweat started to drip from his face onto his robe. He peered into the sky and hoped for something, but his hope faded as he realized nothing was coming.

Chapter Seventy-One: The Galloping Love

Roy Syssian, Biros - "I thought you were never going to stay in Biros for more than a week", Leora said. "You kept visiting every other kingdom", she continued. Roy replied, "I know I was away for a while, but now I am home and here to stay. I want to spend the next few months with you here in the city without going anywhere because I can tell there is a war coming." Leora asked, "Involving Biros?" Roy said, "Not directly, but I believe we will have to fight to support one side. I have already hastened our military efforts." Roy saw the grim look on Leora's face. War was not the common mission that they wanted to pursue.

Roy said, "When there is war, there are spies." Roy pulled a dagger out of his pocket and handed it to Leora. Roy said, "Keep this with you just in case you ever need this. You have already seen what spies are capable of." Leora said, "I have never held one before." Roy said, "You just scream and use it to fend off an attacker until guards come. You need some form of protection." Leora put it in a drawer next to her side of the bed. Roy said, "I hope it does not come to that, but it is better to be ready." Leora said, "Want to take a trip to Dunlow Bridge? I have been wanting to go there with you for a while now." Roy said, "Sure, it seems like a nice day for it."

Roy and Leora walked outside and headed for the stables. Roy could see his white horse in the distance and started to whistle. The horse recognized the whistle and turned around to see Roy. The horse started to lift its legs up and down as it prepared itself for a trot. Leora mounted a horse and started to ride in a circle as Roy went to help her. Roy, with disbelief, asked, "When did you learn to ride?" Leora said, "I had a lot of spare time while you were away. Now we can ride separately and faster." Roy mounted his white horse and said, "Believe me, I don't think you want to ride fast with me." Leora said, "Fair enough, but I do want to go fast today. I want to get even better." Roy said, "You lead the way."

Leora shook the reins and the horse started to gallop at a quick pace. Roy watched as Leora and the horse started to gain speed; Leora's beautiful hair flowing through the breeze. Roy grabbed the reins and instructed his horse to follow. The strong long legs of the white horse accelerated with superior speed. Within twenty seconds, Roy was side by side with Leora on the horses.

Roy looked at Leora who was smiling at him. Roy realized that their love for each other itself had been galloping in a way and had reached new heights. Roy shouted, "I am impressed, who taught you?" Leora replied, "Nollie set me up with someone who taught me the basics." Both of them kept riding for a while until they slowed down at the sight of the bridge. Roy hopped off his horse and extended his hand to help Leora dismount from hers.

Roy said, "It is interesting to think that the last time we were here was when I proposed to you to take you as my wife. Although it was only a couple of months ago, a lot has changed in our relationship and my time as a king." Leora said, "I have been thinking and I want us to try to have our first child. What do you think, are you ready?" Roy, with a smile, said, "I am, I was going to have that conversation with you eventually. You are so perfect I would like to have many." Leora smiled back and said, "You better be around, no more of this constant traveling." Roy nodded and said, "I know, but somehow Lodas is changing, I can feel it. The kingdoms are growing apart after a solid period of unification that has lasted for the last few centuries."

Leora could sense that Roy was still thinking about something and asked, "What is it Roy? There is something else on your mind that you are not saying." Roy said, "Somehow, with my little experience, I must guide Biros in the right direction. Tell me, how do you think I should address the rising conflict?" Leora replied, "You must fight for what you believe in. Behind the doubt, I see a confident king. The question is, what do you believe in?" Roy thought to himself for a moment. He had two separate visions looking out over Dunlow Bridge. On the left, he could see his military preparing for war. On the right, he could see his people living in seclusion and isolated from the cruelty of war. Roy stared directly at Dunlow Bridge for a moment as he thought intently, but his gold and red vision was of no help to him here.

Chapter Seventy-Two: Beloved Traitor

Kip Denvion, Outskirts of Gofon - 'There it is', Kip thought to himself. After traveling for two days straight, he had found his way back to Gofon by himself. Along the way he made a few wrong turns, which extended his journey longer than necessary. Kip had always made the journey while being accompanied by the guards of Gofon, but not this time, so he was just happy to have made it back home.

By now, Kip rode at half speed toward the gates of Gofon. He had consumed all the food and water he had brought with him and he had not rested at all. As Kip slowly approached the gates, he was stopped by the guards who shouted, "Halt and dismount!"

Kip, with the little energy he still had, plopped off the horse and fell over onto his side. One of the guards carefully walked closer and said, "Are you feeling well, boy?" Kip said, "Help me up. I am Kip Denvion, I have just returned from Tyrades." The guard gently lifted Kip up with both of his bulky arms and said, "The boy king. Why didn't you summon our men to retrieve you?" Kip, with a tired and confused look, asked, "What did you call me?" The guard said, "The king's masquerade was a setup. Your whole family could not escape the inferno and perished in the flames along with many others. We are still attempting to find the killer or killers."

Kip dropped to his knees and stared at the ground in disbelief. Kip could not help but reflect on the recent events in his life. From committing murder to now hearing that his family had been murdered all within a couple of days. Kip could not help but to think that something about it was some sort of blind justice. Despite his revered and protected royal status, justice viewed him only as an equal to everyone else.

The guard said, "I am deeply sorry, Kip. Some believe you are dead. You must return and claim the throne." Kip stood up and wiped away the tears from his face. The guard noticed the blood stains on Kip's neck. The guard asked, "What is the blood from? Are you injured?" Kip said, "No, I am fine.

I killed a chicken along the way." The guard suspiciously said, "And the blood ended up on your neck?" Kip said, "I am royalty, you do not believe I know how to slaughter a chicken do you? I was desperate." The guard nodded and said, "Let us get you to the royal chambers. I should have mentioned it already, but my name is Nolan."

Nolan walked with Kip to the royal chambers. Along the way Kip asked, "Who has been leading the kingdom?" Nolan said, "Almost all of the members of the council perished. Jack Haxon was the lone survivor of them and has been working to assemble a new council." Kip said, "How did this happen? Didn't we have guards available to tend to the doors?" Nolan said, "We did, but somehow they ended up being locked inside with the rest of the others. Something or someone must have drawn them in."

In the royal chambers, Jack Haxon was speaking to the new council. He abruptly stopped when he saw Kip and the guard enter. Jack said, "Surprised to see you here. I heard about your time in Tyrades and I was just telling the council about it." Kip walked closer and said, "I was studying the art of fighting, but I just found out about the fire at the masquerade par..., at the masquerade massacre. I can't believe the news about my family." Jack slyly asked, "Do you feel like you are the next king?" Kip replied, "Based on my knowledge of kingship, yes, I am the son of the late king, so it is mine to possess." Jack asked, "Is that blood on your neck, Kip?" Kip said, "Yes, I had a tough time returning to Gofon as I was alone and had to kill a chicken for food." Jack nodded his head and smiled as he said, "Very well, you look exhausted. Go get some rest. The council and I will come to you soon regarding your kingship ceremony." Kip nodded and said, "I look forward to honoring my father and family and serving the kingdom."

Kip and Nolan walked back to Kip's room in the deserted level of the building where his family used to live. Nolan said, "I will watch your door, go get some sleep." Nolan sat down in a position where he could rest but notice anyone approaching. It was unusually quiet, but Kip understood why. Kip crawled into his bed and closed his eyes. In his mind, he could hear his sister in her room practicing her flute late at night. He could also recall his parents laughing and loudly conversing over a couple glasses of wine.

Despite his sad and depressing thoughts and emotions, Kip knew he had to prepare for the next day. One of his two lifelong dreams was going to become a reality. He was going to become a king before becoming a gladiator, which was not the order he was hoping for. Kip slowly dozed off into a much-needed deep sleep as his memories faded away.

The next morning, Kip awoke to the sound of knocking on his door. Kip rubbed his eyes and asked, "Who is it?" Nolan replied, "It is me, Nolan, the council is asking for you." Kip said, "Let me get dressed first." Kip said to himself, "This is it; I better be prepared and not mess this up." Kip looked through his wardrobe for the fanciest attire he owned. Kip saw an outfit he wore to a royal dinner about a year earlier and put it on. Kip opened his door and Nolan said, "Follow me, they are waiting downstairs where we met them yesterday." Kip and Nolan walked down toward the royal chambers where the council was waiting for Kip.

As Kip entered, Jack Haxon called out, "Welcome back, are you ready to shape the future of Gofon?" Kip smiled and nodded as he replied, "With the assistance of the council. Over these past few days, I have learned a lot about becoming a man." Jack said, "Excellent, please be seated in the anointment throne. It is customary that all kings begin their kingship properly with this ceremony."

The council stood a short distance away, observing Kip and Jack. Kip sat down in the throne, which was encrusted with gold and jewels. Jack said, "Close your eyes and let your mind follow my words." Kip calmly closed his eyes and listened intently, anxious to become king. After a few seconds, Jack said, "Loyalty is what makes a king a favorite among his people. Someone who is willing to sacrifice his own son, daughter, wife, hell, even the whole family for the prosperity of the kingdom. We all loved your father for his devout loyalty to Gofon. He even loved you and your family, but loyalty is a trait that you have lost. You will perish as a beloved traitor." Jack pulled out a dagger and thrusted it into Kip's chest. Kip opened his eyes as he gasped with shock and pain.

Jack shouted, "Die traitor!" Nolan charged closer to intervene, but the council commanded the guards in the room to stop him. Jack whispered in Kip's ear, "Say hello to your father for me", before smiling slyly. Jack pulled the dagger out of Kip's body and called out to Nolan, "Kip was being influenced by the king in Tyrades. The king of Biros recently visited and warned us himself. The guards in this room can attest to this. The council and I are here to assure that treason will never be tolerated in Gofon. After spending several months under the close care of someone trying to manipulate him, we were not willing to leave it to chance and have him lead our kingdom. From this day forward, I, Jack Haxon, will be named the king of Gofon as the only remaining council member to survive the royal masquerade." Jack instructed one of the council members to make his anointment.

Jack kicked Kip's corpse to the side and sat in the anointment throne as the council member approached. Jack closed his eyes and waited for the council member to speak. Before the council member could speak, Jack started to smile and giggle to himself. The man asked Jack, "What is it?" Jack replied, "I can already see the people of Gofon celebrating for me." The man said, "Do not worry, there will be a massive festival today to celebrate." Jack replied with a deeper smile, "The festival has already begun."

Chapter Seventy-Three: The Shimmering Hills

Oakley Nodon, Forest Southeast of Sterafia - Oakley limped as he walked slowly alongside Snowstorm. After walking for days, he grew tired and had turned his ankle on a rock earlier that day. Oakley knew that it was nothing serious and he just needed some time before he could walk at his usual pace. Snowstorm walked ahead of Oakley and stopped to look back. Snowstorm curiously watched as Oakley limped closer. Oakley motioned for Snowstorm to sit down and give him a short break to rest. Oakley sat down and began stretching out his right leg and ankle. Oakley knew that the high altitude in the hills was reducing his breathing levels.

As he sat, Oakley was fascinated by the night sky, which seemed to fill the enormous hills with bright green lights. The lights began shifting and swaying from side to side and reflected off the surface of the ground. Oakley and Snowstorm watched for some time. Oakley never had the opportunity to witness this kind of light show in the night sky and thought, 'These hills are something special.'

Oakley stood up to continue on, but Snowstorm walked in front of him staying on all fours. Oakley went to walk past Snowstorm, but Snowstorm did the same thing. Oakley looked at Snowstorm and thought, 'Is this a sign that he is ready to carry my weight and ride together?' Oakley walked to the side of Snowstorm and placed his arm over the tiger. Snowstorm looked at Oakley and then looked straight ahead. Oakley carefully lifted his leg over the side of the tiger and gripped its neck with his hands.

Snowstorm started to walk in the direction they were originally headed in. Oakley looked around; the view was much better a few feet higher off the ground. Oakley could feel each stride Snowstorm took as the movement shifted through the tiger's body. The shimmering lights above lit the path for their return to Sterafia, which, by Oakley's prediction, would hopefully be completed that night. The endless cool breeze blew against Oakley's cheeks as they descended down a hill. After riding for a while, Oakley began to tire from the long journey, but he knew he had to stay awake. Snowstorm would need to be led in the right direction.

After continuing their journey for a couple more hours, Oakley could finally make out some lighting in the distance. Oakley's eyes widened as he tried to get a better look. 'That must be Sterafia', he thought. Oakley extended his arm and pointed in the direction of the lights before grabbing back onto Snowstorm's neck and shaking it a bit. The tiger started to run swiftly with long strides toward the lights of Sterafia.

Before long, Oakley and Snowstorm were passing through the gates of Sterafia. Oakley started heading toward his abode before he remembered that his father's residence was now his. Oakley turned Snowstorm around and started heading toward the other part of Sterafia to his father's old place. After taking off his necklace with the room key, he used the key to open the door. Snowstorm ran ahead into the dark room before Oakley entered.

The residence still looked the same way it had from the day Damien left for battle, the last time Oakley saw his father. Oakley looked around the room before he noticed Snowstorm lying on the ground next to the bed about to fall asleep. Oakley walked over and collapsed in the bed next to Snowstorm. Within a short moment, both Oakley and Snowstorm were deep in sleep, more comfortable than any day in the past few months. Oakley woke up in the morning to the sound of the rustling of Snowstorm pacing around the room. Oakley got out of bed and opened the door to let Snowstorm outside to empty his bladder. The two of them then ate breakfast and relaxed for a while.

Later, Oakley looked up at the sun and noticed it was almost noon on a beautiful spring day. Oakley walked toward the king's estate to meet with Renga. He whistled to make sure Snowstorm would follow behind him. The tiger came running to catch up. Oakley walked up to the king's guards and said, "I am Oakley Nodon, I am here to speak with the king." One of the guards said, "Follow me, but your tiger cannot come inside." Oakley said, "Can I meet him somewhere outside then? I do not feel comfortable leaving Snowstorm alone." The guard said, "Let me go ask him myself."

Within a short moment, the king of Sterafia and a woman walked out to greet Oakley. Renga called out with excitement and said, "Oakley! I have missed you, how is everything?" Oakley smiled and replied, "Great, I have seen and learned far more than I expected." The king said, "This is my new friend, Sakia. She is a survivor from an attack far north." Oakley said, "Nice to meet you, Sakia, you have met the most powerful, yet sincere, person in the whole kingdom." Sakia replied, "King Renga has brought my hope up to new levels. Any friend of his is a friend of mine. Such a ferocious, yet striking, tiger you have there. May I touch it?" Oakley said, "Yes, Snowstorm is comfortable with others when I am around. Extend your hand and allow him to smell it, then you can slowly stroke his fur." Sakia listened to Oakley's instructions and ran her fingers through the dense, soft fur of the tiger.

Renga said, "Tell me what you have seen." Oakley said, "There is a settlement to the southeast named Katorian. They are descendants of Sterafia who resettled there and never came back. They live in snow structures and welcomed me for most of my time away. I intend on returning to them eventually." Renga said, "That is incredible, are they potential allies?" Oakley said, "Yes, they are a lot like us. They are interested in building a greater connection with us." Renga was relieved to hear that.

Oakley said, "That is not all I discovered. There are these blue people from the sea called the Kulvani. They live in the ocean but can venture onto land. I am the only one who has made contact with them. They have grown fearful of living on land among people ever since a kingdom to the north named Torust attempted to raise the dead several centuries ago. Most importantly, they gave me a horn that I can use to summon them when I am close to the coast. They are another ally I have made during my time away."

Renga and Sakia looked at each other for a moment before Renga said, "Torust attacked her town not too long ago, which is why she was forced to relocate here. I have known about Torust for a long time, but I have never built any relations with them. I now recognize them as a consistent threat to the future of Lodas. Sakia, I give you my word that one day we will get revenge for your fallen family and people. Oakley, the news you have shared with us is more helpful and valuable than any words of praise I can give you. I believed in you during your adventure, but what you have achieved far surpassed my expectations. I want to present you with the title of Foreign Affairs Representative of Sterafia. What do you say?" Oakley replied, "Thank you, my king. I would be honored to further serve our kingdom in some way." Renga said, "So what is next for you?" Oakley said, "I will return to Katorian and head further east. There is word that Snowstorm's family passed through there not too long ago."

Simona Molino

Chapter Seventy-Four: Saden

Ria Falune, Torust - "I come with good news and bad news, my queen", Haigar said. Ria replied, "Please have a seat and share", as she sat in the Halls of Absolute alongside her parents. Haigar said, "Chaos has ensued in Gofon. The king and the royal family have been massacred in a fire along with the council and most of the men of influence in the kingdom. A councilman named Jack Haxon has become the new king, so the kingdom is currently in a fragile state. That is the good news. The bad news is that the illness is eradicating many of the towns between us and Gofon, which prevents us from engaging in war with Gofon. I am hopeful that within a couple weeks, the path will be clear for us to advance."

Ria shared this information with her father in ancient Torustian before he responded, "Broken leadership always presents an amazing opportunity to strike. Consider this a sign of luck." Haigar said, "Now, we should just wait for the threat of the illness to settle." Ria nodded and said, "I like this news, but tell me, what is known of this man, Jack Haxon?" Haigar said, "He was a council member before he was king, that is all we know."

Peter approached the table and said, "King and Queen Falune, it is great to see you again. Your presence was sorely missed." Ria replied, "They can only understand me, but I will let them know what you said." After hearing the message through Ria, Jaci said, "We departed only temporarily. Now we must turn Torust into the permanent afterlife for our people."

Ria asked Peter, "Have you heard about the new king in Gofon?" Peter replied, "Yes, hopefully I can be the one to remove his crown and serve it to you, my queen. It is just a matter of time." Ria translated, Tari said, "Later, we shall toast to the news. I surely missed drinking my wine." Ria said, "I do remember how much you enjoyed your wine; I am sure you do miss it, father."

Peter departed from the Halls of Absolute and walked back to his home for lunch. Peter entered the front room and Cazier called out, "Father, I am coming down now." Peter said, "Okay, I was not expecting you to be home, but you can join me for lunch." Cazier came down and said, "Before we eat, I have something I want to show you." Peter said, "Proceed." Cazier said, "Wait here for one minute", before he ran upstairs.

A short moment later, Cazier carefully came down again this time holding a small baby wrapped in a blanket. Cazier said, "He is mine by blood. I knew how much you wanted a grandchild and I wanted to thank you for letting me live the way I am." Peter smiled and walked closer to take the baby. Peter said, "It looks like a boy", as he held the baby. Cazier replied, "Yes, I have named him Saden." Peter said, "I like the name. But Cazier, you didn't need to do this to make me happy." Cazier said, "I know, but I wanted to." Peter said, "What of his mother?" Cazier said, "The lady gave birth to him and nothing more. He is mine completely." Peter looked down at the small baby and said, "I am filled with happiness for you, Cazier." Peter looked into Saden's eyes and could recall a time when he was much younger and Cazier was that small. Peter held out his hand and touched Saden's little fingers. This small child was another extension of Peter's blood and legacy.

Chapter Seventy-Five: The Nature of Dragons

Ryos Pontas, Village of Posbor - "There is an unknown threat deeper south that requires another unified effort from us and Ranfat", Edgar said. The leader of the village of Posbor, Reves Darlo, replied, "What could be of such a threat that you need our help for something you are unsure of?" Edgar replied, "Whatever it is, it can cast fire. Ryos was there with me when we saw the burned bodies; all that remained were remnants of bones and ash." Reves said, "It likely is a dragon and if that is the case, we should not be on the side that upsets it. It would be best for all our villages if we distanced ourselves from it and let it roam freely. Certain beasts of Lodas were meant to roam without obstacles."

Ryos said, "We saw a dragon fly over us a while back. As we were about to fight the yeti, do you remember?" Edgar said, "Yes, I do. I do find it concerning that if it was a dragon, our men were targeted. Dragons usually leave men alone. It is not in the nature of dragons to hunt man. So why did our men perish? Was it a freak accident and bad luck or something we do not know?" Reves said, "Listen, I know you are unsure, but you know we will be here to help if you figure this out and need us. Until then, we cannot help you based on this limited information. Perhaps your men got too close to its food or something else. We may never know. If I were you, I would look to hunt in a new part of the woods."

Edgar said, "That is not like us. We like to remove the threat from our land. Land that, in this case, we fought hard to claim from Staga. If something, even a dragon, wants to try to control us, we will find a way to achieve dominance over it and eradicate it. We will search for the creature and return to you if need be." Reves said, "Good luck, old friend. I hope to see you again, but maybe not too soon." Edgar nodded as he got up to leave and said, "Likewise, Reves."

Edgar and Ryos departed the village of Posbor to head back for Tsirian. Edgar said, "You know, the other villages wanted to murder every one of you. We were the only village that saw potential in your people. Just as you have seen with the yeti and can see in the strife at hand, most conflicts are between us and the creatures around us, but this is a man's world." Ryos said, "When I grew up in Staga, I did not get to see dragons, although I knew they existed. However, the dragon I saw in the sky was massive. I do not know how any force can handle something so powerful and agile, let alone a creature that can blow fire." Edgar said, "We will find a way. Once we get back to the village, we will organize a plan. Just like last time, you will lead the scouting party. You are still so young but are gaining invaluable knowledge and experience. I have high hopes for your future leadership role in Tsirian."

Chapter Seventy-Six: The Weed and the Plant Family

Searleone Vallas, Skyrock - Searleone poured the last few ounces of the liquid into a small, compact vial. Smoke escaped from the vial as the liquid made its way in. Searleone capped the vial and slid it into his robe pocket. Searleone left his potions room and walked out into the sanctuary halls. He could see Voron sitting and reciting something at a table. Searleone called out and said, "Voron, can you come over here?"

Voron nodded with some reservation and stood up. As of late, he had distanced himself from Searleone and the head mage had a feeling Voron was suspicious of something. Searleone walked out onto the balcony before Voron could catch up. Searleone continued until he got to his garden. The water he was pouring into the garden crept deep into the soil supporting the plants. Voron walked up to Searleone and said, "It is coming along nicely, I see." Searleone replied, "Just a little water to supplement the rainy weather we have been having."

Voron stood there for a moment before asking, "Did you need me for something?" Searleone said, "Not necessarily, but I wanted your feedback on part of the lesson I will be teaching shortly." Voron said, "I can give my advice, but you are far more knowledgeable than me."

Searleone looked around the garden and pointed to a weed that was growing on the outside corner. He said, "A single weed can interfere with the prosperity of the whole plant family. There is more that we can learn from nature than we realize. We are a compound of nature after all." Voron said, "That sounds insightful for the lesson. I have something of my own to complement your teachings. I have been working on it for some time now, which is why I have been busy on my own." Searleone asked, "Do you care to share it now?" Voron smiled and said, "I would like for it to be a surprise." Searleone said, "I see, it will have to be a surprise, I suppose."

Searleone looked back at his garden and asked Voron, "Do you mind plucking that weed from the garden for me?" Voron walked closer and kneeled to grab the thick weed. As he did so, Searleone uncapped the vial and doused Voron with the clear liquid, which seeped right through Voron's head. Voron's body flailed from side to side until the headless corpse was completely still. Searleone quickly lifted the corpse and heaved it over the side of the balcony. Searleone looked down as the body traveled for quite some distance before hitting the ground. Searleone murmured, "Be gone disloyal mage." Searleone took the vial and threw it over the side of the balcony. He then walked over to the garden and ripped out the weed that Voron had grabbed.

Searleone looked out over the balcony into the distance, as if nothing had happened. He consistently kept an eye out for any sign of the girl riding the dragon. Searleone turned and headed into the sanctuary halls as he had many mages waiting to hear his lesson.

Searleone entered the lecture hall and walked to the center platform. Searleone looked around the room and peered out at the many faces of the mages waiting for him to speak. Searleone opened his mouth and called out, "Today, I will be lecturing you on loyalty. It is the duty of each and every one of you to remain loyal to Skyrock and to me as your master mage. The penalty for any infractions or breaches of these loyalties can be hefty. Therefore, I expect complete and devout loyalty from you. No exceptions will be tolerated."

Chapter Seventy-Seven: The Much-Anticipated Arrival

Liava Pontas, Dragon Lair - Liava ran her hands along the side of the red dragon. She grabbed onto his side and hopped onto the dragon's back. She wrapped herself in the harness and signaled to the dragon to take off. Within a short moment, Liava and the three dragons were soaring through the midday sky. Liava noticed that the red dragon had grown tremendously and was now the same size as the other dragons. The red dragon could also carry her and fly at an even faster speed than in the past.

Liava looked at the land below to observe nature and ensure that she could protect and preserve it with her new profound ideas and emboldened confidence. Liava did not see any signs of hunting parties that she needed to combat. She continued to fly to the north as the unknown was the focus of her curiosity.

Now, for the first time in her months of flying, she identified one of the villages of the north. She flew lower to scout the village and estimate the size of its population. 'Could the individuals I recently killed belong to this village?', Liava wondered. She could tell that people in the village were looking up at her riding on the dragon. It was in that moment that Liava realized how little human contact she had had in the past several months. Liava thought, 'I have begun to forget what it is like to be a part of a human society.'

Liava continued to pass over the village and stayed on a path flying further to the north. After riding for close to an hour, Liava could hear a loud ringing coming from even further north. In the distance, she could see a large structure high up in the sky. She noticed what appeared to be a large bell being rung on the outside of this citadel high up in the mountain. Liava flew a bit closer until she pulled back on the harness to command her dragon to halt. The red dragon and the other dragons stopped short as their large wings flapped with heavy resistance against the air. The dragons flapped their wings as they remained in the same spot in the sky awaiting Liava's next command.

Liava watched as a man in a dark robe waved at Liava from the balcony of the structure. Liava wondered, 'Who are these people? I have never heard of people living this high up in the mountains. Are they like the villagers? Can they be trusted?' Many thoughts rushed through Liava's mind as she had come to a critical deciding point. Liava reflected on how her recent confidence had empowered her and was helping guide her on her path to change Lodas for the better.

Liava closed her eyes and opened them as she looked at the mountain structure with hopeful thoughts going through her mind. Liava tapped the red dragon's neck and the red dragon started to fly toward the structure with the other dragons following closely behind. Their arrival would be sudden, but bold. As Liava approached the structure, the man continued to wave, but with growing eagerness. Liava, for some reason, had felt as though her arrival was heavily anticipated.